Perseverance Place

Also by Elisabeth McNeill:

Shanghai Emerald
Lark Returning
A Woman of Gallantry
Mistress of Green Tree Mile

PERSEVERANCE PLACE

Elisabeth McNeill

CENTURY

LONDON SYDNEY AUCKLAND JOHANNESBURG

Copyright © Elisabeth McNeill 1991

All Rights Reserved

The right of Elisabeth McNeill to be identified as the author of
this work has been asserted by her in accordance with the
Copyright, Designs and Patents Act 1988.

First published in Great Britain in 1991 by
Random Century Group
20 Vauxhall Bridge Road,
London SW1V 2SA

Century Hutchinson South Africa (Pty) Ltd
PO Box 337, Bergvlei 2012
South Africa

Random Century New Zealand Ltd
PO Box 40–086, Glenfield, Auckland 10 New Zealand

British Library Cataloguing in Publication Data
McNeill, Elisabeth
Perseverance Place.
Rn : Liz McNeill Taylor   I. Title
823.914 [F]

ISBN 0–7126–4655–8

Phototypeset by Input Typesetting Ltd, London
Printed and bound in Great Britain by
Mackays of Chatham PLC, Chatham, Kent

PERSEVERANCE PLACE

1874

The abrupt rattle of a silver teaspoon against eggshell china made a drift of scarlet petals float slowly down from a full-blown rose that stood in a crystal vase in the middle of the tea-table. Like tiny boats they rocked silently among the teacups and Brabazon put out a gentle hand to brush them into her palm. Her golden-coloured eyes behind lowered curving dark lashes were remote and guarded as she tried not to look directly at her mother who sat stiffly upright on the other side of the table. Maria Logan was laughing but her mirth was not genuine for there was a bitter and hysterical note to it.

'You're not serious about this of course,' she said when her burst of artificial laughter was spent. Brabazon lifted her head and looked directly at her mother's face, at the familiar and feared cold, blue eyes; the pendulous and plump white cheeks; the tiny, once rosebud mouth now etched round with pursed lines which showed Maria to be a bitter and dissatisfied woman.

'I'm very serious, Mother. I've made up my mind,' she whispered.

Mrs Logan's eyes flashed, 'You're not old enough to have a mind. You're not eighteen yet, remember that.'

Brabazon said nothing and her mother took silence as acquiescence, relaxing slightly and sipping her tea before she added, 'It's only a fancy of course. You've fallen for his brown eyes and that music – he's a very good musician, I grant you that. Every girl has unsuitable romantic ideas when she's young. You'll forget about him in a week.'

The girl shook her head and said again, 'I'm very serious mother. I'm going to marry Duncan Nairn and I'd like you to be happy about it.'

Maria Logan's composure cracked and her voice rose almost to a scream. '*Happy*! You want me to be happy that you're marrying a tradesman? His father wears a beaver hat with a brass buckle in front like a carter! When his mother was alive she walked about the Kirkgate with her skirts kirtled up like a labourer's wife.'

Though she knew she was wasting her breath, Brabazon tried to defend her lover's family, 'Oh, no. They're very respectable people, Mother. The family has been in business here for hundreds of years. Everyone holds them in high regard.'

Maria's cheeks were no longer white, but mottled with angry red patches that spread to her neck even as she spat out, 'They're brewers and not, unfortunately, big brewers. They run a tumble-down little brewery in the Kirkgate and live beside it in a broken-down house with the smell of hops and malt filling every room. They're tradespeople. You can't marry into that family. My father had a title! He was a baronet. Have you no pride? Don't talk nonsense about marrying a Nairn. I know what it means when a girl marries out of her class. Look what happened to me . . . and even your father's family was several cuts above those brewers!'

Brabazon shook her head as if trying to staunch the tirade but it was useless to plead the case of the Nairn family with her snobbish mother – who regarded herself as socially above everyone else in the crowded commercial port of Leith. The only thing to do was to stick to her resolve and so she said firmly, 'I'm determined to marry Duncan, Mother. I love him.'

Maria Logan slumped in her chair as if her daughter had dealt her a mortal blow. '*Love*. What do you know of love?' Then a threat crept into her voice as she went on, 'If you persist in this nonsense I'll be forced to ask my lawyer to write to your father.'

This did not have the desired effect, however, because the girl straightened her shoulders, raised her firm chin even higher and retorted, 'I didn't want it to come to this. I hoped you'd agree but there's no chance of stopping my wedding now because Father has given his consent already. Duncan wrote to him and so did I.'

2

All the rose petals fell in a cascade of colour as Maria thumped her fist on to the table-top making tea spill from her cup and spread in a brown pool over the beautiful cloth. She ignored the stain, so carried away with fury was she. 'How dare you! How dare you go over the head of your mother who's had sole care of you ever since that man abandoned us three years ago. He left without a backward glance and you write for his permission to marry a brewer's son. You wicked girl! You ungrateful child!'

Brabazon's creamy skin was now showing high colour as well and she had to fight to retain her calm. 'That's not fair. Father has always kept in touch with Mark and myself. He writes to me regularly – you know that because you read the letters! I know you do. He's still my guardian even though he's in Russia and if he says I can marry, no one can stop me.'

With the gauntlet thrown down between them, Maria took refuge in sarcasm which she knew to be her most wounding weapon. 'Of course your father's the most suitable person to give advice on marriage. He's set you such a fine example. He's been an ideal husband and father – ignoring me for years and then running off and abandoning his family when some other woman took his eye. That's a perfect model for you to follow in marriage.'

'Father didn't abandon us. He's left us very well provided for. He gave Mark the timber-yard and he provides you with a big income,' protested her daughter.

But her mother's ears were closed and tears were pouring down her cheeks . . . 'Do you think money makes up for what he's done to me? Anyway you'll have none of my money if you marry against my wishes. You talk about love and tell me that I should be happy to be left here in this benighted place when my husband is living far away with his paramour!'

Remorse for her insensitivity seized the girl and she rose to run around the table towards the weeping woman, saying as she went, 'Please don't cry, Mother. I didn't mean to hurt you . . . but I love Duncan very much and I'd like you to be happy for me.'

Contrite, she knelt by her mother's chair and attempted to embrace the huddled figure but as she reached out her arms, Maria sprang back as if her daughter's touch were repellent to her. Her voice was chilling as she hissed, 'Don't touch me, just don't *touch* me.'

Rebuffed, Brabazon stood up and the guarded expression came down over her face again like a dropped curtain. For the first time she realised how much her mother disliked her. They never embraced and spoken expressions of affection between them had been rare. Brabazon knew the reason was that she too closely resembled her absent father Joshua who, after years of unhappy marriage, had finally broken away from his clinging and complaining wife. The trouble was that though Joshua had stopped loving Maria long ago, her cloying adoration of him had never lessened and when he'd told her that he was going to stay in Russia with another woman, that adoration turned to implacable hatred. Remembering all the weeping and recriminations between her parents, Brabazon's own eyes stung with unshed tears. She looked down on the bent head of her sobbing mother, a woman unloving and unloved, and said as if she were talking to a stranger, 'I'm sorry that you don't approve, Mother but I *will* marry Duncan Nairn. I've made up my mind.'

Maria took plump lace-mittened hands away from her face to reveal baleful bloodshot eyes that poured years of hatred at the girl beside her, 'You'll live to regret it,' she said in a voice so cold that it filled the sunny room with a sinister chill. Brabazon flinched. It sounded as if her mother were giving her a curse as a wedding gift.

A week later the atmosphere in the large house overlooking the grassy spread of Leith Links was still cold and forbidding as Brabazon dressed for her wedding. Mary, her maid, carefully buttoned up the tiny pearl studs on the tight-fitting sleeves of the blue taffeta gown and stood

4

back in admiration. 'My word, you look awfy bonny, Miss . . . it's a pity . . .' and the words trailed off in awareness at having stepped over the line between affection and overfamiliarity.

Brabazon's reflection in the long pier glass seemed to lose some of its dazzle. 'I hope *you* don't think it's a pity I'm marrying Duncan, Mary,' she whispered.

Mary shook her grey head, 'Oh, no Miss Brabazon. He's a fine man. Everybody kens that. There's not a soul in Leith but has a good word to say about him. What I mean is that it's a pity you're leaving here like this – that your mother's taking it so bad.'

She made a gesture with her hand in the direction of Mrs Logan's bedroom where they both knew Brabazon's mother was lying sobbing with the blinds drawn as if there had been a death in the family.

'I've tried to see her. She won't let me in. She says she'll never see me again . . .' the girl's voice was trembling.

The maid, who had been in the house since Brabazon was born, cast propriety aside and put her arms around the slender waist, reassuring the bride with hurried words, 'Don't let her spoil today for you. He's a grand man and if you love him that's what matters. God bless you, Miss.'

There was a knock at the bedroom door and Brabazon's brother Mark, four years her senior and closely resembling their mother in looks, was admitted by Mary. He stood in the middle of the carpet and coughed in embarrassment as he told his sister, 'It's nearly time to go, Brabs. You look splendid . . . really splendid. Er, Mother's told me to have your trunks sent out now as well. Have you got everything?'

His sister nodded. They were both well aware that her mother had forbidden her the house, cast her out of the family, because she persisted in her plans to marry. 'Yes, I've packed all my clothes,' she told him.

Mark nodded and looked around the bedroom at the pictures on the walls and the pretty china on the shelves. 'Haven't you taken something to remind you of your home?' he asked gently. And when Brabazon shook her head, not trusting herself to speak, he pressed, 'Take something. Isn't there anything you'd like?'

She gazed around the room she loved so much. Everything in it was familiar and cherished and it was difficult to know what to select. Eventually her eye fell on a candlestick in the shape of Cupid, with a wreath of flowers at his feet, which had always stood on the mantelpiece and acted as a nightlight when she was tiny and afraid of the dark. 'I'd like to take Cupid with me,' she whispered.

Her brother walked over to the fireplace and picked up the pretty little piece saying, 'I'll send it over to Brewery House with your boxes. We don't need to say anything to Mother about it. Now come on, Brabazon or we'll be late.' And he held out his arm to escort her on the short walk through the lanes behind their home – to the church in the middle of the Kirkgate where Brabazon was to take the step that would cut her off from everything which had gone before and start her new life with Duncan Nairn.

1890

The door of the old nursery on the top floor of Brewery House opened with a muffled groan and a slim, elegant woman with glossy brown hair drawn back from a fine-boned face stepped into the dusty world of discarded toys. A draught blowing in from the landing made a dapple-grey rocking horse with only a few hairs left in its once luxuriant mane and tail move gently on its high metal frame. Wooden spinning tops, an abacus, hoops, broken swords and tattered storybooks were piled in one corner making the room look as if it had been vacated by children moments before. Only the patina of dust that covered every surface showed what a long time had passed since any games were played there.

Brabazon Nairn paused, blinking in the dim light that filtered in through a cobweb-shrouded window, and smiled a little ruefully as she surveyed the relics of her children's past. She patted the rocking horse on its wooden nose and walked towards the casement where, using the heel of one hand, she rubbed at one of the panes until a spyhole appeared in the dust. Lowering her head slightly, she peered through the gap she had made and found herself staring out at what looked like an under-water world, made ghostly and diffuse by thousands of minute bubbles in the ancient, flawed green-tinted glass. Motionless she gazed down at the rust-coloured pantiled roofs beneath her, then her eyes moved over the tilted gravestones around the church next door and onward towards the docks where she could see the tops of the tall ships' masts leaning confidingly together at their berths in the harbour. Beyond them, stretching out like a welcoming carpet to the world, glittered the opalescent waters of the Firth of Forth. It was still early and the morning was chilly but it promised to be a fine day because the sky was cloudless, and the same colour as a duck's egg. Here and there in the vastness soared gulls with their wings curved like archers' bows.

Brabazon's eyes became shadowed and melancholy as she turned her head from the direction of the sea to look eastwards towards Leith Links. The expanse of emerald grass was empty except for the few figures of early morning walkers, some of them lingering under patches of darker colour made by the guardian trees around the perimeter of the grass. She was looking for a particular clump of elms and soon found them, standing beside the gate of the house that belonged to her mother. Above their branches she could pick out the pointed roof of the little tower that stood at the end of the façade of the old house.

Inside the tower, in the room on the ground floor, Brabazon guessed her brother Mark and his wife Amelia would be taking breakfast with a bright fire alight in the hearth and maids bustling around. She saw the scene in imagination – the breakfast room was pretty and comfortable with honey-coloured linenfold panelling and portraits of her own ancestors staring down from the walls. Above Mark's head as he breakfasted, their bedridden mother Maria would be lying speechless and immobile but with her eyes still full of hatred.

The passage of years had not muffled the pain of Brabazon's rejection by her mother. Even now the mortally ill Maria would not receive her daughter, for her malice and dislike were as strong as ever. There had been no point, Brabazon realised, in trying to explain to her mother how much she loved Duncan and even less point in hoping for a maternal blessing. The very sound of the word 'love' drove Maria Logan into the frenzy of frustrated jealousy that had burst out in her parting curse, 'You'll live to regret it'.

As if the words had once more been spoken aloud, Brabazon shivered and laid her forehead against the cool

8

glass of the attic-window. The chill going through her whole body made her shake and she wondered, 'Is this the day my mother predicted?'

Then the silence of the house was shattered by the sound of men's voices and the thud of feet running up and down carpetless stairs. Doors slammed and someone dropped a heavy weight making the attic-window rattle in its frame. Brabazon looked around with a hunted air as if seeking a place to hide among the discarded toys. She staggered a little as the energy drained out of her body; the calves of her legs went limp and she longed to stay hidden, to close out reality and the knowledge that her home was being emptied of all its pretty things. Downstairs the bailiff's men were calculatingly eyeing her possessions, putting a price on everything the Nairns owned and all because her husband's unworldliness had finally caught up with him. Duncan had been forced into bankruptcy by his creditors and, by process of the law, all his possessions except clothes and basic furniture to the pitiful value of twenty pounds were being taken from him.

As she thought about their plight, his wife said aloud, 'No, Mother, I'm not sorry. I'm *still* not sorry. I don't regret marrying Duncan. I'd do it again.' It was a relief to know that she genuinely did not feel any anger towards her husband. She was convinced he had been ill-advised; He'd relied too much on the counsellings of his lawyer and banker – for he had never pretended to be a businessman. If he had been given the choice, Duncan would have become a professional musician instead of a brewer. In fact it was when he was playing the piano at a concert in Leith Town Hall that Brabazon had first seen him. Because he was an only son, however, the option of a musical career was not open to him and he had reluctantly taken over the brewery when his father died. Music he played in his spare time, but the gentleness and sensitivity that made Brabazon love him never left him. She had married him because of those qualities and not because she thought he would excel at making money.

In her eyes, the perpetrators of the Nairns' problems

were the hard-faced men who had driven her husband into personal bankruptcy. Her particular dislike was directed towards the lawyer Willie Ord who, she knew, had urged Duncan into rash expenditure on modernising the old brewery. Ord did not concern himself with the problem of repaying the loans he arranged and when things became difficult, he offered more advances. Finally the burden of meeting the interest grew heavier and heavier until there was no way out but insolvency. Brabazon had watched powerless as her beloved husband aged beneath the burden of his problems. Though he would not agree with her, she suspected that Ord had some private motive in leading her unwordly Duncan into ruin.

These angry thoughts were interrupted by a gentle cough from the doorway announcing the presence of her eldest son, fifteen-year-old Henry. Standing awkwardly on the threshold, he showed open concern on his face and she made herself smile in an effort to assuage his anxieties for she knew he, too, was deeply troubled by the cataclysm that had burst upon his family.

'The lawyer's arrived with some other men, Mama. Father sent me up to find you,' said Henry gently. She smoothed down her hair with an elegant hand, twitched her skirts into place and stepped towards her son who watched her with adoring eyes that reminded her of her father's. As far as Henry was concerned, there was not another woman in the whole of Leith that could match his mother for beauty even when her brow was furrowed with anxiety and her eyes bloodshot with a night's weeping.

'How many men are with your father?' she asked in a voice made light by considerable effort. She did not want to worry her son unnecessarily.

'Five counting Ord. They're in the brewery office with Father, now.'

Brabazon's heart sank. Five meant that the creditors' representatives must have arrived too. Surely they were not going to seize the brewery as well she thought in a flash of panic, which she immediately surpressed as she

10

reached for Henry's hand and said, 'Now don't you worry. Everything's going to be all right. This house was far too big for us anyway and we're only moving across the yard to the Place. Lead the way, my dear, I'll come down with you now.'

Her son felt adult and reliable as he helped her down the twisting attic stairs. Her heavy skirts made a soft susurrating noise as they swept over the steps, bringing back into his mind happy memories of her coming up to kiss him goodnight in the nursery when he was small. The swishing sound always heralded her arrival and made him feel safe and loved.

Brewery House, the home of the Nairn family, was a three-story, rambling old Georgian building that had been put up in place of a more modest dwelling by one of Duncan's ancestors a century before, when Perseverance Brewery was going through a period of prosperity. As the lad and his mother descended the curving stairway, the doors of the bedrooms all stood wide open, revealing men in white aprons piling up furniture, counting out blankets and eiderdowns, and fingering heavy embroidered bed hangings. Brabazon kept her eyes looking resolutely forward so that she could not see what they were doing.

On the second-floor landing her other son, fourteen-year-old Laurence, was leaning over the banisters watching the men bustling around down in the hallway. There was a desolate look on his face as he turned at his mother's approach and, without speaking, she patted him gently on the back. He, too, stepped up beside her on the other side from Henry and in a line they descended to the drawing-room landing. There the big double doors stood open wide and sun was streaming into the room through the three long windows that looked out over the garden. Brabazon loved that room best of all and found it impossible to pass by it without looking in. What she saw made her flinch as if she had been struck, for a burly man was lifting pieces of china off the marble mantelpiece. Instantly she dropped Henry's hand and ran into the room with an anguished cry, 'Not that, don't take that!'

11

The man paused, a tiny piece of pink and white porcelain almost hidden in his huge hand. He stared at her and said, 'I've been told to take everything in here. They've set aside all you're allowed to keep.'

Brabazon swept her hands out towards the other things in the room. 'Take everything else but please leave that. It's mine you see. I brought it with me when I was married. Please don't take it.'

He hesitated but one of the other men intervened, 'Sorry missus. If it was yours you should have said so before. We've been told to pack up everything in here for the sale room.'

Brabazon was frantic and turned to her sons for support, 'Don't let him take my Cupid. It's all I've got from my old home – from my childhood.'

Henry stepped forward, straightening his shoulders and trying to appear adult, 'Can't you leave it?' he asked the packer.

The man had been through many similar scenes before and they always caused him embarrassment. He looked at the woman with her two sons and blustered again, 'I'm sorry but I've been told to take everything.'

Henry said, 'But it's not valuable – only Mother sets great store by that candlestick.'

The boy's loyalty and affection for his distraught mother softened the workman's heart. With a sudden gesture of agreement, he shamefacedly handed over the fragile little Cupid to Brabazon saying, 'Oh, take it then but hide it where the foreman won't see or I'll be in trouble.'

She was still stammering her thanks when Henry said, 'Father's waiting for you, Mother,' and showed her down the stairs.

'The position's quite hopeless!' The speaker, a sharp-faced man in sober black, slapped his hand palm down on to the top of a pile of papers and then sat back in his chair in a satisfied manner as if there was nothing he enjoyed more than pronouncing doom.

The other men around the table stared at him and then moved their eyes towards Mr and Mrs Nairn who sat together at the end. Beneath the table-edge, Brabazon reached out a hand and grasped Duncan's to give him reassurance. His face was drawn and taut with deep strain lines creasing his brow and his dark, curling hair was streaked with silver, which gave his wife a pang for it showed that her dear Duncan was growing old before his time. Though he had the appearance of a man of fifty, he was not yet forty – in the last few months he had aged a decade.

'You'd be well advised to dispose of everything while there's still some goodwill to sell. I know it's only your personal property that has been seized so far but there's still bills outstanding and you can't go on running this business if you're personally bankrupted. No one'll give you any credit.' This speaker was Willie Ord, a rotund man with highly coloured cheeks and a deceptively Pickwickian appearance. His bright blue eyes behind gold-rimmed spectacles looked almost cheerful as he put his dimpled hand on the sheaf of papers in front of him. He was the spokesman for the creditors around the table and sensing their receptiveness, he added with a beam, 'But I've some good news for a change. There's been an offer to buy. It's from Gordon's Brewery in Bernard Street. They're prepared to take the place over for a reasonable sum.' He looked triumphant as he announced this and the smile he bestowed on Duncan was almost a signal to start rejoicing.

Duncan did not respond however, but still looked glum. 'I'd be reluctant to sell,' he said slowly.

'That depends. What do they consider "reasonable"?' asked one of the other men at the table, addressing himself to Willie Ord.

'They'll go to three thousand pounds . . .' he said twinkling through his spectacles. Brabazon gasped and Duncan leaned forward to interject, 'Only three thousand for a good-going concern like Perseverance Brewery? That's not enough. The buildings alone must be worth more than that. What about all our equipment, the drays and the stock?'

One of the other men at the table, an old fellow with a shock of white hair and a white beard who had said nothing so far, joined in on Duncan's side. 'I agree. It's not enough. Three thousand won't even clear the debts.'

Ord nodded sagely as if he, too, agreed completely, 'I might manage to force them up a bit. They could be persuaded to add something for the stock – but it'll be at their valuation. You're not in a position to bargain, you know. You're lucky to be offered anything.'

The last remarks were directed sternly at Duncan who looked at the hostile faces opposite him and protested, 'But this business has been in my family for two hundred years. It has a good reputation – our beer's always good and every piece of equipment we have is the very best. You know that Willie. You know the work we've done on the place, the new pasteurisation plant and everything. It hasn't had time to prove itself yet.'

Willie Ord shook his head and made a tutting sound with his lips, 'Now Duncan, you mustn't confuse sentiment with business. I know the Nairns have been here for a long time but everything has to come to an end eventually. You should think seriously about the offer – before you're forced into bankruptcy in the business as well as personally.'

Duncan was not convinced and shook his head, 'It's hard to understand what's happened. Perseverance has always been profitable, it's only in the last five years that things have begun to go wrong. My father didn't have Excise Duty to worry about and I've been lax about it but if I pay up all the back dues, that should satisfy the authorities. That's why I'm selling Brewery House: it's bringing in a thousand pounds which'll pay off the Excise debt. My family and I are moving over to the Place – there's a flat empty and we're going into it.'

The white-bearded man turned in his chair to gaze at

Brabazon, 'You're moving into the Place?' he asked in astonishment. She flushed and nodded, 'The boys have friends there and it's close to the brewery for Duncan,' she said hastily.

'Won't you miss your fine house?' asked the old man.

Brabazon shook her head. She realised that her questioner knew she was Joshua Logan's girl, born and raised in the big house facing the Links, a woman from a superior and well-off family who had married against her mother's wishes. She raised her head proudly and stared back defiantly, 'I'm happy to live anywhere my husband goes,' she said.

Willie Ord nodded in approval, 'Very sensible Mrs Nairn, very sensible. The Place still belongs to the brewery so you won't have to pay a rent anyway.' Then he turned to Duncan and added, 'If you were to sell to Gordon's however, you'd be able to buy a proper house and Mrs Nairn wouldn't have to go into a flat beside the brewery workers.'

She knew what he was trying to do – make Duncan ashamed for bringing his wife to a tenement flat and she bridled angrily, 'I don't mind living in the Place. It's a very respectable building. It's not a slum if that's what you're insinuating.'

Willie Ord looked shocked, 'My dear lady, of course not! You may rest assured that my respect for you would not allow you to live in a slum, no matter how much you were prepared to sacrifice yourself.'

To her disquiet Brabazon saw that her husband was weakening. Ord's insinuations had undermined his resolve to keep the brewery so she spoke up for him, 'Please don't force my husband to sell his family business. Please give it another chance. Don't make him sell up to Gordon's!'

The faces of the men staring back at her were stern. 'It would be best to sell for what you can get. The business is thousands of pounds in debt,' said Willie Ord slowly. Brabazon turned to Duncan and whispered urgently, 'Don't sell. It's not just for you, it's for the boys as well.

15

The brewery's their inheritance, it's their family business as well as yours. You know how interested Henry is in it already.'

In the duel between herself and Ord she had won the upper hand, persuading Duncan to plead again with his persecutors, 'Give Perseverance Brewery another chance, gentlemen. It's only my personal creditors who're pressing for payment at the moment. The business people we owe money to will wait because they're all old friends and long-standing associates. They know I'll pay in the end.'

'Not all of them are so well-disposed,' said Ord uncovering some of his papers and pushing them towards the beleaguered man on the other side of the table.

As Duncan turned over the sheets, his face went rigid. 'How did you get these?' he asked.

'They were bought up by one of my clients. The holders were glad to be rid of them. The man who owns them now says he'll foreclose if you don't pay up immediately.'

Brabazon leaned across and saw that the papers were unpaid bills: one from a maltster, another from a corn merchant for feed for the dray horses, a third from a cooper and finally one from the supplier of hops. She realised that the situation had slipped out of her husband's control. He was too innocent and honest to combat Ord's guile; for by now she was sure the lawyer was playing some unscrupulous game. Suddenly she heard her own voice sounding strong and confident as she lifted the sheaf of bills and asked Willie Ord, 'How much exactly is owed on these?'

The fat man almost rubbed his hands, 'Just under one thousand seven hundred and fifty pounds. As your husband's lawyer I'm stalling the holder but he won't be put off much longer.'

'Is the holder one of the Gordon's? Are you the lawyer for them, too?' The question came from another of the men at the table and Brabazon sensed sympathy for her as he asked it.

Ord shifted his fat buttocks in the chair and looked uncomfortable, 'As a matter of fact I am, but I must hasten to add that it doesn't influence me in any way. I'm quite impartial. All I'm doing is telling you about their offer which I think is quite a good one.'

'Of course!' said the questioner but his tone of voice was sceptical.

Brabazon saw that the tide was turning in their favour and nudged Duncan who asked, 'If we agree to pay off the Excise bill within a certain time and the other bills immediately after, will we still have to sell up?'

Ord leaned back and said, 'The whole outstandings must come to something like four thousand pounds. Can you raise that amount of money?' It was obvious from his tone that he felt there was little chance of this miracle taking place.

Duncan faced him and said calmly, 'I'm sure it can be raised. I'm selling Brewery House as I've said and the man who's buying is prepared to pay a good price. It can go towards the debts.'

The other men were all watching the exchange sharply and the oldest of them said ruminatively, 'Of course it's better for the creditors if you pay back your debts in full. If you're made bankrupt you'll only have to repay so much in the pound. For my part, I'm in favour of giving you a chance but to be perfectly honest, it doesn't seem that your heart's really in the brewing business, Mr Nairn. If you want to keep the place, why don't you hire a manager?'

'It would be a problem to find a manager's wage at the moment,' said Duncan, not denying his lack of commitment to brewing.

'Our son Henry'll soon be sixteen and starting work,' offered Brabazon but the men around the table shook their heads for they were not prepared to risk their money with a sixteen-year-old.

'I might agree to giving you a year to prove yourself – but only if someone else runs the place,' said a second man.

Ord looked triumphant and said, 'But it doesn't seem that'll be possible.'

17

In the silence that hung over the room it was Brabazon who spoke up, 'I'll run it. I've lived next door to the brewery for sixteen years and heard everything that's gone on for all that time. I know every workman and they know me. I could run it.'

Ord laughed. 'Come, come, let's be serious Mrs Nairn. We're not talking about a sewing circle, we're talking about a brewery.'

Brabazon's eyes flashed fire at him, 'I'm literate and numerate, Mr Ord. I can balance books and calculate percentages. As far as the process work goes, I have Alex Warre the excellent head brewer to advise me. And my husband. Besides, as you probably know, I come from a commercial family. Running a brewery is not beyond my capacities.'

Her dignity and spirit won the day. The other men looked at each other and the oldest of them nodded his head with respect in his eyes. 'It's worth a try,' he said but then paused before adding, 'There's one stipulation however. I don't think Mr Nairn should take any part in the business. Because he's an undischarged bankrupt, it would be best if he relinquished all control. If you feel able to take it on by yourself Mrs Nairn, I'm in favour of giving you the chance.'

She looked doubtfully at Duncan who nodded in agreement and so she drew in her breath and said, 'All right, I'll do it. I'll give you a promise to pay all the debts back with interest and if I don't, you can have the place – lock, stock and barrel.'

Ord was furious. 'This is very irregular, very rash,' he spluttered.

'But it's likely to yield us a better return for our money than selling up to Gordon's for three thousand,' said the old man, rising to his feet and gathering up his papers. Then he walked round to Brabazon's side of the table and held out a hand to grasp hers. 'The best of luck, my dear lady. You're taking on far more than you imagine. I hope you make a good thing of it.'

To her surprise, everyone except Willie Ord agreed

18

and, so to her outward relief but with much secret misgiving, Brabazon Nairn became head of Perseverance Brewery.

On the day that she stepped out of her fine house for the last time, she stared around with new eyes. The building in which she was now to live was called Perseverance Place and faced out into a stretch of the Kirkgate, one of the busiest thoroughfares of Leith which led from the bottom of Leith Walk – the thoroughfare that linked the port with Edinburgh to Tolbooth Wynd and then on towards the docks which gave the place its prosperity and its pride. Leith, the ancient port serving Edinburgh, regarded itself as older, more enterprising and important, even richer than the capital city towering on the hills above it. Edinburgh, said Leithers, was a milk-and-water place whereas Leith was blood-and-guts.

Perseverance Place had originally been a monastic guesthouse, built in the twelfth century by the monks of the priory of St Anthony, who brewed ale in a little brewhouse behind it and after the Reformation this was taken over by an enterprising woman brewer. She made the guesthouse into an inn where her beer was sold to people passing up and down the road to the docks. Three hundred years later, beer was still being brewed in the same premises but the inn had become a tenement of flats in which the brewery employees lived. Their building was four stories high, with bulging ancient walls and a steep-pitched, red-tiled roof set between crow-stepped gables that were studded with embedded clam shells – put there by some seventeenth century owner to frighten away witches. Beneath the clam shells it was possible for those with sharp eyes to pick out an ancient stone slab carved with the date '1604' and one word in antique lettering – Persevere – the motto of the port of Leith.

The tiny, many-paned front windows of the Place stared down into the Kirkgate where there were two shops on the ground floor, one a butcher's and the other a pawn-

shop which advertised itself by displaying three golden
balls hanging from a black metal tripod above the front
door. The real life of the Place however went on at the
back and strangers often missed the opening to the yard
because it looked like a large rabbit hole. It was hard to
believe that a brewery dray drawn by two horses could
actually squeeze through it. Those passers-by who did
find the alley entrance, however, emerged from its darkness into a large cobbled yard hugged between high, red
sandstone walls. To their left as they stood in the alley
mouth was the back of Perseverance Place, the windows
open now, with women leaning out to chat to their neighbours over the tops of flowerpots blooming on the sills or
over the lines of washing hanging gaily out to dry. The
entrance to the flats was also at the back on first-floor
level. The door was approached by a steep stair flanked
by an iron railing on which generations of little boys had
performed balancing acts, much to the terror of their
mothers.

Immediately opposite the alley was the brewery office
which formed the foot of an L-shape, the longest side of
which was taken up by the four-storey brewhouse that
looked lopsided as it teetered up to the sky, terminating
eventually in a tall chimney above a red-tiled roof. Joining
the brewhouse to the Place and the Kirkgate was a high
wall of crumbling stone, in front of which were built the
brewery stables while on the other side was the burying
ground of St Mary's Church where Duncan Nairn's ancestors all lay. The church's truncated spire could be
glimpsed above the wall and its white-faced clock boomed
out the hours for the people living round about. There
was no need to buy a timepiece if you lived in Perseverance Place.

The right-hand far corner and the fourth side of the
yard were taken up by Brewery House, an imposing edi-
fice painted white but built of the same reddish stone as
the brewery and the surrounding walls. An entrance wing
with a pillared portico adjoined the office. Two Grecian
urns balanced on each end of the pediment and a pair of

crouching lions guarded the steps to the door, which had a large brass knocker in the form of a dragon. From a wrought-iron arch over the steps hung an iron lantern that was always lit at night. Along the main part of the house a strip of Greek-key decoration in white plaster ran below the four first-floor windows, each of which had eight panes of gleaming glass. Above them were another four smaller windows, then finally the peeping eyes of three attics. Hidden from view behind the house was a large garden of clipped box hedges, rose arbours and a lawn. Around 1810, the class-conscious wife of the brewer of the day had persuaded her husband to turn the house round so that she could come and go without being seen by the people in the Place. A new front door had been knocked in the garden façade and a sweeping carriage-drive cut through the old walled garden to link Brewery House with Commercial Street, which ran parallel to the Kirkgate. By doing this, the Nairn women were isolated from their workers and social discrimination began. There was a community in the Place about which the isolated women in the big house knew little. Though the gap between the Place and Brewery House could be measured in feet and inches. It was immeasurable in status.

Perhaps because they lived in such a secluded area, the ordinary folk of Perseverance Place regarded themselves as a community apart from the rest of Leith. Through the centuries the many children who had been born and brought up there always thought of themselves as inhabitants of the Place first and Leithers second. They were fiercely proud and proletarian, and because most of them worked for the brewery, the only gentry they acknowledged were the Nairns. It was as much of a shock to them as it was to Brabazon when it was discovered that the Nairns were moving out of Brewery House and coming to live among the ordinary folk in the Place.

Carrying a small wicker suitcase which contained the precious Cupid candlestick packed carefully amongst her clothes, Brabazon walked with her husband across the yard and side by side they mounted the open stairway to the door of Perseverance Place. In his courtly way Duncan opened it for her and stood aside so that she could walk through, but on the worn stone of the threshold she paused and stared back at Brewery House. Its windows sparkled gaily in the sunlight and she knew that already the removal men were carrying the furniture of the new owner through the hidden front door on the other side. Their home had been snapped up eagerly by a prosperous wine importer who owned cellars at the other end of Great Junction Street, but Brabazon's heart ached at the thought of another family in her house. In all her life she had only lived in two and both of them had been beautiful, spacious, calming . . . Now she looked upwards at the windows of the Place and her heart sank. How would she ever be able to exist in a tiny flat surrounded by strangers who were able to overhear and oversee everything she did or said?

From his expression she could tell that Duncan was suffering the same misgivings. It must be worse for him because he had been forced to sell the home of his grand-parents, great-grandparents and their parents before them. When she smiled reassuringly at him, he whispered, 'It won't be for long, my dear. It's only a temporary measure. We'll soon be able to buy back Brewery House. I'm convinced of it.'

'So am I,' she said resolutely, although her secret thoughts were very different.

Their new home was a flat on the first floor of the Place. The building contained eight flats in all, two on each floor. The families who lived there either paid rent to the brewery or else received their home as part of their wages for working in it. Brabazon knew the names of all the tenants, she even knew some of them by sight but nothing about them as personalities. Now she felt as if she were landing in a foreign country, so alien was it all. For years she had lived within a stone's throw of the Place but had never been inside it and could only imagine the dramas of life and death, the tragedies and triumphs, that took place within its walls. Brabazon's life till now had been led, not facing the brewery yard and the Kirkgate, but looking out over gardens to the spread of Leith Links, a very different perspective and another world indeed.

It was only a few steps to their new front door which Duncan opened with a large key to reveal a big, sparsely furnished kitchen with black-leaded range; a bed recess; a scrubbed deal table and four wooden chairs – the bailiff's men had left them nothing else except a blue pottery vase full of mixed summer flowers in the middle of the table. This unexpected sight made tears spring into Brabazon's eyes because they were the only symbol of gaiety and cheerfulness in her new home.

She turned and put her arms around Duncan who clasped her tightly to him muttering, 'I'm so sorry, my dearest. I'm so sorry, it's all my fault . . .'

'No, no,' she was telling him when they heard the sound of their sons' footsteps on the landing and stood apart like guilty children. The boys were laughing and chattering as they came through the door carrying a hamper between them. Thankfully the transition from their stately home to this flat did not appear to worry either of them at all. Dumping his end of the hamper on the ground, dark-haired and mischievous-looking Laurence laughed and said, 'What have you got in here, Mama? It weighs so much you must have it full of stones.'

'It's china and pots, things like that. Light the fire and put on the kettle Henry, dear,' she said.

'We've still got to eat, I suppose,' said Laurence sticking his hands in his pocket and wandering around the flat peering at everything, 'where am I going to sleep? Which room will I have?'

'There's not much choice,' said his brother, 'You'll have to sleep with me because there's only two rooms and a big cupboard. We'll sleep here in the kitchen in the box bed. Look it's over there in the corner.'

Laurence looked into the bed recess and shrugged, 'I'd rather sleep in a cupboard than share that with you. You

23

shout and kick all night in your sleep. Can I have the cupboard, Ma? I'll put a cot in it.'

The boys were still scrapping and arguing about places to sleep when there was a knock at the door which Duncan opened to reveal a wiry, freckled little woman with straggling red hair escaping from a large bun on the top of her head. She carried a plate covered with a white cloth, and a mouthwatering smell of freshly baked pancakes seemed to hang around her like a veil.

Duncan said in a welcoming voice, 'Oh, Nellie, come in, come in: you're the first visitor at our new home.' To Brabazon he called, 'It's Nellie Warre, my dear, the wife of Alex the head brewer . . .' He was obviously afraid she would not recognise the caller but Brabazon nodded and smiled because she did know Nellie though they had only ever exchanged a few words.

'I saw your laddies coming up and thought you might like something nice to eat,' said a flustered Nellie.

'That's very kind. Henry's making tea. Come in and take some with us,' said Brabazon pulling out a chair.

Duncan gestured at the flowers in the middle of the table and asked, 'Was it you who brought us the flowers too, Nellie?'

Nellie shook her untidy head, 'No, they're from Minna, my neighbour at the top. Ye ken Minna Meirstein from the pawnshop, Mr Nairn? We're a' – we're a' that sorry about what's happened . . .' Her voice faltered as she looked at Brabazon whom she had always admired from afar for her gentility and ladylike demeanour. 'If there's anything I can do for you, just ask,' said Nellie gathering her courage.

Brabazon took her new neighbour's hand, 'You're very kind,' she said.

Nellie flushed scarlet and coughed as she replied, 'Well, we're your neighbours, aren't we? The Place is good at looking after its own and my Alex says the folk who work in the brewery're like his family. We've got to stick together, haven't we?'

Duncan nodded, 'There's been Warres in Perseverance

24

Brewery for as long as Nairns have been here. It was a great relief to me when Alex said he'd stay and help my wife. She couldn't take over the business without him.'

Nellie was genuinely shocked, 'Where else would he go? We're just thankful you didna' get selt up. Alex'd never work for Gordon's. They're a rotten bunch along there and their beer's no' a patch on ours . . . I mean yours.'

Duncan laughed and said, 'You're very loyal. Now sit down, have a cup of tea and tell us about our neighbours. We'll have to get to know everybody . . .'

Nellie was soon in her element, sipping tea and regaling the Nairns with stories of the Place.

'Well, Mr Nairn, you know us Warres of course – we're on the left of the top floor. We've a grand view out to the harbour but that's another thing. There's me and there's Alex and our laddies, Pat, Gideon and Robert. We've Baby Elsie as well. She's only two and she was a bit of an accident as they say. Ye ken how it is . . .'

Laurence who was sitting on the floor listening to the recital nodded and said, 'I know Pat. He and I are friends. He's the same age as I am.'

'He's fourteen,' confirmed Nellie, 'and he's in the brewery with his dad . . . I hope you'll not be paying off lads, Mrs Nairn?'

'If I am, I won't be paying off Pat,' said Brabazon who already knew how highly the Warres were valued for their labour.

'That's grand,' sighed Nellie and re-launched into her recital, 'My next-door neighbour on the top is Minna Meirstein and her husband Abe. They're Jews, you know. Don't go out on Saturdays and all that . . . they came here from some place with a queer name in Russia when they were just young things, but they've done well have the Meirsteins. They own the pawnshop at the foot of the building. They dinna give any favours but they dinna cheat either. Everybody in Leith uses them when times are hard.' She paused embarrassed, suddenly remembering that times had become very hard for her listeners.

25

'Go on, Nellie. It's very interesting,' Duncan urged her gently, recognising that she thought she'd made a gaffe.

'On the floor above you old Happy Anderson has the wee flat on the right. No' very big but that's all she needs because she's on her ain since her man died. He was a carter with you, Mr Nairn. Maybe you remember him, a wee fellow with a big carbuncle on his cheek?'

Duncan nodded, 'Yes, I do, he died about four years ago, didn't he?'

'Is her name really Happy? Was she christened that?' Henry's voice came from the corner where he too was sitting entranced.

Nellie gave a cracked cackle. 'Bless you no. That's her nickname. She's called "Happy" because she's that gloomy all the time. No matter what you tell her she sees the black side of it. If she heard the King was coming to call, she's worry in case he fell on the stairs and broke his leg. She's like that. It's a joke with everybody.'

'Doesn't she mind people calling her Happy?' asked Brabazon.

'Not a bit of it. She thinks they're paying her a compliment. She's a good old soul, though, with a kind heart underneath it all. She's looking after Elsie for me right now and she's aye ready to help folk when they're in trouble . . .'

Trouble again, thought Nellie, I wish I could think before I open my mouth; but encouraged by the attention of her audience, she plunged on. 'Next door to Happy, we've the Cairns. I'm not sure if they're a blessing or a curse.'

'I think I've seen them,' said Brabazon, 'Is one of them a huge woman with black hair?'

Nellie nodded, 'That's Ruthie. Once seen never forgotten is Ruthie. What a size that woman is! She must be six foot and her muscles are like iron. Alex says he wouldn't like to meet her on a dark night. Folk say she's a wrestler. She runs a sort of club for laddies in Salamander Street. She teaches them to box, can you believe it?'

'Her brother Bobs is pretty strong too,' said Duncan,

'He works in the cellar at the brewery and can roll more barrels a day than any man we've ever had.'

'Bobs is the youngest of them. He's the same age as my Pat though he looks a lot older. They're gypsies I think, they're a' that black. Tho' Bobs is big, he's gentle, not like Ruthie who's a terror. On Saturday nights they all go out in a gang and get fu'. The noise they make coming home is something terrible, shouting and singing. Nobody's brave enough to tell them to keep quiet though. There's four of them and the only one that's not a giant is Rosie, the second one. Even Ruthie's scared of Rosie. God knows how she does it but she can quiet them. And you wouldn't think it to look at her, wizened and thin as a scarecrow. You've maybe seen her, Mrs Nairn. She works in the shoe shop on the Kirkgate.'

Brabazon had never bought a pair of shoes in the Kirkgate in her life. Hers, till now, had all been handmade but she nodded and asked, 'What about the fourth Cairns?'

'That's Eck. He helps Ruthie with the boxing club. He's a bit simple is Eck but he's no trouble to anybody, not wild or anything like that. They all look after him.'

Her listeners were by now becoming slightly confused. The building had begun to seem like a teeming anthill. 'What about our neighbours on this floor? Who lives in the flat opposite us?' asked Brabazon.

Nellie's face lost its look of enjoyment. 'It's Tom Lambert and his wife Irene. You dinna want to have anything to do with them. Lambert's in the brewery, too, but he's bad lot . . . Alex says so, anyway. Irene's funny. She doesnae speak to anybody. If she meets me on the stairs she scuttles past like a crab. She has a terrible life with him, I think. He's aye knocking her about. They've no bairns living, though she's had a few and lost them. God knows why she stays with him.'

Duncan and Brabazon looked at each other. They had only that morning been consulting the staff list of the brewery and decided that economies had to be made. Some men would have to be dismissed and Lambert's name was the first they had picked out.

27

At that point the sounds of returning footsteps were heard on the stairs and when the church clock boomed out twelve Nellie rose to her feet with a gasp. 'Is it that time already and me without any dinner made for the men coming in? I'll have to run. If there's anything you need, Mrs Nairn, just give me a call. And welcome to Perseverance Place!'

With a wave of the hand, she left.

'You shouldn't do anything too hastily,' Duncan warned her when Brabazon had sat down to make a thorough study of the record and account books of Perseverance Brewery. After a few days it became obvious that the place was working at a loss; the wage bill alone was more than the weekly incomings. Duncan, she knew, had been too soft-hearted to refuse a place to a son of an employee or to pay off any man too inefficient, old or infirm to continue working effectively.

'We can't just hope that people will leave of their own accord,' she told him eventually in despair. 'I know how much you hate being strict, but I'll do it for you. We have to cut the work force by at least five.'

There were twelve men working in the brewery plus six pensioners, one of them Happy Anderson, who received small payments every week.

'Who's to go?' she asked Alex Warre who, after an initial few weeks of suspicion on his part, had become a trusted ally. There was no use asking Duncan. He could not bring himself to fire anyone.

'I'll write you a list,' offered the big, gruff brewer and next morning he produced it, written in careful copperplate script on a sheet of paper torn from a child's exercise book.

She read five names . . . two old men could be dispensed with and mollified with pensions. They would still cost money every week but a good deal less than a wage.

'Neither of them'll mind, they've been wanting to stop working for ages but didn't say so in case Mr Nairn

28

wouldn't be able to give them their pensions,' Alex told her.

'Tell them that's quite safe,' said Brabazon ticking off their names.

Alex pointed out the next name, 'That lad's an idle young sod. He doesnae deserve his money. I ken that he's been round at Gordon's asking for a place. Let him go.'

Brabazon ticked off the name.

'Then there's Tom Lambert,' said Alex.

She looked up at him and asked, 'My neighbour, you mean?' She had met Lambert on the stairs several times and he seemed to mock her as he stood aside for her to pass. Her sharp nose noticed that he always smelt of beer.

Alex nodded, 'Aye. We'd be better off without him. He drinks more than his pundy every day – far more – and he makes trouble with the other men, picking fights and saying things about the boss.'

Brabazon shivered, 'About me?'

Alex nodded, 'Not just you though. He's aye been the same. The boss is on one side and folk like Lambert on the other. It's a kind of a battle for them.'

'But what excuse do we have for firing him?'

'We don't need one. We're cutting back. We're not brewing as much as we did this time last year. We've only one vat going at a time and we used to have two or sometimes three. We don't need extra men.'

'I know, but if Lambert goes from here, he'll lose his flat won't he? It's part of his wage.' Brabazon had also seen Lambert's raddled wife Irene slinking up and down the stairs like a scared cat, just as Nellie had described. She would feel guilty about causing that woman any extra grief.

'If he wants to keep it tell him he can pay a rent. If you're that softhearted missus, make it low. He'll not refuse.'

She put her long finger on the last name. 'This can't be right. You know that Duncan always promised a place for your boys. You can't mean that I should fire your Pat?'

Alex nodded his grizzled head, 'I do that. Pat's not keen on brewing. He's aye talking about joining the army, but his mother doesnae want him to leave home. His uncle's working with a house-painter in Leith Walk and he says he can get Pat in there. Splashing about with whitewash'll suit him fine.'

There was a note of disappointment in the voice and Brabazon sensed that Pat and his father were at logger-heads. Alex could not imagine any son of his wanting to do anything other than work at Perseverance Brewery, but from infancy Pat had been a rebel – constantly in conflict with his father. If house-painting had been the career Alex selected for his son, Pat would surely have wanted to be a brewer.

'All right,' she said, 'but remember that if your other boys want to come in here, there'll be a place for them.'

Alex nodded, 'Gideon's next. He's a tough wee lad but he's set his heart on being a policeman. His mother and I don't think he'll grow big enough though and maybe he'll have to be a brewer instead.'

'Then there's Robert of course. How old is he now?' said Brabazon.

'He's eleven. There's time for Robert, yet,' Alex told her, and she could see from the way he said this son's name that the lad was his last hope for another generation of Warres at the brewery.

As soon as all was decided, she made up wages in brown envelopes and walked out into the yard where the men were taking a mid-morning break and drinking some of their daily pundy of beer. They took it in the morning, at midday and in the middle of the afternoon and con-sumed about five pints a day each. They said they worked better for it. A few men drank more than their share but unless the consumption became blatantly prodigious, the Nairns and Alex turned blind eyes.

She walked among them, handing out their wage pack-ets and when she reached the men on her list, paused beside them to break the bad news of dismissal as tactfully as possible. Everyone took it stoically until she reached

Lambert. He was sitting on his folded jacket in a patch of sunlight with his brawny arms crossed around his knees and did not rise to his feet when she approached. From the way he stared at her she knew he guessed what was coming.

Bending low she handed him his wages and said, 'I'm sorry, but I'll have to give you a week's notice. You'll finish next Friday. You can keep the flat though. Alex's made arrangements about the rent.'

He glared up at her, blue eyes glinting malevolently behind reddened lids.

'Will I? That's awful kind of you. Are you sending me off?'

She nodded, 'Yes, I'm sorry.'

'You're nothing of the kind. You're like that man of yours, a damned fancy piece that thinks you're better than us. But you're one of us now, aren't you Mrs Nairn? And you don't like it.'

She turned to walk away and he shouted after her, 'You don't fire your favourites, do you. Alex Warre's still here and so are all his cronies. You watch out Mrs Nairn or you'll be in trouble. Folk don't treat Tom Lambert like dirt and get away with it!'

She was shaking when she reached the sanctuary of her office and sank down in a chair with heart hammering and black spots swimming before her eyes. The malice in Lambert's eyes when he looked at her had been truly terrifying and she wished with all her heart that she had been able to send him out of the Place, out of their little community altogether. He was the rotten apple that could spoil an entire barrel.

Her distress was so overpowering that she felt she had to escape from the confines of the brewery and the enclosed yard for a little while. In the world outside, she knew, the sun shone and the open space of the Links, where she had once loved to walk, beckoned. On impulse she put on a rather battered old bonnet of Leghorn straw and pulled a thin lace shawl, one of the relics from her days of prosperity, over her shoulders. Then she locked

31

up the office and without telling anyone where she was going, headed for the alleyway into the Kirkgate. Once there she paused and breathed the air like someone savouring wine. Leith always smelt delicious. Mixed with the aroma of their own brewing beer were mouthwatering scents wafting over from the chocolate factory and the sugar refinery three streets away. Overlaying those came the resinous scent of pine forests as the saws in her brother's timber-yard, at Timber Bush on the other side of the Kirkgate, ripped into the hearts of the tall trees her father shipped in from Scandinavia and Russia. Then there was an underlying smell of fish which wafted in when the breeze blew from the East, plus a taste of tar and salt from the docks. It was the mixture of smells she had delighted in all her life, the perfume of her native place.

She walked quickly down the Kirkgate, past the busy shops and tumble-down tenements that were packed full of families living cheek by jowl with each other. Though she thought that her present home was a comedown from Brewery House she realised that, compared to the slums of Sugarhouse Close, the Shore and Jubilee Alley, she was living in a very respectable building indeed.

She knew now where she was going – to visit Mark and Amelia and enquire about the health of her mother. She had not been there for several months and though her mother had given orders that Brabazon was not to be admitted into the sickroom, she knew that her brother and sister-in-law would be concerned about her failure to call. Her route led her past Trinity Hospital where a group of old sea-men sat on a low wall, their weatherbeaten faces turned up to the sun as they yarned together. They were waiting for their pensions from the mariners' fund because this was paying-out day. At three o'clock the ancient, iron-bound chest in the hall of the hospital would be unlocked and the keeper would distribute the small sums that kept many old seafarers and their families from destitution.

Brabazon had never been so aware of the value of

money as she was that afternoon. She had walked past the old mariners many times before but without realising exactly what it meant to have to count the pennies, to measure out money into small sums that bought food and coal, clothes and rent, a pint of beer and a twist of tobacco in a torn-off piece of newspaper. She smiled at the old men and said 'Good day' as she passed. They returned her greeting gravely, sharp old eyes assessing her, and when she went on up the paved street, she knew they would have their heads together talking about her for they all knew who she was. Some of them might have sailed in her father's timber ships. They'd all have heard about Duncan's bankruptcy and though the shame of being talked about had worried her before, today it seemed unimportant. It made her more at one with the ordinary people who walked the Kirkgate.

Soon she was at the Links which were bathed in the sun's full brilliance. People were strolling across the grass, some of them nursemaids pushing babies in high-wheeled carriages; others were truant schoolboys kicking footballs. Promenading couples walked arm in arm, the women shading their heads beneath frilled parasols. Brabazon herself had played here as a child and had strolled on the grass with Duncan when they first met. Now she paused and gazed across at her brother's home. The windows glinted through the trees inviting her in. She turned and walked across the grass towards the wrought-iron gate.

Old Mary was dead and the maid who opened the door was young and trim in a long black dress and frilled apron. She knew Brabazon and smiled, holding the door for her. 'The master and the mistress are in the parlour, madam. I'll tell them you're here,' she said. Mark appeared behind her and cried out, 'I thought I saw you coming up the path. Come in, come in! We're taking tea. You're just in time.'

Mark and she had always been friends. The problems with her mother had not divided them although he had to tread a narrow line for fear of angering the old woman. Now that she was mute and immobile, he still respected her wishes as far as he was able but he was fond of his sister and concerned about the troubles that had overtaken her. He put a tender hand on her arm and guided her towards the little turret room. Feeling emotional, she walked beside him, noticing pieces of furniture and pictures that she remembered from long ago. Her sister-in-law Amelia was lying on a sofa beside the fire which was lit in spite of the warmth of the day.

"Melia's not been well,' Mark told her, 'so I try to be with her every afternoon. The office's not far away after all.' He was a more uxorious husband than his father Joshua, thought Brabazon.

Amelia's illness was obviously pregnancy. She looked as plump and satisfied as a broody hen as she sat up against silken cushions. 'Isn't this dreadful?' she asked Brabazon, laying her hands on her swelling stomach, 'It's my fifth. I'm simply terrified. The last delivery was such agony.'

Brabazon sat down in a chair by her side, surprised at this outburst of familiarity. Amelia had always kept her at arm's length before, confining herself to conventional politeness whenever they met.

'I hope everything goes well for you,' she murmured and Amelia smiled sweetly showing small, perfectly shaped teeth. 'I trust in God, my dear,' she sighed.

Of course, thought Brabazon, you would say that. Amelia's father was a clergyman after all.

Her brother came up with a cup of tea in his hand and said, 'You're looking well, Brabazon.'

'What a pretty shawl,' added Amelia, fingering Brabazon's lace.

Their effusiveness made her suddenly realise that they were worried about her and because such concern made her feel awkward, pride made her straighten her back and say, 'I'm very well thank you,' in a carefree voice. For the rest of her short visit, she talked about her mother's unrelenting sickness – she was no better and no worse. The doctors said she might live for years. No one mentioned Duncan or his troubles. Then Amelia dominated

34

the rest of the conversation telling her sister-in-law about the big estate she and Mark were hoping one day to buy outside Edinburgh.

'All the best families are moving out of Leith now, you know. It's getting so crowded and rowdy. Not at all as it used to be. The big people have left already but of course we can't make any plans while your mother's so ill . . . People we know have found this lovely place with forty acres and such a pretty house! It needs a lot of things done to it, but the workmen are in now and they'll move out by the winter. One day we'll have a place like that, too.'

The unspoken addition of 'when your mother dies' hung on the air between them.

Brabazon smiled and said, 'I hope you find something pretty, 'Melia.'

Her sister-in-law looked pensive, 'Wouldn't you like to live in the country, too, Brabazon?'

'Not at the moment, I'm afraid. What I want to do is buy back Brewery House. Anyway I wouldn't want to leave Leith. I'd find the country too quiet.' It was the first time she had actually admitted to herself that she was planning to get Brewery House back. For the first time, too, it seemed like a possibility.

As soon as the door had closed behind Brabazon, Amelia gazed at her husband and asked, 'Wasn't that dreadful, so embarrassing. I do hope she didn't come to borrow money or anything. The poor soul looks very shabby and tired.'

'I'm sure it wasn't to borrow money, but I'm worried about her too,' said Brabazon's brother.

Amelia sighed and put the back of her wrist against her forehead. 'That husband of hers is such a wastrel, bringing shame on the family the way he's done. Everybody's talking about them. I thought she looked very drawn. Why did you tell her she was looking well?'

Her husband replied, 'I couldn't say that she looked ghastly, could I? It would worry her more. Anyway you admired her shawl and I thought she looked very shabby.'

'Yes, I had to say something. That sort of lace is so old-fashioned and hers is quite yellow with age. Poor Brabazon.' Amelia sank back against her pillows with a martyred air.

'Something has to be done about her. I'll write to Father and ask for his advice,' Mark decided.

In spite of their efforts to cover up, Brabazon was disquieted as she walked home. The shawl felt awkward on her shoulders and she resolved to put it away in her box when she reached home, for she could tell by the way Amelia had handled it that it was unfashionable. By the time she had walked half the length of the Kirkgate, however, her spirits rose – for the looming shape of Perseverance Place hove into sight. 'I'm going home. Duncan will be there and so will my boys. I'm a lucky woman in spite of all that's happened,' she told herself and then she laughed inside at the next thought that struck her, 'I wonder what Mark and Amelia would say if they knew I'm about to start learning how to be a woman brewer?' she asked herself.

It was Alex Warre's idea. 'In the old days the brewers were women. How'd you like to try your hand, mistress?'

She looked doubtful. 'I don't think I'd manage it. How could I learn?'

'I'll teach you. It'll take a bit of time but there's no hurry is there? You should learn how to make the beer because we need an extra brewer now that we've cut the work force and if anything happened to me, there'd be nobody to take over, would there?'

Neither of them mentioned Duncan so she was well aware that Alex knew about the creditors' stipulation against her husband having a hand in the business. Duncan had in fact welcomed his freedom and spent most of his time practising in St Mary's Church where he was organist on Sundays. His beloved piano had been sold at the breaking-up of Brewery House and he'd missed it sorely until Mr Templeton, the minister, gave him permission to play the organ at the church as often as he liked.

The morning after her visit to Mark and Amelia, Brabazon went to work in her oldest clothes and when she met Alex, told him, 'Well I'm ready to start as your apprentice brewer. Let's begin at once.'

With a grin he waved a strong bare forearm towards the roof of the brewery building and said, 'Kirtle up your skirt then and we'll begin at the top.'

Her ankles and shapely calves were exposed but that didn't matter to either of them as she climbed the narrow ladder leading to the upper floors of the brewhouse tower. The warm heady air made her head swim slightly and she fought against a tickling in her nose that made her want to sneeze. When they reached the first level, her guide did not pause but went on climbing until they reached the malt store tucked away under red clay roof tiles. Ancient beams of roughly hewn oak criss-crossed above their heads and Alex had to bend slightly to avoid knocking himself out against them. As she negotiated her way after him, she realised why it was that he always walked with a slight stoop.

Thrusting a hand into an open sack of grain he held a cupped palm towards Brabazon and said, 'Taste it.' She looked at the golden seeds of barley in his calloused hand and carefully picked out a few. 'No, no, take a handful like this and chew them,' he told her, so she too dipped into the loosely shifting grain to gather up enough to make a decent helping.

Raising her palm to her mouth she nibbled cautiously before smiling and telling him, 'But they're delicious. They've a very crisp taste.'

'That's how it should be. It's malted barley and the first thing a brew master – or mistress – has to do is taste every sack that comes in from the malster. When you've done it long enough you can tell which farm the barley comes from. If they try to slip in a few sacks from a different place, you'll be able to pick them out at once. Perseverance Brewery always buys East Lothian barley, from a place near Drem. I've never been there myself but I can tell their grain the minute I taste it. The Nairns have always bought the best.'

Impressed, she bit into a few more grains savouring their nutty flavour. 'It tastes so rich and ripe,' she said.

'Barley's very important but so's everything else,' Alex told her, 'Now come over here and look at this.' Lifting a full sack as easily as if it were a bag of feathers, he heaved its edge over the metal lip of a large hopper and sent a stream of golden grain down into the pipe leading to the next floor. 'Sacks of barley come up to the top here on a hoist from the yard and when I've tested them, they're poured down into the grist mill like this. Now we'll go down and start the mill working.'

They clambered back down the ladder which Alex always used in preference to the stairs that ran down the middle of the building and on the next floor he pulled down a switch on the wall to start the steam-engine of the malt grinder, the grist mill. Its pistons groaned into life and rattled like an old man grinding his teeth. Then slowly the air filled up with minute sparks of dust that glittered and gleamed like motes of gold in the diffused sunlight coming through tiny slits of windows in the thick walls.

Brabazon watched while Alex tested the ground barley from a bucket at the bottom of the grinder. He rubbed it reflectively between his fingers, muttering in a low voice, 'You've got to get the right feeling.'

'How do you know when it's right?' she asked impressed.

'By your fingers. It should feel as soft as silk – not like dust and not like grit but like very fine sand. Feel it. You'll learn by doing it. That's the only way.' But Brabazon wanted to sneeze again and was forced to hold her hand to her nose. Alex laughed, 'The grist mill aye does that to folk at first. When I started working here as a laddie, I sneezed without stopping for a week.'

'How old were you then? she asked.

He thought for a minute, 'I was ten I think. My father was head brewer, that was nearly thirty years ago.'

'Is it going to take me as long as that to learn everything?' she asked in alarm.

'Och, no, you'll have it at your fingertips in about ten years,' he told her with a laugh.

The noise of the machinery was insistent in their ears and Alex had to raise his voice to make himself heard. 'Before Mr Nairn put in his steam-engines, the machinery in here was worked by water-power. We've a grand stream running under this building, you know, and we've the best well in the whole district. There's breweries in Edinburgh that'd pay big money for it. It's so sweet and pure. The old monks knew what they were doing when they sank that well.'

'Is it why Gordon's are so keen to buy us?' she asked.

'It is. Their well's not a patch on ours, it has a kind of salty taste but ours tastes like honey. It's the liquor from here that makes our brew so special.'

She had been the wife of a brewer long enough to know what the word 'liquor' meant in a brewhouse. No brewer ever talked about water. She realised she'd have to learn a whole new language as well as so many other things in her new rôle.

'What happens next?' she asked.

'We put the grist, the ground-up barley, into a vat and start mashing it. Now this is where the magic comes in. Not everybody can make a good mash, just like not every woman can cook. Some folk just dinnae hae the hand for it.' Next to the grist mill, a brew was mashing in a big vat from which a faint steam was rising. Alex looked satisfied and said, 'This was started at seven o'clock this morning. I mixed it myself – two parts malt to one of liquor. It's heated up to 149 degrees – nowadays we use the modern thermometer things but in the old days we could tell the right heat by holding a glass over the top and watching how it steamed up.'

'How long is it left heating?' she asked.

'About an hour. You judge it yourself – you just know

when it's right.' His methods were more instinctive than scientific she realised and as her face expressed disbelief at this, he said, 'Look, I'll show you a trick. You'll know when the liquor's at the right temperature to add to the malt without using any fancy thermometers if you can see your reflection clear as glass in the surface. That's the sign it's ready.' At this prompting she climbed a little set of stepladders and leaned over the edge of another vat of water heating for the next mash. To her surprise a woman was staring back at her from its surface – a woman with pale ivory-coloured skin, well-marked dark eyebrows and a curving mouth; she saw the thick brown hair drawn back from a middle parting and curving like silk over both ears; she saw her own dark-fringed golden eyes with new lines of worry and concentration at the corners and recognised that she, Brabazon Nairn, was still beautiful. The sight gave her confidence and she was looking happy when she descended again.

Alex was still enthusiastically pouring out information. 'When the malt and liquor are properly mashed, there's a slotted bottom to this vat and we run off the wort from there.'

'What's the wort?'

He was a patient teacher who answered all her questions. 'The liquid that comes off the mash is called the wort and at first it's very strong but we go on sparging – that's spraying – the grist for a bit longer till it gets weaker. When we've got out everything we can, we sell the draff that's left behind for cattle feed. Folk come and collect it. We don't get much for it but it's aye money.'

Her head was beginning to swim slightly and she could not make up her mind whether she was confused by so much information or sickening for some illness. She must have looked strange because he asked her anxiously, 'Are you all right, Mrs Nairn?'

She shook her head, 'I feel rather weak.'

To her relief, he laughed and said, 'I was wondering when that'd happen. If you're not used to it, the air in here can mak' you drunk. You'd best go home and have a lie-down. I'll tell you the rest tomorrow.'

She drowsed for a long while against her pillows while a whole vocabulary of new words ran through her head – *liquor, wort, grist, draff*. And Alex had warned her that was only half of it. How could she remember everything? Would she ever be able to do such a job as brew beer? Then she remembered Mark and Amelia in their grand house and her own reflection, so ladylike and composed on the surface of the heating vat. The memory made her laugh.

Next morning Brabazon woke early and stretched her arms high above her head in bed. Duncan cocooned in blankets, stirred in his sleep and muttered a few words. She slipped out on to the floor and pulled the bed curtains tight behind her to keep the dawn light away from him. The early morning was glorious and over in the tree-filled churchyard a chorus of birds was greeting the rising sun. From her kitchen window, she saw a trickle of silver smoke rising from the brewery chimney.

Alex Warre looked surprised when she pushed open the brewhouse door. 'My word, you're early,' he said.

'I saw the smoke and wanted to know what's going on. There's still a lot to learn, isn't there? It's too lovely a morning to lie in bed anyway.'

He smiled and noticed with gladness how much more carefree she looked than on the previous day. 'Today we'll start fermentation. I've lit a fire under the big copper with the wort in it and when it boils I'll add the hops.'

There was a little sack at his side full of what looked like pale-green dried petals. She loved the pungent aroma of hops and lifted a few to inhale the the smell that often seeped like a wraith through the Kirkgate.

Alex told her, 'Taste one. Hops're good for folk. They eat them like cabbage over in the Low Country. It makes me mad when thae do-gooders in the Temperance Hall up Bernard Street preach against beer. When I was a laddie, folk knew that beer's better than any doctor's medicine!'

41

Brabazon laughed, 'You're biased.'

'Maybe I am but I'm no weakling and when I was a bairn, we were a' given a glass of beer in the morning. Nane o' us were peely-wally looking things like some of the bairns brought up on milk.'

They began work at once and by mid-morning had run off the wort and hop solution. When she saw the spent hops left behind, Brabazon looked wistful and said, 'That's the stuff we used to use for mulching our roses in the garden at Brewery House.'

'Aye, it's good for flowers. I'll send this lot over to the new folk to keep the garden sweet till you get it back again.'

She was surprised that he had seemed to be able to read her mind and also that he accepted without question that the Nairns would one day recover their old house. There was no time to chat however because he was showing her something else. 'Now, mistress, this is the stage that's most important. Watch while I add the yeast.'

It was a ritual.

As head brewer Alex kept the key to the yeast store, a little wooden cupboard in which the putty-coloured wonder-worker was stored. He stressed the importance of keeping the store absolutely clean for even an airborne infection could turn the yeast sour and spoil a brewing. Then, holding a shining brass bucket under her nose, he said, 'This yeast's fine. Take a sniff of it. If it was off, you could tell by the smell.' She sniffed, hardly daring to breathe on the thick sudsy contents of the bucket. It smelled like baking bread and made her hungry.

'It's ten years since we had any bad yeast in here,' said Alex proudly as he climbed like a high priest up a stepladder to the top of an enormous, brightly gleaming copper vat. 'Go to work,' he told the yeast as he poured it in. And looking down at Brabazon, he explained, 'It'll take three days and all that time we've to keep a watch to make sure it doesn't get too hot or too cold . . . We heat it up or cool it down and guard it like a newborn bairn in a cradle.'

For the next three days she could hardly bear to stay away: time after time she climbed the ladder to peer over the rim of the brewing vat and watched the progress of the working yeast. It seemed to be alive and at first worked slowly, raising shallow patterns, like the sculptured decorations on panne velvet, on the surface of the liquid. Then, as activity increased, the whirls and scrolls puffed up in size; as she gazed at the ever-moving pattern she remembered her fascination with a toy kaleidoscope that she was given by her father when she was a child. The fermenting yeast exerted the same spell on her and even when she was in bed at night, she visualised it beneath her closed eyelids and wondered what pictures it was drawing on the top of the brewing beer.

After a couple of days, thick white suds of activated yeast threatened to overflow the vat and Alex showed her how to scrape them off into a bucket with a long wooden shovel. 'Don't waste it. It can be used again as long as we keep it clean,' he told her and showed her how to store the wonder-worker in its scrubbed cupboard.

On the third day be pronounced that the beer was ready. 'How do you know?' she asked.

'Well, I just know by the smell but you can test it with a hydrometer. You know what specific gravity you want and when it's reached that, it's ready. We stop fermentation by cooling the vat down. We pour cold water down its sides.'

'And then you have beer?' she asked hopefully. The whole business seemed to be so long and drawn out. But the end was not yet in sight and Alex laughed as he shook his head.

'It's no' as easy as that. We've still to rack it into barrels and let it settle for four days before we add the fining . . . but, don't worry, Mrs Nairn, after all that you'll have Perseverance Special.'

Finally, on the tenth day after her education in brewing began, Brabazon stood in the cellar with her workmen, her husband and her sons. She was holding up a glass of clear golden liquid that shone and glimmered like molten amber.

'Taste it, it's your first brew,' said Duncan proudly.

She sipped cautiously. The beer was cool and slightly effervescent on her tongue. When she swallowed, the taste was pure and refreshing. 'I think it's delicious,' she pronounced to the watching faces. Then Alex poured out more glasses and passed them round before he raised his own towards Brabazon. She felt nervous as they all took deep draughts.

Duncan was the first to speak, 'It's an excellent brew. One of the best.'

Alex agreed. 'Aye, it's splendid. We'll call it Mrs Nairn's Number One.'

'But I didn't make it, you did,' she demurred.

'No, you were there all through. You touched everything I touched and tasted everything I tasted. If you weren't a good influence it wouldn't have gone well. A brew works differently for different folk, some cannae do it . . . but you can, Mistress Nairn. Here's to you!'

She beamed with genuine pleasure as she watched them raising their glasses in the air, 'Here's to Mrs Nairn's Number One,' they chorused.

1893

It was Saturday night and Brabazon, dressed in a thick serge skirt and wrapped round with a black woollen shawl, was shopping in the Kirkgate.

As she shouldered her way through the jostling crowds she felt her purse bumping against her flank in the skirt pocket. It did not weigh very heavily because she had paid the wages of her workmen that morning and had been depressed by how little was left to feed her family. Now, like so many other black-shawled women that night, she was out looking for bargains from the brightly lit shops and stalls that were anxious to be rid of their perishable goods before Sunday. There was a rueful smile on her face as she peered in the windows where tempting goods were displayed under hissing gas lights. Her life had changed so radically in only a few years that it was difficult to remember she had been Mrs Nairn of Brewery House who never set foot in tradesmen's shops, but sent her servants out to do the buying for everything from a roast of beef to a packet of pins; Mrs Nairn whose order was delivered with alacrity by the best grocer in Leith; Mrs Nairn who was greeted with respect by the people she favoured with her custom.

Those thoughts were running through her mind as she stood, basket on her arm, in front of Donaldson's, the butcher's on the ground floor of Perseverance Place. Beside her two skinny little boys in ragged clothes and bare feet were scrabbling through a pile of half-rotten fruit and vegetables thrown out by a greengrocer's stall in the middle of the street. As a contrast to their obvious hunger Donaldson's window was a glory to the eye and an evocation of sumptuous dining, with legs of lamb and snake-like oxtails hanging from a polished brass rail along the top of the window. Succulent roasts of beef were displayed on the gleaming white tiles beside pyramids of lamb chops with paper crowns on their shanks, piles of scarlet mince and coils of sausages. In the middle sat the pièce de resistance, an enormous pig's head with its ears upright, its eye sockets smiling and its mouth propped open in a grin by a scarlet apple. Its neck was wreathed with red-berried holly because Christmas was near.

Brabazon sighed at the sight of the pig and mentally counted her money. She had enough for some pieces of stewing mutton which would make a filling meal if she added lots of vegetables. Pushing open Donaldson's door, she stepped inside. Behind the counter the proprietors stood side by side like Tweedledum and Tweedledee. They were both enormously fat, red-cheeked and jolly – just like their grinning pig. Tom Donaldson, the master butcher, wore a straw boater, a pristine white coat and a long blue and white striped apron tied round his vast waist. He was gaily sharpening his knife against a long whet iron and shouting as he worked, 'Cheap mince tonight, lots and lots of sausages . . . potted haugh and mealie puddens!'

Beside him stood his best advertisement for the quality of their wares, his wife Lily who was famous in Leith for two things: her love of finery in clothes and her fluent tongue which could outswear anyone – in a port where sailors had imported curses from all over the world. Donaldson was immensely proud of his Lil. Not only was she a living example of how good was his beef but she was also a safeguard against unruly customers. She was always smartly dressed but on Saturday nights, the biggest trading night of the week, she surpassed herself and customers would come from far and near to see how the butcher's wife had chosen to dazzle her clientele.

From the doorway Brabazon saw that tonight Mrs Donaldson was decked out like a Music-Hall star in a low-cut, purple satin gown with enormous rosettes of darker purple ribbon on her shoulders. On her head she wore a black hat, all cocked up on one side and adorned with a bird made of purple feathers, its beak pointing down at her cushiony breasts which rose like twin mountains of marshmallow out of the top of the gown. A little white apron was kirtled round her waist but Lil did no cutting. Her job was to wrap up the orders passed over by her husband and as she bustled to and fro behind the white marble counter, customers could see that her tiny feet were shod in high-heeled black patent slippers with big purple ribbons on the insteps. Lil had very elegant feet and always wore her skirts short to show them off.

Seeing Brabazon Nairn, she waved a be-ringed hand and invited the customer right inside, 'Come in, love! What's it to be tonight?' Some of the shop-owners in the Kirkgate had adopted a condescending attitude to the Nairns when Duncan was bankrupted and they'd moved out of their big house, but Lil had always been kind and treated Brabazon courteously. Though she said nothing, she seemed to sympathise.

'I think I'd like some stewing mutton – not a lot,' said Brabazon cautiously, leaning her full basket on the counter-top but unaware that any other woman doing the same thing would have received a volley of abuse from Lil who was jealous of the cleanliness of their premises.

'Mutton it is,' cried the butcher joyously throwing two fistfulls of mutton pieces into a large square of paper which his wife grabbed, wrapped up and handed over without weighing. 'That's eightpence ha'penny,' she said and Brabazon knew she was being given a great bargain for there was at least one and sixpence worth of mutton in the package. With a grateful smile she groped in her purse for the money. When she paid, all she had left was twopence farthing.

Lil's sharp eyes missed nothing. She saw how little there was in Mrs Nairn's purse and felt pity for the proud, reserved woman who had been brought down so abruptly from her comfortable life. Impulsively she reached over to the meat cutting block and grabbed a marrow bone which she wrapped up and handed to Brabazon with the words, 'That'll make you a pot of soup for Sunday, Mrs

Nairn. Go on, take it. It's nearly closing-time and we'll no' be able to sell it now.'

A ragged woman who was standing behind Brabazon pushed forward and said, 'If you're throwing bones out Lil, chuck one my way. I could do wi' a marrow bone.'

The butcher's wife leaned her fat hands on the counter and glared fearsomely at the interruption. 'You'll have nothing of the bloody kind. Get your whippet's arse out of my shop before I come round and kick you from here to Hell!'

The cheeky woman didn't even flinch because, although Brabazon did not know it, her presence had restrained Lil's tongue.

The basket was heavy and darkness was closing in as she slipped into the alley that led to the brewery yard. At the foot of the steps up to the door of the tenement building, she paused and stared around. The yard was dark because the lamp over the back door of Brewery House was unlit and only a few lights glimmered in the windows. In front however, she guessed, all the windows would be blazing. The wine merchant's family had literally turned their backs on Perseverance Place. At that moment she made a resolve. 'When I buy the house back, I'll make the front door on this side again. I'll put things back the way they used to be when it was first built.'

In her own home, the lamp was burning softly casting a golden glow over everything. The room looked warm and comfortable, for bit by bit she had made it welcoming. Her sons sat one on each side of the gleaming black-leaded fireplace. Both of them were reading. Henry's head was stuck in a heavy leather-bound book but Laurence was immersed in the local newspaper, absorbed in the sporting news his mother correctly guessed. 'Where's your father?' she asked as she set her basket down on the table.

Henry lifted his head and said, 'In the church still I think. He went out to practise about an hour ago. Will I go over and fetch him for you?'

She shook her head, 'No, I'll go myself. He'll have

forgotten the time. You boys set the table. I put a pie in the oven before I went out and it should be ready now.'

She welcomed the chance to listen to her husband playing the organ in the empty church and the walk back would give them a rare opportunity to talk without being overheard. It was not that she had secrets to impart, but rather that she relished being alone, absolutely alone, with her beloved Duncan. Even when they were in bed at night, she was always painfully conscious of the thin partition wall that divided their bedroom from the kitchen where Henry slept. Laurence, as he'd said at the beginning, had made up a cot in the hall cupboard where he slept with the door open for fear of suffocation. His mother did not object to this arrangement because she understood the pleasure it gave her son to retire to his private little burrow every night.

St Mary's church was approached through a high wrought-iron gate in the Kirkgate which was rapidly emptying of shoppers and filling up with people in search of pleasure in the taverns and in the music hall at the end of Tolbooth Wynd. Soon there would be drunks fighting in the gutters and police hauling off brawlers for a night in the cells. Duncan rarely stayed out so late.

The door at the end of the aisle creaked slightly as she pushed it open and slipped inside. Music flowed out to meet her like a wave, surging with energy and intensity, soaring to the timbered roof and vibrating against the stained glass of the windows. Duncan always played with passion, but tonight there was a fury and grief in the piece he had chosen that disturbed his wife. She slipped silently into a pew at the back and felt her body tremble and throb with the fury of the sounds coming from the organ. It disturbed her when she realised that her husband, sitting bolt upright in a pool of light from a bank of candles in front of the gilded organ pipes, was so totally immersed that he did not even know she was there. Anxiously she hurried up the strip of red carpet and put a hand on his shoulder. How thin he had become, she realised with a shock.

'What are you playing? Who wrote it?' she asked him.

Startled, he lifted his hands and turned his face towards her, 'No one. I'm making it up as I go along. Do you like it, my dear?'

'It's magnificent but it makes me feel sad . . . more than sad, it makes me want to weep. Come home Duncan, supper's ready.'

Without rising he put both arms around her waist and said in a whisper, 'I love you so much.'

Deeply moved, she laid her own hands on the top of his dark head. She had always admired Duncan's thick, curling jet-black hair but it was greying quickly now and she wanted to defend him from the ravages of time. 'I love you too,' she told him with passion in her voice.

He hugged her more tightly and his voice was muffled as he said, 'I'm worried, Brabazon.'

She moved her hands down to his shoulders and knelt beside him, 'What about? Everything's fine. The brewery's been slow to turn round but we're surviving and the debts are being paid off every month, even though it's taking longer than we thought it would. Don't worry Duncan.'

'It's not that. You're far better at running the place than I ever was. It's something else. I think something's going wrong with me.'

Her body felt suddenly very cold and goose pimples rose on her arms. The silence of the church became threatening, the candles flickered as if they were about to go out and plunge them into haunted darkness. 'It's all the anxiety you've had for the past years. You're tired, that's all,' she said firmly, but when he looked up at her she saw that his dark eyes were pools of misery. Her tone changed and she whispered, 'Tell me about it, Duncan.'

'It's been going on for a long time. At first I thought I was imagining it and I've been practising my music more and more just to find out . . . but I don't think I'll be able to play much longer.'

She shook her head in violent refusal to accept such an idea, 'Duncan, the way you were playing when I came in

50

was simply wonderful. There are concert performers who can't play as well. You're famous throughout Leith; people come to this church on Sundays from Edinburgh for the pleasure of listening to you!'

'Hear me out Brabazon, I'm finding it harder and harder to play. My body's not doing what I ask of it. My hands are losing their strength and they ache so badly that I can hardly bear the pain sometimes. I didn't want to speak of it to you. I hoped it would cure itself but it's getting worse. Something's happening to me and I don't know what it is.'

She refused to believe that another blow might strike her dear husband. 'No, no,' she told him stoutly, laying her face against his cheek, 'I won't let anything happen to you. You're only tired and suffering from anxiety. I've heard it does that to people sometimes. You must rest and I'll feed you up. Come home to supper now, please. The boys are waiting.'

For several weeks after Duncan's outburst in the church, his wife watched him carefully but he did not talk of feeling unwell again and she thrust her worries about him to the back of her mind. Christmas passed and on the last night of 1893, she and her family listened to the church clock striking twelve and lifted glasses of their own beer to each other with great solemnity. Brabazon felt tears pricking her eyes as she surveyed her growing sons: Laurence so dark and dashing like his dear father, but with something dangerous in his face that was missing from Duncan's; Henry, the image of her own father, brown-haired, hazel-eyed, earnest-looking but, in his case, without Joshua's devil-may-care dash. Henry had inherited the Logan looks with the Nairn nature while Laurence's legacy was the other way around.

'Your father and I want you both to know how much we appreciate the way you're settling down to working,' she said to them.

Henry grinned, 'Oh well, the brewery's ours as well. I enjoy being there and learning things from you and Alex.'

Her pride in her oldest son showed. 'You'll make a good brewmaster yourself one day. Alex was saying that the other day,' she told him and did not notice the cloud that passed over the face of Laurence as she spoke. Henry had left school and gone into the brewhouse when they'd moved from Brewery House but Laurence had stayed on for a while and it was only a year ago that he'd started in the stables. His mother believed he preferred working with the horses to making beer and was unaware of his secret resentment at being put into a position inferior to his brother. From childhood Laurence had felt that Henry was his mother's favourite child and he longed for her to bestow that wondrous smile on him as well.

New Year's Day was the only holiday the brewery took but on 2nd January, Brabazon was at work again, bustling here and there, supervising, taking part, giving orders. She was happy to be back in the sweet-smelling warmth of her brewhouse and while she went from place to place, she had a sudden realisation that she would never want to return to being the idle lady of the big house with nothing to occupy her except embroidery and gossip. There was a good side to almost every upset in life, she reflected.

In Perseverance Place Nellie Warre was also happy and singing hymns as she peeled potatoes at her kitchen sink under the window overlooking the brewery yard. At her feet little Elsie was playing with a ball on the floor and Nellie glanced down with delight at the bent golden head. Being given a wee lassie after three laddies was a glorious blessing and she redoubled her hymn-singing efforts. She was well launched into 'Onward Christian Soldiers' when her neighbour Minna Meirstein stuck her head round the corner of the unlocked front door. Minna's terrible jet-black wig was slightly askew on her head and her face was flushed with excitement.

'Vat's all the din about?' she asked but did not want

an answer, she had more to say, 'Look out of your window, Nellie, and tell me vat you see,' she hissed.

Nellie laid down her paring knife and stared through the steamed glass. 'It's raining. There's a dray just come in. Laurence's driving it. Alex's going into the cellar . . . What's to see, Minna?' Her face was puzzled as she turned to look at the agitated woman.

'Are you not seeing Mr Nairn?'

Nellie peered again, putting her face closer to the glass. 'Oh aye, there he is standing at the corner of the stables. He doesnae look very well, puir soul.'

'Poor soul indeed! He's drunk!' Minna's voice was full of indignation.

'Surely not!' exclaimed Nellie turning around with shock on her face.

Minna nodded, 'A scandal, that's vat it is. He's bringing more trouble on that poor voman's head. Drunk – at this time of the day!'

Nellie's face was deeply concerned as she looked out again. Even little Elsie had got up from the floor and clambered on to the wooden draining board so that she could see into the yard. Duncan Nairn was leaning against the stable wall with his hands out at his back as if to brace himself up.

'He was staggering about all over the place ven I saw him,' said Minna self-righteously.

Nellie wiped her hands on her apron and said, 'That man's no' drunk, Minna. He's ill. He's no' a drinker. Not like some. Come down and help me get him back to the house.'

Duncan's face was white and he was gasping when the two women appeared at his side. Nellie took his arm and said, 'We'll take you back up the stair, Mr Nairn. Lean on us.'

He shook his dark head, 'No, Nellie. It's all right. Just leave me be for a minute. I was walking over the yard when my legs seemed to buckle under me. I'll be fine.'

Nellie shook her head firmly, 'You cannae stand here

in the rain. Mrs Nairn'll see you. We'll help you up the stair.'

'I'll bring you a nip of Abe's brandy,' added Minna who was regretting her first hasty assumption.

Nellie's warning against letting Brabazon see him in such a state made Duncan acquiesce and when they had installed him in his own arm chair with a glass of brandy and hot water in his hand, she said, 'I'll go for Mrs Nairn now.'

'No, no!' Duncan cried out, 'No, don't tell her. I don't want her to know. It was just a moment of weakness. I'm perfectly well now. Abe's brandy's done the trick. Please say nothing about this, because it'll only worry Brabazon.'

Brabazon was in the fermenting room on the ground floor of the brewhouse when her brother walked in. He looked askance at the picture she presented, with her sleeves rolled up to the elbows, her skirt kirtled almost to her knees and a large wooden shovel in her hand. 'What are you doing? Surely you don't work like a labourer?' he could not keep the astonishment out of his voice.

She wiped her hands on her coarse apron, looked down at the heavy boots on her feet and said defensively, 'We're short-handed. Some of the men haven't come in today – hangovers, I expect. Anyway you can't brew beer in silk and slippers, you know.'

'Brew beer? What would Mother say! We thought you were only running this place, not making the beer as well!' exploded Mark. 'Why doesn't Duncan sell up rather than put his wife to work like a labourer? Where is he anyway?'

Brabazon looked angry. Any criticism, even veiled, of her husband roused her rage. There was no way she was going to tell her brother that Duncan was probably playing the church organ at that very moment. She knew he would regard that as a dilettante occupation. Instead she went into the attack, 'What exactly do you want?' she asked leaning on her shovel, 'I'm sorry I can't spend time talking with you but this vat's fermenting and the yeast

54

must be scraped off.' She pushed past him and started scooping away the thick creamy suds. In the shiny copper side of the vat at the far end of the room, she saw distorted reflections of herself and her brother. She thought Mark looked like a black scarecrow with long thin legs and an elongated face.

His voice was kinder as he started to speak, 'Brabazon, I know you've had several offers to buy from Gordon's. I've lots of friends in business in Leith and I know quite well that they're prepared to pay six thousand pounds for your brewery. Why don't you just sell up instead of slaving like this? I wrote to tell Father what's going on and he's very worried about you, too. He's anxious to give you money if you need it.'

She turned slowly and stared hard at him, 'Yes, I've had letters from Father. He's a good father though he's so far away. He's always kept in touch with me.'

Mark nodded, 'It's because of Mother that he can't come back to Leith, you know. It was part of their separation agreement that he stay away from her.'

'She made it as hard for him as she could but I suppose you can't blame her really. I think she loved him very much once and nearly went mad when he left her,' said Brabazon. Maria Logan's children stared sadly at each other remembering the past and Brabazon's voice was softer when she spoke again, 'It's kind of Father to offer me money but I can't take it. Duncan's pride would be hurt. It would mean I was turning to someone else – to another man to help me out of problems. Duncan doesn't know Father and Mother's always treated him with such snobbery. You understand, don't you Mark?'

'If you won't accept help from Father, let me give it to you – or lend it if that's what you prefer,' said her brother. 'I'll give you two thousand pounds. You're my sister and it hurts me to see you working like a common woman.'

'And I'm from such a good family . . .' she mimicked her mother's voice as she spoke and could not help her sarcastic tone.

Mark ignored the cutting edge and went on reasonably,

'You're not going to help yourself or your family by carrying on like this. Everybody thinks you'll have to sell up in the end. It's the talk of Leith. You'll have plenty of money if you'll only sell to Gordon's.'

'Duncan won't sell,' she was definite about that.

Mark looked exasperated, 'Of course he will if you tell him to.'

'Then *I* won't sell if that's what you want to hear. I'm determined to persevere . . .' She gave a little laugh as she said the word, and added, almost musingly, 'Persevere at the Perseverance Brewery!'

'Be reasonable, Brabazon. Gordon's is a good offer – and if you have my two thousand as well you could buy a little shop.'

She made a scoffing noise, 'What sort of "little shop"? A hat shop perhaps? Something ladylike no doubt? I don't want a shop! I'm developing a feel for brewing and anyway I'm surprised at you for joining up with Gordon's against your own sister. Go away. I've work to do.'

But her brother stood his ground and his face was grim as he told her, 'Brabazon, you must see sense. I came here today because your husband's behaviour is causing a lot of scandal. He's the talk of Leith.'

She went very still and glared at him. So Mark knew where Duncan went all the time! He knew about the hours playing the church organ. 'What do you mean? Why shouldn't he spend his time making music. It's lovely.' Her brother's face was stern as he stood his ground, 'This has nothing to do with music. I came here today for a purpose, Brabazon, and you can't get rid of me until I've said what I came to say.'

She stiffened, 'What do you mean?'

'Don't pretend. It's a disgrace! Not content with being a bankrupt, he's starting to drink as well. The man's never sober. Folk are talking about him, pointing him out in the street. He staggers around like a sailor in a gale. I'm your brother and I'm ashamed for the family.'

She was furious, her eyes flashing and her lips trembling, 'It's a damned lie. The only drink that ever crosses his lips is beer and that not very often. It's shameful to talk about him like that – *shameful!*'

The tears were pouring down her cheeks not only because of her rage but also because, at that moment, she accepted what she had been shutting out of her consciousness for a long time. Duncan *had* been acting strangely; he had trouble keeping his balance and something was the matter. Her wall of reticence cracked and she turned brokenly to her brother, 'Oh my God, Mark! What is wrong with him? He's not a drunkard but I'm scared he's sick.'

She put both hands to her eyes and sobbed in fear while Mark held out his arms to comfort her. 'My dear, I'm sorry. If Duncan's ill, you must call in the best doctor you can find. I'll pay the bill.'

Brabazon shook her head and said through her tears, 'He won't see one. I've suggested it already but he won't hear of it. He thinks what he needs is peace of mind and I agree with him. He's been through a terrible time . . .' She was not prepared to think the unthinkable, that her beloved husband might be seriously ill.

Mark realised that he was treading on dangerous ground, 'Perhaps you're right, but remember my offer if you change your mind.'

When he went away Brabazon stood leaning on her tall spade with a harried look on her face. She could not concentrate for the rest of the morning and at midday she slipped across the courtyard to seek Duncan and question him about his strange behaviour. When she opened the door of the flat, she saw him slumped in sleep in his armchair with an empty glass on the floor by his side. She sniffed at it: the glass smelt of brandy and doubts assailed her. Perhaps Mark was right after all, perhaps her husband *was* drinking secretly. The sound of her beside him woke Duncan and he blinked distractedly before he smiled. She went straight into the attack brandishing the glass at him, 'Have you been drinking brandy?'

He nodded, 'Yes, I have. Minna gave it to me. I felt a bit peculiar this morning and the brandy helped.'

Terror seized her. She spoke anxiously, 'Are you all right? Can I send for a doctor?'

He shook his head, 'No! I feel fine now. I went out without any breakfast that's all and felt faint. Don't worry, Brabazon, sit down and tell me what's been happening in the brewery.'

She fought with herself to appear reassured and told him, 'I had a visit from Mark this morning.'

'Is your mother worse?' Duncan asked.

Brabazon shook her head, 'No, she's the same. It was something else. He came to offer me money and to persuade us to sell up to Gordon's.'

Duncan's head drooped and when he spoke his tone was hesitant, 'Their last bid was six thousand, wasn't it? Perhaps we should accept that, Brabazon.'

She was horrified. 'What? After all we've been through? We've nearly come through the worst, we're nearly making a profit again!'

Duncan shook his head hopelessly, 'I know what Mark feels and I understand. He hates to see his sister working like a labourer. And I've not been helping you enough.'

She ran across the floor and put her arms around him. 'Don't be silly. You're not going to turn snobbish on me, are you? I told Mark people don't make beer in silk and slippers. I enjoy working. You may not believe me any more than Mark did, but it's true. I wouldn't want to sit in a drawing-room doing cross-stitch and producing babies like the precious Amelia. I want us to be clear of debt and buy back Brewery House one day.'

Duncan was not reassured, 'That'll take years, Brabazon. Perhaps it would be better to move away from here altogether so that you don't see the old house every day. I've seen you gazing out at it when you think I'm not looking. It's a sort of symbol for you, isn't it?'

She protested, 'It's a target. When I look at it in the morning I think about the day when we'll own it again. But I'm not unhappy here. I've come to love the brewery as much as I loved the old house. I love its funny little doors and those stone arches in the cellar that the monks built. I'm sure the ghosts are friendly and if we give up and allow the Nairns to be put out, they'd be furious! Our boys have to inherit Perseverance, Duncan, that's very important. We can't be the ones to break such a long connection.'

'Oh, Brabazon,' he murmured, 'I can't make you do anything you don't want to. I never could.'

His voice was slurred and for a second she stiffened, remembering the brandy. Fighting against the suspicion she asked, 'You sound strange, are you all right?'

He stared bleakly back at her and suddenly his shoulders drooped. 'I'm tired, so deadly tired even when I do nothing,' he said in a flat monotone.

'Let me make up your bed. Let me ask Minna for another glass of brandy. I'll send out for a bottle of whisky if that'll help you.'

He shook his head and she noticed that his hands were trembling when he laid them on top of his book. He did not seem able to grasp it and it slipped to the floor with a thud. 'Duncan, tell me the truth. What's the matter?' she gasped.

There was dread in the eyes that looked into hers. His words were low and measured, 'I feel as if I'm freezing up. Sometimes I think I'm imagining it, but on days like today it's almost impossible to move. I feel as if I'm turning into a statue!'

She was panic-stricken. 'You're exhausted. You need to rest. You've been worrying about Perseverance for years without telling me. I'm going to force you to take things easy. Come into the bedroom and lie down. I'm going to cosset you.' Her strength and energy flowed out to him in a wave of anxious love and he grasped her hands gratefully as he rose tottering to his feet.

That evening before she closed the brewery, Brabazon slipped out of a little door in the back wall of the brewhouse. It was a very ancient door, made of worm-holed and splintering oak planks of a tremendous thickness which were bound together in a criss-cross pattern by heavy bars of pitted iron, and with a handle made of iron too, a huge boss that took two hands to turn. It led directly into the church's burial grounds and because it was hidden from view by a thicket of ivy, only the Nairns and the Warres knew of the door's existence. It was never locked because the key had long ago disappeared. Brabazon used it from time to time as a short cut to the church or the Kirkgate if she was working in the brewhouse.

It was so low that she had to bend her head to get through and she heard the low groan of protest the hinges made when she pushed them open. The fresh, green smell of ivy greeted her on the other side as she pushed her way through to reach the path between the grass-covered graves. The door of the church stood open and she could see lights burning up beside the altar. That was where she was going, to pray for Duncan. In a few seconds she was kneeling quietly in the empty silence with her forehead held in her cupped hands.

Slowly a feeling of peace and tranquillity came over her. One by one, she felt her taut muscles relaxing and a series of disconnected prayers ran like eddying water through her mind . . . 'Please God, help my dear husband get his strength back. Make him well, dear Lord, *please* make him well.' She did not ask for anything for herself, not even for Brewery House. She knew that if she was to succeed in owning it again, it would have to be through her own efforts.

She was totally relaxed and almost asleep, when a hand was laid gently on her shoulder and the voice of Mr Templeton, the minister of St Mary's, spoke in her ear, 'I'll have to close the church now, my dear. It's nearly seven o'clock. Shouldn't you be going home? You've been here for over an hour.'

As she lifted her head, Brabazon realised how cold and stiff her body had become. There was darkness all around except for the lamp in Mr Templeton's hand and with the return of consciousness, euphoria left her. The strained look in the eyes that she turned towards the minister gave him a pang of concern and he felt a rush of sympathy for poor Mrs Nairn.

'Something's the matter my dear. Do you want to tell me about it,' he said sitting down in the pew beside her.

'I don't know really. I feel frightened in a way, more frightened than I've been since all our troubles began.'

He sounded consoling, 'Everyone in the parish admires you tremendously, Mrs Nairn. The way you've coped with your vicissitudes is admirable. I've heard that the brewery's doing better, too, these days and the boys are both helping you there. You should be proud.' She noticed that he did not mention Duncan and wondered if he had heard the rumours that had brought Mark to see her.

Her words rushed out in reply, 'Mr Templeton, I'm worried about Duncan. He's ill; he's tired all the time these days.'

It was comforting to hear again the same words she herself had used to her husband a few hours before, 'He's probably exhausted. He's been through a terrible strain and some people are able to bear that sort of thing better than others. Duncan has always been very sensitive. His energy has been sapped. If he can take things easy for a while, he'll be his old self again.'

She nodded, 'That's what I told him. I said he should come here more often and play the organ. It's such a pleasure to him – but he hasn't been doing that so frequently, has he?'

The minister frowned for a moment, 'No, he hasn't and when he does, he seems to be having trouble. He makes mistakes and he never used to. I thought it was because he was losing interest in his music.'

'Duncan'll never lose interest in music. It's his life. He should have been a musician, not a brewer, then he'd have been a great success – poor Duncan,' sighed his wife as she rose, pulling her shawl over her shoulders. She walked to the church door with Mr Templeton and before they parted at the iron gate opening into the Kirkgate, he asked her in a light way, 'Has Duncan complained of any specific pain or feeling of illness?'

The lamplight was shining on her face and she looked like a figure in a Rossetti painting when she answered, 'He said a strange thing. He said he sometimes thinks he's turning into a statue. He feels as if he's freezing up little by little.'

It was good that the night was dark and she did not see the start the minister gave when he heard her words. After his supper a solemn-faced Mr Templeton called on his friend Dr Allen with whom he occasionally played chess, but he soon showed he had not come for a game. He'd come to talk about the Nairns.

'I was speaking to Mrs Nairn tonight and she told me that Duncan's ill.'

'He's not been to see me but I've heard talk in the town that he's hitting the bottle,' said Allen disappointedly folding up the chessboard.

The minister shook his head. 'I don't think it's that. There's something more seriously wrong I'm afraid though I didn't say so to his wife, but what she said was no real surprise to me. He's told her he feels as if he's freezing up and I've seen him staggering around in the church but I'm sure he's not been drinking. He moves so awkwardly – I've seen him sitting at the organ trying to play as if his hands weren't his own, and he used to make such magnificent music. He's made St Mary's famous.'

Allen nodded, 'I know that well enough. There's not a church even in Edinburgh that has music like ours on a Sunday. We're lucky at St Mary's.'

'Haven't you noticed he's making mistakes that he never made before?' asked Templeton.

'Maybe he's getting forgetful,' mused Allen, 'but it's not like him. I'll look in and see him. I only hope it's drink for his family's sake. Something can be done about that.'

The minister looked shocked, 'Why? What do you mean? What could it be?'

Allen pulled a book out of the shelf behind him and said solemnly, 'I don't like speculating about things like this but what you say makes it sound like paralysis agitans

62

– Parkinson's disease. That feeling of freezing up could be the start of some sort of palsy. Don't you go showing either of the Nairns that you're worried. I'll call in on him with some excuse and maybe he'll tell me more about his trouble, so that I can make a proper diagnosis.'

The chance for the doctor to visit the Nairns was to come sooner than anyone expected.

When Brabazon was in the church praying for her husband's return to good health, her son Laurence sat in the Warre's flat having supper with his friend Pat. There was always enough to fill an extra plate and Nellie, who never grudged hospitality, was watching with pleasure as the boys wiped the last vestiges of stew gravy off their plates with big chunks of bread.

Laurence leaned back in his chair and sighed, 'My word that was great Mrs Warre.'

She grinned like a little elf, her pointed chin on her fists and her sharp eyes looking straight at him. 'I hope you're helping your ma these days, Laurence,' she said.

His dark face was surprised, 'Aye, Mrs Warre. I'm working in the stables with the dray horses. I like it fine but – '

'But . . . ?' she encouraged him.

He shook his head, 'But I'm like your Pat. I want to see the world. One day I'll leave Leith and do a bit of travelling. The brewery'll be fine because Henry's quite happy to live here for the rest of his life. He's not like me. My feet are itchy.'

'You'll maybe be able to go one day but your mother and father need you now,' said Nellie sternly and it sounded as if she were giving him advice. She did not want to speak about his father's illness but felt she had to warn the boy of what she feared might lie ahead.

When Laurence and Pat went down into the Kirkgate after their meal, the rain had stopped and the air smelt heady with the mingled sea smells of tar, salt, oil and coal smoke. Pat sniffed appreciatively and said, 'Leith's

perfume. Smell it Larry. Come on, let's go to the docks.'
They set off running until they reached the maze of streets
with evocative names – Elbe Street, Baltic Street, Jamaica
Street, Salamander Street – which led to the quays and
jetties where cranes towered above the roof tops and tall
masted ships were lined up. Flags of all nations could be
seen fluttering above the dock wall and the sight of them
made the hearts of both boys thud with longing for adventure. Though it was evening, men were still bustling
about: loading and unloading ships; shouting; hauling;
cranking up cranes and hoists. The work of Leith Docks
never ended.

Arm in arm the lads wandered along a wharfside laid
with huge, flat stones, worn in the middle by the passage
of thousands of cart wheels. They stood with their hands
in their pockets watching the crew of a Russian merchant-
man casting off the ropes for departure, like the cutting
of an umbilical cord, and the sense of excitement that
always attends a ship's moment of sailing made them itch
to feel deck planks under their own feet and smell a head-
on breeze as they cut their way into the North Sea.

'Where's that ship going?' Pat asked an older idler who
was standing beside them.

'St Petersburg,' he said with longing in his eyes and
Laurence sighed, 'God, I wish I could go too. My grandfather's in St Petersburg. I wonder what it's like there?'

'Your grandfather's a real old lad. He ran off with a
Russian woman didn't he?' said Pat.

Laurence nodded, 'So they say. My mother doesn't talk
about it but I've heard the local gossip. The Russian
woman was a countess or something. It made my grandmother take to her bed with jealousy. She's never got up
for fifteen years.'

Pat laughed. He was as avid for adventure as his friend
and his urge to get away now made him excitable, unable
just to stand and stare. With a sort of a leap he turned
his tall, straight body and ran off down the quay to
another berth where a ship from India was unloading.
Huge chests of tea were being slung down from the hold

64

and a delicate scent filled the air. Pat threw his cap in the air shouting, 'God, I hate house-painting. I want to go to Calcutta, Bombay, Madras, Benares . . .'

Laurence joined in, chanting names of all the foreign places he could remember from school geography lessons: 'Helsinki; Hamburg; Penang; San Fran-cis-co; Rio; Man-da-lay!'

Shouting like children and pushing each other as they ran, they dashed along the quay, declaiming more names of distant places: 'Marmunsk – Gibraltar – Osaka – Sydney . . .' Each tried to outdo the other and by the time they reached the dock gate, they were breathless and dishevelled. When Pat yelled out 'Vladivostock!' they looked at each other and Laurence shrugged. He couldn't think of another name. They had run through their gamut of foreign places.

The same strange excitement still gripped them both, however. 'Come on, let's walk along The Shore,' said Pat to Laurence, who hesitated for a second until challenged by his friend, 'You're not scared are you?'

'It's awful rough down there especially after dark. I've been told to keep away from The Shore. You know the stories – even the policemen have to go about in pairs.'

'If you're scared I'll go on my own. You'll have to grow up sometime Larry.'

'I'm *not* scared,' said Laurence squaring his shoulders.

'Have you any money?' asked Pat, producing a sixpenny piece from his pocket.

Laurence searched in his own and brought out a shilling so, very daring, they walked across the muddy open space opposite the dock gate till they found themselves on the broad pavement of the most notorious thoroughfare in Leith. The Shore stretched along the side of the Water of Leith at the point where it debouched into the sea. One side was the water of the inner-dock basin and floating about half-way up, tethered to the dock wall, was a wooden jetty where passengers disembarked from the ferry that ran between Leith and Fife. The water looked viscous and oily, so filthy that even the few seagulls bob-

65

bing about on its surface looked dirty and depressed. On the surface, bits of stick and sheets of cardboard were floating. During the day old men could be seen sitting with their legs hanging over the dock wall, fishing in a desultory way but none of them ever seemed to catch anything.

After dark, all the action in The Shore took place on the other side of the street which was fringed with a continuous line of buildings, some tall, some low, with higgledy-piggledy roofs covered in grey slates or red clay tiles. Lines of windows, like curious eyes, stared out across the dock water. At street level almost every door led into a tavern, a beer hall or a gin parlour; a few of them palaces of cut glass, glittering with glowing gas jets and shining brass, mirrors and polished woodwork, but most were sordid, sawdust-floored drinking dens. All of them, even the most squalid, were packed with people that night because it was payday and the stevedores were drinking up their wages.

Clutching their money Pat and Laurence went into the first bar which was clean and fairly quiet by Leith standards. They only witnessed two small fights which were quickly quietened by a proprietor who had arms like sides of beef. With bravado the boys drank a pint of beer each, specifying loyally that it had to be Perseverance. Around them prostitutes were squealing together as they drank their gins. The boys tried to act coolly, not eyeing the made-up women, not showing any surprise at this other side of Leith. When they were fortified by the beer, they felt brave enough to try another bar and walked along the pavement till they came to the most famous saloon of all, The King's Head on the corner of The Shore and Bernard Street. By this time it was pitch-dark outside and the din that burst out of the bar when they pushed open its brass-handled door was deafening. They had to fight their way in through a press of sweating, odorous bodies.

After another two pints were ordered, they huddled together and counted the coppers they had left. There was

66

not enough for another round and they were preparing to leave when a man shouldered his way through the crowd and clapped a hand on Pat's shoulder.

'Hey, young Pat! What're you doin' here? Does your mother know you're out? Come on, lad, I'll buy you a beer!' he shouted.

'It's Uncle Angus, my mother's brother,' explained Pat to Laurence as two pint glasses full of ale were thrust into their willing grasp.

Angus and his friends were generous. They had been stevedoring on a huge clipper out of Bremen and money was burning holes in their pockets. This time the beer went straight to Laurence's head. At first he felt slightly giddy but then his sight became hazy and his legs felt as if they were made of cotton wool. He heard his own voice as if the sound were coming from far away. Everything seemed very funny and he laughed a lot.

What jerked him back to sobriety was the outbreak of an argument between Pat's Uncle Angus and a broken-nosed man who had been buying drinks for a raddled woman at the corner of the bar. She was dressed in tattered finery and her face was painted with round, rouged cheeks like Judy in the Punch and Judy show that performed for children on the Links every summer. Suddenly Laurence became aware that this hideous woman was shouting and pointing a finger at him.

'That cheeky lad's got real dreamy eyes hasn't he . . . look at them, eyes to drown in.' She leaned towards him and breathed gin in his direction. 'Eyes like yours get women into bed, my lad. Do you want to poke me?' she asked. Her friend turned on Laurence with his fists bunched and Angus, who was about half the other man's size, intervened.

'Leave the laddie alone. He's not done anything.'

The woman only leaned nearer to Laurence, gratified at having caused jealousy in her man. 'Come on big eyes, tell me, do you want to poke me?'

Laurence shook his head at which the woman's escort turned on him with a shout, 'Not good enough for you is she?' He was now bent on fighting, no matter what the excuse.

The one who'd caused all the trouble stood back with arms crossed across her scrawny chest and a smile on her grotesque face. She urged her furious defender on by accusing Laurence, 'Used to better are you? Hear that Sammy, he's too good for the likes of me!'

Before the boys knew what was happening they were all hustled out into the roadway. Pat's uncle was stripping off his jacket and facing up to a group of other men, all similarly jacketless and spitting on their knuckles. Laurence remembered stepping forward with his hands held high in the boxer's classic defensive position and then everything went black. Someone had hit him full on the chin with a terrible uppercut and he'd fallen backwards, literally poleaxed. When this happened, Angus, with the cunning that distinguished his sister Nellie and his second nephew Gideon, dodged under the flailing arms and sprinted off towards his home in Baltic Street.

Laurence regained consciousness when water from Pat's cap was poured over his head. As he turned his face aside and spluttered, spitting foul dock water out of his mouth, he asked, 'What happened?'

'You were laid out with one punch,' said Pat not bothering to conceal the admiration in his voice, 'What a punch! I've never seen anything like it. It was that fellow Lambert from the building that hit you. He just came up from nowhere and let fly. Thank God he didn't try to hit me.'

'Help me up. I can't lie here all night. I want to go home.' Laurence groaned. He felt as if he'd been run over by a steamroller.

Their journey along Bernard Street was slow because they had to stop every now and again while Laurence staunched his bleeding nose with a blood-soaked handkerchief. When they turned into the Kirkgate they saw to their surprise that it was after midnight and the street was almost empty except for a few straggling revellers like themselves, blank-eyed men clutching half-empty bottles

68

and a tousled woman being wheeled along spreadeagled on top of a fruit merchant's barrow.

When Pat left Laurence at the door of his flat he whispered, 'Good luck. You're going to need it. When your mother sees your face she'll kill you.'

Next morning Brabazon stuck her head around Laurence's cupboard door and then reeled back in horror. 'What on earth has happened?' she gasped surveying the sprawled, bruised body on the bed. He was wearing a bloodstained shirt and the cupboard reeked because he had been sick into a towel at the side of his bed. 'What's happened?' she repeated, shaking him by the shoulder. The answer was a groan and she realised he could hardly open his swollen eyes. 'My God, I'll send for a doctor,' she cried and ran back into the kitchen calling on Henry to dress quickly and run for Dr Allen.

When a doctor's gig was seen driving into Perseverance Place, an atmosphere of gloom descended on the residents because no one called out a doctor unless serious illness had struck. Minna Meirstein saw Allen's gig first and rushed out of her dark flat to find out where it was going. After hanging over the stair head, she gathered up her skirts and went running back to tell Abe. 'He's gone into the Nairns' on the first floor.'

'So?' said Abe sipping his morning cup of tea.

'It must be Mr Nairn! You know vat happened ven Nellie and I brought him up from the yard. The man's very sick.'

Abe muttered a Hebrew blessing and his wife was shamed into silence.

Dr Allen was an old friend of the Nairns who had often been entertained in Brewery House during their days of prosperity. When he entered their small flat in Perseverance Place he could not help comparing it with what the family had enjoyed in the past, but Brabazon was too taken up with the matter of Laurence to notice his awkwardness and hurried him inside.

69

'It's my son – my youngest boy. He was fighting last night and his face is terribly bruised. He says his head is aching fit to burst and he's been very sick.'

She showed the doctor into the tiny cupboard where Laurence lay and he knelt beside the bed, gently handling the recumbent boy's head and asking him questions, 'Can you see? Have you double vision?'

When he'd finished his examination he came through to the kitchen where the rest of the anxious family were assembled and said, 'He has a touch of concussion. He must be kept quiet for a few days but he'll be all right. He says one of your neighbours hit him.'

Brabazon looked astonished, 'Pat Warre? Pat's his friend, he was out with him last night.'

'No, it was somebody called Lambert. They met on The Shore.'

Brabazon wondered what Laurence had been doing on The Shore but those speculations were swept aside by the mention of Lambert's name. It filled her with terror for she had never forgotten his threats when he was dismissed. She's passed him several times on the stairs since that day and he always shouldered her aside rudely or else swore at her under his breath. She was really afraid of him for she was sure he was a man who nursed his grudges, allowing them to swell and grow into something poisonous with the passage of time.

In spite of having delivered his reassurances about Laurence, Dr Allen showed no sign of wanting to leave and Brabazon poured out a cup of tea which he sipped while he sat down beside Duncan and launched into conversation.

'How're you keeping, old friend? I haven't seen you for some time,' said Allen, laying a kind hand on Duncan's shoulder. The other man shook his head and muttered 'Not so well, I'm afraid,' in reply. Then both men looked at Brabazon and she realised they wanted to be alone, so hastily she and Henry pulled on their outer clothing and went off to work, shutting the door firmly behind them.

The first thing that Allen noticed was how slurred Duncan's speech sounded but his brain seemed unaffected and he was able to answer all the doctor's questions, though it occasionally took some time for him to enunciate the words. He seemed to be relieved to have the opportunity of talking about his problems and told his friend that he'd first felt a problem in his hands. They were often stiff and did not respond to the messages from his brain. Then a pain started in his back and spread to his arms. When it was really bad he found it difficult to walk straight: the ground seemed to lurch beneath his feet. He'd managed to hide his suffering from Brabazon for a long time but recently his hands had started fits of uncontrollable shaking, so that he could no longer play the organ or even hold a teacup without spilling its contents.

As he spoke the doctor looked intently at him, noting the slurred words and the fact that although he was recounting frightening symptoms, his face was almost expressionless. He looked like someone talking about a subject that was totally disinteresting to him.

When Duncan stopped speaking, Allen put a sympathetic hand on his friend's shoulder and said with a false cheerfulness that did not deceive his patient, 'Don't you worry about this, Duncan. I know a good chap in Edinburgh who specialises in cases of this kind. If you don't mind, I'll call him in to have a look at you. We'll come back this afternoon. He'll be able to advise me on how to treat your case.'

Before he left the Place, the doctor went over to the brewery and told Brabazon that he was bringing in a specialist for a second opinion. Her face was frightened as she asked, 'For Laurence?'

Allen gave himself a shake, he'd forgotten about the concussed boy. 'Oh no, Laurence will be quite all right. It's for Duncan. I think he needs treatment and I know a good man. I've told him I'll come back this afternoon. Can you be there, Brabazon?'

She nodded. Her mouth was so dry she was unable to speak. It seemed to her that a nightmare was starting.

The man from Edinburgh, Dr Summers, was grey-bearded and fashionably dressed. He swept into the flat like an emperor, stripped off his gloves and started examining Duncan without a by-your-leave.

'Look this way; look that way; hold out your hands; stand up; stand on one leg . . . you can't? Then sit down.' When he wanted Duncan to strip, he made a gesture to tell Brabazon that she should retire and she went out into the landing where she paced slowly back and forward with her arms crossed under her shawl for what seemed like an eternity. When the door eventually opened she looked up, her face expectant and hopeful. Surely these clever men would be able to do something to help Duncan, but Summers' face was not reassuring and he walked over to stand beside her at the little stair window overlooking the yard and Brewery House.

It was not his way to beat about the bush. He came straight to the point. 'I'm afraid the prognosis is not good, Mrs Nairn.'

'Prognosis?' She did not recognise the word.

'Duncan's not going to get better, Brabazon,' said Allen who was standing behind the specialist with a stricken look on his face. She went stiff. 'What do you mean?'

Summers sighed, 'He's showing the first symptoms of a disease called paralysis agitans. I'm afraid it's progressive.' Such scenes always distressed him and he adopted a hard manner as a kind of protection.

To his relief, the woman stayed calm, only asking, 'What can be done for him?'

'Nothing – I'm sorry. In time he'll become more and more immobile. His brain'll be unaffected however, although his speech is likely to be difficult to understand quite soon and as time goes on he won't be able to walk.'

'Are you telling me that he'll be unable to move but he'll always know what's happening?'

'Yes.'

'Oh dear God, that's the cruellest part!' she cried, but still she did not break down. When the doctors left, she stood weeping silently at the landing window but after a

72

few minutes, she composed herself, wiped her eyes and went in to comfort Duncan.

1894

The damp and dimly lit pawnshop owned by Minna and Abe Meirstein was a changing-house for the gossip of the whole Kirkgate. Nothing happened to the many families living in or around the ancient street without Minna hearing the news: births; deaths; marriages; infidelities; illnesses; parental rifts; illegitimacies; inheritances; hopes won and hopes lost were grist to her mill.

Like a bedraggled parrot, shoulders hunched up high and wig tilted on her head, she sat behind the protective wire shield of her counter and watched everyone who went past her window. Sometimes, unaware of her sharp-eyed scrutiny, they lingered to peer inside at her display of broken-ribbed umbrellas; trays of cheap jewellery; chipped china; a melodeon with flowers painted on its sides; a solar topee that had gone a shade of dingy yellow; a case of moth-eaten stuffed birds and a rack along the back from which an assortment of clothes hung.

If the passers-by were known to her, she beckoned them inside and listened avidly to anything they had to tell. Whatever she gathered was passed on to the next caller. She had her favourites, however, and there were a selected few people she rarely discussed with outsiders. The Nairns were among this special category. But Minna's closest friends were her neighbours, Nellie Warre and Happy Anderson and there were *no* taboo subjects among the three of them.

Because the Meirsteins closed their shop on Saturdays, Friday was their most important working day and for many of the porters and labourers working in the docks it was also payday. When the rush to pawn or redeem was over, Minna was able to relax with her cronies who always popped into the shop on Friday night when the church clock was striking eight. They knew that Minna would be sure to have some news to pass on and all three looked forward to this gossipy time as a highlight of their week.

It was Happy who started talking about Laurence Nairn. 'That youngest laddie of Mrs Nairn's is fair running wild these days, ever since his father took bad. I hear him coming home in the wee sma' hoors. You'd think he'd help his mother more – Henry does, he's a grand laddie.'

Nellie flushed. She knew that her son Pat and Laurence Nairn ran as a pair and wondered if Happy was implying that Pat was leading the Nairn boy astray. Her son was a few months older after all.

'My Pat's giving us trouble too,' she conceded, 'He's going through a time of life when laddies mak' trouble. Pat's that discontented. He's no' happy in Leith. He wants to get away. It's fair worrying his dad . . .' Her voice trailed off as she remembered the arguments and shouting matches between her husband and their eldest son. Things were reaching the stage where she was beginning to realise that only Pat going off on his travels would bring peace and quiet back to her little home.

Minna nodded sagely, 'I think Mrs Nairn favours the eldest laddie and the other one's a bit jealous. He's fond of his mother, too, but he's not as able to show it. That'll be the reason he's running vild. Poor souls, they dinna hae their troubles to seek, do they? Mr Nairn's bad.'

Happy agreed, 'I saw him trying to cross the yard to the brewhouse yesterday. He was walking as if he was as drunk as a puggled monkey. How long's he going to be like that?'

Minna was the local medical specialist and was consulted about symptoms and diagnoses by anxious neighbours. When she looked searchingly into someone's face, they were disconcerted and wondered if she saw illness there. 'Am I all right, Minna?' they'd ask. Now she shook her head so vigorously that the wig slipped down slightly to one side as she pronounced her verdict. 'He'll no' get better. But it could take a long time. Some folk go on like that for ten years or more.'

'Ten years!' gasped Happy.

'Oh, poor Brabazon,' said Nellie. It was the first time she had openly referred to her neighbour and her husband's employer by her first name.

The conversation was interrupted by the sight of Laurence and Pat bursting out of the alleyway beside the shop. They were laughing and pushing at each other as they walked along; tall, eager young men intent on a night of fun and drinking. The women looked at each other and Nellie sighed as she said, 'I didna mean to tell you yet but our Pat's decided to join the army. He told me today and asked me to break the news to his dad. I was hoping he might change his mind . . . but there's not much chance. I think he's going out to celebrate. I hope they dinna wake you up coming home the night, Happy. You'd best put some cotton wool in your ears when you go to bed.'

The two young men shouldered their way through the crowds in the Walk and when they reached Tolbooth Wynd they started running, carried along by unleashed vitality after a day's confinement at work. Pat Warre and Laurence Nairn were closer to each other than to their brothers. Only four months separated them in age and ever since childhood they had vied in a companionable way. Unknown to his mother at the time, Laurence had made his way into the brewery yard when he was still a toddler and had joined up with the gang of workers' children that played there. Pat and he became immediate friends and their closeness had grown through the years.

When they were seated together in The Bells sipping their first pints of beer that night, Pat suddenly went quiet and said, 'I've news for you. I'm joining up.'

The smile on Laurence's face faltered. He knew that Pat and his father Alex had been at cross-purposes for a long time and he had listened many times to his friend's

76

threats of leaving Leith, but now he had really decided to go.

'When?' he asked, his eyes scrutinising Pat over the rim of his glass.

The other boy shrugged his broad shoulders, 'Tomorrow. I'm sick to the teeth of the smell of paint. I'm going up to Leith Fort in the morning and signing on. My mother's telling my father the news tonight.'

Laurence's feelings were a mixture of envy and regret at the realisation he was about to lose his closest friend. 'He'll take it badly,' he said.

'I know. But we're getting on each other's nerves. It's best if I go away. He's got the other laddies to push into the brewery. Gideon'll never get into the bobbies. He's too wee. Even if they give him a glass of beer every day for ten years he'll no' make five feet eight. You'll have him in the brewery with you in a year's time. I want to join the army.' Pat was definite and spoke without any of his usual irreverence. This was very serious.

Seeing the shaken look on his friend's face, however, Pat's mood changed and he leaned back in his chair with a laugh saying, 'It's a good thing you've got on your best celluloid collar. Drink up. We're going out to have a night we'll remember for the rest of our lives.'

'God, I wish I could go into the army with you,' sighed Laurence.

'Sign on too, then,' said Pat.

'I can't. My father's ill and my mother's working herself to death over there. I can't leave her.'

'Your father never was much help and your mother's got Henry. You could sign on if you wanted to,' said Pat.

'*Henry!*' Laurence's voice was sharp, 'He's the perfect son. Everything is "Henry this" and "Henry that". "Henry doesn't go out drinking", "Henry doesn't come home late at night". It's always been the same, but Henry can't deal with the waggons or the horses. The brewery needs me . . . I feel responsible in a way.'

'In that case, if you're determined to stay, let's get as drunk as Law Lords!' said Pat.

77

They headed for forbidden and dreaded territory, The Shore. It was the first time they had been back since Laurence had been knocked out by Lambert, but now he was bigger, stronger and fortified by beer so the two of them walked with a swagger as they pushed open the door of The King's Head. By this time it was dark and the prostitutes were lined up on the pavement, a raddled army. They sold their bodies along the street notorious to seamen of all nations, and their prices were low because none was in their first youth or beauty.

Pat and Laurence knew that anybody going with a Leith tart was taking a dangerous risk. Yet they were fascinated by the whores. Half-repelled and half-attracted, they watched the techniques of the women who solicited beside The King's Head.

As the night drew on they lost all sense of time and Laurence was semi-drunk when Pat suddenly grabbed his arm and whispered, 'Look at those two over there. They're tarts. What do you say we make a play for them?'

Screwing his eyes up, Laurence focused on two women standing together at the end of the huge mahogany bar. Both looked quieter and more respectable than the other streetwalkers. They stood with their shoulders half-turned to the gathering as if they were ignoring the men eyeing them. One, a big-breasted and black-haired woman with large golden hoops hanging from her ears, was older than the other who was slim and looked like a child dressed up, because she wore a large hat with a blue and white spotted ribbon around its brim and white gloves which nervously clutched a tatty pelisse around her shoulders. Laurence thought she resembled a quivering whippet.

Pat had his eye on the woman with the golden earrings. Downing the last of his beer, he said, 'I'm off to the army tomorrow and I've never had a woman. What the hell, why not? Come on.' Before Laurence could stop him, he was shouldering his way through the crowd towards the whispering couple and Laurence followed in time to hear his friend saying without preamble to the woman with the black hair, 'How much?'

She did not protest that he had mistaken her but smiled in a motherly way, eyeing his muscular young frame as she told him, 'A pound, dearie.'

'That's too much. I'm good. You should be paying me,' said Pat cheekily.

The smile on the woman's face grew broader and she looked at him indulgently, 'Lovey, I've never paid a man in my life and I'm not going to start now, even for a fine young chap like you.' Then she slowly ran a hand down Pat's arm in such a sensuous way that both young men felt lurches in their stomachs. Any warnings they had ever heard against going with bad women were forgotten. Like Pat, Laurence found himself thinking, 'What the hell!' and in his turn he smiled at the girl who looked like a whippet.

'I've got five shillings,' lied Pat, grabbing the big woman's hand.

'Oh, all right, you're just a kid,' she said. When she smiled, deep dimples popped into her cheeks and her eyes disappeared in crinkles of flesh. Now that he was near her, Pat could see that her hair was dyed and she was as old as his mother but this was no time for backing out because, to his surprise and a certain amount of alarm, she took his arm and started to lead him out of the bar.

As he was leaving, Pat pushed Laurence towards the second girl who was cowering in the corner watching the transaction with her friend. 'Five bob for him too,' he told her, adding, 'And be gentle with him – it's his first time.'

The girl's lips were trembling as she looked at Laurence. He recognised that she was as afraid as he was. Emboldened by her nervousness, he said, 'Five bob then?' She nodded and headed for the door without speaking.

In front of them the black-haired woman and Pat, arms linked, walked quickly along the pavement. She seemed vastly amused, 'First time is it, dearie? How old are you?' she asked.

His bravado was disappearing slightly but he didn't want that to show so he blustered, 'What d'ye mean, first time? I've been dipping my wick for years . . . I'm joining up tomorrow. I'm celebrating tonight.'

She laughed a deep gurgling laugh, 'You can't fool me lovey. I've had more first-timers than you've had hot breakfasts. Don't worry, I'll break you in before you go off with the boys. What about your friend? Is he a man of the world too?'

'No, Laurence's not done it yet . . .' In a muddled way Pat recalled the many conversations he'd had with Laurence, speculating about how you did it and what it felt like. His stomach lurched as he realised he was about to find out. What if he didn't get it up? What if Laurence managed it and he couldn't? Suddenly he felt sick.

She sensed his fears and slyly rubbed his cheek with a motherly hand, 'Come on. There's no point hanging about in the street when I've a cosy bed waiting,' she whispered.

It was only a short distance to where she turned off into a narrow entry and led him up a twisting, stinking staircase to a dim room. All he could see was the bed – huge, high and covered with brightly coloured quilts. A feathered hat was perched on one of its brass posts and a tangle of discarded clothing was strewn over the floor.

'You can call me Bertha,' she whispered as she stripped off his clothes with a practised hand. First the jacket, then the white shirt and finally the trousers which she pulled down in a businesslike manner leaving Pat stark naked on the bed. Then she pulled her dress up over her head and revealed that she was wearing nothing beneath it except a tightly laced corset. All Pat's fears about not being able to react in the required way disappeared when he saw her plump body bursting like whipped cream out of the whalebone. She climbed on to the bed beside him and giggled, 'You've got the equipment anyway. Now let's see what you can do with it.'

Laurence and the young girl walked more slowly along the pavement, not linking arms and keeping a fair distance between them. 'What's your name?' he asked her.

He saw the startlingly clear whites of her eyes sliding towards him beneath the ridiculous hat as she said,

'Daisy'. He couldn't think of anything else to say after that and, in silence, they climbed the same narrow staircase as Pat and Bertha but went up one more floor to an even tinier room. There was no finery spread over this floor and no feathered hats on the bedpost – only a bed with a dirty patchwork cover and pillows without pillowcases.

The girl stood shivering nervously in the middle of the floor and gazed at Laurence who looked back nonplussed. All ideas he'd had about a night of passion left him abruptly at the sight of the dirty bed. He was sure it was infested with bugs. The girl took off her hat and put it carefully on the floor. 'Have you the five shillings?' she asked and her accent was not the familiar tones of Leith. She sounded sort of fancy-spoken.

Nodding, he fished into his pocket and brought out a handful of coins. When he counted them out they came to five shillings and twopence which he put on the floor beside the drooping hat. Daisy had been watching carefully as he counted and now nodded too, reaching out a hand to push the two extra pennies in his direction but he did not reclaim them. All he wanted was to escape as soon as possible without having to get into that bed with his trembling companion. Now that her hat was off he could see that she had a sleek head of dark hair coiled into a huge loop at the nape of her neck. Her profile was strange and reminded him of something . . . then suddenly it struck him! She looked like an Egyptian goddess that he'd seen carved on a sarcophogus in the museum in Edinburgh. She had the same slanting eyes and high-bridged nose.

'Is this your first time?' she whispered and when he did not bother to lie, she told him: 'Mine too. Bertha brought me out with her. She said it'd be easy. She said the man would know how to go about it. She said it'd be over before I knew what happened.' She sounded on the verge of tears.

'I could try,' offered Laurence and she looked at the money on the floor before she nodded.

'Oh all right,' she said and slipped out of her dress,

81

revealing a white bodice and long underskirt. Wearing these as well as her boots she climbed on to the bed and lay down.

Looking at her lying there like a human sacrifice, Laurence felt deflated. 'I don't feel like it any more. I'm sorry,' he said.

She turned her face into the ticking of the pillow and her voice came back in a muffled way. 'It's my fault. If the woman who runs this house finds out what's happened, she'll beat me till I'm black and blue.'

He was backing towards the door now and stuttering, 'Don't tell her. Keep the money. I don't want it back. What're you doing in this place anyway?' As she sat up he could see that she was even younger than he had imagined, probably no more than fifteen.

The prospect of being allowed to keep the money stopped her sobbing and she told him, 'I'm an orphan. My mother was a lady of quality and my father was killed on a trip to South America. The news broke my mother's heart and she died a year later. I was eight when I was put in an orphanage in Edinburgh but I ran away to Mrs Duncan who has this house. She bought me clothes and sent me out with Bertha. This's my first night. God knows how I'm going to be able to do it.'

Laurence stood with his hand on the door handle gazing at her. She was really the most astonishingly beautiful girl he'd ever seen, 'Then don't,' he said.

She was crying now, tears slipping over her alabaster cheeks. 'What else can I do? I've nowhere to go, nobody to care if I live or die. It's this or starvation.'

Laurence's sympathy was fully awakened now, but his libido had disappeared. He indicated the money on the floor, 'Take it. Owe it to me. I'll come back and collect one day.' Then he left.

Downstairs Pat was having a very different experience. He had never felt anything like it in his life. All his fears of impotence proved groundless as he plunged into a squealing Bertha. He felt like a king, an emperor, a lord of the universe and wanted to raise his head and yell his triumph to the world. Once was not enough for him. He wanted to do it twice and when he turned to Bertha for a second time, she gave her giggle and said, 'No, no. What a lad you are! You've not paid for the first time yet.'

He stopped and the realisation dawned that he hadn't enough money. He'd not really expected her to take him up on his offer in the bar. Everything had gone on from there and he only had a couple of shillings in his pocket. What would she say when she found out? He rolled over on his back, rampancy deflated, and she turned on her side beside him so that her huge breasts flopped against his arm.

'What's the matter? Tired are you?'

He jumped out of bed and started to pull on his clothes. 'I've only two bob but you wait here and I'll go home and borrow the rest from my brother. I promise I will,' he told her. She took the news surprisingly calmly and was still smiling as she looked back at him from the pillow.

'I guessed as much. Tarts usually ask for cash in advance, lovey, but I fancied you and I was just out showing that lassie Daisy the ropes, so I thought I'd slip in a free one. It's your first time and you going off with the army an' all. Go on home but come back when you're on leave and have some money in your pocket. I'll be happy to see you.'

Laurence was waiting at the bottom of the stairs to their flats when Pat loomed up beside him and said, 'My God, I'm knackered. You should have seen me. I did it four times and she gave me it for nothing, I was so good! How'd you get on with the skinny one?'

Laurence was looking sheepish. 'All right.'

'Only all right? Hell, it's the most wonderful thing that's ever happened to me. I can't describe it. Anything I've heard about it isn't true. It's better. I bet you didn't get it up. Is that what's wrong? You didn't make it!' He was pushing his friend playfully in the chest and was surprised when Laurence punched back in anger. 'I did so. You needn't think you're the only one with a cock. It was fine. I've got a headache now, that's all. I'm going up to bed. Goodnight!' And he ran upstairs quickly before Pat found out that he hadn't lost his virginity after all.

1895

For the rest of her life Brabazon Nairn was to remember 1895 as a bad year. By the time the church clock struck the hour of its beginning, she had accepted that Duncan's illness was never going to improve. Though she hid her concern, little by little she charted the deterioration in him.

It was proving to be a long hard grind trying to turn the brewery round to profitability, but having always to pretend to Duncan that one day he would recover his health was worse. The effort of appearing cheerful taxed her reserves of strength and composure: sometimes she longed to scream out in frustration.

At night she lay chastely in bed beside her sick husband stilling his quivering body in her arms till he fell asleep. Then she stayed awake and unsatisfied, staring at the dim square of their window until morning. Her mind was full of worries about her business and her sons, especially Laurence who was a problem. Since Pat Warre went off to the army, he had been deeply disruptive and dissatisfied and when the news came that Pat was being shipped out to India, that unsettled him even more. He fought continually with Henry who became more shy and withdrawn, taking solace in books and music, or wandering Leith in search of antiquities when he was not playing St Mary's organ. Henry was almost as gifted musically as his father and on the days that Duncan was able to stagger across to the church to listen, he was often moved to tears by the intensity of his son's playing. Laurence was musical, too, but because of his father's and brother's proficiency and the praise they received, he had chosen to ignore his gift.

After a broken and sleepless night, Brabazon was working in the brewery office on a cold January morning when her brother Mark appeared in the doorway wearing mourning. He looked bleakly at her and said, 'It's Mother. She died last night. The funeral's at St Mary's on Wednesday. Do you want to come, Brabazon?'

'Of course. What about Father, does he know?'

'I wrote him last week warning him it was near. She was in a coma at the end. His promise to her was that he wouldn't come back to Leith while she was alive but he took a ship from St Petersburg last Friday and he should be with us by Wednesday.

Brabazon nodded. She felt no grief at the loss of her mother who had been hard and unloving towards her only daughter, but her heart rose at the thought she would see her father again. They had not met since she was fifteen.

On Wednesday morning, the funeral procession of Maria Logan snaked from her fine house across the Links, through a little alley, over Constitution Street and up to the church. The dead woman's daughter was waiting with her own sons beside a freshly dug grave in the iron-railed enclosure that was the burying place of the Logans. Beneath the veil that shrouded her face she was scrutinising every mourner in the line that followed the coffin.

She picked him out at once. Her father, Joshua, was an unmistakeable figure all wrapped up in a sable coat that swept the ground and a gleaming top hat. With his golden-topped cane and his neatly clipped, grizzled beard he was by far the most impressive person in the gathering as he walked beside Mark, and his daughter stared at him proudly. Her memories were not wrong – he was elegant, assured, polished, a gentleman. She glowed at the thought that she was his daughter.

Because of the biting cold Mr Templeton wasted little time and Maria Logan was buried very swiftly. After the last clod of earth was thrown in, Joshua walked around the mourners to grasp his daughter in his arms. 'Brabazon! Let me look at you. My dear, are those your sons?

How often I've thought of you, how often I've longed to speak to you directly instead of writing letters.'

His voice had a foreign intonation as if speaking English was strange for him. He smelt of cheroots and some spicy hair dressing. The touch of his arms made her feel safe. There were tears in her eyes when she looked at him. 'Please come home with me Father and meet my husband. He's sick and can't come out.'

Joshua charmed Duncan as he charmed everyone else. He remembered his parents; he remembered the brewery in the days of its glory and talked with confidence of it being prosperous again. His optimism gave his daughter a fresh impetus to her life. More than ever she was determined not to give in; to win through; to prove Willie Ord and all the doubters wrong. The week that Joshua spent in Leith was seven days of pleasure for her and on his last night he came around to invite Brabazon's sons to dine with him in a fashionable Edinburgh restaurant.

Henry and Laurence were astonished and delighted by this invitation, but it was obvious that their grandfather considered it nothing unusual to ride up the hill from Leith in a hackney carriage and sit down at a table in one of the best dining establishments of the capital.

Joshua won their hearts by talking to them like men of the world. Looking around the half-empty room which was decorated with gilt paint and crimson velvet curtains looped up by golden cords, he said, 'This is a not a city for men who like pleasure. It's too discreet.'

Greatly daring, Laurence said, 'I prefer Leith.'

His grandfather smiled at him, 'You're right. I prefer Leith too. It's got guts. It's more vital. Edinburgh's so polite! Leith isn't polite – and I like that. Do you boys know that you're descended from a pirate? They say that's how my great-grandfather made his fortune – by piracy out of Leith.'

His grandsons gazing at him could well believe it. Laurence, thinking of his own desire to travel the world, asked, 'Why did you leave Leith, Grandfather?'

Joshua recognised a kindred spirit in the young man

before him and said, 'I'll tell you that story when we're having dinner. Let's start . . .' They ate quails and braised beef, roast mutton with caper sauce and an iced confection of a pudding that shivered on their plates. They ate melting French cheese and drank the best claret and champagne, finishing with cognac. By the time Joshua had lit his post-prandial cigar, the boys were relaxed and easy with him.

'You were going to tell us the story of your life,' prompted Laurence sitting back in his chair.

'I hope you take a lesson from it. I've done things that I shouldn't have done, I'm afraid,' was the reply.

'What sort of things?' Laurence wanted badly to hear this story.

'I married your grandmother for one – and had two children by her – then I left her. I shouldn't have done that.'

Henry, reflectively twisting his brandy glass, said, 'If you hadn't we wouldn't be here.'

'True.'

'Why did you leave?' Laurence was curious about every aspect of his grandfather's life. He had not been able to talk with anyone so openly since Pat went away.

'I didn't love her. I married her when I was twenty years old: don't ever marry too young. We'd known each other from childhood. Her father was my father's friend. They owned ships between them. It seemed the ideal match – on paper. But I was green. I was as randy as a stallion. I could hardly wait to get into bed with her.'

Henry looked embarrassed at this disclosure, but Laurence nodded in such a way that Joshua knew his assessment of the boy was right. This one would appreciate sensuality.

'It didn't take me long to find out that she bored me. She was a tedious woman. I left her alone a great deal and when I did go home, she spent her time complaining or else she tried to ingratiate herself with me, twisting her hands – like this. I used to wish she'd swear and throw things but she never did. She was too well brought up,

too ladylike, from a very respectable Edinburgh family –
the sort of people who'd put up with having a murderer
in the family but never complain in case the neighbours
found out.'

Neither of the boys had ever seen their grandmother
and Henry asked, 'She couldn't have been like Mother
then?'

Joshua shook his head, 'Not a bit. Your mother's got
spirit. She's like my mother. When anyone annoyed her,
she'd really shout! I was terrified of her.' This was difficult
to believe and both boys laughed but Joshua's face sobered quickly as he went on, 'I fell in love when I was
twenty-eight – in Russia. I bought timber there. I tried
denying my feelings and came home, but it wasn't any
good. I couldn't forget her. When I left I salved my
conscience by providing well for my wife and children.'

Laurence leaned forward in his chair and asked
urgently, 'Did it last? Your love affair I mean.'

Joshua nodded, 'Yes, I'm still with her. Her name's
Olga.'

'Have you married her?'

'No. I couldn't because your grandmother was still
alive. We'll marry now though – we've four children, you
know. They'll be happy to be made legitimate.' And he
laughed throwing back his head, puffing cigar smoke into
the air.

Laurence was delighted. This was a man he could
respect, a man who could be an example for him. If Henry
wasn't with us, I'd tell him about Daisy, about the fever
I've felt for her ever since the night we met, he thought.

As if guessing the young man's thoughts, his grandfather turned towards him and said, 'You're like me. It
won't be easy for you.' Then he turned to Henry and told
him, 'You're different – you're a fine man like your father.
Look after your mother, Henry, she needs all the support
you can give her.'

After Joshua sailed away, Brabazon felt deflated and fearful. It was as if all the terrors closed in on her again and there was no one to fend them off. With dread in her heart she waited for the next calamity and it was not long in coming.

Early on a March morning after a night of bitter cold, Brabazon slipped on the faded, old green velvet cloak that she used to wrap herself up in for her journeys to and from the brewery and slipped across the yard. She had a feeling of deep disquiet which she could not explain and nothing would satisfy her unless she could go and have a look at her latest vat of beer which had been fermenting satisfactorily the previous evening. The brewery was silent and very cold when she pushed open the door and it seemed as if a draught of icy wind was blowing through the ancient buildings. It ruffled her cloak like a cruel intruder, making her spirit sink. She knew that whatever happened a fermenting brew must not be allowed to grow cold.

Everything was still and silent as she walked into the vaulted ground floor. A fermenting vat did not make any sound but she could always sense its activity. Now instinctively she knew that her brew was dead. The cold air had killed it.

Heart thudding, she hurried up the stepladder to the top of the vat and bent over. Instead of a landscape of fascination, a surging pulse of activated yeast, there was only a flat and sullen surface that glittered ominously beneath the rays of her lamp. The yeast had stopped working. She dropped her head in anguish. There were orders to fulfil; she had customers anxious for supplies. Two days ago, she and Alex had started this and now it was ruined. What had happened?

A quick check proved her suspicions to be correct. The heating system that kept the brewhouse at an even temperature was extinguished and the chill air circulating inside the old building came from the tiny door that led into the church burying ground. By some terrible mischance it had been left open. She examined the handle, twisted and turned it in her hands. It was not sticking.

This could not have been an accident. Someone had turned off the heat to the vats and made sure that disaster would strike by opening the churchyard door.

Alex and Nellie Warre were wakened by a rapid hammering at their front door. 'Who's that?' asked Nellie sitting bolt upright in their box bed, 'Go to the door Alex, it's not six o'clock yet. Something must've happened.'

When Alex drew back the bolt he found an agitated Brabazon on the step. 'Somebody's killed the vat. It's cold and dead. Come over and see for yourself,' she gasped without apology for waking him so early.

A few minutes later they stood stricken in the brewhouse, regarding the ruin of their work. 'We'll just have to run it off. There's nothing else for it,' said Alex.

'Somebody's been in here. I know it. I'm sure of it. Neither you nor I would have left that little door open. But who knows about it except us and our families?' Brabazon was angry. 'It couldn't have blown ajar because it's too heavy. Why did it happen at the same time as the boiler going out? It's been deliberately opened.'

He soothed her, 'No, no. It *must* have blown open. We'll start again, missus, don't be downcast, we'll just start again.'

'You mean we'll persevere,' said Brabazon bitterly.

Alex's face was thoughtful as he worked through the morning and at lunch-time he sought out Brabazon to tell her, 'I've been thinking. It's funny this happened now. I heard the other day that Gordon's well is nearly dry and they're desperate for good water. And there's another thing. A man stopped me in the street last week and offered me fifty pound if I'd leave you and take another job.'

She was astonished, 'Fifty pounds! What did you say?'

'I said five hundred wouldn't be enough for me to leave Perseverance Brewery.'

She looked at him with gratitude, 'Thank you Alex. Bit it's odd, isn't it?'

Next day Willie Ord the lawyer arrived to tell her that

one of the major creditors, a grain merchant, had called in his bill.

She looked at him with distaste and suspicion, 'But I've been paying him back bit by bit. The debt's gone down a lot,' she protested.

Ostentatiously he consulted the papers in his hand, 'Umm, yes, but you still owe him two hundred pounds. He's had business problems himself and he says he can't wait any longer. After all it's been several years now, hasn't it? If the word get around that he's forcing things, other creditors might panic and push you into liquidation after all.'

His spectacles gleamed in a kindly way at her and she wondered how anyone so wicked could manage to look so benevolent. Her hands were shaking and she gripped one tight in the other to try to settle herself. 'What should I do?' she asked.

'Well there's still Gordon's offer on the table. But if you won't take it, you'll have to raise two hundred pounds by tomorrow. It's a pity this has happened, Mrs Nairn, just when things seem to be going well for you at last. Your beer's good I hear.'

She glared at him balefully but he went away smiling as cheerfully as if she'd been as sweet as honey. When he'd gone she sat in her office, elbows on the desk and head in hands, trying to think. The aroma of stewing hops filled the air because Alex had wasted no time in starting another batch after their disaster. The smell seemed to clear her head so she could enumerate her problems – first, and worst of all, she had no spare money and no assets left which could be sold. Her mind threw up possibilities and rejected them one by one. For Duncan's sake it was still unthinkable to go to her brother or her father and ask for a loan. Yet she had to find the money – and quickly.

She hurried home to where Duncan lay feebly in his armchair. As she poured out the story his eyes showed profound concern.

'Perhaps we *ought* to sell the brewery,' he told her but

she shook her head. Every obstacle she met made her more determined to hang on as long as she could. She had no wish to sell especially when she had already surmounted so many obstacles. When he recognised her determination, he thought for a bit before he said, 'In that case, try to sell this.' He lifted a shaking hand and, following his gaze, she found herself staring at the gold signet ring he wore on his index finger. It had been secretly saved from the bankruptcy sale.

'But it's your family ring. It was worn by your father and his father before him.'

'That doesn't matter. It's a crisis,' said Duncan.

'You're right. It is a crisis. I've got a ring, too, and a brooch my aunt left me. That's what we'll do, we'll pawn them.'

Easing the signet ring off his finger was difficult for illness had made his hands swell, but the application of soft soap and warm water eventually made it come loose. When she slipped it over his knuckle, a deep mark was left where he had worn it for so many years. When it was tied safely into the corner of her handkerchief, she lifted a floorboard beside their bed and brought out a small, green silk-covered box containing what remained of her own jewellery. Inside was a ring with a diamond set in the middle of two clasped hands; Duncan's mother's betrothal ring. Most imposing of all was her own aunt's brooch, a large square sapphire surrounded by tiny diamonds. Tying them up safely as well, she ran down the stairs to the pawnshop where Minna and Abe were leaning on the counter, watching the passing crowd through the grimy glass in their doorway. Without preamble she laid her handkerchief on the counter, untied it and asked in a gulping voice, 'What can I raise on these?'

Abe carefully lifted out the rings and screwed a jeweller's eyeglass into his left eye to examine the stones. It seemed an eternity before he pronounced judgement. 'They're old and they're bonny but they're not very valuable. The brooch is the best. It's worth about fifty pounds.'

Brabazon had put out her hand and pushed Duncan's ring to the side of the counter. If possible, she wanted to save it for him. By the way the couple behind the counter looked at each other, she knew they recognised the significance of her gesture.

'That ring you've got there's worth about ten pounds because it's heavy gold,' said Abe nodding at it.

Brabazon sighed. things were desperate and ten pounds made a difference. 'How much altogether? How much for everything?' she asked.

Abe furrowed his brow. 'Ninety pounds?' he suggested.

Minna saw the look on Brabazon's face and jumped in. 'We might be able to make it a hundred. Vhat do you think Abe?' she asked him.

He squinted at her in surprise but what he saw made him turn to Brabazon and nod, 'Yes, I could do a hundred.'

They were disappointed when her face fell, 'Is that all? It's not that I think . . . It's just that . . .'

'How much do you need?' asked Minna. There was no point beating about the bush Brabazon decided. It was best to be honest. 'I need two hundred by tomorrow but I've nothing else to sell. I'm desperate.'

Abe turned and took a heavy key from a hook at the back of the counter. 'How do you want it?'

'What do you mean?'

'How do you want it? In notes or in coin?'

'Anything. I just need the money.'

'We'll lend it to you – at interest, mind. And we'll have to take all the jewellery as security.'

As he was speaking, Abe was bending down and unlocking a huge iron safe that filled most of the wall behind him. When its dark door swung ajar, Brabazon caught sight of stacks of silver and piles of deed boxes. He counted his finger down the boxes till he came to the third which he pulled out and laid on the counter. Then he unlocked it with a tiny key on his watch chain and revealed that it was full of money – notes and coins, gold sovereigns. He dipped in a hand – in much the same way as Alex dipped for hops – and brought out a brimming fistful. Very slowly and carefully, he counted two hundred sovereigns in stacks of fifty on to the counter and then pushed the piles towards Brabazon. She looked at the money in disbelief. 'When do you want it back?' she stammered.

'Keep it as long as you like. But don't forget out interest,' said Abe.

'How much will that be?'

'Two hundred at five per cent per annum – ten pounds a year. You can pay it off monthly if you like.'

'You're sure – only five per cent?' Brabazon had lived long enough in Perseverance Place to know that Abe and Minna charged more than fifteen per cent on loans.

Abe looked irritated as if his patience was being tried. 'I said five didn't I?' he asked pushing his glasses up the bridge of his large hooked nose. Impulsively she reached both hands over the counter and took his. She wanted to kiss him but was afraid at how he and Minna might react. Instead, stammering her thanks, she gathered up her money, signed the promissory paper they pushed at her and ran out of the shop with Abe's admonition ringing in her ears, 'Watch how you go with all that money. Don't leave it in the flat when you're out.'

It did not stay in her keeping very long because that same afternoon she paid off the grain merchant and later Willie Ord came around to tell her the remaining creditors had been assuaged. They had decided to go on as before because, as they well realised, even if repayment was slow it was in their own interest to have their money repaid in full rather than settling for the terms of a bankruptcy.

'Mind you, I don't think you're being very wise. As your adviser I have to tell you that it would be far easier for you to go bankrupt and pay them all off at less than the debt,' said Ord to Brabazon.

She shook her head, 'But that would mean I'd lose Perseverance Brewery and also I don't want to do things that way. I'd feel dishonoured. I *want* to pay in full. I want to be clear of debt and able to hold up my head again.'

1895 was also a bad year for a girl living on a small croft on a remote island in the Outer Hebrides. She had never heard of the Nairns, nor they of her but their paths were destined to cross.

Mhairi McKay was a blithe sixteen-year-old with a mass of thickly curling yellow hair and a face like a spring flower opening to the sun. Nothing had ever bothered her, not poverty nor hard work; not bitter winds in winter nor the cutting teeth of an autumn gale. Until the night she went to a dance and met Dugald Stewart.

He'd been watching her for a long time, slinking along behind stone walls as she worked in the field with her father. Stewart was a tall, straight man with dark hair and a solemn face, a regular churchgoer and very pious. People would have called him handsome if there had not been a slyness in his eye and a cruelty in the line of his mouth that Mhairi was too young and innocent to spot. She was flattered when he sought her out because he was the richest man in the district; a farmer with fifty acres and a real house with two rooms on the upper floor. Mhair's family, and the others around her, tilled one field which they rented from a distant landlord and lived in a turf-roofed hovel. While her admirer ploughed his fields behind a pair of horses, the crofters scraped at their earth with long-handled mattocks and contented themselves with growing potatoes and cabbages for their own feeding. Their inhospitable ground would yield nothing more. If she could marry a man like Stewart, the troubles of all her family would disappear.

At the dance Stewart paid her compliments in his slow voice and brought her two glasses of whisky which she drank rather than disappoint him. When her face was flushed and her eyes sparkling, he suggested a turn in the fresh air. In a hayshed beside the hall where the dance was being held he suddenly turned on her, pushed her on to a bale of hay and held her hands in his strong grip.

'Kiss me,' he ordered when she turned her face away from his whisky-smelling breath.

'No, no, let me go!' she cried in terror.

'Kiss me.' His voice went softer, 'Then I'll marry you. We'll have vases on the mantleshelf and a brass bed with lace around it.'

She listened to his words and weakened. The whisky made her too feeble to protest when his hands began stroking her tiny breasts. Then all at once he went wild, threw himself on her and ripped at her clothes. She screamed and fought against him, pummelling at his back with her fists but it was too late. He was bigger than she, and wild with lust. Less than a minute later she lay weeping and deflowered, hair and clothes disordered, watching him pull up his pants. When he'd dressed he left her and was nowhere to be seen when she limped back into the hall.

Three months later Mhairi had changed. Her vigorous hair had gone lank and lost its colour. Her pink cheeks were white, her blue eyes dark-shadowed. 'It can't have happened,' she told her friend Chrissie. 'He was only in me for a second – how it hurt! It can't have happened like that. I can't be having a baby, *can I?*'

For weeks she hoped that her fears were groundless but the moon waxed and waned and still no bleeding came. Even when her belly swelled like a ball beneath her belt she went on hoping, but one day she put her hands on her stomach and felt a faint flutter deep inside and knew there was a baby there.

She had not seen her ravisher since the night of the dance but on the evening the baby moved she walked along the path to Stewart's house. Primroses spangled the banks and furry catkins swung from the branches of the hazel trees. The countryside looked so lovely that Mhairi felt hope rise within her. He must have meant all those things he'd said about the vases on the mantelpiece and the brass bed. The reason he'd not come to see her since

97

the dance must be because he was busy planting his corn. When he heard her news, he'd be delighted and they'd marry straightaway.

There was smoke coming from the chimney stack at the side of the thick heather thatch of his home. It was a snug place, better-built and bigger than any other on the island because he was the most prosperous man around.

As she drew nearer to the cottage Mhairi saw that a dog-cart stood in front of the door and recognised it as belonging to the minister from the church up the road. His daughter used it sometimes to drive from cottage to cottage on her charitable visits. Mhairi's family never received any of those calls because they were Roman Catholics and did not attend the minister's church but walked five miles over the moors every Sunday to Mass.

The cottage door stood open and voices came out. The minister's daughter always spoke loudly and her words came over very clear, though the man's replies were lower and sounded like rumbling water.

'I've persuaded my father to agree at last. He'll marry us, Dugald. He's fixed it for the seventeenth of October.'

Mhairi slipped up to the open door and looked inside. There were vases and jugs along the mantelpiece and a fine peat fire burning in the grate. A rag rug lay on the floor and a picture of Queen Victoria hung on the wall facing the window. Around the room were good pieces of furniture and a piano with fluted red silk behind its fretted front stood in a far corner. The minister's daughter and Dugald Stewart stood hand in hand before the fireplace and they looked around in surprise when she coughed. His face never changed when he saw who the caller was.

'Have you come for the pitcher of milk I promised your mother?' he asked in a level voice and walked towards her, leading her out to the cowshed at the back of the cottage. When they were out of earshot he turned on her, 'What do you think you're doing spying on us? Get away home with you.'

She looked dumbly at him and wondered how this terrible thing had happened. He was still a handsome man in his early thirties but now she realised that his mouth was hard and his eyes shifty and cold.

'I have to speak with you,' she whispered.

'What about?'

'I'm having a baby.'

'Whose is it?'

'It's yours of course! I was a virgin when you had me at that dance. I've never been with anybody else.'

'How do I know that? You were easy enough for me. You'll have been putting it about as easily for other men. You Papes are all liars.'

A wave of nausea filled her mouth and she swallowed quickly, 'That's not true. You filled me with whisky and talked so sweet to me that I believed you. You cheated me. Then you took me – I didn't know what you were doing till it was all over.'

He laughed, 'You're a crofting lassie. Who'd believe that story?'

'But it's true. What are you going to do about me and the baby? It's yours.'

'I don't believe you. Anyway I'm getting married in October to Miss Robertson in there and not you nor anybody else is going to stop it. You'll have to find another father for your bastard.'

She wanted to attack him, to flail him with her fists but when she stepped towards him with fury evident in her face, he grabbed her by the wrists and said, 'I'll deny it. You can't prove it. You were birling and flirting with other men on the night of the dance. It could be any one of them.'

When she walked home, the tears in her eyes made it impossible to see the primroses any longer. All colour seemed to have drained out of the world.

She told her mother about the baby that night and had to cradle her head beneath her folded arms in an effort to avoid the blows that were rained on her. 'You loose little bitch! You harlot! How're we to keep another bairn? There's not enough to eat for us all as it is.'

'But what about him, what about Stewart? He's as bad as me. Worse – because I didn't know anything.'

'It's different for men. Women should keep themselves pure. You've disgraced us all.' There was no reasoning with her furious mother. Her father's reaction hurt her more however because, although he did not rage at her or beat her, his face showed shock and disappointment when he heard the news. She could see that she had injured him.

She was the oldest child of the McKay family with no brothers to stand up for her because the other children were two little girls. It fell to her father to go to see the man who had ruined his daughter. He walked over to the farm next day and stood leaning on a field gate till Stewart deigned to come over and speak to him.

'What do you want?' he asked abruptly.

'I've come to find out what you're going to do about my lassie and her bairn,' said Peter McKay.

'Nothing. If she says I'm the father she's a liar. I'm getting married in October and if you spread the news about me getting your girl with child, I'll make you suffer: you can be sure of that.'

He owned land all round and had money in the bank. He was a friend of McKay's landlord and both of them knew it. Besides, Mhairi's father relied on the extra seasonal work this man provided and which would be denied him if he forced the issue. With loathing on his face, he stepped back from the gate and walked away disconsolate, his black and white collie dog trailing at his heels.

In the stables of Perseverance Brewery, Laurence sat on an upturned bucket with his aching head in his hands. He did not look up when he heard his mother's hurried footsteps on the cobbles. 'Why didn't you come when you heard me calling?' she demanded.

At this he raised his head showing reddened eyes, 'I've a headache. I was just on my way.'

She did a quick turn on her booted feet like a dancer

100

about to launch into a spirited step. It was one of her signs of rising anger. Her voice was tense as she accused him, 'You were out till after midnight last night. I heard you coming home. I don't know what's come over you. You used to be such a good boy.' Her younger son sat hunched in front of her with a lock of dark hair hanging down over his forehead. A smell of stale beer came off him and she had no doubt what had caused his headache. Ever since Pat Warre went away, Laurence had been disruptive and surly.

She sighed loudly as he replied, 'I suppose you mean I'm not like your precious Henry.'

'I've never made any difference between you. I love you both the same,' she told him still angrily.

'In that case let me be. I'm growing up like a normal man, that's all – not like Henry,' he almost shouted, and rose to his feet to start clanging around with buckets of oats for the horses who were shifting their hooves uneasily on the floor of the stalls. Any argument between humans upset them.

Brabazon left then but her parting shot was, 'You miss Pat Warre, that's all that's wrong with you. He'll come back – he must get leave some time.'

Laurence had to fight to stop himself from swearing, 'Mother, he's gone to India. He won't be back for years,' he spat back, feeling very sorry for himself. He hated to realise that since Pat went away he had been lonely and resentful, wishing that he too could don a scarlet coat and sail to distant lands. What was worse, however, was the way he was still obsessed with Daisy. The girl with the strange exotic profile and sleek shivering body was never out of his mind. Many times after he'd been drinking with his cronies, he wandered the pavements of The Shore looking for her but she seemed to have disappeared.

He thought about his brother – responsible, clean-skinned, innocent and virginal. Henry knew nothing of the other face of Leith and would run a mile from the delights of The Shore. He was happiest playing the church organ and had taken over Duncan's duties of providing the

101

music for Sunday services. Laurence was positive Henry had never been with a woman, had never even considered it. He remembered Pat's lyrical description of his night with Bertha and wondered if it would be like that with Daisy. What a fool I've been giving her five bob and running away! he told himself not for the first time.

When work was finished for the day, he did not go home but, still wearing his working clothes, ran over the yard and into the Kirkgate. He headed for The Shore. This time he did not linger and watch but went straight to The King's Head and asked the man behind the bar if he knew Daisy. The answer was a shake of the head and a shrug. 'Tarts are ten a penny down here,' said the man, 'Won't another one do?'

Laurence knew where Bertha lived and was soon knocking at the door of her room. After several sharp knocks, she opened it, rubbing her eyes with her knuckles and clutching a dirty wrapper over her mammoth breasts.

'Do you know where Daisy is?' asked the young man on her threshold.

'Daisy? What Daisy?' She was stupid because she'd just woken up.

'The thin girl that was with you about six months ago – the night my friend and I met you in The King's Head. My friend's name was Pat . . . he went with you and I went with Daisy. She told me you'd taken her out because it was her first night.'

Bertha made a ticking sound with her tongue. 'Oh that one! She kept on weeping and wailing and one night a sailor beat her up so she went up to Edinburgh on the tram. She said she knew somebody there. She's probably walking Rose Street now. She thought she'd get a better class of customer there!' Bertha gave her throaty laugh.

The horse-drawn tram took what seemed an age to toil up the slope of Leith Walk and it was an hour later when Laurence found himself in Rose Street. Though Leith was less than two miles away, this felt like a different country. The pubs were much grander, with stained-glass windows and vast saloons, and there was one every twenty yards or so. He went in and out of them until he was dizzy. From time to time a woman put out a hand and touched his arm in invitation and every time he was surprised because they were all so well-dressed that he would have taken them for ladies if it had not been for the urgent words they whispered.

'Do you know a girl called Daisy?' he asked one of them but she shook her head, uninterested in passing him on to anyone else. It was not until he'd asked in the fifteenth bar that he picked up her trail.

'I'm looking for a girl called Daisy. I'm her brother,' he told the barman.

'Is she a tart?'

'Yes.'

'What's she look like? We know a couple of Daisys.'

'She's very thin and she's got dark hair. She's very young, looks a bit like a leggy horse.' He didn't want to say she reminded him of a whippet because it didn't sound complimentary, although he'd greatly admired her angular shape.

'There's one comes here that looks like that. She was in earlier. If you stick around, she'll probably be back. It's not late yet.'

He positioned himself in a corner where he sat clutching his glass of beer and facing a large engraved mirror in which he could see whoever came through the bar door. More than a hour passed before she entered. In the mirror he saw the door swing open and for a moment no one was there but then she appeared, framed in darkness, almost sliding round the door jamb like a snake, pouring herself into the big room in such a sensual way that his heart skipped a beat at the sight of her. She was wearing grey, a long fitted coat and a floor-sweeping skirt that made her look as elegant as a fashion plate. Her hat was black with a plume of scarlet feathers at the side. The feathers and the way she slid through the doorway were the only sign that she might not be a respectable girl.

Laurence stood up and looked straight at her. The impassive expression on her face seemed to shiver and crack and her eyes lit up, but she did not smile. Instead she walked towards him and whispered, 'Are you looking for me?'

His throat was visibly pulsing with emotion above the collarless shirt and he nodded. 'I owe you five bob, don't I?' said Daisy, gently taking his hand.

He laid his glass on the table and hand in hand they walked out into the gaudy street. That night Laurence discovered that Pat's description of lovemaking was an understatement. What was more important was that he fell deeply in love with Daisy.

The summer passed with young Mhairi McKay growing rounder and rosier as Stewart's child inside her came nearer to being born. She was in a state of strange tranquillity in which nothing worried her. Her mother had forgotten her original anger and seemed more tender towards her oldest child than she had ever been before. There was pity in her eyes when she looked at Mhairi.

On a late summer afternoon the birth pains took Mhairi by surprise because she was not due for several more weeks. With a gasp she bent double in agony as she worked with her father tying up stooks of corn in their field behind the cottage. She lay down among the stubble and looked up at a bright September sky where a wind from the sea was sweeping banks of fleecy clouds over a vastness of blue.

Her father helped her into the low door of their home and she crawled into the bundle of dry heather that was her bed. Then agony descended like a huge cape, muffling her and shutting out awareness of everything else. Behind her closed eyelids she saw jagged streaks of scarlet like lightning flashes as pain ripped through her body. Her mother, busy with milking the cow and preparing food for her husband and the younger children, paused beside the labouring girl every now and again to put a hand on her brow and whisper consolingly, 'It doesnae last. It passes.' But as darkness came and there was no sign of the girl's labour advancing, she began to worry and sent for one of her neighbours who was skilled in helping others through childbirth.

Half-conscious, Mhari heard them whispering over her. Her mother's voice said, 'It'd be best if it didna live.'

The neighbour said, 'It'll probably be dead. It's only a poor wee thing judging by the size of the head.'

Another spasm gripped the girl and she gave an anguished scream. She felt her mother pulling off the cover that had been spread over her legs and someone's hands pushed them apart. The neighbour leaned over her and said encouragingly. 'It's nearly there lassie. Gie another push and you'll hae it oot. Dinna waste your strength yelling, just push and push.'

Mhairi concentrated and pressed down as hard as she could. Every muscle in her small body tensed and the effort sent such agony through her that she lost consciousness. When she recovered from her faint there was a blessed silence and an absence of pain. For the first time she realised that the noise she'd been hearing had been her own voice shrieking out. The women around her were now talking in soft clucking voices and she heard her mother say, 'What a bonny wee laddie!' Her son had been born.

They let her sleep for most of the next day and when she woke a peat fire was glowing scarlet and orange in the hearth and her mother was standing beside it with a bundle in her arms. Her face was unusually soft and gentle and her voice soothing when she came walked over to Mhairi on the bed and said, 'He's a grand wee soul, the living image of a bairn I had years ago – before I had you. He died though, poor wee soul. I called him Calum . . .'

'Then I'll call this laddie Calum, too,' said Mhairi and started to cry for she was only sixteen years old and felt so unhappy. Having a baby was not a joyous experience for her. In fact everything about growing up and becoming a woman had proved to be a disappointment.

Her weakness was not allowed to last long. Childbirth

105

was a black and white matter in their society. Women either died or were expected to take it in their stride. Mhairi was young and strong so within two days she was back in the field stooking the sheaves but this time with a baby tied to her back. Though Calum was very small when he was born, he gained weight quickly and proved himself to be a contented child. All Mhairi had to do was give him her breast every few hours. He suckled greedily, mouth clamped tight over her tender nipple and almost as she watched him, he seemed to expand and bloom like a rosebud.

She watched her child with fascination. She had not wanted to bear him, had carried him without thinking about the future and given birth to him in agony; but as she held the child in her arms, she began to love him. This was her son. This boy was hers and had nothing to do with the perfidious Dugald Stewart except that his seed had been planted in her to allow the child to grow. She delighted in him, marvelling at his miniature perfection. All the tears that resulted from his conception were forgotten.

As the baby grew, the neighbouring women came to see him and exclaimed in admiration, 'My word what a bonny wee laddie.' They were only speaking the truth because the child was well-made and blonde with bright, intelligent blue eyes and a placid disposition like his mother. Clear in the eyes and in the interrogatory voices of the neighbours was one question, 'Who's the father?' There were not many candidates for the honour of siring such a perfect child, for young men were rare in the crofts. They either went off fishing for most of the year or joined the army. The land was tilled by old men and women assisted by children.

Mhairi and her family did not satisfy their curiosity but allowed them to go on wondering. So they sat in the open doorways of their homes in the tumble-down little clachan in the evenings, casting speculative eyes on every man under the age of eighty who passed up and down the rutted path that led to the harbour four miles away. It

106

was surprising that no one guessed the truth because Mhairi was beginning to see distinct resemblance between her baby and his tall, proud father. Calum had Stewart's face but, thank God, not the shiftiness of his eyes or the cruelty of his mouth. None of the gossips picked out Stewart as Calum's sire, however, because they thought of him as being so much above a crofting lassie.

Mhairi was happily suckling her bairn one evening when her mother who was stirring a huge black cauldron of soup over the fire, suddenly turned and asked, 'Have you decided what's to happen to that wee laddie?'

The soporific effect of the drowsy baby suckling at her breast had made Mhairi almost drop off into sleep but she was startled into wakefulness by the question. 'What do you mean?' she asked looking at her mother with fear in her enormous eyes.

'He's a bonny wee soul but you realise we canna keep him. What're you going to do about him?' Mhairi's mother voice was sorrowful. This was hard for her because she loved the child too.

Mhairi seemed to shrink. 'I haven't thought about it,' she said. She knew that there had been girls in the district who'd abandoned their babies at birth. They were left to die on the seashore where their poor wee bodies were found naked on the shingle with waves lapping over them. She hugged Calum to her in terror. 'I thought we'd be able to keep him here with us. There's plenty of other bairns around who don't have fathers.'

Her mother's face was set. 'It's not that, Mhairi. It's because we can't afford another mouth in this house. It's all right when you're suckling him but he'll soon need other meat. We canna find it. I've been speaking to the priest and he says we should send Calum to an orphanage.'

'Oh, no, they're awful cruel to the bairns in those places!'

'But he'll have to go some place. My sister in Glasgow's no bairns of her own – none that's lived anyway. I was thinking she might take him.'

107

Mhairi thought about her aunt, a stern woman who had gone into service in Glasgow when she was twelve years old and married a man whom she nagged ceaselessly. Not that he didn't deserve it for he drank heavily and on the rare occasions when their aunt and uncle visited the croft, the little girls had to hide themselves away because he tried to put his hand up their skirts. Mhairi hated them both. She knew they had little sympathy with children.

'Oh Ma, can't Calum stay here with me? I'm his mother . . . I'll work harder to help feed him.'

'It's not working harder that's needed. It's more land or more money. We're taking as much as we can out of the croft already and the landlord's putting the rent up again next term-time. We can't grow any more and your sisters are getting bigger and needing more food. I live in fear of falling wi' another bairn myself. If I did I'd go down to the sea and drown it. It breaks my heart too, Mhairi, but that bairn canna stay here.'

'You're not saying I should drown him?' Mhairi looked terrified as she gazed at her mother.

'Of course not. He's too big anyway. If we were going to do that, we should've done it on the first night but I just couldn't when I saw him – he's that bonny. If you won't let him go to the orphanage or to my sister, you'll have to ask Stewart to take him in or at least provide for him. It's the least he can do.'

That night Mhairi wrapped her baby up in her shawl and slept with him held tight to her heart. By next morning she had made up her mind what to do. After drinking a bowl of curds for her breakfast, she rose from the table and picked up the baby from his wooden cradle at the fireside. Her parents and round-eyed little sisters silently watched everything she did but no one asked where she was going when she left the house.

It was a fine day and she knew where to find Stewart. After walking for about two miles, she breasted the brow of a hill and saw a man and a horse in the middle of a field far below. It made a striking picture, half of the field

108

was green and the other half purple-black, the colour of freshly turned earth. Stewart was ploughing early in order to be finished before his wedding which was at the end of that week.

She clambered down through the heather bushes on the hillside and stood watching from a gateway in the stone dyke. Stewart was a fine-looking man, tall and broad-shouldered. She hoped Calum would inherit that vigorous frame but nothing else. Oblivious of her presence, he was pacing in a measured way up and down each furrow, his booted feet pressing down into the rich earth. Over his head birds wheeled, fighting for the worms the gleaming ploughshare exposed. A sturdy bay mare was harnessed between the shafts of Stewart's plough and she pressed steadily forward with her head lowered and the breath from her distended nostrils silvering in the crisp morning air.

Holding her baby close, Mhairi walked up the side of the field and positioned herself at the top of the last furrow facing down towards the man and horse approaching her. When he came close, she held out the child and called out to Stewart, 'This boy is your son.' He had seen her from half-way up the furrow but given no sign. Now, without looking at her or the baby, he pulled on the reins, turned his horse and re-positioned his plough so that that metal share was cutting into a fresh stretch of green stubble. Mhairi might have been a scarecrow for all the attention he paid her.

If he hoped that she would be gone by the next time he reached that part of the field he was disappointed. The girl still stood there, face white and hair flying in the breeze. This time she held out her baby and asked, 'What are you going to do for your son?'

Again he ignored her. Making clucking sounds with his tongue to the horse, he cracked his whip derisively in Mhairi's direction and went back down the field. Bleak-faced she watched him go and sat down at the wall foot to await his return.

The third time he came towards her, she asked, 'Are you going to help this boy?'

His resolve to ignore her snapped. Pulling on the reins to stop the horse, he stared straight at the girl holding his son and said only one word, '*No!*'

Like a conscience she shadowed him all day, moving along the wall as he ploughed up and down the field. Each time he came to the end of his upward furrow, she was always there. He went away for a spell in the afternoon but she did not leave herself, only lying down in the shade of the wall lovingly suckling her baby and staring up at the blue sky where birds tumbled over her head. Her face was tranquil and impassive. In the late afternoon he returned and each time he came up to her with the plough she held out the child, but each time Stewart told her, 'Go away! It isn't mine.'

When evening drew near, shadows clustered in the corners of the field and the birds settled down in their night-time nesting places. By now the field was a carpet of black and Stewart was ploughing his last furrow. Clucking encouragingly at the mare, he came up the hill watched by the tired and hungry girl.

This was her last chance. Before he reached her, she stepped out from the place where she was standing and walked down the final strip of unturned sods towards him. Then, in front of the labouring horse, she bent down and laid her baby on the ground. Very carefully she arranged her son's shawl; he was asleep and she stood looking at him for a few seconds, before she turned and walked back to the edge of the field.

Dugald Stewart stood with his hands on the plough handles and his face thunderous. Silence engulfed them both. The mare Jess, whose harness had been jingling joyfully as she'd trudged up the hill, stopped dead. The sweet earth beneath the silver ploughshare broke and fell apart like crumbling cake. The sound of it softly breaking was the only noise to be heard. Mhairi watched tensely, seeing Stewart's fists tighten on the plough handles before he urged the horse on in fury. 'Get up Jess! Go on, get up.' Lifting one hand he rattled roughly on the reins, pulling the bit up in the mare's soft mouth.

But Jess stood stock-still, head down, sniffing the sleeping baby. When her head was jerked up by the tugging on the reins, her eyes rolled and she snorted in alarm. Though Stewart cracked his whip over her haunches, she would not move. Wild and raging now, he was keenly conscious of the girl watching him from a few yards away. Her hands were knotted tight in front of her breast and she looked as if she were praying.

With a curse Stewart stepped away from his plough and went forward to the mare's head. The baby lay in a heartbreaking bundle at his feet but he ignored it.

'Are you going to plough right over your own son?' asked Mhairi in a tense voice.

'If you're mad enough to leave him there I will,' he told her.

'That'll be murder. You'll hang for it.'

'You're mad!' he yelled and hauled on the stubborn mare's bridle. 'It'll be your own fault. What decent mother puts her bairn beneath a horse's feet? No one can prove I saw it lying there in the dark.'

'Lift him up. He's yours. He'll be a braw man one day,' pleaded Mhairi.

'He's not mine! You can't prove it.' He was obdurate. She tried another tack. 'If you don't want him then give me some money to raise him.'

'You're a thieving, greedy bitch. You're foisting another man's bastard on me. I could have you up in court for this. Lift your bairn and get away home with you. I'll not take it and I'll not pay for it. I've better things to do with my money.'

Mhairi was weeping now. 'What sort of man are you who would drive a horse over your own child? You'd leave him down there to die wouldn't you? My God, you're wicked. I hope he's inherited nothing from you.'

'Lift it,' he shouted, his face scarlet with rage, 'Lift it or I'll walk right over it. I've got to finish this field before it's dark.'

'Walk then, walk over your own son and you'll rot in Hell for it.'

'I don't care about Hell. Lift that bastard!'

He was almost screaming as he laid the whip over Jess' back. Stung, the horse leapt in the air but, by a miracle, when she came back to earth her huge hooves missed the baby's head by inches. In spite of ill-treatment Jess would not step forward and drag the plough over the child.

'That horse has a better heart than you,' sobbed Mhairi. Now she realised fully what sort of a man she was dealing with. He was a devil and there was no use pleading with him. Tears poured down her cheeks as she accepted defeat, running forward with her arms extended, kneeling down and lifting her son off the ground. When she raised Calum up, she held him out to look at his face, cuddled him close, kissed him and brushed the earth off his shawl with trembling hands.

'No good will ever come to you. I curse you. You'll never have another son,' she told Dugald Stewart and ran off into the gathering darkness carrying her baby.

When Mhairi reached home, her mother was sitting alone beside the smoking peat fire.

As the door was pushed open, Mrs McKay lifted her head and stared at her daughter, 'He sent you away?' she asked.

'Aye,' said the girl with a sob in her voice.

'He didna gie the bairn anything?'

'Nothing.'

The two women met in the middle of the bare floor and Mhairi carefully placed her baby in her mother's arms.

'Look after him well, Mam,' she whispered.

Mhairi's mother bent her head over the child but her daughter could see the tears glittering in her eyes. She had never seen her mother show signs of tearfulness before.

'I'll look after him,' was the muttered reply. Then in an effort to explain the situation to her daughter the older woman said, 'It's best if *you* go. You wouldn't want him to be sent to strangers. But, oh bairn, I'll miss you sore.'

With one arm she hugged Mhairi close while they clung together sobbing, but their lives were hard, their expectations harsh, and their tears quickly spent. She added in a reassuring voice, 'You'll come back, lassie. It'll not be forever. It's best this way. We can raise him easier if there's one less mouth to feed and besides he's a laddie. He'll be able to do a man's work when he's bigger.'

Mhairi nodded, 'I know, I know. Don't say it again. I've made up my mind but I'll miss him and you all so sore . . . so sore.'

Mhairi was sitting with her friend Chrissie on a bank in the waning sunshine. The baby was on her knee, blinking his brilliant eyes in the light. He was smiling.

'I've been afraid to love him. I've really tried not to. I thought then I wouldn't feel so bad when I leave him – but I love him anyway. I can't help it.' Mhairi looked helplessly at her friend who lived on the next croft. They had been confidantes since they were little older than the child they now passed back and forth between them.

'It's too bad of your folk to send you away,' said Chrissie.

Mhairi defended her parents stoutly. 'They're not sending me. I'm going. It was me or the bairn and I chose to go.'

Chrissie was one of the few people who knew the identity of Calum's father and her face was angry as she looked at her friend nursing the little boy who reached up at his mother's face with plump, dimpled hands.

'I hope that Dugald Stewart rots in Hell,' she said, 'I saw him yesterday coming back from church with that new wife of his – a stuck-up besom she looks. Everybody's saying he married her for snobbery and she married him because he's money in the bank. But he's a grippy devil, she'll no' get much out of him. They'll make a sorry pair.'

Mhairi said nothing as she gently prised open her baby's fingers for he had firm hold of her long curly hair. She smiled at him, not minding the pain. Chrissie longed

113

to comfort her friend. 'Don't you worry Mhairi. You'll be able to come back soon and see Calum. When you've saved a bit of money, you can come home. I've a big sister working in Inverness and she comes every year for a whole week! And he'll be quite safe. Your mam'll look after him well.'

'I know that. She loves him already. She says he's like the wee boy she had that died. When she said it was either me or him that had to go, I knew I'd have to be the one. He's a laddie, you see. When he's bigger he'll be a better help than me on the croft and right now he doesna eat as much as me. My wee sisters'll be up and married by the time he's taking a man's meal.' Her voice became heartfelt, 'Isn't it awful to be poor, Chrissie? Isn't it awful when you haven't enough food for everybody in your family?'

The other girl nodded. Poverty ruled in her home as well. She was the youngest of thirteen and had brothers and sisters that she'd never seen scattered across the world – in Canada and Australia. Her mother's anguish when she talked of those distant children she would never see again harrowed Chrissie's heart.

'When are you going away?' she asked Mhairi gently.

'They said I should stay till he's three months old. He's so big and strong now that he's needing more than my milk, so I've been weaning him. I'm off to Aberdeen next week.'

'But you'll come back. The nuns'll be kind to you in that convent you're going to. Nuns're like that.'

Mhairi's face was set as she looked at her friend, 'I don't want to go to a convent, Chrissie. It's my mother and the priest who've cooked it up between them. He's got me a place in the convent kitchen, but I hope they don't think I'm going to take any vows because I won't. I don't believe in anything. I used to think that God was looking after me but now I'm not so sure.'

Chrissie was a Protestant and unsure about the vows taken by nuns. 'They're holy women. They'll be kind to you. You'll be able to come back soon,' she said reassuringly.

Mhairi nodded dumbly and dropped a bird's feather on the top of her son's silken head. Then she said in a faltering voice, 'But if I come back he won't be mine. He'll be my mother's bairn by then. He'll not know me. I'll be a stranger. If I've to go away to Aberdeen, I might as well stop away altogether. It'll hurt even more if I keep coming back.'

Chrissie put her arms around her friend and whispered, 'I'll keep an eye on him for you, Mhairi. He's a fine laddie. You mustn't worry.'

The tears began to flow from both of their eyes and Mhairi, giving way, sobbed on the other girl's shoulder, 'I'll stop remembering. I'll not think about my home or my family or my baby. I'll have to blank it all out. Oh Chrissie, I dinna want to go away!'

Two days later Mhairi climbed up on to the back of the carrier's cart that was to take her to the harbour to board the little boat that would carry her to Inverness on the first leg of her journey to Aberdeen. She sat smiling stiffly as her sorrowful father heaved her box up beside her. At the cottage door, her mother held up wee Calum, raising his little hand in farewell to the girl on the top of the cart. Mhairi's two sisters huddled weeping together, their eyes swollen and their cheeks blotched. They could not understand why their big sister was leaving. When the cart turned the corner of the narrow lane, Mhairi strained for a last sight of the huddle of grey stones and turf that was her home, and the waving people whom she loved so deeply. Then she put her head in her hands and wailed her grief to the unheeding wind.

The convent of the Immaculate Conception stood on a corner, behind an immensely high stone wall on the road that led from the harbour up into Old Aberdeen. Over the top of the wall trees peeped, their branches waving

115

like captive hands. It looked as if they were desperately reaching for light and freedom.

There were iron spikes set around the wall top and only one gate, which was made of green-painted wood, with a small door set in the middle of it. There was a bell pull in the wall and when Mhairi yanked at its enamelled handle, she heard its voice ringing out somewhere in the distance. After a long time the door opened a chink to reveal a woman's face surrounded by a stiffly starched white wimple. This face raised finely arched eyebrows in interrogation but did not speak.

'I'm Mhairi McKay. I've come for the job in your kitchen. Father Malloch from Inverlochy sent me.'

The door opened wider but still nothing was said. The nun beckoned abruptly with her hand and Mhairi stepped inside. She was nervous and gabbled to the woman, 'There's a man coming up from the harbour with my box. I hope you're expecting me. Father Malloch said he'd written you a letter.' The nun only nodded and grimaced, putting her forefinger to her lips in a sign that speaking was forbidden.

Inside the wall was a huge garden laid out in neat squares of finely tilled black earth. Nuns, with their skirts kirtled up and sandals on their feet, were working in the beds, digging them over for the winter. A cluster of neatly pruned fruit trees stood together in the middle of a patch of lawn and the big trees around the perimeter of the wall looked like guardians against the outside world. Mhairi, who came from an almost treeless island, did not know that they were ancient chestnuts. In the spring pink and white candelabra blossoms would glow brightly on them, but now they looked bare and threatening.

The house was grim and as Mhairi followed the striding nun up a broad gravel path, she felt herself go chill at the sight of it. Built of bleak grey granite hewn in enormous blocks, it stared at her through narrow, slit-like windows that resembled hostile eyes. A serrated parapet ran along the top and made her remember pictures of ancient castles that she had seen in her school history book. Its iron-studded door looked like the entrance to a dungeon. On a broad terrace in the front of the house, other nuns were walking with their heads bent and hands crossed in front of them. Their black habits only added to the gloom of the scene. A thin drizzle of rain was falling but that did not seem to worry the walkers.

Mhairi's escort led her around the house to what was obviously the kitchen area, for when she opened a back door the smell of baking bread flooded out and made Mhairi's mouth water. She was very hungry.

Inside a cavernous and gloomy kitchen a nun wearing a white apron was rolling out pastry on a marble slab, while in the corner an immensely fat woman in ordinary clothes was washing dishes. Her arms, sticking down into the water, were blotched purple with cold.

The pastry-making nun nodded briefly to Mhairi and indicated the woman washer who stepped forward. Also without speaking, this woman took Mhairi's arm and led her down a dark passage to a tiny room that contained two iron beds, a line of clothes hooks along one wall and nothing else.

'You'll sleep in here with me,' she whispered.

'Don't they ever speak?' Mhairi whispered back.

'Not on Wednesdays. It's silence day. They'll be speaking again tomorrow.'

'You're a savage! You're utterly and completely ignorant!' The nun's face was flushed as she confronted Mhairi, who looked uncomprehending as she stood in the front hall with her arms full of kindling for the stove in the nuns' refectory.

'What do you mean by trailing through here with all that wood? It should be taken in at the back door. And look at you! Dirty apron, hair flying, untidy as a tinker. You've been here for two weeks and you're still as savage as if you'd come out of the glens yesterday!'

'There's no glens where I come from.'

'Don't be insolent. Go round the back.'

117

'But it's such a long way by the back door. It's quicker this way. Anyway I've got to hurry, the cook's waiting for me to peel potatoes in the kitchen.'

'You were given legs to walk with. You're bone idle like all you Highland wastrels.'

Mhairi wanted to throw the wood down on the flagged floor and run away, as far and as fast as she could go. Her life was a misery. Having grown up and spent her life in the open, she took badly to living in narrow confinement behind high walls. She had always existed among wild hills and heather-covered moors, but now she was a prisoner, like a caged bird, as closely watched over as if she had taken vows.

As the days passed she slipped deeper into despair. During the long nights she felt genuine fear when darkness came and the nuns closed the front door, turning its huge key. She'd never been locked in anywhere before and she lay in bed, her milk-filled breasts aching, in the dark, cold dungeon below stairs, beside Jean the snoring cook, listening to the brooding silence that seemed to fill the rest of the building with an atmosphere of melancholy.

Her work was hard and unrelenting and she was frequently told that she had been taken in as an act of charity. She and Jean were expected to attend day-time services with the nuns but were excused those during the night. They needed their hours of dreamless sleep to replenish their energies for their unremitting toil in the kitchen. When they did go into chapel they knelt at the back while the lessons were read and hymns sung by the sisters in voices of ice-like purity. Instead of making her feel closer to God, the hymns chilled Mhairi's heart. She began to think that any religion that was as strict and rigorous as that practised by the unsmiling nuns was more of a punishment than a celebration of joy.

On the dull, rainy afternoon when she was berated by the angry sister, her sorrow became too strong to bear any longer. She collapsed in a fit of weeping in the kitchen, huddling on a chair beneath the window with her fists knuckled into her eyes, sobbing as if her heart would

118

break. Jean, though slightly half-witted, was kind-hearted and fussed about panic-stricken, waving her arms and remonstrating with the weeping girl.

'Aw lassie, dinna greet,' she pleaded laying a large, chapped hand on the quivering shoulders. When this elicited no response, she tried another tack, hunkering down and peering into Mhairi's face, 'I'll mak' you a piece,' she offered. Jean's cure for any attacks of depression or sadness was a thick slice of home-made bread liberally spread with black treacle. She liked it best when the treacle slithered over the edges of the crust and seeped into the bread so that it took on a blackish colour. Consoling herself with those pieces was how she had achieved her immense girth.

'If I eat any more pieces, I'll not be able to walk far less work,' moaned Mhairi through her sobs.

But having succeeded in stopping the weeping, Jean grinned happily, rose to her feet and cut a doorstep slice of bread. Then she dipped her knife into the treacle tin and brought it out dripping, black and oily. 'I'll mak' ane for mysel' when I'm at it,' she murmured savouring the smell.

Mhairi accepted the offering and bit into it. The taste was cloyingly sweet but somehow it did cheer her up, though not so quickly or so well as it cheered Jean. How fortunate to have so little care that a treacle piece could restore your happiness! Yet Jean led a lonely life. She was never allowed out of the convent and might as well be a nun for all she saw of the world outside. She'd already told Mhairi that she'd been a foundling, left by her unknown mother at the convent gate, wrapped in an old bit of blanket.

'How old were you?' Mhairi had asked, thinking heart-breakingly of Calum.

Jean had puzzled, 'Oh, just wee. Just a bairn. I was lucky I didna dee. It was an awful night o' wind and rain the sisters told me.'

The thought of the abandoned baby lying at the gate in the rain made her breasts sting and tears came to

119

Mhairi's eyes; she missed her own child so dreadfully. Her arms longed to hold him, her hands ached to stroke his golden head. Remembering this, she started weeping again. 'I hate it here. I miss my home. I miss my baby,' she sobbed.

Jean shook her head, 'The sisters said you'd a bairn and that was why you were coming here. They said you'd sinned just like my ain mither sinned.'

Mhairi raised her head with anger in her eyes, 'I did not. I never knew what was happening to me. They don't know anything about what life's really like in the world. They're so cold and narrow-minded!'

'No, no they're not bad. There's ane or twae that are old bitches but the others're kind enough. Just do what ye're telt and you'll be fine.'

'I'll never be fine. I can't bear the idea of spending the rest of my life in this place,' sobbed Mhairi. She felt pity for Jean who knew nothing else and expected nothing better.

The new kitchen maid's obvious depression exasperated the fastidious sisters as Mhairi trailed from task to task, hair untidy and face sullen. The chief housekeeper, Sister Ursula, was always in and out of the kitchen chivvying her. 'Hurry up. Try to look grateful. You don't know how lucky you are to be here. What would have happened to you if we hadn't taken you in? No decent house would have a maid with your history.' She aimed a cuff at Mhairi's head but missed and cuffed Jean instead.

Mhairi resented being bullied by Sister Ursula but it was her words that hurt the most. Nettled, she turned and protested, 'I'm not a bad girl. I've never done anything wrong.'

'What do you call having a baby without a husband? When your priest wrote and asked us to take you in, he told us your story. You're a little harlot! God will make you suffer for your sins.'

'Then why doesn't he make the baby's father suffer, too?' asked Mhairi. Homesickness, loneliness, longing for wee Calum and a terrible yearning for the open moors and the sea had turned her from a pretty, chubby girl into a gaunt figure of misery in spite of Jean's generosity with treacle pieces. The thick, butter-coloured hair that had been her glory was hidden beneath a cotton mobcap that was pulled down around her brows and her once sparkling blue eyes were red-rimmed and puffy because of the tears she'd shed. Her future stretched before her like a desert and she wanted to die.

'I want to see the Mother Superior,' she suddenly said to Sister Ursula who glared back in horror.

'She hasn't time for the likes of you!'

'I want to see her. I've something to tell her,' persisted Mhairi and was obdurate in refusing to speak to anyone else. The Mother Superior was an august being whom Jean talked about as if she were a deity, but Mhairi had never seen her – far less spoken to her. Now she seized on the idea of asking for her release by pleading her unsuitability for life in a convent. Surely a Mother Superior would understand!

The study was on the first floor overlooking the garden and when she was granted an interview, Mhairi went up the stairs with apprehension in her heart. She had brushed her hair, washed her face and put on a clean apron, but she had not rehearsed what she was going to say except for the opening sentence, 'I want to leave this place.'

The Mother Superior was sitting behind an enormous desk with a carving of a tortured Jesus on the Cross on the wall behind her head. When she stood in the middle of the carpet Mhairi was acutely aware of the nun's sharp grey eyes watching her intently. There was something about the starkness of the stiff wimple that accentuated the eyes of all the nuns and made them hypnotic. This woman did not look friendly, not like a 'mother' at all.

'Well? You asked to see me . . . I haven't much time.' The voice was cool and very well-bred.

Mhairi cleared her throat, conscious of her own soft Highland burr. 'I want to leave this place,' she whispered.

Then she lapsed into a silence which seemed to last

121

forever. The Mother Superior stared at her reflectively before asking, 'Aren't you happy with us?'

There was no point telling lies, 'No.'

'What do you want to do? Where do you want to go?'

There was nothing the girl wanted more than to go home but she knew that was impossible. 'I don't know.'

'Have you any family or friends in Aberdeen?'

She shook her head and stood staring at the crucifix while the nun considered her sadly. Father Malloch at Inverlochy had written explaining this child's background. He'd told about the poverty of the crofting family and the speculations about the identity of the illegitimate child's father. The girl had said he was a very respectable farmer in the neighbourhood but Father Malloch doubted if she were telling the truth. She was fantasising, he suspected, and said in his letter that he hoped working in the convent among the holy sisters would redeem Mhairi and guide her towards the religious life.

They would not have taken her in had he condemned her out of hand, but he did not do so. In fact he wrote that she was a very intelligent and innocent girl who had been misguided; not a bad girl; rather a victim of circumstances and her own carnal impulses. All she needed was to be shown the path of righteousness.

'If you leave us, how can we recommend you to anyone else? Sister Ursula tells me that you're not working very hard.' The Mother Superior sounded disappointed.

'That's not true. I try but everything's so strange and I'm so unhappy . . .' She was not going to plead that she had never seen a cooking stove or a kitchen sink before she'd arrived at the convent. She remembered the taunts about glens and Highland wastrels. Life on the croft was basic and she was not accustomed to the niceties required by the nuns. They worried about things like the correct way to lay plates and glasses on the table; the right forks and knives; the crisp laundering of table napkins. All these things seemed mysterious and unnecessary to Mhairi.

The Mother Superior shook her head, 'Perhaps you're

right. I don't think you're suited for convent life. I agree with you that it's been a mistake.'

Mhairi's face expressed relief but that disappeared when the figure behind the desk continued, 'However we have a responsibility towards you. You were given into our care by your parish priest. You're only a child. We can't just turn you out.'

'Oh, turn me out! Please don't worry about me. I'll be all right.'

'Don't be silly. You're a child who's already proved herself to be irresponsible. Have you any idea of the dangers and temptations of the outside world? You fell quickly enough back home in your own village. I think the best thing to do is for me to try to find another convent that'll accept you and train you for something that you can work at later – a sewing maid perhaps or a cook. I'll write to your priest and tell him what's happened. He may have some suggestions. In the meantime I expect you to work hard, give us no more trouble and attempt to be grateful.'

By the light of a thin candle Mhairi counted her money. She had four coins: a florin given to her by Father Malloch when she'd left Inverlochy; a shilling and a silver sixpence which was all she had left of the money her father had scraped together for her fare to Aberdeen; and the last coin was a silver threepenny piece that had been presented to her when she was eight years old by a titled lady, patron of the village school, because Mhairi was the only one in the classroom who had been able to recite Tennyson's poem about the Charge of the Light Brigade by heart. She kept her money stitched into the hem of her skirt and knew it was safe because she wore the same skirt every day.

When the coins were laid out in a little line on the floor she sat back on her heels to contemplate them. The dozing Jean watched from bed and asked, 'What're you doing lassie?'

'Have you any money, Jeanie?'

'Aye. I have.'

'How much've you got?'

'I've a golden sovereign. The sisters gave it to me as my wages last year.'

The nuns obviously did not pay much, thought Mhairi. She asked again, 'Is that all?'

'It's more than you've got.' Sometimes Jean wasn't so daft.

'Would you lend it to me if I promise to pay you back.'

'What d'you want it for?'

'I want to go away.'

'Where to?'

'I don't know. Just away. If I stay here I'll die.'

Jean leaned up on her pillowy arm in the bed and stared sadly at the girl on the floor. 'I'll miss you,' she said. In the flickering candlelight she looked old and for the first time Mhairi realised that she was well into middle age, but the simple-hearted soul had no idea of how old she was because dates of birth meant little to her.

'Jean, listen! I've got to go or this place'll kill me,' whispered Mhairi.

Her companion, recognising desperation, rose with bare feet slipping on the cold linoleum of the floor and walked across to the clothes hanging from the line of hooks on the wall to grope in her skirt pocket. Out came a tiny leather purse and when she put her fingers into it, they emerged triumphantly holding up a coin that sparked fire in the candlelight. There was nothing else in the purse but Jean handed the sovereign to Mhairi who took it reverently. It was her ticket to freedom.

Impulsively she kissed the cook on the cheek, promising in an excited voice, 'I'll pay you back. I swear I will. Look, I'll write down an IOU and you can keep the bit of paper in the purse till I send back the money. What's your full name so I can put it on the note?'

'My name's Jean. You ken that fine.'

'Jean what – Jean Brown, Jean Smith, Jean what?'

'I don't know. Just put "Jean". I don't think the sisters gave me another name.'

'I'll put Jean Cook,' said Mhairi and she carefully wrote her promise to repay one sovereign on a scrap of paper and placed it in the leather purse.

When it was after midnight she deemed it safe to leave. The convent was as still as a tomb and she had taken care to leave the window beside the locked back door unlatched before she went to bed. As she climbed through it to freedom, Jean held a candle to light her way.

'How're you going to get over the wall? It's got big spikes on it,' she whispered as Mhairi landed safely in the flowerbed outside.

'There's a bit where the spikes are broken behind the potting shed. I'll climb up on to its roof and then up to the top of the wall. Don't worry. I'll manage.' She was filled with energy and optimism, happier than she had been since she'd left Inverlochy. Before she ran off over the grass, she pushed her head back inside the window and kissed Jean on her moist, plump cheek. 'Don't forget me, Jeanie. And don't worry about your sovereign. I'll send it back as soon as I'm able.'

'I'm not worried. God bless you.' Mhairi's lips felt the tears running down.

The branches of the big trees rasped together as if spreading the news about her escape when she ran beneath them. Because she was unused to trees, they made her afraid and she was glad when she reached the open space in front of the shed. A ladder lay on its side in front of a cold frame and she propped it up against the wall. The shed was low but its grey slated roof sloped steeply upwards nearly to the parapet of the wall. Like a crab, she clambered up the roof on her hands and knees, not caring that the skin was being scraped off her shins. All she was afraid of was that the noise of her departure would waken one of the nuns. After what seemed like an age she reached the part of the wall where the iron spikes were broken. Only three or four had lost their fierce prongs but the space was wide enough for her to slip between. Crouching high above the ground, she paused and looked down. It was a mistake for the distance terrified her and her courage almost gave out. If she jumped and broke a bone, what would happen to her? Should she just give up the whole idea and run back to bed? When that thought struck her, she remembered her misery in the convent and took her courage in both hands. She had no choice but to jump.

It seemed that she sailed down through the air for an eternity with her skirt billowing up around her in spite of the money in the hem. As she hit the ground, she remembered the days when she and the other children had played at jumping off the turf roofs of their homes and bent her knees so that when she landed, she rolled over sideways. Luckily for her the ground was soft and she found herself on a grassy verge that was deeply covered with a drift of dead leaves from the trees bordering the road. She lay gasping and winded for a few moments before she realised that she hadn't broken any bones. Then she gathered up the little bundle she had thrown over before she jumped and started running down the street towards the sea. She had no idea where she was going.

A fever of love had Laurence Nairn in thrall. Day or night he thought about Daisy: he could not work; he could not eat; he could not sleep. He was obsessed with her. Every waking thought he had was about Daisy – wondering where she was, what she was doing, who she was with. These speculations were agonising for him.

As soon as the horses were bedded down for the night, he was out of the brewery, up to the flat to change his clothes and on to the tram car to Edinburgh. She kept him in thrall by treating him in a cavalier fashion. Sometimes she did not turn up at their meeting place; sometimes he saw her strolling in the street with another admirer or even picking up a client and disappearing in the direction of the house where he knew she shared a room with another prostitute. They took night about to use it, because they were both young and pretty girls and were making more money than any other women on the street. When his jealousy became so painful that he was almost ready to kill himself for her, she won him round by honeyed sweetness that started the whole cycle again. She said he was her man; the only man she enjoyed making love to; the only man who had her for nothing.

On a December night of bitter cold and keen wind that cut into the people out walking in Edinburgh's grey streets, he reached the Kenilworth pub at eight o'clock but she was not there. When the clock struck ten and she had still not arrived, he was so bitterly angry and disappointed that he would have picked a fight with anyone who looked at him twice. As he was finishing his pint of beer, draining the glass angrily and slamming it down, he saw her slinking in her strange animal way around the corner of the door. The effect was so erotic that he felt himself stiffen in anticipation of making love to her. Soon she was standing beside him, stroking his arm in apology and whispering, 'I was held up. I'm sorry.'

His anger drained away like water through sand. Now he was only jealous. 'Business?' he asked gruffly because a constriction in his throat made it difficult to talk.

'Don't be like that. You know you can't keep me, can you?'

As they walked out on to the pavement together he groaned, 'Daisy, give it up. Why don't you try to get a place as a housemaid or something? Maybe you could work in a shop . . . let's get married, let's be together always.'

She flashed the slanted eyes at him as if she were putting him under some kind of a spell. 'Don't be silly,' she murmured, 'I make more money in a week than a housemaid makes in six months.'

'But look what you do for it!'

Her face under the lamplight was hard and ungirlish, 'It's better than being a housemaid. You don't have to come to see me if you don't want to. I'm saving my money. One day I'll be able to be anything I like – a lady of property perhaps.'

'Daisy! You could catch some disease before that.'

'Is that it? Are you scared in case I give you something? Then stay away. I don't ask you to come here hanging around after me. Go back to Leith! Don't worry about me, I know what I'm about. One of these days I'll find a rich man to set me up with servants and a fine house. You see if I don't!'

He groaned. She was torturing him. 'I love you Daisy. What about *love*?'

She stopped in the middle of the pavement and looked at him. For a second he saw in her face the vulnerable girl that she had been on the first night they'd met. 'I love you too. You know that, but what good would it do us if we were poor? What would we have if we married now? Two rooms in a Leith tenement; thirty bob a week if we're lucky! We'd be rich at that. I've seen people starting off in love and ending up in misery. That's not for me. I don't like whoring but I do it. It's my job to tease and entice and I've come this far so there's no point stopping now. If you don't like it, you know what you can do! Are you coming home with me or aren't you? Make up your mind because I'm off.'

He went with her of course. They walked downhill past Queen Street and Heriot Row till they came to Stockbridge where the road crossed the Water of Leith. While Daisy went inside to check that the old woman who owned the house where she roomed was well and truly asleep, Laurence leaned his arms on the parapet of the bridge and watched the slow water flowing underneath. In a little while that same water would be pouring past The Shore where he'd first met Daisy. There were times when he wished that he'd never fallen in love with her but he could not help himself. She fascinated him.

His reverie was broken by a low whistle and he saw her slender figure silhouetted in dim light in the open doorway of the first house on the north bank of the river.

She was beckoning to him and he went to her, powerless to resist.

He could not believe that people could make love with such abandon, could lose themselves in each other till the whole of the world outside no longer mattered. When their passion was spent, he lay holding her as she curled by his side and whispered in her ear, 'Say you love me, say you love me again,' he pleaded.

She laughed and put a hand on his dark head as she whispered back, '*I love you*. I don't suppose I'll ever love anybody else as much in the whole of my life.'

'Marry me then.'

She rolled away from him, 'Stop that. We've been through all that tonight already. Every time we're together it's the same thing. I'm not going to marry you. I'm not going to stop whoring. Either we go on as we are or we stop.'

'I hate knowing that you're out on the street picking up any man who'll pay the price. You could be murdered. There's some odd types about – especially in Edinburgh.'

'No odder than in your precious Leith, believe me. But you needn't worry. I didn't mean to tell you yet but I'm going off the street, I've found a protector.'

Laurence felt as if she'd stabbed him in the heart. 'Who? When? Why didn't you say so before?'

'He's looking for a place for me. A nice little house in Trinity, he says. You can come and visit me there. He won't know.'

'Who is he for God's sake?'

'He's a businessman. I'm not sure myself what he does and I don't ask questions. They like it that way. But he's very grand and gentlemanly – and not demanding either. Not like you!' She rolled back giggling and pushed her face into his chest. He ran his hand down her silken back and fought with a desire to hurt her, beat her, grab her by the long straight hair that fell around her shoulders like a curtain.

'I can't bear this,' he said at last.

'You needn't worry. I've told you, he's not demanding.

He's quite old in fact. Must be about seventy. He wants a pretty girl to show off to his friends. Can you believe it? He pays me for going out with him two nights a week – Mondays and Wednesdays. He can't do much else I'm afraid, but he likes to try.' Her voice gurgled away in laughter that made Laurence leap out of bed and start pulling on his clothes, 'Shut up Daisy! Don't talk like that. You know what you sound like: you sound like a whore!'

The hard look was back on her face when she sat up in bed, 'But I am a whore, my dear. You're just lucky that I don't ask you to pay for sleeping with me.'

In a fury he shouted, 'All right, I'll pay!' and threw a handful of coins on to the bed cover where they lay glittering in the lamplight. Daisy was out of bed now, gathering up the money. Naked, in the dimly lit room she looked like a Greek goddess; slim, tall and small-breasted. The sight of her made his heart leap again. She came over to him in her feline way and wrapped her arms round his neck. 'You're not going, not like this. Stay a little longer Larry, come back to bed.'

He could feel her nipples against his shirt and he groaned as he sank his head towards her.

Brabazon stirred in her sleep when she heard her son coming in. Slowly she returned to consciousness and sat up in bed, squinting to see the time on the little clock that stood on the mantelpiece beside her Cupid candlestick. It was half past one. He wasn't stumbling around so, thank heavens, he must be sober.

The wind was howling through the courtyard and she lay listening to it for a few moments before she remembered that Alex Warre had stayed in the brewery the previous evening to mend the grist mill which had broken down. It was a matter of urgency to get it going again because they wanted to start their last brew of the year, and he had told her he would make sure it was working before he went home to bed.

130

If there was ever any problem in the brewery she worried, and now wakefulness claimed her. Rising quietly from bed she slipped over to the window. To her surprise and disappointment she saw that a light was burning in a tiny window on the brewery's top floor. Her heart sank for she realised that it meant Alex was still tinkering with the grist mill.

Hastily she threw on her thickest clothes and topped them all with the old cloak before she slipped out, closing the door soundlessly so as not to disturb Duncan. Inside the brewhouse she drew a deep breath, savouring the lingering aroma of sugar, malt, yeast and hops. She had never ceased to love the sweet heady smell of her work place. There was no one on the ground floor but her fears had been correct for above her head she could hear the sound of Alex hammering away at recalcitrant machinery. She did not call out, but threw back her cloak and walked through the dark hall to a corner where the steep and rickety ladder led up to a trapdoor above her head. The main stairway led up from the front door but the ladder was the quickest way up, although the most precipitous. It had terrified her when she first began working in the brewery but in time she had become so accustomed to it that she was no longer afraid of its flimsiness and now she hardly noticed how it swayed under her weight as she ascended.

There was no sign of Alex on the next floor where the mashing vats stood cold and silent so she kept on climbing. The sounds from above were growing louder and she knew he was on the highest level among the sacks of malted barley.

When her head popped above the last trapdoor, she called out to the shadows, 'What's the trouble Alex? Is it worse than we thought?' A hissing Tilley lamp was standing on the floor and around it he had cleared a space on which he had spread out the pieces of the grist-grinder's machinery. There were cogwheels, metal bars, screws, nuts and bolts. The first stage of the beer-making procedure could not start if the grist mill refused to work

131

properly and Alex was still trying to restore it to its former accuracy.

In the dimness she saw his sturdy figure squatting under the low eaves. To her relief his voice was confident as he called back and he held out a cogwheel towards her. 'Oh, it's you mistress. Nearly finished. I've found the bit that was causing the trouble. I've put that mill together and taken it apart again four times – but this time I think I've solved the problem. It was lucky I remembered we kept some spare parts downstairs. It's going to take a wee while longer but I'll have it going by morning.'

'It's a quarter to three,' she said in a horrified voice, 'Why don't you go home and start again tomorrow. You must be exhausted.'

He shook his head and she realised that he looked as if he were enjoying himself with his shirt sleeves rolled up and his face smeared with grease. 'Och no. I'll not stop now. It's nearly done. I'll just get this mill going and the mash'll be ready to start first thing. That brew's got to be going before the year's end or we'll miss the New Year trade.'

She was immensely relieved: because of the broken mill, they were out of grist completely and every day lost set them back. 'It's good of you to take all this trouble. Nellie must be worried about you.'

He shrugged it off, 'It's no trouble. I'm as keen as you are to start the mash on time. When I've got this going, I'll stoke the boilers and have everything ready for the brew starting. Gideon came over with my supper a couple of hours ago and they won't worry about me because they aye know that if I'm no' at home I'm in here.'

Not for the first time Brabazon felt inexpressible gratitude. Alex *was* Perseverance Brewery really, for he could tackle any problem and without him she would never have been able to run the business; it would have been sold long ago. Because of him however, it was almost in profit and Perseverance beer was much respected by their customers. In 1896 they were planning to double their output.

She sat down on a pile of sacks in a corner and said, 'Isn't it funny? It always seems that when things are going well, there's a little imp waiting to mess them up. And I never can understand how it is that Gordons hear about each setback. They've been at me again. They must have heard how ill Duncan is and think I'll give up now.'

Alex raised one eyebrow at her in an unspoken question and she shook her head, 'No. I'm not going to sell. I'm determined to keep going. We've worked too hard, you and I. I suppose I'm just mulish. I want to pay off *all* the debts, save some money and buy back Brewery House. Silly, isn't it? I don't suppose I'll ever do it.'

It was a relief to be able to talk to Alex so openly, to treat him as a confidant and her voice was wistful because Duncan's growing disability made it difficult for him to converse with her any longer. She knew that he understood what she was saying, but his own replies were slow and stumbling.

'You'll do it, missus. I've faith in you,' said Alex solemnly and she was reassured by his confidence. Carefully and neatly he worked away in the lamplight as Brabazon watched, but she felt her head beginning to nod and exhaustion overwhelmed her. She stifled a yawn, but she did not want to leave him working alone and offered to help.

When he looked over at her he noticed how white and strained she was. Poor soul, he thought, she's tired out! He wondered at her stamina and ability to look after a sick man and run the brewery as well. She was making a good fist at it too.

He remembered the fine Mrs Nairn of the days before the bankruptcy. That lady had been a remote, beautifully dressed woman of fashion, but now she was sitting beside him on a pile of sacks in an old cloak that was so threadbare and faded a beggar wouldn't wear it. Life hadn't treated her well and he felt she deserved better.

Half-shaking his head he told her, 'No, I'm nearly

finished. You go on home Mrs Nairn and get a bit of sleep.'

'I wish you'd call me Brabazon,' she said suddenly, 'It's my name. It makes me feel very formal and distant when you call me Mrs Nairn. Nellie calls me Brabazon now, you should too.'

He laughed, 'All right – Brabazon. I'll start this mill working and be home myself in an hour but you go on. I'll lock up when I let myself out.'

'There's one thing I can do before I go. I'll fetch you up a pundy of beer. You must be parched after all this work,' she said rising stiffly from her seat.

'That's a good idea. It'll go down fine,' he told her.

She climbed down the ladder again and went over the yard to her office where she poured off a mug of ale from the little wooden pirn she kept beside her desk for the entertainment of customers or favoured visitors. Carefully tightening up the wooden tap so that it wouldn't drip on the polished boards of the floor, she carried the mug back up the stairs of the main building for she could not manage the ladder and stop the beer from spilling at the same time. When she reached the first landing, something made her pause. Then a wave of cold air made her stiffen and she felt her blood freeze. In the deep shadows she thought she saw the figure of a man, looming large and very still. He was only an arm's length from her.

'Who's that?' she whispered hoarsely but there was no reply. She wished she had brought a lamp instead of relying on the light of the moon and her heart was hammering in her breast but, gathering her courage, she took a step towards the shadowy figure. It receded in front of her and seemed to disappear, drifting off into the enormous room where there were many hiding places among the vats and boilers. Very frightened, she hurried on to the next floor where Alex was still working in his comforting pool of light.

She was shaking as she handed him the beer. 'I thought I saw someone down there,' she said trying to make her voice light but she could not control her face which showed the state she was in. He looked intently at her.

'Where?'

'On the first landing, standing in the corner watching me.'

His voice was kindly, 'Och, I ken that one. He's often there. This place's full of ghosts. I've seen him on that landing, too, in the night time. There another old fellow in a long kind of goonie that watches me in the cellar sometimes. I've offered him a pundy but he never takes it.'

She gave a little gasp. 'I've never seen any ghosts here before,' she said only half-reassured.

'They're worse in the winter-time,' he said with a shrug as he drained his glass and put it down on the floor. Feeling less afraid when she saw how matter of factly he accepted her strange sighting, she offered to fetch him another pint but he shook his head, 'That was grand stuff but you'd better not bring any more or I'll no' be able to see what I'm doing. We're making pretty strong beer these days. No wonder folk want to drink it. You go home now Mrs . . . Brabazon. I've just heard the kirk clock striking half past three. And don't you worry. The ghosts in here never hurt anybody. They just don't want to leave. Maybe we'll hang about frightening folk when our time comes, too.'

The wind was punishing when she pushed open the door and battled her way across the yard. It was a relief to be able to snuggle down into her warm bed beside Duncan and she hoped fervently that it would not be long before Alex, also, was safe at home. Her last thought before she drifted into sleep was of immense gratitude towards him.

By six o'clock when her alarm clock went off, the wind had died down and there was a strange stillness in the air that Brabazon knew meant bitter frost had the outside world in its grip. It was still dark when she opened her eyes and all the memories of a few hours previously came flooding back. Now wide-awake and alert, she lay listening to the silence outside and decided to go back to the brewery to check that the grist mill was running smoothly. Alex should be allowed to sleep. It was her turn to take over the responsibilities of overseeing the brew. When she stepped out into the yard, she saw to her surprise and disappointment that a light was burning in the top floor. Her heart sank. Surely he could not *still* be up there!

She began to run. To her growing alarm, the front door was unlocked as she had left it earlier, but there was no sound of industry, no hammering or movement from the top floor. The place was silent as she grabbed an oil lamp from a table behind the door and her hands were shaking so badly that it took several false strikes of the Vesta matches before she succeeded in lighting it.

'Alex! Alex!' she called out urgently but no voice called back to her.

Holding the lamp above her head Brabazon mounted the stairs. She was too concerned to worry about meeting ghosts. She told herself that Alex must have fallen asleep over his work – he could hardly be blamed for he'd been at it for hours. It was not like him, even so, to forget to extinguish the lamp. He was always so anxious about fire.

On the top floor his pile of tools lay neatly stacked beside a folded dirty rag. The cogwheels, the nuts and bolts had disappeared and the lamp stood beside the tools, its light flickering weakly inside its glass globe. She looked around in surprise and relief. The work was finished. He must have gone home. Then she saw his jacket thrown down in a corner and panic tightened her throat, though she did not know why. Holding up her lamp she called out again, now very frightened. Forcing herself onwards, she walked around the cavernous room, pulling aside sacks of barley in case Alex had lain down behind them and gone to sleep. But only frightened mice scuttled away from her feet as she searched the hidden corners beneath the sloping eaves, brushing aside cobwebs and turning over sacks far too flimsy to conceal a body. She found nothing.

Flickers of light from her lamp sent terrifying shadows

leaping on the white-washed walls and Brabazon recoiled from them. Instinctively she sensed something was very wrong. Her next step was to run across to the trapdoor in the far corner and climb down to the floor below, where she made another fruitless search. She examined the hopper and the grist mill and saw that everything had been put back together. It was ready to switch on. She pulled the handle and with a groan and a shudder it began grinding, pouring out fine grist. It was working perfectly. Not only had Alex fixed it, but he had also filled the hopper with grain as well. Everything was prepared for a day's work. She told herself he must have gone home fuddled with sleep, forgetting his tools, his coat and his lamp. The theory did not sound very likely, but she held on to it desperately.

With the noise of the machinery pounding in her ears, she descended to the ground floor going backwards down the last flight of the ladder – holding the lamp carefully in her right hand. She knew how many rungs there were and, as always, she counted all twelve of them off in her head as she went. On the eleventh rung her foot reached out searching for the next, but did not find it. Instead she felt the sole of her boot pressing into something soft – into a body. Her heart leapt as she screamed. When she turned her head to look down over her shoulder, she saw Alex's body lying in a crumpled heap at the foot of the ladder. She knew he was dead before she touched him because of the strange way his head was turned.

Shaking, Brabazon knelt on the floor beside the sprawled body and started to turn him over when she suddenly realised that she should leave things as they were until the police arrived. Alex's brown eyes were open and staring: he looked astonished. Death had obviously come on him unawares. She gently closed his lids with careful fingers and her tears fell on his weathered cheek, lying glistening on the skin like dew drops. She did not wipe them away.

The first thing she had to do was break the news to Alex's family. Running like the wind, with her cloak flying out behind her, she crossed the dark courtyard and plunged up the stairs. Her neighbours were awakened by the thudding of her feet on the stairs and the pounding of her fists on the wooden panels of the Warres' door.

Nellie opened it and Brabazon grabbed the little body in her arms, gasping out, 'Oh, Nellie, Nellie, I'm so sorry, something's happened to Alex. Waken your laddies and I'll send Henry for the police.'

Nellie's face seemed to shrink and her eyes went saucer-wide, 'The police? Has my Alex had an accident then?'

Brabazon was weeping, 'Yes, he's had an accident. Oh, he's dead, Nellie. Someone's pushed him down the ladder.'

From half-way up the stairs the heads of the two Nairn boys were staring at their frantic mother. Henry took in the news first and ran downstairs to fetch a policeman. It only took a few minutes before there was a crowd of people bending over the pathetic heap on the floor of the brewery. Brabazon stood behind the men with her arm around the shoulders of Nellie who was gulping and sobbing convulsively over and over again, 'Oh my Alex, my poor Alex!'.

Henry had quickly found two policemen patrolling the Kirkgate and the most senior of them knelt down beside Alex's body. After a few seconds, he pronounced, 'The poor soul's dead all right but he's not stiff yet, though his jaw's flexed. He canna be dead for long. Get somebody to fetch a doctor Mrs Nairn will you?'

She nodded to Laurence telling him to go and said to the policeman, 'He was alive at half past three this morning. I saw him then. We were fixing the grist mill. It was nearly ready when I left and you can see he's put it all together. That shouldn't have taken him more than about another hour . . . half past four or so . . .' her voice trailed off and she hugged Nellie closer.

The second, younger policeman was kneeling down beside the body now, and sniffed loudly before he said, 'He smells of beer. He's been drinking.' He exchanged a significant glance with his colleague and Brabazon read their thoughts.

Her voice was vehement as she said, 'He wasn't drunk if that's what you're thinking. He only had one pint of beer. I gave it to him myself. He didn't want any more. He was anxious to get home.'

'Well he slipped and fell down the ladder anyway,' said the young policeman. 'Has he been ill, did he get giddy turns or anything?'

He looked at Nellie as he spoke and the little woman shook her head, 'He was very fit was my Alex. And he knew that ladder well. He'd never fall on it. He's been going up and down it all his life. He'd be more likely to trip on the stairs.'

'Then it must have been the beer,' said the first policeman sadly, rising to his feet, 'It needn't take much. It was very late and he must've been tired. It was an accident.'

Brabazon was beside herself, 'I think he was pushed. I think there was someone else in here last night. I saw a figure on the stairs. Alex said it was a ghost but now I'm not so sure . . .'

Immediately she saw it it had been a mistake to mention ghosts. The policemen looked at her as if she were hysterical and the elder one shook his head, 'Now, now, madam, you can't say things like that. You'll only distress people. It's obvious he's fallen.'

She asked angrily, 'Why's he lying on his chest then? He always went down the ladder backwards.'

'Falls are funny. He could have twisted over . . .'

Brabazon could see that no one would listen, but it was important to her that Alex Warre did not go to his grave labelled as an accident victim who'd fallen to his death when drunk.

The senior policeman came over and patted her arm, 'Come on now, Mrs Nairn. There's no need for you to feel guilty because you gave him a glass of beer. Like I said it was an accident.'

'No, no,' said Brabazon and Nellie together.

Their protests were so disturbing that Roddy, the oldest

139

policeman, who had been a friend of the dead man, decided to call a halt to the harrowing scene. He laid Alex's jacket over the body that was beginning to stiffen with rigor mortis and said to Gideon, 'Take your mother and Mrs Nairn up the stairs, lad. We'll put your father on a stretcher after the doctor's had a look at him and bring him upstairs then.'

Brabazon would not give up and pleaded with him, 'Please listen. Don't write it off as a drunken fall. It wasn't that, I'm sure. There must be some other explanation.'

The policeman looked hard at her, 'Well you don't think he jumped, do you?' he asked coldly and she had to agree. It was obvious that she was going to get nowhere with him for he'd made up his mind. As she turned to leave with Nellie, Brabazon saw Alex's red neckerchief lying on the floor beside his body. Swiftly she bent down and picked it up. It felt damp to her fingers and when she raised it to her nose, a sharp smell of beer assailed her. For a second she wondered if the policemen were right. Had Alex been drinking after she'd left him? She sniffed the neckerchief again and, all of a sudden, her sharp and discriminating nose gave her the answer. The beer that soaked the cloth did not come from Perseverance Brewery! She knew the smell of her own brew too well to be deceived. This was another brewery's product and it must have been brought in by someone who had been with Alex after she'd gone home. But who?

1896

Alex Warre's coffin, followed by his mourning family and neighbours, was being carried out of Perseverance Place when the ferry bringing passengers into Leith, from Inverkeithing in Fife, came steaming up to its jetty moored beside The Shore.

One of the passengers standing on deck in the cutting teeth of a snow-filled wind was Mhairi McKay. She held her arms crossed across her breast and kept her shawl pulled up over her blonde head as she stared in astonished wonder at the bustling town to which her wanderings had brought her.

Leith was enormous. The island-bred girl had thought that Aberdeen was busy, but she realised that it didn't compare with this place. Through drifts of sleet she gazed across steel-grey water at a crowded landing place where tall, steep-roofed houses were packed so close together that not a tree or even a blade of grass could grow on the street facing the water. Over to her left she saw lines of docks filled with ships; a Martello watchtower stood on the end of a street gazing out to sea; there were phalanxes of stone warehouses all dotted with tiny, iron barred windows. She saw works' chimneys piercing the grey sky above the roof tops; the cones of a sugar factory were belching forth smoke and sweet smells; and there were busy people everywhere, so many and so confident that her spirit quailed at the sight of them.

'Well this is Leith! We've arrived,' said a woman standing beside her in a satisfied voice – as if there were nowhere better.

Mhairi glanced shyly at her, 'It looks awful big,' she said hesitantly.

'It's the grandest place in the world. Folk come here from all over. We've got negroes and Indians, Eskimos and Dutchmen – you name them, we've got them in Leith. It's a pity the haar's so thick or you'd be able to see Edinburgh up there on its hills. It's very grand, but I like Leith better.' She gestured towards the South with a woollen-mittened hand.

'I've heard tell that Edinburgh's a bonny place – with lots of work,' ventured Mhairi. It was to the capital that she intended to direct her steps. A kindly carter who'd given her a lift on the Stonehaven road out of Aberdeen had advised her that the folk in Edinburgh were aye crying out for servant lassies.

The woman had keen, inquisitive eyes and she stared at Mhairi from beneath the rim of her bonnet, 'What kind of work are you seeking? Have you relations in Leith?'

There was something in her calculating look that made Mhairi lie, 'I've an auntie.'

'Where does she live? What's her name? I ken a lot of folk. I'll maybe know her.'

Like a scared animal Mhairi shrank back saying, 'She doesn't live in Leith, more like Edinburgh. Up on the hill . . .'

'What hill? Calton Hill? Haven't you her address?'

'Yes, Calton Hill.'

'There's some fine houses up that way.' The woman looked meaningfully at Mhairi's shabby clothes before she added, 'Is she a servant up there?'

Mhairi bristled and took on an air of defiance. The questioner was too curious and her persistence alarming. Although she knew it to be unlikely, the idea struck her that perhaps the nuns were looking for her and this woman had got wind of a blonde runaway. Her imagination ran riot and she took care to give this acquaintance the slip when the ferry boat tied up and its passengers began filing ashore.

When she disembarked from the boat on to the cobbles of The Shore, it was early afternoon and the street was so crowded that people eddied around her like the water of the sea. Immediately Mhairi found herself being harried by persistent beggars, mostly women who clutched

142

at her skirt and pushed their undernourished babies towards her. She drew away from them in alarm and was relieved when the barracking stopped as soon as they recognised her own shabbiness.

Clutching her little bundle, Mhairi followed the teeming throng along the waterfront. Around her were leathery-skinned men smelling of tobacco and the sea; painted women giving off the scent of perfume and gin; skinny children, some carrying enormous baskets. Others, more sly and light-fingered, worked the middle of the throng. She felt a tug at her skirt and when she turned quickly, she noticed a ragged boy slipping like a wraith into the crowd. He hadn't found anything in Mhairi's pocket though, for what was left of her money – eight shillings and two pence farthing exactly – was still stitched into her deep hem. If she wanted to spend anything, she'd have to find a quiet corner to unpick some of the stitches and extract a precious coin.

The more prosperous ferry passengers climbed into hansom cabs that lined up waiting for custom along the water's edge, but Mhairi followed the less affluent along a muddy lane that was almost blocked with huge carts pulled by equally huge horses. The sleet was piercingly cold and above her head the grim Martello tower stared out to sea. It had the look of a prison; its narrow windows and parapet top made her shudder with the memory of the convent. She made up her mind to look for work in this place. It was so big there must be someone in need of a servant and she felt too intimidated to travel on any farther. If Edinburgh was bigger than this, it would swallow her up completely!

Without any idea of where she was going Mhairi hurried on for a couple of hundred yards till she found herself in a broad thoroughfare. Here imposing buildings with rounded bay windows facing the pavement bore the names of wine merchants and shipping companies in gilt letters. Through the glass she caught glimpses of white-collared clerks bending over high desks. It was unlikely that she would find a place among them so she continued on her way, arriving at a busy junction that made her shrink back in horror when she saw the press of horses, carts, men pushing barrows and messengers on bicycles contending for space with clanging tram cars that bore down, bells ringing. To escape the throng she dodged into a street on her left which was quieter because there was no wheeled traffic there, except for men pushing barrows. Without knowing it she had found the Kirkgate.

As usual its shops were busy, its pavements full of people. Mhairi stood at one end of the narrow street and looked up into its snaking length, seeing how it twisted off between lines of ancient buildings and brightly painted shop fronts. Behind her was another broad thoroughfare that she guessed led up to Edinburgh judging by the volume of its traffic, but she turned away from it and walked towards the Kirkgate that seemed by contrast to open up and welcome her.

At the head of the street a man was lounging in a padded, black leather chair set on the top of a stationary open cart. He was brandishing a pair of evil-looking pliers and above his head a huge flag showing a garish mouthful of grinning. teeth was strung from a rope between two poles. Mischievously he called out to the girl who was so obviously an innocent new arrival, 'Got toothache, miss? I'll pull your choppers without pain!'

Mhairi drew back with one hand going involuntarily towards her mouth and he grinned down even more widely from his perch.

'Ever had toothache?' he asked her in a kinder tone when he saw how pretty she was.

She shook her head. On her other side a black-skinned old man with a short frizzle of grey hair and a flat, wide nose, who stood juggling a line of coloured balls in an endless flow, called out in a broad Scots accent, 'Just as well you havena. That yin hauls oot stumps like stabs from the grund.'

'That's not true, Malabar! I don't hurt my patients,' riposted the tooth-puller.

'You'll no hurt them if they've a couple of tots in their

bellies afore you start on them!' retorted the old man who went on throwing and catching his mesmeric line of multicoloured balls in a stream of orange, green, blue and red as he spoke. He gave Mhairi a conspiratorial look and said, 'He bribes folk to go up there and hae their teeth pulled – he'll gie you a shilling and a tot of rum. If you don't yell, he'll gie you another threepence!'

A little crowd had gathered in expectation of seeing some victim yield up a tooth to the pliers and they laughed at this sally. The dentist unabashed shouted back cheerfully, 'I wouldn't waste my money on you anyway, Malabar. You've no teeth left to pull.' But he leaned forward from his perch and spoke to Mhairi, 'Come on up, miss, I'll wheek out one of your teeth so's you'll no ken what's happened. You'll no miss it. I'll take one at the back. And I'll pay you a shilling. A bonny lassie like you'll draw a good crowd. You're no' a greeter, are you?'

'I'm no' a greeter but I'm no' needing any teeth pulled either,' said Mhairi stoutly and ran off into the crowd. There had to be easier ways of earn a shilling in Leith, she thought.

The shops fascinated her. To Mhairi, who had never seen their like before, they were magnificent. There were no shops with shining glass windows on her island and she had not wasted enough time in Aberdeen to wander along Union Street. However now that she was in Leith and anonymous among such a throng, she felt safe enough to spent the afternoon taking in the glories of such a cosmopolitan place.

She paused at Donaldson's the butcher's with its immaculate cuts of meat so neatly displayed inside. She gaped at sparkling rings displayed in a pawnshop window. She admired dress shops where wasp-waisted headless figures sported elegant gowns. She lingered for a long time in front of a shoe shop where rows and rows of high-buttoned boots made her look down at her own poorly shod feet and heave a regretful sigh. Her boots had burst their seams after her journey from the North, for she had walked most of the way. Suddenly she realised how hungry she was and went in search of something to eat. For the first time in her life Mhairi saw oranges and bananas, piled up high in pyramids of colour on a stall in the middle of the roadway. Very daring, she decided to try a banana and slipped into an alley to take a few coppers from her skirt. Having made her purchase she stood eating it as she peered through the door of a grocery store, sniffing the delicious scent which came wafting out. She did not know she was smelling freshly ground coffee. In fact she had rarely even tasted tea.

The din, colour and strange new aromas of the Kirkgate entranced her so much that she forgot the passing of time until she saw that the shopkeepers were starting to shutter up their windows and a church clock boomed out the hours . . . *Five, six, seven!* The night was beginning and music was filling the street, drifting out of the doors of public houses.

Exhaustion and hunger struck her all at once and Mhairi knew the time had come to find somewhere to sleep. She longed for a real bed, with a mattress and covers like the one she'd had in the convent. During her trip from Aberdeen she had walked most of the day and slept in haystacks or farm sheds at night. Sometimes dogs had heard her and set up a wild barking, but she was lucky and had always escaped detection. She felt at ease in the countryside and was unfamiliar with towns, not knowing where to look for a convenient hiding place in Leith. There was nothing for it, she decided, but to spend some of her precious hoard on a night's lodging.

For a farthing she bought two more bruised bananas and walked back to the top of the street. The dentist and his cart had gone but the juggler was still there so Mhairi asked him, 'Excuse me sir but do you know a place that lets out rooms?'

He was surprised at her politeness and actually paused in his juggling to answer, 'There's a hotel doon Great Junction Street . . .'

'Is it – is it cheap?'

'No, it's not; but if it's a cheap bed you're needing,

146

you'd best try The Shore. There's ane or twae places there. Ask for Nanny Grey's, she rents rooms to lassies. Dinna gie her more than a shillin'.'

The Shore in gaslight was a different place from what it had been during daylight hours. Now it had turned into a bacchanalia and the noise coming out of the bars was ear-splitting. A shouting crowd had gathered around a couple of men who were fighting in the middle of the roadway, while under the lamp-posts knots of garishly dressed women stood urging on the combatants with shrill yells.

Mhairi approached a shrieking blonde in the first group she came to and asked, 'Excuse me, is there a lodging-house called Nanny Grey's near here?'

The woman was wearing a green satin dress and had a long feather boa around her neck. She looked at the shabby girl in surprise before she answered with a question, 'New here are you?'

Mhairi nodded, 'I came off the ferry from Fife today. I'm looking for a room.'

A thinner, younger woman stepped out of the shadows and said fiercely, 'Then you'd better get back to Fife. There's plenty of us here as it is.'

The be-feathered woman gave her a shove, 'Get on with you, she's just a country lassie. Can't you tell by the look of her? Needing work are you dearie?'

The last question was directed at Mhairi who nodded and said, 'Yes, I was hoping to find something here.'

'I can tell by your voice you're from the Highlands,' said the stranger, 'So am I. You'll go on back there if you've any sense.'

There was nothing Mhairi could reply to that, but her stricken face made the woman soften. She pointed up the pavement and said, 'Oh, folk never listen! Go on up there for three doors. Nanny Grey's is the red one, but don't give the old bitch more than a shilling because she only changes the sheets once a month. And take a tip, dearie, tomorrow morning get yourself on the ferry boat again. Don't hang around here if you know what's good for you.'

147

The figure that answered the door to Mhairi's knock gave a laugh and said, 'I thought I'd be seeing you again. Was your auntie out then?' It was the curious woman from the ferry. She stood back and held the door open when asked if there was a vacant room.

'There might be. How long do you want it for?'

'I'll be off tomorrow I think.'

'Uh, only one night. You're not staying then? For one night it'll cost you a florin.'

'I've only got a shilling.'

'You learn quick,' said the landlady.

The room contained only a bed which was dirty. The sheets and blankets smelled sour. Mhairi decided to sleep in her clothes, but what she wanted most of all was to have a wash for she was a fastidious girl. She was afraid, however, that if she asked for water Nanny Grey would charge her more and she had to save every penny for her cash was dwindling fast. She lay down on top of the bed and covered her feet with her shawl. In spite of the din that was going on in the street outside, she fell asleep immediately and it would have taken a full-scale war to waken her.

It was early when Mhairi arose after her night in the dingy lodging house. There was no one else stirring in the building. She combed her hair carefully, replaced her blouse with the clean one from her bundle, rubbed her boots clean with spit and a bit of rag, and arranged her shawl over her shoulders so that its frayed edges were hidden. She knew that if she were to succeed in finding work, it was necessary to look tidy and respectable.

When she'd finished dressing, she looked at herself in the cracked mirror above the room's empty fireplace and was relieved to see that travels and troubles hadn't marked her. In fact her looks had improved since she left the convent. Freedom suited her and days spent in the open on the way down from Aberdeen had given her skin and eyes a clear bloom, also making her hair gleam with a glorious sheen. She looked young and healthy, well able to do a hard day's work.

Mrs Grey must have heard her moving about because when she descended to the hall, a door creaked open and the landlady's face beneath a dirty nightcap peeked out. She gave a sly grin and said meaningfully, 'Off are you? Come back if you don't find what you're looking for in Edinburgh. There's plenty of ways of making money in Leith for lassies like you if you're not too fussy.'

'I'm looking for a kitchen maid's place,' Mhairi told her primly. She was beginning to understand what sort of house she'd wandered into.

'What a waste and you such a bonny lassie! You can do better than that,' said the woman grinning again.

Mhairi felt brave enough to face Edinburgh now.

The tram would cost her a penny said a little boy waiting at a stop at the bottom of Leith Walk, so she decided to walk the whole way. The rain and sleet had stopped overnight and a fitful sun was shining, allowing her to see the buildings of the capital city rising on the horizon before her as she trudged along – drawn ever onwards by the lure of clustering turrets, church spires and a brooding castle that looked like a resting dragon lying along a spur of hill.

Footsore, for the blisters she had acquired on the way down from Aberdeen had not yet healed, she eventually found herself at the end of Princes Street where she paused in astonishment. Although impressed by Leith, she had never seen such a magnificent sight as the broad thoroughfare which now stretched ahead of her. On one side was a line of trees and pretty gardens; on the other stood shops and houses more grand and imposing than anything she had ever dreamed about. The Kirkgate paled into insignificance beside it. Every day was presenting her with more and more marvels, she reflected.

A friendly policeman with a Highland accent directed her to an agency that provided work for domestic servants. It was on the first floor of a house in Castle Street and Mhairi was so overcome with awe in the imposing office that she could hardly stammer out her name when interviewed by a stern woman wearing pince-nez, a beautifully laundered high-necked white blouse and a long black skirt.

'Have you any references?' was the first question fired at her. The eyes behind the pince-nez did not look encouraging as they regarded Mhairi's ragged clothes.

'References?' Mhairi did not know what she meant.

'Do you know anyone of good standing who'll vouch for your character or any employer who can say that you're a good worker?'

'The priest at home, Father Malloch of Inverlochy, will vouch for me,' said said and then wished she hadn't because she remembered that he would probably blacken her name to anyone who enquired after her. She had run away from the convent, after all.

'A priest?' Ice came into the woman's voice. 'Are you a Roman Catholic then?'

Mhairi nodded. 'The priest knows me and all my family,' she said proudly and was surprised when the interviewer shut her notebook firmly. 'I'm afraid we don't find places for anyone who isn't a member of the Church of Scotland. We cater to a very respectable clientele,' she snapped.

Shaken and confused, Mhairi was shown the door but before she left she had the presence of mind to turn and ask, 'Are there any agencies that do find jobs for Roman Catholics, please?'

The woman appeared to be softened by the politeness of the 'please' and she nodded. 'Try Dundas in Hanover Street. They're not as fussy as we are.'

Dundas' office was on a ground floor and this time it was staffed by men. A cluster of office boys giggled and whispered when Mhairi entered. Their merriment made her blush and wonder what they found funny about her until, as she waited at the end of a line of would-be domestics in the reception room, she realised they did the same thing whenever any woman under forty came in.

After an hour's wait she was interviewed by an old man

150

with a fringe of grey hair, and gold spectacles perched on his nose.

His opening question was the same as previously, 'Have you any references?'

She had her answer ready this time, 'I've only just left home. I've never been in service before.' He glared and she added hastily. 'The priest'll give me a character.'

He did not flinch at this. 'And where's home?' he asked.

'Inverlochy on the island of Benna.'

His face clouded, 'Hmm, crofting country. You won't have any experience of proper housework then?'

'I've worked with my mother.'

'In a bothy?'

It was a dismissive word for an island cottage but, quelling her resentment, she nodded. To her disappointment he shook his head, though his voice was kinder than the previous interviewer's, 'I'm sorry but we need girls with experience of a good house, girls who know what's what in a proper kitchen. Come back when you've acquired experience and can offer us something more definite.'

He had no suggestions to make as to how such experience could be found without a job and she did not dare tell him about the convent. After her discouraging start Mhairi trudged the streets all day, but was turned away everywhere she enquired for work. When night came she was so tired that she was even reconciled to spending a penny for the tramcar fare to return to Leith which, compared to the chilly grandeur of Edinburgh, was beginning to feel like home.

The following day was equally depressing. Mrs Grey watched her going out again with a sceptical eye and it was plain to see that she knew how little money the girl had left and how long she was likely to survive as a lodger. On the third night, after another fruitless search, Mhairi counted her remaining coins over and over again but could not make them come to more than four shillings and eight pence. Walking the streets in search of a place made her hungry and though she was reluctant to buy

151

food, she knew that it was essential to keep up her strength. The expenditure on nourishment and having to pay for a bed each night was rapidly eroding her reserves. She was sitting on the bed worrying when Mrs Grey came knocking at her door.

First she asked if Mhairi had found herself a position and when the answer was a depressed shake of the head, she went on, 'I've some cheaper rooms in the house next door.'

'How cheap?' asked Mhairi, thinking if a room was cheaper than the one she was in already, it was difficult to imagine what it would be like.

Nanny Grey grinned, 'Four bob a week but nothing at all if you'll see sense and take a turn along the street at night with the other lassies . . . then you can give me a cut of your earnings.'

Mhairi felt herself shrivel up inside in horror. The memory of being raped by Dugald Stewart came back vividly.

She recoiled against the wall and protested, 'I wouldn't want to walk the street. I'm looking for a decent place and I'll find one any day now.'

'You've not had much luck though, have you? Use your head. Who'd hire a maid that's as shabby as you? But you're a bonny one and you're young. You should be out there making easy money with my other lassies. They sometimes bring in three pounds each a night because business is good just now. There's ten timber ships, five wine luggers and two navy ships in the harbour, not to mention the other boats that come and go. The men off them have plenty of money.'

'But I'm not a prostitute!' Mhairi's face was flushed and she was shaking at the thought of what she was being asked to do.

'Don't try any fancy stories with me. You haven't an auntie on Calton Hill either, have you? You're only a lassie but you know what's what. You're not any innocent wee thing. I can tell. They've a green look . . . and you haven't got it.'

152

Mhairi shrank back from her landlady, terrified that her story was written on her face – terrified that the birth of Calum had marked her in some way that picked her out as a fallen woman. It was no good protesting that she had sinned only once. Her experience in the convent had taught her that once was enough. She felt dirty and debased. She had been deliberately trying not to think about her baby and had almost succeeded, but now her thoughts went back to him and she felt a stab of terrible pain at the realisation of what she had been forced to leave behind. Here she was among strangers, among people who had no love for her, and she felt a wave of painful yearning for her home and the security of her family. She longed most of all to hold Calum in her arms. The thought of him brought tears to her eyes and, sobbing, she shouted, 'I'm not a prostitute, damn you! I'd rather die of starvation than sleep with a man for money.'

'There'd be no sleeping in it!' sneered Mrs Grey, 'They don't stay around long enough for that. You're a daft besom. I've given you a chance and you haven't taken it so you'd best get your bundle and leave.'

Mhairi did not argue or change her mind as she had been expected to do. She was so angry and frightened that she did not stop to think. Five minutes later she found herself on the darkening street. A leerie with a long pole was patrolling the pavements setting fire to the gas jets on top of the lampposts; some small boys were kicking a ball desultorily as they straggled home; the first of the prostitutes were taking up their positions in doorways. As Mhairi looked around, she was seized by terror, and wondered where she was going to spend the night.

The wind off the sea was knife-sharp and the grey colour of the evening sky had hinted that snow was on its way. Eager to escape from The Shore and all its threats of violence, Mhairi turned her steps in the direction of Leith Links where she walked slowly beneath the skeletal arms of tall, leafless trees. A swirl of sea-mist lay over the broad expanse of grass as she walked around looking for a place where she could sleep. She was not afraid of the open air but here there were no secret places; no nooks or crannies; no place that would be safe from bitter weather, prying eyes or dangerous interference. She prayed that she would find an empty shed or some abandoned building in which to hide and, in search of such a sanctuary, turned her feet towards the network of little lanes and back alleys running down into the Kirkgate.

She tried garden gates but they were all locked. If she lingered too long at likely places, Mhairi found people watching her suspiciously. She was almost frantic with fear when she saw the squat tower of St Mary's Church looming up in front of her like a beacon of hope, and hurried towards it. Soon she was standing outside its iron gates, peering between the iron bars at the grey silhouettes of the leaning gravestones. Lamplight from the street behind her sent strange shadows flickering over the scene, but Mhairi was not afraid. She felt that ghosts could not hurt her: there was far more reason to be afraid of real people.

The gate gave a loud creak as she pushed it open and ran quickly up the path to the church door. When she tried the handle it did not yield, and she sobbed in despair. When she turned back to the path she was frightened to see that the first flakes of snow had begun to fall, drifting down steadily and inexorably. Her feet felt cold and wet in her broken-soled boots. Every bone in her body ached because she'd been walking around the hotels of Edinburgh looking for work since early morning, and had eaten little all day. If she did not lie down soon, she knew she would drop. The church had no porch and the direction of the wind meant that soon snow would be piling up on its broad step, so she could not lie there.

With her shoulders huddled up against the cold, Mhairi wandered obliquely across the churchyard towards the far wall of the burying ground – thinking that she might find some shelter against a tilted tombstone. Looking from left to right for a suitable place, she staggered on until she found herself beside a thicket of ivy growing on the tall wall. Her spirits lifted. The ivy was so thick and bushy, so ancient and knotted that it would make a good shelter against the snow. Inside its depths she would be able to keep dry. Bending low, she crawled beneath the tangled tendrils like a burrowing animal. Above her head she heard angry birds rustling, disturbed in their night-time perches by her intrusion.

It was only when she was really deep into the bush that she realised it was drooping over a small wooden door which was sunk into the wall. The door had a metal handle made of twisted iron bars and shaped like an orange. With hope in her heart Mhairi used both hands and turned it. Round it went; the handle was obviously kept well-oiled by someone. She pushed against the door with her shoulder. Without sticking, it slowly opened and she stepped into a vault of blackness, closing the little door behind her.

Duncan Nairn was too ill to attend Alex Warre's funeral and had been forced to stay at home as the sad procession slowly paced along the Kirkgate.

His illness was gradual but inexorable though there were times when Brabazon still allowed herself to hope that he might become better. That hope was always dashed because after what looked like a few days of improvement, when his speech would be miraculously unslurred and his spirits high, he always fell back again and became worse than before.

Until Alex was found dead Duncan was still trying to get up every day and in the evenings Gideon Warre often helped him to stagger haltingly across to the church to listen to his son practising the organ.

Henry was very conscious that he had not yet reached his father's level of musicianship and would stumble and make mistakes if he heard Gideon and Duncan coming in, so they took care to enter quietly so that he did not know he had an audience. Then his music was so ecstatic that it brought tears to the eyes.

The shock of Alex's untimely death, however, and his own inability to help Brabazon in her reaction to it, set Duncan back very badly. He longed to console her, to tell her not to blame herself, but the words would not come and all he could do was groan and stammer.

Brabazon at first attempted to conceal her anger and doubts about Alex's death from her sick husband, but she was unsuccessful. In the end she felt she had to tell him of her fears that Alex had been murdered – 'Why, why?' she would rage, 'who would do such a thing, Duncan?'

Mutely he'd shake his head and try to hold her hands in his palsied ones. When she saw how much she was distressing him, she'd be overcome with remorse and apologise, 'I'm sorry, my dear. I shouldn't be going on like this. Alex's dead and we can't do anything about it. Now I'll have to help Nellie and his family.'

She had already told Alex's sons that they had jobs in the brewery for as long as they wanted, and she reassured Nellie that their flat was also safe. They could live there rent-free forever. Alex's Nellie was stoical in widowhood, but her pain and anguish showed in her set face. She never blamed Brabazon for her husband's death but always refused to discuss the police verdict. 'If they say he'd taken too much beer and fallen down the ladder, let's leave it at that. Arguing about it willnae bring him back.' she pronounced firmly.

As Brabazon watched the widow trying to carry on living after such a tragedy, the reality and the significance of her own husband's frailty struck her and she accepted at last that he would soon reach a stage when he would be a speechless invalid; a mind without the ability to express itself, a body without the power of movement. And then, awful thought, he would be dead.

Duncan was indeed growing worse and on the days when he was low, it was almost impossible to make out what he was trying to say. The day after the funeral he was very bad indeed and Henry was sent for Dr Allen, who looked very solemn when he arrived for he had been expecting such a summons.

'How's Duncan sleeping?' he asked Brabazon before he went into the bedroom to examine the patient.

'All right once he does fall asleep but he finds it difficult to drop off and often stays awake till morning, shaking and quivering. The tremors have become much worse. You told me to give him aspirin but it doesn't seem to work any more,.

'I'll write him out a prescription for veronal. Give him one at night and if that isn't enough to give him a decent night, put the dose up to two.'

'Is veronal dangerous? Could I overdose him?'

The doctor shook his head, 'Not with two or even three. It would only be dangerous if he took a dozen. Then he'd die of pneumonia probably. But the time comes with this disease when the patient needs a strong sedative. Veronal will make him sleep and bring him peace for a little while.'

When Dr Allen went into the bedroom he saw that an armchair had been positioned in the window from which Duncan had a good view of the yard. He sat in it now constantly rubbing his thumbs and index fingers together: he was a distressing sight because his head and jaw were wracked by uncontrollable tremors. Controlling his own face so that he would not show shock at the change in his friend, the doctor closed the door behind him.

Brabazon could hear their voices as she waited in the kitchen and when Allen returned she could tell at once that the position was even worse than she had imagined.

'He's approaching the terminal stage,' said the doctor in a low voice.

'How long?' she whispered.

He shrugged, 'God knows. The disease itself won't kill him, he'll die of a stroke or, as I said, pneumonia. I'm sorry Brabazon, but you'll have to prepare yourself for a bad time.'

When she went into the bedroom after the doctor's departure, her husband was sitting staring ahead, immobile except for the trembling of his limbs and face. As if nothing were amiss, she said, 'Wouldn't you like someone to help you over to the church or take you for a little walk. It'll soon be dark and it'd do you good to have a bit of fresh air.' But he shook his head and muttered a few words which she did not catch. Still trying very hard to act naturally, she said, 'I'll have to pop across to the brewery shortly. We're starting production up again tomorrow and I've to check that everything's safe over there before I go to bed. I'll miss Alex.'

He muttered something again and she bent closer. When she was beside him, he managed to grab her hand and stammered, 'Brab – Braba – Bra-baz-on. You – won't let – me suffer too long like – this – will you?' The intelligence and pleading in his eyes communicated with her own heart, although his face showed no expression. 'Help – me,' he whispered.

'Of course I'll help you. You mustn't worry. I'll nurse you myself. I'll not let you suffer in any way Duncan. When you need me all the time, I'll close the brewery. I'll not sell it, I'll close it.'

With a terrible effort he shook his head. 'No. no! I don't – want to suffer – too – long. *Help me*. Only you can . . .'

The last words were said with fierce intensity and, shocked, she realised what he was asking. She put one hand on the crown of his grey head and tried to project some of her own vitality into his wasted body. Her touch seemed to soothe him and after a few seconds he calmed. The trembling grew less.

'I'll help you, my dearest,' she told him with a different inflexion to her voice. The false cheerfulness had vanished and she sounded like someone taking a vow.

'Promise,' he whispered.

'I promise that I'll help you do whatever you want Duncan. You have only to tell me,' she said solemnly. It was the only way to calm him.

'Thank God,' he said in a heartfelt voice.

At that moment Brabazon heard someone coming into the flat. She glanced through the half-open bedroom door and saw it was Gideon Warre. He was a stocky young man with a cheeky face and a cow's lick of tow-coloured hair that stuck up at the back of his head like the cockade on a Highlander's bonnet. Gideon normally looked like Puck, a joker, and was always distressed that because of his snub nose and cherubic cheeks, everyone assumed he was years younger than his actual age. Very few people ever took him seriously. Because of his father's death, he was solemnly dressed in black but he still looked young and schoolboyish.

Brabazon was glad to see him and went into the kitchen to grasp his arm and ask, 'Can you stay with Duncan for a little while, Gideon? Dr Allen's been to see him and he's upset. I have to go over to the brewery soon to check everything's all right and Henry's out playing the organ. Heaven alone knows where Laurence is!'

Good-natured Gideon nodded, he was always ready to help. She bustled about lighting the lamps in the flat and preparing an invalid supper before she left. When Duncan had been fed, Gideon sat on the floor beside him and lifted up a newspaper that had fallen from the nerveless hands.

'Do you want me to read this to you?' he asked, holding it out.

Duncan slowly shook his head.

'Do you want to sleep?' asked Gideon.

This time Duncan managed to speak, 'N-n-n-n-no. Talk to – me'

Gideon did not ask what he should talk about for he knew that the sick man welcomed any distraction. He began with a pensive look on his face, 'It's a funny business about my father, isn't it? There's something wrong but I can't put my finger on it. I just know. I've always wanted to be a policeman, Mr Nairn. I'd be good at it. I get feelings and I notice things . . . I've often gone down to the police station asking how to join but they always throw me out. That big sergeant Roddy MacDowell laughs at me because he says I'm too wee for a bobby. You've got to be five foot eight and I'm only five two and a half. Roddy's six foot two, lucky devil. My mother says I'll never grow big enough . . .'

Duncan's eyes were interested as he nodded and Gideon

went on. 'You see, they said my dad's death was an accident. But my mother's told us she never saw him the worse for drink all the years they'd been married. And there's something else. He was lying face forward, as if he'd been pushed. Mrs Nairn noticed it too. She said he always used to come down that ladder backwards. It was safer.

'Then there was what Mrs Nairn told me afterwards. She said the beer that soaked his neck-cloth wasn't Perseverance's and I'm sure she knows. The police pooh-poohed that and said she couldn't tell for certain. But she's a grand nose on her my dad always says – said.'

Duncan was watching the boy intently. Gideon's face had lost its expression of cherubic innocence as he looked up in the lamplight and swore fiercely, 'I'm sure of one thing. I'll find out who did it and why. Even if it takes the rest of my life. And I'll be a policeman yet, you see if I'm not.'

Brabazon had encountered Henry returning home on her way out. He'd paused in the doorway watching her putting on her cloak before he asked, 'Where are you going at this hour Mother?'

'Across to the brewery. We start work again tomorrow and there's no Alex to help. I want to make sure everything's ready.'

'I'll go for you. It's dark now. You look tired.' But Brabazon knew she would not sleep soundly if she did not check that the boilers were working and the place was securely locked. The responsibility of running Perseverance on her own was weighing heavily on her. She brushed his offer aside saying, 'No, you stay here with your father. Gideon's in with him now but he'll have to go home soon. I'll have to check everything myself.'

Her son told her, 'Alex once said you're as good a brewer as he was. You'll have to trust your own judgement.' His encouragement gratified her and she smiled sweetly at him, thinking what a support he was to her.

160

'I don't know what I'd do without you,' she said laying a hand on his cheek. She often made such gestures of affection to him, unaware that they rankled sorely with her other, absent, son whose recent prickliness was making him unapproachable. Tonight, though she did not know it, he was in Rose Street searching for Daisy.

There was no one about in the Place as she crossed it and the brewery was warmly silent when she unlocked the big door of the brewhouse. For a few moments she paused on the threshold and felt fear knot her stomach as she remembered the last night she'd been there and found Alex dead. Wishing that she had accepted Henry's offer after all, she stepped into the darkness and the pool of light cast by the lamp fell around her feet like a protective shield. She was grateful for it.

Acutely conscious of every creak and rustle in the building, she pulled off her cloak and set about checking that the vats were clean; the yeast cupboard safely locked; the floors swept; the boilers stoked; the grist mill's hopper full to the brim with golden grain. All she had to do next day was pull the switch and start it going: she recovered her confidence and her fears were driven away. She had put on her cloak again and was on the point of returning home to bed when she heard the noise. It was not like the usual sounds of an old building settling down for the night; this was a soft whimper and it was coming from somewhere above her head.

She did not call out: she did not want to lose the advantage of surprise. Tiptoeing up the stairs to the next floor where the silent grist mill stood, she was reluctant to investigate the darkest corners and felt her legs trembling.

Under the thick rafters of the roof the air was very still. Arm upraised, Brabazon stood like a statue and shone her light from corner to corner. There was nothing unusual to be seen at first, but then her heart gave a leap as she caught sight of what looked like a body lying beneath a pile of sacks in the lee of the brick chimney stack.

On closer inspection she saw that the body was that of a girl. Yellow hair had escaped from its pins on to the rolled sack the sleeper was using as a pillow. She was little more than a child and looked like a sleeping angel, but her innocent appearance did not soften Brabazon's heart. Angrily she grabbed an extended leg and shook it hard.

Mhairi sat up in terror at such a rough wakening. In her bemused state she found it difficult to realise what was happening, but soon discovered that an angry woman was shouting at her, 'What do you think you're doing here? How did you get in? This isn't a lodging-house. You'll infect my yeast . . .'

In rage Brabazon became truly fearsome because her eyes flashed fire and she drew her brows together like an infuriated witch. Mhairi's first reaction was to put up both arms to protect her head from blows and it took a few seconds before she could collect herself sufficiently to understand what the woman was saying. 'Who are you? Who let you in here? What do you think you're doing?'

'I'm Mhairi McKay. I'm sorry. I came in by a wee door in the back. It wasn't locked. I didn't think I was doing any harm. I won't touch anything or steal anything. I've nowhere else to go,' her apologies were jumbled and incoherent, and she was shaking.

'Get up and out of here before I call a policeman,' hissed Brabazon, but she was relieved that this was only a young girl – a stray who had wandered in for shelter.

The girl didn't speak and made no effort to defend herself as she went stumbling towards the stairs.

Brabazon, hands on hips, grimly watched her go but there was something about the bedraggled figure that made her rage seep away and as Mhairi was reaching out for the newel post of the stair, she was suddenly called back, 'What's this? You've left this.'

The realisation of what she'd nearly lost made Mhairi turn round and run back to retrieve her bundle. It contained all she possessed.

Brabazon saw the tears, and the evidence of poverty. Her features softened . . . something had to be done about this waif. 'Haven't you a home to go to lassie?' she addressed Mhairi.

'I have – in Inverlochy – but that's far away. I've been in lodgings but my money ran out. I'm looking for work you see.'

Brabazon knew the perils of street-life and could guess what prospects there were for a girl without training or connections. This lassie was pretty and innocent, one of the pieces of human flotsam that were frequently washed up in Leith. Pity pierced her heart and she asked, 'Are you hungry?'

Mhairi nodded. In fact she was starving. Bananas and bread, which was all she had eaten for twenty-four hours, were not sufficiently filling to keep her going for long.

Brabazon told her, 'I own this place and I've been making sure it was all locked up for the night. If you come back to my house with me, I'll give you something to eat and we'll say nothing more about you breaking in.'

Mhairi's eyes expressed her doubts. The innocent trust in people which she had enjoyed until she was sixteen had been eroded and Brabazon did present an odd image in the long cloak that smelled as if it had been left out too long in the rain. To Mhairi she could be just another Leith witch out to exploit a stranger. But closer examination on her part showed that the fearsome eyes were honest and the demeanour that of a lady. The voice was well-modulated and very genteel, reminding Mhairi of the titled lady who used to visit the village school, the one who'd given her threepence for reciting Tennyson. With a nod and a quavering smile, she agreed to accompany Brabazon.

Henry had his feet on the gleaming fender reading a book when his mother pushed open the door.

'Is your father comfortable?' was always her first question, at which he nodded and reassured her. Then he noticed that she had a stranger with her, a ragged girl with yellow hair and a flushed face who stood awkwardly in the doorway while Brabazon explained, 'Look what I found sleeping in the grain store. I brought her back for

163

a meal.' Henry gaped in astonishment, as much at the calm way his mother was accepting the girl's invasion of the brewery as anything else. When she was brought nearer to the firelight he saw that she was a slender little thing with delicate features and eyes of startling blue. The light coming down from the gas jet above the fireplace made her tumbled hair glow as if it were surrounded by a halo.

'Sit down girl,' said Brabazon imperiously, 'What's your name again?' The answer came in a whisper and Henry liked the soft Highland accent that made every word sound like a caress. His mother was bustling about saying, 'I'm Brabazon Nairn and this is my son Henry. How old are you?'

'Nearly eighteen.' In fact only just seventeen was more accurate but Mhairi wanted to be thought adult.

'What would you like to eat?'

'Anything – just anything. It's very kind of you.'

'Hmm,' said Brabazon looking at her unexpected visitor. 'You've not had much success job-hunting by the look of you. When did you last have a proper meal?'

There was no point in lying, 'About ten days ago I think. I've been eating a lot of bread and I'm awful tired of the things called bananas.'

She ate two plates of soup and a large piece of cheese before washing everything down with a mug of warm milk. It was the milk that was her undoing because while Brabazon was brewing a pot of tea, Mhairi fell asleep in her chair with her fair head lying on the white tablecloth.

'Poor wee thing, she's exhausted,' Brabazon said softly.

When Mhairi woke next day the first light of dawn was coming through the window of the flat. She was lying on a folded rug in front of a fireplace with a quilt covering her, but had no recollection at all of how she had got there. What awakened her was a young man with dark curling hair who now bent over her grinning.

'What have we here? You look like a mermaid. Let's see if you have feet,' and he lifted the corner of the quilt. Then he laughed, 'Too bad. No fins.' Surprised and slightly discomfited by Mhairi's frightened reaction, Laurence stood back and said, 'All right, it was only a joke. I'm not going to hurt you.'

Before any reply was necessary from Mhairi, Brabazon came into the kitchen pulling a plaid wrapper over her nightgown and scolding irritably, 'Don't bother to tell me any of your tales about where you've been all night, Laurence. I can guess. You've been on the razzle! I only hope you'll be able to work because we're starting production up again today and there's a lot of time to be made up.'

He backed off into the next room, placating his mother as he went by saying, 'All right, all right. I'll be over there in good condition before you can count to twenty.' He was in a good mood because he'd spent an ecstatic night with Daisy.

As this scene was going on, Mhairi stood up awkwardly, straightening her clothes, smoothing her hair and picking the bedding up off the floor. She watched Brabazon bustle around putting dishes on the table, poking the fire in the grate, opening the oven door and testing the heat with her hand. When she began running water into a pot of oatmeal, Mhairi went across and offered help, 'I can do that for you. I'm good at making porridge.'

The pot was handed to her without a word and Brabazon went back to her own room to dress. Mhairi could hear her speaking gently to someone in there, 'Are you feeling better today? Would you like some tea? Let me push up your pillow . . .'

On hearing the word 'tea', Mhairi filled the kettle and set it in the middle of the now glowing coals. When Brabazon reappeared, it was steaming briskly.

'Thank you very much for being so kind to me. I'm sorry I collapsed like that last night,' Mhairi told her and was warmed with a friendly smile and a reassurance.

'You were exhausted. One minute you were sitting there drinking milk and the next you were sound asleep. What are you going to do now? Have you any money?'

'Oh yes, I've still some,' said Mhairi proudly.

'Have you enough to go home to your parents if you don't find anything here?'

'Oh, I can't go home. There's not enough . . . I mean, I don't want to yet. I want to give this place a try. I've a feeling I'll find a situation today.'

Brabazon looked searchingly at the fresh face by her side. 'If you don't find a place and if you haven't the fare, come back here and I'll give you the money to go home. That would be the best thing for you to do, I'm sure.'

Mhairi thanked her and, as payment for Brabazon's hospitality, insisted on washing the dishes, stoking the fire, sweeping the floor and brushing the rug that lay in front of the fireplace and which had served her as a mattress. Then, repeating her thanks, she went away.

Brabazon leaned on the windowsill and, with pity in her eyes, watched the little figure walking bravely across the yard. She had no doubt that the poor lassie was about to experience another day of disappointment.

Before she herself went over to the brewery she settled Duncan for the morning. He sat in bed white-faced and impassive, but still handsome, as she fed him with porridge and milk, anticipating everything he wanted. He liked her to talk to him without expecting a reply and she gave him the account of Mhairi. 'Poor child, she's so down-at-heel. I can't imagine anybody giving her a place in a house or even a hotel kitchen. I told her I'd give her the money to go back to the islands. She's got the most beautiful soft lilt to her voice. I could see Henry hanging on every word she said and understand why, it was like music.' Duncan smiled and she was pleased at having made him cheerful. 'I think she's sure to come back soon. She doesn't want to go home for some reason but she'll see sense in the end because she's not the sort who ends up on the street. At least not without a struggle, she's a good girl, I'm sure of that.'

The subject of their discussion, as Brabazon predicted, experienced another fruitless search for work. No one was hiring kitchen maids off the street, especially ones with broken boots and no references. By evening, Mhairi was so exhausted that she expended another penny on the tramcar fare back to Leith and sat on the cold top deck with her head down and her shoulders bowed in utter dejection.

Henry was standing at the end of the Kirkgate watching Malabar the juggler perform when a tramcar from Edinburgh disgorged its passengers on the opposite pavement. Last off was the girl with the lovely voice whom his mother had brought home the previous evening. As he watched, he saw her sway when she climbed down from the tram. Her face when she stared up and down the street in an aimless way was tired and dejected. She looked like a lost child and it was obvious that she was almost at the end of her tether.

Breaking away from the spectators around Malabar, Henry ran across the road and touched her on the shoulder as she was turning in the direction of The Shore. She paused and looked up at him with troubled eyes. Then she smiled, making a deep dimple appear in one cheek. He felt a wave of sympathy break inside him as he asked her, 'Where are you going?'

She shrugged, 'I don't really know. I've enough for another night's lodging and I'm going to try again tomorrow, but it really looks as if nobody'll give me work. I've hardly any money left and I owe Jean in the convent a sovereign. She'll be wondering what's happened to it because I promised to send it back soon.' She was talking without thinking, words spilling out of her like water from a pitcher.

Henry stood with a look of surprise on his face, 'The convent?' She didn't look like a runaway nun – all that hair! He'd always been told they shaved their heads.

She realised why he was looking so amazed and laughed, 'I wasn't a nun or anything. I worked in the convent kitchen.'

'Where? Here in Leith?'

'No, no. In Aberdeen.'

'My word, you've been around for somebody your age. Why don't you go back there then?'

She frowned, 'Have you ever been in a convent? Of course you haven't, and I'm sure you've not been in prison either but that's what it's like. I'll do anything rather than go back.'

He felt even more sorry for her and said encouragingly, 'Don't give up yet. Something'll turn up. It always does. Come home with me. My mother'll be glad to give you supper. She's good at working things out and she might have some idea of where you can find a place.' His voice was so earnest that Mhairi's reluctance to impose herself once more was swept aside.

'If you're sure she won't mind,' she said and Henry took her arm to lead her back to the Place. He was feeling chivalrous and proud.

Brabazon did not look surprised to see Mhairi again and, with a smile, brandished a big serving spoon to indicate that she sit down at the table where Laurence was already eating. Henry gravely pulled out her chair as if she were a grand lady before he sat down himself. The supper was a mouthwatering stew with plenty of vegetables and mashed potatoes and Mhairi tried not to fall on it like a ravenous animal.

Although he seemed indifferent, Laurence was watching intently and was vastly amused by the attention Henry paid to the stranger. Perhaps he was taking an interest in women at last. About time! thought Laurence who often jeered at his brother for being a cissy who was terrified of the opposite sex. He was very far from being terrified himself and looked with an experienced eye at Mhairi. Hmm, marvellous hair if you liked that colour, and unusual eyes. She was pretty enough, but countrified and very young; a real innocent. She and his brother would suit each other well – a green pair. A smile passed over his face at the thought, but he could not resist taunting Henry and started to put himself out to be charming to the visitor.

While she was very easy, almost sisterly, with Henry,

168

Laurence's attentions obviously embarrassed and disturbed Mhairi. When he leaned over to pass her a plate and contrived to touch her hand, she reddened and almost flinched away. Laurence's face showed his annoyance and he sat back in his chair watching the supper-table tableau distantly. When the meal was finished, he pulled his coat off a hook behind the front door and went out without saying goodbye.

'What are we going to do with you? I can't have you sleeping in the brewery I'm afraid,' said Brabazon, suddenly speaking her thoughts aloud. Mhairi looked flustered and rose to make her departure, 'Oh, I know that. I'm grateful for what you've done already. I'll go back to The Shore. There's cheap lodgings there. I'm sure I'll find a job tomorrow. I heard about an agency that supplies maids to hospitals – I've not tried it yet.'

Brabazon shook her head, 'The Shore's not the place for a girl like you,' she said disapprovingly. Then she put her chin on her hands and lapsed into thought, Mhairi, in an effort to repay hospitality in the only way she knew, collected the dishes to be washed and was filling the sink when her hostess sat upright with a smile. 'I've got it, I've got it,' she told Henry. 'Run upstairs and ask Mrs Anderson if she's ever thought of taking in a lodger. She's always complaining about being lonely and frightened on her own at night. This lassie here will solve her problems!'

Then she turned to Mhairi and said, 'Would you like to be a lodger with Happy Anderson? If she takes you, can you afford to pay anything?'

Henry laughed, 'Maybe she should meet Happy first, Mother. She could drive Mhairi mad with her gloominess.'

Brabazon looked at Mhairi and said, 'You've a contented nature, I can see that. You wouldn't mind an old woman that moans a bit, would you? That's how she got her nickname. Her real name's Jessie and she's a decent old soul. Though she'll probably not say so, she'll appreciate your company as well as a little extra money. You

169

run up and ask her Henry, she's always had a soft spot for you.'

Her son rose from his chair and left the flat while Brabazon asked Mhairi, 'Now let's work out how much you can afford to pay.'

The real answer was nothing because there was little left in the hem of the skirt and no immediate prospect of earning any more, but Mhairi said stoutly, 'I could pay up to three shillings a week.' She was too proud to admit to poverty and trusted in her luck to find her a job soon.

'Oh, that's too much,' said Brabazon who had a suspicion of the truth. 'If she takes you in, give Mrs Anderson half a crown and say you'll buy your own food. She'll be very glad at that.'

Everything was arranged in a few minutes. Grumbling and groaning, Happy Anderson came limping down the stairs with Henry to inspect the would-be lodger – while Mhairi stood to attention.

'She's a good respectable girl,' said Brabazon as a sort of introduction.

'Mmm, you canna tell these days,' said Happy standing back with her arms akimbo and eyeing Mhairi's shabby clothes, but she did not look really displeased.

It was not in her nature to reveal pleasure however and Brabazon pressed on encouragingly, 'She'll help you in the house and run your messages.' Happy was always complaining about having to go up and down the steep stairs to her flat.

'Mmmm, I havena many messages what with living on my own,' muttered Happy, furrowing her brow.

Behind her, at the table, Mhairi could see Henry practically doubled up with laughter and his hilarity was so infectious it was difficult to stop herself smiling as well. As she fought to repress a chuckle she realised she was happier than she had been since she'd left Inverlochy.

In the end Mrs Anderson agreed. 'All right I'll try it for a week – only a week, mind – till we see if we get on.'

'What rent would you like her to pay?' asked Henry.

'I hadna thought. I wasna thinking of takin' in a lodger.'

He smiled engagingly and said, 'How about two shillings?' As he spoke he glanced at Mhairi to see if this sum suited her and she nodded with a smile, hiding her misgivings at the realisation that she had only enough money for one week's rent. Yet she was optimistic for it seemed as if her luck were turning. Surely she'd find a job before the week was out!

'That'll do fine,' said Happy, fighting to keep the doleful expression on her face because inside she was actually very pleased. The rent was welcome enough but just to have this pretty, smiling lassie in the flat would be grand company for her.

Perseverance Place took Mhairi McKay to its heart. After being plunged in gloom by the unexpected death of Alex, the inhabitants were cheered to see such a pretty stranger in their midst, with her smiling face and cloud of golden hair.

They gossiped about her and vied with each other to help her. The first gift she received was a pair of boots from Nellie who had the same-sized feet. 'They pinch me something awful. She'll have to break them in,' she said when she took them to Happy's door.

Minna Meirstein noticed how shabby Mhairi's clothes were and guessed that she possessed little more than she stood up in. Meeting the girl on the stairs, she laid a wrinkled hand on her arm and said, 'I've some bonny dresses in my shop that folk put in for pawn and never redeem. Come on down with me and take a look. There might be something you'd like.'

She pressed a sprigged cotton dress with a white crocheted collar, a tweed skirt and jacket, and two blouses on Mhairi. Only the girl's proud determination to accept nothing more made her refuse the offer of an emerald-green taffeta ballgown with a sweeping train and a bustle. 'I'd never wear it Mrs Meirstein. I've only been at one dance in my whole life and it wasn't a grand one . . .' Her smile dimmed a little as she spoke and Minna guessed

171

that there were unhappy memories connected with that occasion.

'Vell, if you do go to a ball, you know vhere to come for the dress,' she said.

The Cairns sisters wanted to help as well but Rosie was too tall and Ruthie too broad for anything of theirs to fit Mhairi. They gave her a coat and it swept the floor around her feet, the sleeves dangling down below her hands. Even Happy laughed. With the return of the coat, Ruthie was frustrated in her inability to do something for Mhairi – everyone else except the Lamberts had done their bit for the girl but nobody counted Lambert anyway. She was not going to be left out of the great philanthrophy effort and puzzled about what she could find for the lassie.

Happy was worried about her lodger's inability to find work. 'If she doesn't get a place soon, she'll be off,' she said and worried about losing her new companion. Every time Mhairi came back to the flat from job-hunting, Happy sensed her disappointment.

'Poor wee soul, she's no' likely to find a place in service. She sounds that Hieland and looks as if she's run away from an orphanage!' Happy told Minna Meirstein who, in turn, told Ruthie.

On the fourth day of Mhairi's stay with Happy, she was beginning to rehearse what she would say when she had no money left and was forced to accept Brabazon's offer of the fare back to Inverlochy – at least it would be easier to be hungry and penniless there than in Leith. Then came a knock to the door of Happy's flat and it was Ruthie asking to speak to her: 'I've a friend who works in Taylor's chocolate factory off Jubilee Street. She says there's a job going there. If you're interested, go along and ask for Mrs Young – she's in charge of the packing shed.'

Mhairi ran along the street towards the chocolate factory and when she walked into the succulently smelling shed where the sweets were boxed, she found that Ruthie had prepared the way for her. 'Let's have a look at you. We've been expecting you,' said a grey-haired woman in a flowered apron, who inspected Mhairi's hands, then stood back and took in her appearance before she decided, 'All right, you're clean anyway. I'll give you a try. Sit down there at the end of the bench and sort out all the sweeties with wee violets on top. You'll have to watch you don't eat too many or you'll lose that narrow waist. We let our lassies eat all the chocolates they want when they start but you soon go off them.'

Mhairi had never tasted a chocolate that looked as delicious as the violet-and rosebud-trimmed confections lying on the table of the packing room but she told Mrs Young, 'I'm not very fond of sweeties.'

The forewoman laughed and said, 'They all say that in case we think they'll be stuffing themselves. Don't worry lassie, we don't mind you eating one or two. It's when they're taken away by the boxful that we call a halt.'

That night a transformed Mhairi ran up the stairs and burst into Happy's flat. 'I've got a job Mrs Anderson and I'm being paid ten shillings a week! Ten shillings and all the chocolates I can eat!' It seemed like a fortune to her.

As she went down the stairs next morning on her way to work, she met Henry Nairn and told him her news. He looked pleased and said, 'I'll tell my mother. She was quite worried about you after she got over her fright at finding your hiding place. She said it was like finding the baby Moses in the bulrushes!'

'Good for Ruthie,' Brabazon said. 'That lassie'll be all right now. She's a bonny wee thing and won't have to work in the chocolate factory for long. Some young fellow'll snatch her up.'

Henry's face clouded. He was timid with women and had never walked out with a girl. How different from Laurence! thought his mother, for though she knew nothing of Daisy, she was well aware of her second son's interests.

The sad longings for Inverlochy, her baby and her family,

which had made Mhairi so miserable in Aberdeen merci-
fully began to fade after she started working.

Now that she had a permanent address she wrote home
pouring out her love for Calum, and asking her mother
to make sure that news of him was sent to her. She had
already written a letter from the convent but had not
stayed there long enough for a reply to be received. She
was the only member of her family who could read and
write and used to be the one who wrote any letters for
her parents. Because her little sisters were not yet old
enough to take over the task, she hoped that her letter
would be given to Chrissie to read and send a reply. She
knew that Chrissie would guess the sort of things she
wanted to hear about little Calum.

When Mhairi held her first pay-packet in her hand a
week later, she remembered Jean and knew that there
would be a second letter to be written when another week
was over and another pay earned. In Happy's flat two
weeks later she counted out the money for her rent and
also set aside another little pile for food. What remained
was to go towards the repayment of her debt – a whole
ten shillings! As Happy watched with curious eyes, she
wrapped the precious half-sovereign in cotton and stitched
it round like a little parcel, explaining its destination as
she did so and saying, 'It mustn't get lost or stolen.'

The tiny parcel was addressed to Jean Cook at the
Convent of the Immaculate Conception in Old Aberdeen's High Street and with it Mhairi enclosed a note
saying she was well, living in Leith and working in a
chocolate factory. 'I'll be able to send you the other half
of your sovereign very soon,' said her letter. What she did
not remember was that, like Mhairi's parents, Jean was
illiterate. One of the nuns would have to read the letter
to her.

Every day she went to the factory she felt happier and
happier. She enjoyed going to work, dressing up in a long
overall and covering her golden hair with a white kerchief.
The factory always smelt delicious though she quickly
came to dislike the oily taste of chocolate on her tongue.

The girls in the packing department where she worked were kind to her and she was making friends. She passed the time by singing with them as they all sat in lines carefully placing chocolates in lace-trimmed boxes. Mhairi quickly learned the words of their songs and had a sweet voice which soared like a lark's now that it was filled with new happiness and hope.

On her fourth Friday, she was happily piling dark ginger chocolates in tempting arrangements when Mrs Young, the forewoman, walked up beside her and said in a stern voice, 'There's a man in the office to see you.'

Mhairi was surprised, 'Me? But I don't know anybody here except the folk in the flats.'

'Aye it's you he wants right enough. Come on, leave that, he's waiting in the office.'

Mhairi's heart missed a beat when she saw a policeman standing with hands clasped behind his back in the office where she queued on Friday nights to receive her wages. He looked her up and down before he said ponderously, 'You've been a very silly girl, haven't you?'

Genuinely confused, she stared from him to the forewoman. The factory manager, looking very grim, had by this time joined them. 'What's wrong? What have I done? What do you want with me?' Mhairi asked in amazement.

'The nuns sent a letter down to the police station from Aberdeen about you. You ran away from their care, didn't you? And you stole money from the convent'

'Stole money! Of course I didn't. I've never stolen anything in my life. How can they say that? It isn't true.' She was shocked and on the verge of tears but fought to control herself.

The policeman shook his head as if her protestations only confirmed her guilt, 'Now don't tell lies. You took a sovereign from a poor, half-witted woman in the convent. Then, to do you justice, you seem to have felt remorse because you sent half of it back. That's how the Sisters knew where you were. There's only one chocolate factory in Leith.'

'But Jean *gave* me the sovereign. I left her a receipt

promising to pay her back. I'll send off the other half tomorrow. Ask my landlady Mrs Anderson. She knows all about it, because I told her.'

The policeman still shook his head, 'The nuns tell a different story. They didn't say anything about a receipt in their letter. All they know is that you took a sovereign and ran away after a priest left you in their care. You've been a naughty girl from the start – an illegitimate baby and all.'

Mhairi was incapable of anything but tears now. No matter what she said, they were not going to believe her. What good was it trying to explain the circumstances that had brought her to Leith? The character painted for her by the nuns would stand. 'Please don't send me back,' was all she said through her sobs and to her accusers it sounded like an admission of guilt.

'Take off your overalls and get your shawl. I'll have to take you down to the station,' she was told.

In the packing shed everyone had stopped work and stared as Mhairi was led out of the factory. It was the same when she was shepherded through the streets to the police station in Queen Charlotte Street. She knew the people watching were all speculating about what she had done.

Roddy MacDowell, the station sergeant, was a bigoted Protestant who disapproved strongly of the Catholic church. A flicker of sympathy came into his eyes when Mhairi retold her story, but he re-read the letter that lay on his desk top and shook his head sorrowfully. 'They say you're a fallen lassie, that you had a bairn and no father for it when you were only sixteen years old. They say you need to be looked after, to be protected from yourself.' he tut-tutted at Mhairi as if she were an unrepentant sinner.

Her pleas fell on deaf ears and she was locked in a little cell where she sat huddled with arms folded over her chest. She had no idea what was going to happen and abject misery seized her. Outside she could just hear the rumble of voices which, after a while, included a woman's. Then there was a slight commotion in the doorway leading to the cells and Brabazon Nairn walked in with the sergeant.

'What on earth's happened?' she asked Mhairi, 'Mrs Anderson's in an awful state about you. Ruthie heard you'd been arrested and I've come to find out what's going on. I've heard the police story, but what's yours?'

When Mhairi told her, Brabazon nodded. She'd already heard Happy's defence of Mhairi. 'But why didn't you tell us about your baby? The nuns say you were put into their care because you'd given birth to an illegitimate child.'

Mhairi lifted her head and looked back defiantly, 'I have a baby and I miss him sore, very sore. The father promised to marry me but changed his mind, and my family couldn't keep both of us so I was the one who had to go. My baby's a boy, you see. He'll be able to work on the land one day. But I wasn't sent to the nuns, Mrs Nairn, I went there to work as a kitchen maid and I hated it. I can't tell you how much I hated it. That's why I ran away.'

Something stirred in Brabazon Nairn's heart. There was an unspoken communication between the two women and, a loving mother herself, she guessed what pain it must have caused the girl to part with her baby. She knew Mhairi was telling the truth. Turning on her heel she left the cell, motioning to the sergeant to follow her. In the hall outside she told him, 'Let her go. She's sent most of the money back and will send the rest. The nuns are only being vindictive I think. I'll stand surety for the girl if that'll do any good.'

'The sergeant was not only a religious bigot, he was also susceptible to pretty women. He remembered Brabazon from when he'd attended the scene of Alex Warre's death and now her magnificent dignity, and the girl's golden hair, won his grudging sympathy. 'If you vouch for her good behaviour Mrs Nairn, we'll give her a warning and let her off. I don't like to think of a poor lassie being sent to a nunnery if she doesn't want to go,' he said.

The chocolate factory took Mhairi back but she had lost her pleasure in the work because some of the girls now regarded her askance and muttered about her behind their hands. One day she overheard one saying to her neighbour, 'There's no smoke without fire I aye think,' and Mhairi's cheeks burned as if she were really guilty of the sin that had been ascribed to her.

Her neighbours in Perseverance Place, however, were even kinder to her than before. They really took her to their hearts as her story went from flat to flat. Old Happy now treated her like a daughter and the other women always stopped to chat if she met them on her way to and from work.

She stopped going out in the evenings with the other factory girls and spent all her spare time in the Place as if it were a sanctuary from the outside world. Spring came, followed by summer's long sunny evenings and Mhairi would bring out a blanket to sit on the stone steps with all the gossips, and listen to the stories.

Henry Nairn was as lonely as she was. When not working or playing the organ, the eldest Nairn boy went wandering alone along the dockside where he sometimes sat for hours watching ships loading and unloading their cargoes. Unlike his brother he did not yearn to sail away with them, for he had the gift of being content and was quite reconciled to spending the rest of his life in Leith. He knew his parents needed him and he enjoyed the feeling of being trusted and relied upon. Anyway the place of his birth was a continual pleasure to Henry. His roots went deep down into its soil, piercing through the paving stones to the ground that had not been countryside since Roman legions had landed on the shores of the River Forth.

He had his favourite places and could often be seen standing in the crowd watching the jugglers or the mountebanks selling patent medicines at the end of Leith Walk; he walked along Leith Sands or lingered on the Links to watch other boys playing football. Sometimes he felt as if he were watching the familiar scenes from afar and all the time he longed for a companion, someone he could talk to.

With his brother Laurence, there was no common ground. Laurence taunted him about his innocence of women and Henry didn't reveal that he was curious about women, too, because they terrified him. His idea of the perfect woman was his mother whom he worshipped. The thought of finding one for himself, marrying and sharing a bed with her, scared him so much so that he doubted it would ever happen. When Laurence made fun of his timidity, Henry wondered 'Is there something wrong with me? I must be odd. I can't be normal.'

From the beginning of their acquaintance Mhairi felt confidence in Henry and could converse easily with him, forgetting that he was a man, one of the enemy, for she no longer trusted the male species. She was unable to feel so easy with Henry's brother, however. Laurence's knowing eyes upset her.

One warm summer night, as she was sitting on the stairs with the other women, Henry passed by carrying sheets of music in his hand. 'Where are you off to then?' asked Happy, beside Mhairi.

He grinned at them, 'I'm going to the church. There's a big wedding on Saturday. Some wine merchant's daughter's marrying a lawyer's son from Edinburgh. I'm going to give them a special fanfare but I have to practise it first.'

Happy nudged Mhairi, 'You go over with him and listen to the music. He's a grand player this lad.'

'Yes, come,' said Henry eagerly. He had often longed to invite her to walk with him, but had never been able to summon up the courage.

Now, to his delight, Mhairi rose to her feet and said, 'I'd like to. I'm fond of music but I don't know much about it. My father's a grand singer – but he sings in the Gaelic of course.'

She sat in the church while Henry positioned himself in front of the organ and, after a few snatches, launched into a soaring anthem. It was glorious, magnificent, full of pomp and majesty. Mhairi sat entranced, with her eyes closed, imagining lines of magnificently garbed courtiers marching along behind a king in cloth of gold. When he'd finished and come back to sit beside her she looked bedazzled, her eyes glowing and lips parted. 'That's wonderful! What was it called?' she asked.

Gratified by her reaction he said, 'It was *The Arrival of the Queen of Sheba* . . . Handel wrote it. I thought it would suit a very grand wedding rather well.'

Beaming she told him, 'If I got married to that music, I'd feel like a queen.'

Daisy Donovan – for that was her real name though she used several others – smoothed the gleaming satin of a fishtailed skirt over her narrow hips and admired herself in a long pier glass. Then she turned slowly on her heel and looked at her reflection over a bare shoulder. Satisfaction was evident on her face which had become narrow and predatory. She was literally glowing with health and good spirits, her skin complemented the dazzling cloth she was wearing. Her hair, too, had a silky sheen in the light of the gas jets that lit the room.

Laurence sat in an armchair watching her. His hands were in his pockets and his long legs stuck out into the middle of the carpet. To see her full reflection, Daisy had to keep stepping over them, lifting her tight skirt a little every time she did so. It was obviously causing her a good deal of irritation.

'I wish you'd go home. What are you doing sitting there? I told you I was going out with my old fellow tonight. We're going to the Assembly Rooms.' As she held a beautiful necklace up to her neck, there was a new look on her face – satisfied and greedy. 'You'll have to get out of here quickly,' she told Laurence's reflection in the glass. 'He'll be here in a quarter of an hour and he's always very prompt.'

'Tell him you're finished with all this. Pack your bag and come away with me!'

180

Daisy grimaced, preened herself again, then turned to stare as if he had taken leave of his senses. Her eye ran up and down Laurence's long body, meaningfully looking at the flannel shirt and working boots. Then she laughed, throwing back her head and revealing her gleaming white teeth. 'Go away with *you*? Where to?' she asked cruelly. Then it was back to her reflection to fan herself with a plume of ostrich feathers lifted from the bed. The inference was obvious.

He held his arms out to her but her eyes were hard in the mirror. 'We've been through all this so often I'm tired of saying it. If you don't like the arrangement we have now, you should stay away. I'm saving money, I'm living well. Do you seriously imagine that I'd give this up for some filthy flat up a stinking stair in Leith.' She threw out one hand indicating the comfortably though vulgarly furnished room.

He groaned, 'I won't always have to live in a flat beside the brewery. We're doing better these days. My mother's talking about buying back Brewery House. It's her dream.'

Daisy leaned on the end of the bed and laughed again, 'Your mother's a crazy woman. Everybody knows that – wandering about Leith dressed like a scarecrow and working like a navvy when she doesn't have to. And her such a lady! How do you think she'd react if you took me home as your wife? The old snobberies would come out then I can tell you. I'm a tart, Laurence! I look like a tart. I talk like a tart and my aim is to keep on being a tart until I think it's time to stop. I'm no fallen woman. I like my life. It's a lot more comfortable and easier than living in Leith surrounded by squawling bairns.'

He was out of the chair now and reaching for her hand, 'Oh Daisy I hate it when you talk like that. I remember what you were like that first night. I love you and I know you love me no matter what you say. That old man who keeps you means nothing.'

'I look after him. I do what he wants because he means money and no matter how much beer you sell, you'll never be able to match him for that. Now get out of here. I don't want him to see you.'

Laurence was always distraught when she talked about her rich lover. A stab of hatred and jealousy lacerated his heart whenever she mentioned the man. 'Why have you become such a bitch Daisy? What's happened to you?' he shouted at her, his face flushing red in fury.

When she spat back like an angry cat, he grabbed her wrists and shouted, 'You're a bitch, a bitch! You're driving me mad and you do it deliberately.' He shook her hard and shouted again, 'Don't you?'

He was stronger than Daisy and a wrench of his arms threw her on the floor. They wrestled on the carpet until her piled-up hair escaped from the arrangement of cunningly placed pins and fell around her shoulders. He could tell from her voice that he had succeeded in frightening her, 'Let me go Laurence, you're spoiling my dress. Let me go, you're hurting me,' she wheedled.

He pinned her down beneath his weight and said menacingly, 'I want to hurt you. Sometimes I think I want to kill you. That's the only way I'll ever have you to myself. You're like a sickness that won't go away.'

The eyes that looked back at him were dark hazel with deeper brown flecks through the irises. He stared into them as if trying to read the mind of his mistress, but there was a shield in front of them. Daisy kept her secrets even when she was scared. When he realised what he was doing, his voice changed and he slackened his grip, 'You love me, don't you Daisy?' he asked in a different tone.

Now she went into the offensive, ferociously she fought to free her arms and to his surprise, he saw tears glistening on her thick lashes.

'Damn you, Laurence Nairn, damn you! I do love you. I wish I didn't. It'd be much easier. I wish I didn't love anybody or anything. Get out of here. Just go!'

He rose to his feet and bent down again to help her up. They stood staring wordlessly at each other and then she stepped nearer to him, wrapping her arms sinuously around his neck. The lips she pressed to his face, laying kisses on his cheeks, his eyelids and his mouth, were very cold. 'I love you. I've never loved anybody else and I never will,' she whispered and then she sent him away.

As Laurence wandered through the familiar streets, an affecting scene was being enacted in his home at Perseverance Place. Taking tea by the fire with his wife, Duncan had suddenly slumped forward in his chair in a deep faint.

Terrified, Brabazon at once jumped to her feet, shouting for Henry who was in the next room, 'Come here, come here! Something's happened to your father.' And then she sent him for the doctor.

Henry had only been gone a few minutes before Duncan's eyelids fluttered and he returned to consciousness. He looked up and whispered, 'What happened Brabazon?'

'You fainted my dear. Lie still. Henry's gone for Dr Allen.'

'That's good,' whispered Duncan weakly. Then after a pause, he spoke again, 'It's time we found out what to expect. I'm not going to get better. You know that don't you my darling?'

She nodded but did not allow herself to speak.

'I want to know how long I've left. That's important,' said Duncan as he tried to sit up.

Brabazon put a restraining hand on his shoulder, 'Lie still a little longer, my dearest. Lie there till the doctor comes. We'll face this together . . .' And she lay down beside him on the rug in front of the fire, folding him in her arms as if he were a child.

It was not late when Laurence reached Leith and joyous crowds were queuing up for the cheap seats at the Music Hall where a celebrated comedian was billed. Laurence usually loved the ear-splitting music and vulgar jokes but tonight he had no heart for it and walked past the inviting doors with his shoulders hunched up almost to his ears.

The Kirkgate was busy – was there ever a time except in the middle of the night when it wasn't? he wondered. He strode on past groups of friends without acknowledging their greetings. He was burning with love and rage, with jealousy and desire. Daisy was like an infection in his body. He knew all her faults. She could consistently rouse him to speechless anger, but he was not able to shake himself clear of her. She was always in his mind. Her teasing sensual smile, the look of stillness that sometimes came over her when they were together, haunted him day and night. His hands tingled with the memory of her silken skin as he'd held her pinned down on the carpet.

The lamp on the stairway of Perseverance Place had gone out and when he entered the narrow door in darkness he heard sounds of scuffling and muffled shouts coming above his head from behind Lambert's front door. Then came the sound of a woman's voice pleading, 'Don't Tom, don't hurt me. Oh *don't* . . .' As Laurence paused on the landing he flinched at the sounds of thumps and the muffled screams of a one-sided fight. It was not the first time he had heard the brute of a man beating his wife.

Suddenly he felt angry for all the brutality around him, for the cruelty that people inflicted on each other. Jumping forward he took a violent kick at the flaking door. 'Leave her alone you bastard or I'll break the door down and give you a taste of your own medicine!' he yelled in fury.

As if he had pressed a switch, the sounds of the beating ceased.

In the flat above Mhairi had also been listening to the same horrible noises. The beating had begun while she'd climbed the stairs, after being in the Kirkgate to fetch some snuff for Happy, and she had hurried past the door with her heart thudding in terror. She longed to be able to help Irene Lambert but did not know how and was very thankful for Laurence's decisive action. She was also surprised because she had not thought of him as being particularly chivalrous. Lambert was such a foul-mouthed bully that most people in the Place turned their heads the other way when they heard him berating or beating his pathetic wife.

184

When Laurence barged in to his own home, he found his mother and father cuddled together on the hearth rug. He paused in the doorway with an expression of astonishment on his face. Completely without embarrassment Brabazon rose to her feet and said in a composed voice, 'Your father's not well. He fainted. Henry's gone for the doctor.'

Full of remorse at having been absent from home not only on that particular night, but also on so many before, Laurence knelt by his father. And he was found in that position when the front door opened again, admitting his brother and Dr Allen who bustled up to Duncan, shouldering the brothers aside as he did so.

'Let me look at you, old man,' he said, as he helped him to sit upright. Then he turned to the young men and said, 'Carry your father next door to his bed. I'll examine him there.'

The resulting examination was not as worrying as had been feared. Duncan, Allen pronounced, was suffering from strain and exhaustion. 'He's trying too hard. He's not admitting to being ill. Does he still get up every day?'

Brabazon nodded. Her composure was impressive but the tightness of her hands clutching nervously together gave away her feelings as she watched everything the doctor did.

'I don't think he ought to do so any longer. He should stay in bed and rest,' said Allen.

Brabazon knew this meant that Duncan's last stage of life was being inaugurated. She looked with yearning at her husband as she spoke. 'All right, Duncan will stay in bed now. He really can't walk any longer, though he's been trying very hard.'

The sick man, waxen-faced, staring back at her, eyes sharply intelligent and a terrible contrast to the rest of his vacant face.

'Now you must tell us what to expect,' she said turning her own eyes from Duncan to the doctor.

The pretence was completely gone and Allen's discomfort showed before he said, 'Well, as I told you in the beginning this is a progressive disease.'

Hands extended, open-palmed and upwards like a supplicant, Brabazon pleaded for more information, 'So what's next? Tell us. What can be worse for my poor husband than this?'

'Do you want to talk about it in front of him?' asked Allen.

She nodded, 'Yes, he wants to know as much as I do. We discussed all that tonight before you came.'

How the shuddering man in the bed could be said to discuss anything was a mystery to the doctor but he respected both the Nairns and asked, 'How's he sleeping? Is the veronal still working? He's going to need bigger doses soon.'

'I'm giving him three tablets each night but it doesn't always work.'

'Do the tremors stop when he's asleep?'

'For a little while but not so well as they used to.'

Allen had recovered his professional manner and he talked as if to another doctor, 'Yes, that's what happens. Does he suffer from cramp?'

She shook her head. 'Not yet.'

'It'll come and it'll be very painful. He'll need someone to massage him. The legs are often affected very badly. Can he still swallow?'

She nodded, her eyes full of dread at what their future held. 'Yes, he can,' she said slowly.

'That's good. But soon he'll have to be fed on liquids,' said the doctor.

The stricken couple looked at each other and as if answering a question, Brabazon nodded at Duncan before she said, 'What we want to know is will he always be aware of what's happening? He won't lose his mind, will he? He's worried about that. He wants to keep his dignity.' Her voice cracked over the last words for it was Duncan's dignified reserve that made her love him. Her husband's eyes, fixed on her face as she spoke, slowly filled with tears and she laid her hand on his, patting it

186

gently as she told him, 'It's all right, Duncan. It's all right.'

'He won't lose his mind,' said Allen in a solemn voice. These people were his friends, he had been a guest at their wedding and now he was having to tell them terrible things. It was bad enough when death was quick for his patients but this agony could last for a long time yet because Duncan Nairn had been comparatively young and in good condition when the illness first struck him. He hoped Brabazon would not ask the question he dreaded but of course she did, 'How long has he got, Doctor?'

He took refuge behind professional jargon, 'Death isn't imminent. This disease can be protracted. A patient may live for ten years from the onset of symptoms.'

'Ten years . . . Duncan's been very ill for three already and there were signs it was coming before that . . .' Then she rallied and said hurriedly, 'I want to know what I can do to make him comfortable. I'll do anything, just tell me.'

Allen felt helpless for he knew there was little that could be done when this cruel disease had a sufferer in its grip. 'I'll change his medicine. Till now you've been dosing him with aspirin by day and veronal at night, haven't you? I'll prescribe hyoscine to calm his tremors during the day. Let's try it anyway – three doses a day. It should bring an improvement in his symptoms. Feed him on things he doesn't have to chew – and if you can afford it hire someone to look after him when you are working. Don't leave him alone.'

When he was leaving the flat, the doctor paused at the front door and looked intently into Brabazon's face as he said with deep sympathy, 'You must take care of yourself too. You can't go on like this, you know. If you fall sick, what's going to happen? Have you considered selling the brewery? And remember what I said about hiring help. You're going to need it.'

Her skin was paper-white and her eyes looked exhausted, but her spirit was undiminished. 'Duncan wouldn't want anyone else caring for him. He's been trying so hard not to be a trouble. I'll go on as I'm doing and the boys'll help too, especially Henry.' She did not say whether or not she would sell Perseverance Brewery. 'Whatever Duncan needs, I'll arrange.'

'At least let me prescribe a tonic for you. You're going to want it,' said Allen taking his pad out of his pocket and scribbling something on it.

When the doctor left she re-settled Duncan among his pillows, smoothed his coverlet and then walked back into the kitchen to tell her sons what Allen had said. They listened solemnly although nothing was really a surprise to them. The inexorability of their father's disease had been accepted long ago. Henry jumped from his chair and went over to Brabazon, laying an arm around her shoulders and whispering, 'Don't worry Mother. We'll help you. We'll do everything we can. Laurence and I could run the brewery by now. You've trained us both well.'

She looked up at her eldest son and grasped one of his hands, 'I don't know what I'd do without you, Henry,' she sobbed.

Watching them, Laurence smarted with resentment and stood up quickly, making the dishes on the table rattle together with his violence.

'Why only him? I care as well! I'm trying to help too!' he snapped and stormed through to his cupboard where he flung himself down on the cot and lay fuming. 'She doesn't trust me, not like she trusts Henry. She doesn't value me. He's the one she relies on, he's the one she loves the best. My father's dying; Daisy's playing double games and my mother prefers my brother . . . I want somebody to love me, just me! I want somebody of my own.' He turned on his front and lay overcome with misery, his face pressed into the pillow. He wanted to weep but thought tears were unmanly.

Everyone in the Place knew that the doctor had been called to Duncan, and Nellie came knocking at Brabazon's door with offers of help before breakfast was ready next morning. 'The doctor told me he needs someone to be with him all the time, he needs a nurse really,' Brabazon told her.

'I'll help,' offered Nellie.

Brabazon shook her head, 'That's kind of you but you've your own family to look after and anyway, he needs someone here all day; someone with nothing to do but look after him, read to him, give him his medicines and keep him interested.'

Brabazon had been awake half the night worrying about what she should do, wondering if the time had come to sell the brewery. Since Alex's accident, Willie Ord had been to see her on three occasions, each time bringing an increased offer to buy her out. She'd laughed at him, secure in the knowledge that her order books were filling up and people were pleading with her to sell them Perseverance beer – which was enjoying a great reputation in Leith and even people in Edinburgh had started wanting it as well. Every penny earned, however, had to go back into running the business and Brabazon was, if anything, personally poorer than she had been when she'd first taken over the brewery. What irked her most was the fact that she had not yet been able to raise enough money to repay Abie and Minna and give Duncan back his signet ring.

In the middle of the night, as she thought about this, she decided to send Henry around to Ord's law office and tell him she had changed her mind. She'd sell after all. She was looking so bleak, Nellie asked anxiously, 'Are *you* all right?'

Brabazon shook her head, 'Not really. I've just realised how selfish I've been. If I wasn't so pig-headed I'd have given up a long time ago but now I'll have to sell the brewery I'm afraid.'

Nellie's face showed a mixture of emotions, primarily shock and then regret. 'Oh no, not yet. You've tried so hard and so did Alex . . .' Her voice trailed off and Brabazon knew that she was thinking that her husband's dedication, which cost him his life, might turn out to have been in vain.

'Do you think I'm being selfish hanging on, Nellie?' she asked, 'Don't you think it would be better to sell up so that Duncan can have a comfortable time before he dies – because that's what's going to happen. Dr Allen spelled it out for me clear enough last night.'

Nellie responded, 'But what'll happen to you when he does? You're still a young woman and you've made a place for yourself here. Will you move to the country like other widowed ladies?'

She had never talked so directly to Brabazon before and the effect was everything she wanted. The woman by her side straightened, stood taller than before and seemed to change her attitude. 'You're right. There's all sorts of things to consider before I really make up my mind. Anyway Duncan doesn't want me to sell. He thinks the same way as you do. Oh, Nellie, I'll give it a chance for a bit longer. But who can I find to look after him when I'm working? Who'd be kind to him?'

Minna Meirstein was the next person to appear on the stairs, bustling down with a china bowl in her hands. 'I've been making soup and thought I'd bring some down for Mr Nairn. It's good strengthening stuff,' she said pushing the bowl at Brabazon.

Minna, with her knowledge of the neighbourhood, was the perfect person to seek out a suitable carer for Duncan so Brabazon told her about the doctor's verdict and the old woman wrinkled her brow saying, 'Now let me think. There must be someone . . . I'll ask around for you.' Later, as she and Abe were unlocking the pawnshop, Minna saw Mhairi running through the alley and into the Kirkgate. The girl had overslept and was hurrying for fear she would be late for work. Because Abe and Minna were childless, they watched their neighbours' bairns growing up with yearning and when Mhairi first came into Perseverance Place, they had been struck by her golden beauty.

'Poor bairn, she's too young to be turned out in the

world. What was her mother thinking about?' Minna always asked her husband when they talked about the girl's story, a subject upon which they often speculated as they waited for custom in their shop.

'Poverty, poverty! Don't you remember what it's like to be poor?' Abe asked his wife. She nodded sagely as the memories of hunger and persecution came back, making her even more sympathetic towards Mhairi. As well as giving her clothes, she sometimes pressed bits of lace or pieces of cheap jewellery into her hand when they met.

When evening came Minna was sitting in the sunny courtyard with Nellie, waiting for Mhairi to come home. Eventually the girl came round the corner of the alley and paused beside them with a smile. Minna put up a hand and detained her, 'We're talking about Mrs Nairn. We're all saying that she's looking that worn-out. She vorks too hard.'

Surprised, Mhairi nodded, 'I know. She never stops.'

'She's needing someone to help her,' said Minna. 'Who do we know that would come and not ask for too much in the way of vages?'

The older women looked at each other with raised eyebrows before Minna turned her eyes towards Mhairi. 'How're you getting on these days?' she asked. 'Sick of chocolate yet?'

'I don't eat it. I never liked it much.'

'Vhat about you helping Mrs Nairn?'

'I'd be glad to if she'll have me.'

'I'll ask her,' said Nellie jumping to her feet. Everything had worked out exactly as she and Minna had planned.

And so it was arranged. In exchange for her food and five shillings a week, Mhairi was to look after Duncan while Brabazon was at work. Her rent to Happy was paid by Brabazon, half in money and half in pitchers of beer which were carried over by the one of the Warre boys every morning. Happy thrived on it and even put on weight, telling Mhairi when she sipped it, 'When I was a lassie naebody drank that fancy feckled tea. They took

191

beer and did weel on it.' For once she did not find anything gloomy to say.

Mhairi did not miss the chocolate factory. A peaceful life in Perseverance Place suited her far better. She enjoyed running down the stairs every morning to the Nairn flat, always arriving before the boys had finished their breakfast. Little by little, Brabazon relaxed enough to allow the girl to take over the running of the house. Mhairi did the shopping and, under the direction of Happy who had been a cook in a big house before she married, learned to cook delicacies like sweetbreads and steamed fish for the invalid.

She found she had a talent for producing tempting dishes as well as a gift for nursing. With infinite patience and kindness, she spooned the food into the patient's mouth and wiped his face like a baby when the meal was finished. She was as happy as she had been during the first weeks of Calum's life. When the work of the flat was done she read to Duncan, administered his medicines and, when cramps started to seize him as the doctor had said, she learned to massage his arms and legs.

As she rubbed the oil on to his wasted limbs, he watched her gratefully and though he was not able to voice his thanks very clearly, she could pick up his thoughts in the peaceful silence of the little room.

Brabazon told Mhairi, 'I'm so grateful to you. Duncan's a lot calmer since you came and I don't worry about him so much. You've taken a load off my shoulders.' She had come home that night after a hard day's work and found to her delight that her husband was dozing peacefully and a delicious smell of baking filled the kitchen. 'Mmm! What a lovely smell. What are you making?' she asked.

Mhairi looked very pretty as she straightened up from the grate where she was baking pancakes on a large flat griddle. Her face showed that she was both pleased and embarrassed by Brabazon's compliments. 'I love working here. I'm very fond of Mr Nairn,' she stammered, 'I thought you'd like something tasty for your tea so I made these. Happy showed me how.'

'You're a good learner,' laughed Brabazon picking a finished pancake and biting into it.

They did not hear Henry coming in at the doorway and he paused silently on the threshold watching his mother sitting with her head turned towards the white-aproned girl at the fireplace. In the black-leaded grate the embers of the fire glowed and cast glimmers of light on Mhairi's crown of golden hair. The scene was like a painting of domestic tranquility. The spell was broken however when Mhairi noticed him in the doorway and smiled in his direction. His mother followed her look and called out, 'Oh, it's you Henry. I didn't hear you. Come in, sit down and join us.'

Overwhelmed with some emotion that he could not explain, he said nothing as he pulled out a chair. His mother noticed his confusion and the reverent way he looked at Mhairi who bustled about laying a place for him. She was happy for him.

Later that night, Brabazon had gone to speak to Duncan and Henry was alone with Mhairi in the kitchen. With an effort he summoned up his courage. 'The Fair's coming to the Sands next week. I was wondering if you'd like to go with me on Saturday night. It's always exciting. You've never been have you?' His voice sounded stumbling and awkward in his ears as the words he'd been mentally rehearsing came rushing out.

Mhairi smiled. 'No, I haven't but I've heard about it. I'd love to go.'

His face lit up as if she'd granted him an enormous favour and he said in a stronger, more confident voice, 'I'll come up for you at five o'clock next Saturday then. It's a holiday for the brewery and when she's not working my mother likes to be alone with father. She won't mind if you go out.'

Mhairi nodded. 'I'll be ready,' she whispered.

Three times a week Gideon Warre went boxing in Ruthie's gym; he did exercises to lengthen his spine and on the first of every month surreptitiously measured himself against a scratch on the whitewashed wall of the lavatory his family shared with Minna and Abe next door.

In the gym they called him the Mighty Atom because he was so tough and so small. When he put on the gloves and battered away at bigger men, his face was looking into their waists. People sympathised with him and wondered about his sanity in accepting such challenges. They were amazed when he laid out his opponents.

He drank his daily pundy of beer and ate everything his mother piled on his plate but on the first day of May he discovered that in a year he had succeeded in growing only half an inch. He was finally forced to accept that, now he was eighteen years old, there was little chance of growing any taller. He was five foot three, and the height for a police cadet had to be five foot eight. But Gideon was not one to accept defeat even when it was staring him in the face. He resolved to find another way to make himself indispensible to the police force. He was sure it was possible if he put his mind to it. 'Five foot eight's a daft rule anyway. Look at Napoleon!' he said to himself, and set out for a brisk run around the streets of Leith before darkness came. If he couldn't be tall, he could at least make himself supremely fit.

'Hey shortie,' called some idlers on the Kirkgate when he emerged from the alleyway into the Place and they were taken aback when he turned on them with fists up and a dangerous light in his eye. When angry, Gideon stopped looking like an errant schoolboy and became a small bundle of sheer menace. They backed away from him with their hands up placatingly and saying, 'All right, all right, Gid, only joking!'

He ran on down the road in the direction of the sea with his mind full of frustrated dreams: himself in uniform, whistle and truncheon at his waist, helmet on head, striding along the pavement casting terror into the hearts of all wrongdoers. But there was a more serious side to his ambition. The death of his father still rankled and

Gideon longed for the opportunity to clear Alex's name of drunkeness.

As he ran past the people around him, he knew which women were prostitutes and he could pick out the men who were their pimps; he knew which local thief was looking unusually prosperous and who had been spending more money than usual on beer. His sharp eye detected pickpockets about to lift purses from the unwary and if he'd had the power of a police uniform behind him, he would have taken great pride in arresting them. 'I'd make a great policeman. I know I would. I'll make them take me on,' he swore to himself. He'd raise their apprehension rate by several hundred per cent!

By this time he had reached Albert Dock when the sound of a great splash was followed by that of people shouting, and Gideon saw men running towards the dockside. One was carrying a lifebelt, another hauled a coil of rope while a third ran along balancing a ladder on his shoulder. The rescue team was going into action. At the water's edge a man was struggling and not helping his chances of survival by gulping down mouthfuls of water as he tried to shout. No one looked too anxious to jump in to his aid, because the water was unusually filthy even for Leith. Drownings in the dock were common and an idler beside Gideon commented, 'He's off that boat over there. Fell over the dockside. He's drunk. He'll no' last long.'

Without hesitation Gideon leapt into the water and reached the struggling man with a few strokes of his powerful crawl. But the man tried to cling to him, grabbing him around the neck in a fierce embrace. He was twice the weight of Gideon and unless something was done very quickly, he was going to take them both down to the bottom of the dock. Realising the danger, Gideon delivered one of Ruthie's best right hooks to the jaw. The man went limp in his arms and then it was easy to turn him on his back and tow him to the dockside, where hands reached down and hauled them to dry land.

Someone threw a coat over Gideon while a squad of

helpers lifted the unconscious sailor and ran with him a short distance to the shoreside dispensary, where a huge bath was always kept filled and warming over a slow burning fire. It lay in wait for the resuscitation of those who lost their footing along the slimey sides of the dock.

The water was pressed out of the victim's lungs and he was laid in the bath where the temperature made his chilled blood flow again. Within half an hour he had recovered completely and was shouting for more rum.

'Whae went to the trouble of saving this yin?' asked an old woman helping in the bath-house.

'Wee Gid Warre,' she was told.

'What a warrior that laddie is! He should get a medal for his trouble,' she said, wiping wet hands on her sacking apron. As he overheard her, Gideon's great idea came to him. He knew how he was going to persuade the police to take him on.

'Away home laddie an' grow another foot.' Sergeant Roddy at Leith police station grinned cheerfully at the boy presenting himself as a candidate for the force. Roddy was used to the lad because since he'd left school Gideon had been turning up at the station about once every six months, hair slicked down and face glowing, to ask if he could be taken on as a trainee.

'But I've grown nearly an inch since the last time I was here! Measure me. And I'm tough. Didn't you hear about me saving that man in the dock yesterday?' he asked.

'I heard all right. You'll get a safety medal but no uniform. One sailor saved doesn't change the regulations, you know.'

Gideon leaned his elbow on the desk in a man to man way, 'Aw come on, Roddy. You ken fine that you'd rather have me on the beat than some of those long drinks of water you've got.'

'Listen Giddy. I'm telling you. There's nothing I can

do. You may be the local hero but I canna help you. Away home and keep out of trouble.'

As it turned out Gideon Warre received two safety medals for his activities that week because on Friday night, as he was strolling on The Shore, a small boy happened to plunge into the water and was also saved by him.

'By Jove and they say lightning doesnae strike in the same place twice,' said Sergeant Roddy when he heard the news on the night the Fair opened.

The fairground brought a surge of excitement to the whole town. People everywhere could hear the strains of music wafting inland with the breeze and it seemed as if the whole of Leith had turned out for the fun. Tightrope walkers, jugglers, preachers bawling about sin and Redemption to unheeding ears: all competed against bands and hurdy-gurdies to delight the crowds of dancing children, smiling men and women.

Mhairi's face was a delight to Henry as they walked together through the show-ground. Her eyes sparkled and her lips were slightly parted as she gazed from side to side like a child seeing a Christmas tree for the first time. He longed to be able to touch her, to feel her hand on his arm but though they strolled through the crowds quite close to each other, she did not slip her arm through his. Linking was a recognised sign of something more than friendship. It was the first step towards engagement.

'I'll win one for you,' Henry announced when they reached the canvas-backed coconut shy and, to his own surprise, his second ball knocked a coconut off its stand.

It was presented to Mhairi and she shook it a little as she held it to her ear. 'There's water inside,' she gasped in delight.

'It's not water, it's coconut milk. It's very good for you, they say,' Henry told her proudly. He had never enjoyed himself so much before.

In the middle of the fairground, the din drew them towards the biggest attraction of the evening – the boxing booth. It was housed in a tent large enough to accommo-

197

date several hundred people, and a flourish of multi-coloured flags flew from its two tall supporting poles.

A large man with his belly straining at the front of his waistcoat, and a fierce black moustache which made him look like a theatrical villain, was shouting out the attractions to be staged within. He had a voice that could be heard for half a mile and crowds came running from all over Leith when they knew that the fights were about to begin. They were eager to pay up for the spectacle because it was certain that blood would flow. The boxing booth was Leith's equivalent to Nero's Roman games. A frisson swept their ranks as the busker announced – 'Roll up, roll up! The Fearsome Fly will fight Killer Jack. Roll up, roll up! The Champion will take on any challenger from the crowd!' His voice grew portentous as he declaimed his boxer's qualifications, 'The Champion is one of the few men ever to knock down John L Sullivan. He has *never* been beaten! He is a *killer*, ladies and gentlemen. Don't come in tonight if you're squeamish.'

Of course they flooded in when they heard that. The promise of blood-letting excited them all.

Henry and Mhairi stood in the press of people listening to the shouted invitation, while others filed past clutching their shilling entrance money in their hands.

'Are you coming then?' asked a voice at Henry's elbow and he turned to see Ruthie Cairns with her brothers. Ruthie was all dressed up in a long cape piped in scarlet and gold, and her face was shining with excitement.

Henry shook his head. 'I don't think so. I wouldn't like to see anyone get hurt.'

'Aw don't worry about that. He'll no' get hurt. Come on in. It'll be special tonight. You'll see a real fight for a change, not a fixed one. That's right, isn't it Bobs?'

She turned to her brothers who were squeezed into tight black suits and wore floppy cloth caps set at dashing angles. Simple Eckie grinned and nodded but Bobs said confidentially, 'You don't want to miss this, Henry. Not when somebody you know is fighting.'

Ruthie hissed conspiratorially, 'Dinna let on. It's a

secret. Hurry up, come on or you'll no' get a good seat.'
She gave Henry a firm push.

'Do you want to?' Henry asked Mhairi, who looked
doubtful. Like him, she was not anxious to see blood.

The busker saw them hanging back and urged them
on, 'Roll up, roll up! Tonight you'll see heroism. There's
a ten-guinea purse for anyone who lasts three rounds with
the Champion.'

The arrival of Laurence decided the issue. He pushed
his way through and slapped Henry on the shoulder,
'Hey, what're you doing here? This isn't your usual sort
of place, is it? Come to see the fight, have you? You'd
better lay your bet early before they cotton on.' He looked
challengingly at Mhairi as he spoke, teasing her with his
eyes. It surprised him how enchanting and doll-like she
looked in the flaring lights. She was wasted on Henry. A
note of grudging admiration crept into his voice as he
spoke again to his brother. 'I'd put on a half guinea if I
was you. It's a sure thing.'

'What is?' Henry was bemused.

Laurence's voice sank to a whisper, 'Don't you know?
I thought that was why you were here. It's Gideon. He's
going to take on the Champion. Ruthie's been training
him for weeks. Come on. The tent's almost full. We can't
miss it.'

The first bouts were depressing affairs with superannu-
ated old men or callow youths slamming half-heartedly
at each other. The crowd barracked and yelled in frustration at the lack of either skill or blood until the master
of ceremonies climbed into the ring and held up a hand,
yelling out, 'Now we come to the big event of the night.
The Champion, ladies and gentlemen!'

The band struck up a fanfare as the Champion made
his entrance. People gasped at the sight of him for he was
a giant, almost six foot six inches tall. Once upon a time
he must have been magnificently muscled but now his
biceps and pectorals hung loose; his skin had a jaundiced
colour that was an indication of the fondness for alcohol
which had ruined his career and reduced him to boxing

in a fairground tent. As he threw his leg over the rope, he brushed his nose continually with his left boxing glove and made funny hissing noises. The Champion's brain had been pounded into pulp. That did not mean that he was not dangerous, however. Once fighting, he would punch and punch until his opponent was driven to the floor.

Mhairi clutched Henry's arm as she watched the mountainous figure holding his arms above his head in the ring. His eyes were blank and it was obvious he was performing by rote. 'Oh, poor Gideon. That man's going to kill him,' she sobbed.

Henry looked at Laurence standing beside him. 'Don't you think we ought to stop it or something?' he asked urgently.

Laurence looked down his nose, 'Gideon's going to win I tell you. Bet you half a crown!'

On the far side of the tent, Henry saw Sergeant Roddy among the throng, 'There's the police sergeant over there. I'll go over and ask him to stop it.'

Laurence laughed, 'Don't be daft. Roddy's betting on Gideon as well. If you try to stop it, it'll be you who's punched to pieces. Shut up and watch.'

In the ring the Champion gave an animal grunt and spread out his enormous arms. Then there was a scuffle in the crowd where a half-drunk young man was being helped up by his friends. He looked tall and strong, but he was a plant from the management. He barely had time to take his stance before the Champion delivered the punch that made him lie down on the ring floor feigning unconsciousness.

The ringmaster was beaming broadly now as he called, 'Come on, that didn't last long did it? Do we keep our ten guineas tonight or will someone else have a try for it?'

'I'll take the challenge,' called a voice from the middle of the audience and an arm was stuck up in the air. When Gideon made it to the ringside, a howl of hilarity rose.

'Aw no, it's wee Gid Warre!' People were laughing and

rocking back and forward on their heels with delight, 'Wee Gid Warre' they yelled in disbelief.

Unabashed, Gideon bent down to go through the ropes and posed in the middle of the canvas with his arms upraised in joking imitation of the Champion who stood in his corner looking astonished.

And no wonder. Gideon's head was barely level with the big man's breast; he was less than a quarter of the Champion's weight. Seeing the humourous potential of the bout, the ringmaster pranced into view, too, and held up a hand to silence the laughter. 'I know it's funny. This lad's a joker, isn't he? Hey sonny, are you sure you know what you're doing? Does your mother know you're out? You know we're not responsible if you're killed?'

'I won't get killed.'

The ringmaster pretended despair, 'Ladies and gentlemen. I've tried to persuade this lad to see sense. On his own head be it. The Champion will take the challenge!'

Another voice cried, 'In that case, I'll be Gideon's second and make sure there's fair play!' Ruthie Cairns came climbing into the ring now. Having cast aside her cape, she revealed herself to be dressed in a boxer's singlet and a long tight pants like men's underwear. The crowd howled again, their whistles and catcalls ringing out in an ear-splitting cacophony.

The ringmaster could not believe his luck at the way the evening was going. This was too good to miss. 'The fight will start in fifteen minutes,' he announced and ran back to the tent door to rustle up more spectators. 'There has never been a fight like this in Leith!' the crowd inside heard him roaring, 'Roll up and see our Champion against a featherweight! Roll up and see a local laddie's act of heroism. If he's still on his feet at the end of *one* round I'll give him a guinea myself.'

There were soon more than five hundred people packed into the tent, all sweating, all excited and all eager to see David take on Goliath. Just before the flap was tied down, a party of two elegantly dressed men each with a pretty woman on his arm appeared. When one of the men spoke it was in a toff's voice, 'There's nothing like a good fight to sharpen the appetite for supper.'

Impressed, especially when they offered to pay double for a good view, the ringmaster himself pushed a way for the party through the press of people till they reached a wooden stand at the back. 'Climb up there, gents and ladies,' he said, 'You'll see every drop of blood and believe me there's going to be plenty.'

When he was stripped down to his shorts and singlet, Gideon looked as if he were still a boy. The cow's lick of hair at the back of his head was somehow very pathetic as he danced on his toes, making feints and passes at an imaginary opponent. Mhairi shivered as if she were about to see a human sacrifice. She looked around in a rising panic but the packed ranks made it impossible to escape. The Nairn brothers stood one on each side of her and she took a step back in order to be more protected by them.

Neither Laurence nor Henry noticed her discomfort, however, because they found it impossible to take their eyes off the ring where Ruthie was preparing Gideon. Sergeant Roddy, his better feelings activated, and his face grim, bent down to Gideon to whisper, 'I'm not going to let you go in there. He's going to kill you Gid. Are you listening? I'm going to tell the big bloke that you're throwing in the towel.'

'Come on Roddy. I know what I'm doing. Stay and help Ruthie. I need somebody in my corner,' was the reply. Shrugging, Roddy took hold of a sponge and a bucket of water but he did not look very enthusiastic.

Then the bell rang its sharp tinny note and the Champion came lumbering out of his corner with arms weaving to and fro and his Neanderthal head lowered. Gideon ran lightly forward on his toes, dodged beneath the flailing arms and planted a punch on the yellow abdomen. The Champion gasped and bent his knees slightly. His face showed mild astonishment, but he brushed Gideon away like someone batting off a wasp. The crowd howled in glee.

Driven against the ropes, Gideon stood with his fists up defending his head against an onslaught of punches, at every one of which the crowd yelled. In return he found he was battering uselessly against the wall of flesh that was his opponent's vast stomach. The round seemed to go on forever and only when Ruthie yelled out in protest did the showman ring for its end. Instead of lasting three minutes, it had gone on for four and a half. If Ruthie had not called and Roddy not been a policeman, it would have been even more protracted.

When Gideon staggered back to his corner a trickle of blood was coming from his right nostril. The ringmaster called out, 'He's lasted one round. He's earned himself a guinea. Here lad . . .' and he strode across to lay a golden coin on the floor at Gideon's feet. 'Want to give up now?' he asked hopefully but Gideon shook his bleeding head.

Round two opened with the crowd chanting 'Champion, Champ-ion!' every time the big man aimed. When a punch connected, they cheered, 'Kill him; kill the little bastard!'

Later Ruthie swore it was because they'd called Gideon 'little' that the tide turned. Each time he heard the word he seemed to gather himself together, bounced on his feet like a rubber ball, paused for a second and, on tiptoe, drew back his arm to shoot a ferocious jab at the battered face looming over him. Fortunately for him, and unfortunately for his opponent, the Champion's head was often lowered in an effort to locate his miniature assailant.

The enormity of Warre's nerve turned the feeling of the crowd towards him especially when his nose started pouring scarlet gore, and the howls grew louder when the Champion was seen to stagger after dropping his guard and leaning forward long enough to give Gideon the opportunity to hit him on the right eyebrow. It had been cut so many times before that the old scar burst open, covering his face with blood.

The yells of the crowd could even be heard in Persever-

203

ance Place where Nellie was gossiping with Minna, blissfully unaware that the shouting came from a crowd baying for the blood of her second son. Had she been able to listen properly, she would have heard Ruthie's voice, two rounds later, calling Gideon a wee hero and almost suffocating him in her embrace.

The Champion was stretched out like a fallen mountain in the middle of the floor and the ringmaster was squeezing water from a sponge on to his unconscious face.

'You've won, Gideon, you've really won!' cried Ruthie again and again.

'Great,' said Gideon and fainted.

'A good try but he didn't make it,' called the ringmaster, leaving the Champion's recumbent body and stepping across to Gideon's.

The spectators hissed and in a surge they moved forward threatening to invade the ring, so he tried to placate them by saying, 'It's a double knockout but it was such a good try I'll give him another sovereign!'

'Don't be daft,' yelled Ruthie, 'If he doesn't get his proper purse, I'll knock your bloody head off.'

By this time Sergeant Roddy had succeeded in reviving the victor who sat on the floor bemused, while bedlam broke out around him. Bet-takers were trying to slip away without paying those who had made wagers against the Champion; women were screaming in panic and a group of young men were trying to climb over the ropes to get at the ringmaster who was forced to cry out, 'Of course I'll pay him! I was only joking.'

He waved wildly at a girl in the doorway and she fetched a red velvet bag into the ring. Like a courtier, the showman bent down and placed it before Gideon who stared at it as if he could not believe his eyes. Then he got up and raised his arms above his head while the crowd went mad around him. Bloodied and battered Gideon's puffed lips opened in his old cheeky grin. The cheers were deafening.

The young people from Perseverance Place were delirious with glee. 'He did it, he did it!' Laurence called out

204

and his companions threw aside all reserve in their relief and pride. Laurence hugged Henry, Henry hugged him back and they they both hugged Mhairi who giggled as she was pressed tight to first one chest and then the other. Her bonnet was knocked askew and her legs were trembling with the force of emotion she'd felt during the terrible fight. Each time Gideon had been hit she'd closed her eyes. She'd hardly seen anything of what had happened, but Henry's yells had made her look through her fingers at the last scene and now she was glad she had not missed it.

All of a sudden, as she clutched at the arms of her escorts, she realised what she was doing – she was touching men and was not afraid to do so. When Henry looked down and saw her hand on his arm, his face went soft; Laurence, too, smiled at her abandon and was surprised at how much he enjoyed the touch of her hand. With a grin, he turned towards the girl and hugged her for a second time but by then her innocent rapture was over and she drew away from him.

His face fell and he drew back, looking up to watch the dancing, shouting people all around. His eye lighted on the fashionable group on top of the wooden stand. They were cheering and one of the men was throwing his hat in the air while a woman clutched his arm. She was beautifully dressed in brilliant blue silk with a dashing feathered hat and she was laughing excitedly, head thrown back. His heart missed a beat and he leaned forward to see more clearly. Yes, he was right! The woman was Daisy.

The sight of his brother looking so happy as he escorted Mhairi out of the tent was bitter for Laurence because his jealousy burned like a fire within him at seeing Daisy with a man. That was no aged admirer! That was a young toff and she'd been hanging on to him as if he were a treasure. Laurence could not bring himself to join the revellers who followed Gideon, perched high on the shoulders of Bobs and Eckie Cairns, back to Perseverance

205

Place. Instead he walked all the way to Trinity and waited for his mistress.

It was dawn when she came home in a hackney cab, her feathers and silks drooping. As she stepped up to her front door, Laurence came out from behind a large bush in the front garden and grasped her arm.

'What did you think of Gideon Warre's fight?' he asked.

'Whose fight?' She was exhausted and wan.

'Gideon Warre's. The boxing match you watched on Leith Sands. What did you think of it?'

She didn't bother to lie, which annoyed him even more than if she had done. Instead she shook his hand away and said shortly, 'I enjoyed it. I thought it was exciting – almost as good as sex.'

'Who were you with? That wasn't your old fogey. The excitement would have killed him.'

'I was with friends. You don't own me. I do what I like and go where I like. Leave me alone.'

By now they were inside the house, arguing and glaring angrily into each other's faces.

'Who is he? Is he paying for you too? What are you playing at Daisy?'

'What business is it of yours? I've told you already if you can't keep me, I'm free to go to somebody who can.'

'Daisy, for God's sake. I love you. I think about you all the time. You're driving me mad. You can't love anyone else the way you love me. You couldn't love him in bed the way you do when you're with me . . . could you?' His memories of their frenzied, biting lovemaking acted on him like a drug. In spite of his anger and jealousy, there was nothing in the world he wanted more at that moment than to make love to her. Though they had been lovers for so long, his fever for her had never abated. The more he was with her, the more he wanted her.

She sensed his change in mood and put a hand on his face, talking in her coaxing whore's voice. 'Laurence, Laurence; don't be silly,' she cooed, 'Don't be jealous. It's you I love and you know it. Come upstairs with me. I'll make you happy. I'll show you who I love. Come on . . .' Trailing him behind her like a child, she led him up the stairs to her enormous bed.

It was noon before he woke. For a few moments he lay confused, wondering where he was and what had happened. Then he saw Daisy's sheet of hair spread out on the pillow and turned to stroke her hunched right shoulder. The sun was glinting through the drawn linen blinds and glittering off silver-topped crystal bottles on the dressing-table. Daisy, he thought, was amassing valuable possessions very rapidly. Her taste, which had been vulgar only a short time ago, was changing. She was living like a lady now. At the touch of his hand, she shrugged and murmured something which he could not hear so he bent forward to ask her, 'What did you say?'

'I said get dressed, Laurence. It's time you left.'

Disappointment killed his arousal and he fell back against the pillows, disappointed and deflated. 'Why? It's Sunday. I want to make love to you again and then we could go out and promenade along Princes Street like a real couple.'

She was fully awake now and he could sense her quick mind swinging into action as she prepared one of her sweet lies – 'That would be lovely. What a pity I've arranged to visit an old friend.'

'One of your clients you mean? Surely they all spend Sundays with their families? Isn't that the way these respectable men go on?'

She giggled, 'Now don't be jealous again. I thought I'd cured you of that last night. No, it's a woman friend – she's been sick – I promised to take her some beef tea.'

He laughed. The idea of Daisy bearing beef tea to anyone's sick bed was too unlikely to credit. He could not help admiring her effrontery. 'You must think I'm stupid,' he told her.

But she knew her power over him and turned on one side to burrow her face in his chest, sighing, 'Well, perhaps there's not too much of a hurry. Perhaps we could have a little more time together,' And then she kissed him with lips apart so that he forgot everything else but his

207

need for her. What happened after that was the most ecstatic experience he had ever had with her.

When eventually he rose to dress, Daisy lay beautifully unashamed – like a naked Venus on top of the tumbled sheets watching him. His heart soared when he saw there were tears in her eyes. Seeing him scrutinising her, she wiped them away with a hasty hand and whispered, 'I do love you Larry,' She was the only one who still called him that. 'I wish you'd believe me. I've loved you since the moment we first met and you were so kind to me. Do you remember that night?' It was something they had never discussed between them till now. He sat down on the bed and took her hand as she continued, 'I don't want you to forget – ever – no matter what happens. I *love* you. But it's impossible for us to be together all the time. I could never settle down to be a good wife to anybody. You know that. There's some sort of devil in me and it's the same with you really. I didn't realise it the first time we met, but it's there. We'd tear each other apart and I'd go mad if I couldn't live the life I want. Sleeping with men is the way I'll make my fortune. It's the only thing I can do really well. I know what they want and I give it to them, but it doesn't mean that I give them my heart too. It's just a transaction, Larry.'

His face was stricken and she put a hand on his cheek as she went on, 'Don't argue, dearest. I don't care about them. They make love to me and they pay for the privilege. I've got to make as much as I can while I'm still young because it won't last, but as far as real love is concerned, it's you I'll always remember.'

It was the old Daisy, the frightened girl who'd first cast her enchantment over him, that was speaking and he looked questioningly at her. 'What are you trying to say? Are you telling me something, Daisy?'

She stroked one hand down his hard flank and smiled her coquette's smile. Their moment of real intimacy had passed and her normal disguise of double-dealing came over her again. 'Of course not. What could I be saying? You're always suspecting me, aren't you?'

'Can I come back tomorrow?' he asked.

'Yes darling, come tomorrow. Come late and you can stay all night,' she told him as she kissed him goodbye.

When Laurence returned to Perseverance Place there was a party going on in the cobbled yard. Brabazon had brought two hogsheads of beer out of the brewery, and Mhairi was bustling around handing out full glasses to everyone who came to congratulate Gideon on his victory. The hero himself sat on the bottom of the stairs beside frail Duncan who was installed in a wicker armchair in a patch of sunshine.

Laurence took a glass of beer and wandered across to where Gideon sat. Sergeant Roddy was standing beside him with his hands in his pockets and as Laurence approached he heard him saying, 'All right Gid. I'll see what I can do. It's no' very regular but I'll tell them you're special.' He gave a grin before he added, 'And in return, stop thae wee laddies jumping into the dock every time you pass by. You've saved another three in the past week, haven't you? When we take you into the force, you'll have to have a word with them. If they keep falling in like that, you might be too busy to fish one of them out some day and that'd be an awful pity.'

Gideon flushed and looked down into the glass of beer in his hands, but he didn't say anything. His mother turned to Laurence with a smile and said, 'Oh, I'm awful proud of my laddies. And wee Elsie too, of course.'

He warmed to her and grinned back asking, 'How's Pat these days, Have you heard from him?'

She nodded happily and patted her pocket. 'I've a letter here from Pat. The postie brought it yesterday. He's in the North West Frontier fighting the Pathans – and he's been made a sergeant.'

'I hear they're awful wild those Pathans, but that part of the world's very bonny,' said Laurence wistfully.

'They'd have to be pretty wild if they're worse than the folk in Leith,' said Nellie looking at the marks on Gideon's face. Both eyes were black and blue, and his lips were so swollen that he could hardly speak.

Ruthie Cairns who was hovering around Gideon and his mother joined in the conversation and told Nellie, 'You're a lucky woman having a family like yours. Look at Gideon here – the best pupil I've ever had in my gym. I wish you'd persuade him to go professional, Nellie. He'd end up in New York punching hell out of the Yanks, I'm sure of it. He's the makings of a world-class boxer. Pat's a grand fellow too and he'd have made a great prize-fighter as well if he'd stayed at home. I hope he remembers all the things I taught him – then he'll be able to stop thae Pathans quick enough. He had a punch on him that could fell an ox but he couldna outbox Gideon. Oh my word, but I'm proud of him! I wish he'd go in for the bantam-weight title of the world.'

Nellie's face sobered because she knew how sensitive Gideon was about his height. She always worried about him, always piled more food on his plate; and Ruthie's use of the word 'bantam-weight' rankled with his mother just as badly as it must have done with Gideon himself. 'He's maybe wee but he's awful tough,' she said defensively.

Ruthie, sensing her mistake, nodded vigorously, 'Tough's not the word Nellie. He's a hero! The whole of Leith's proud of him today.'

They all toasted their battered victor while the sun shone down on them. The only family missing from Gideon's celebrations was Tom Lambert's but no one cared, and no one noticed Irene's sad white face watching the party from behind the grimy glass of her window on the first floor.

Laurence went through the afternoon in a beer-induced haze. The sun beat down as he wandered from group to group making conversation, but thinking all the time of Daisy and counting the hours till he could return to her. A little germ of worry was working away in the back of his consciousness. She'd acted so strange before he left her; she'd seemed so unusually soft and gentle – she was up to something! But what? She'd said come late. How late was late – eleven o'clock? Midnight? By half past nine he could contain himself no longer and slipped away from the last remnants of Gideon's celebrations to walk to Daisy's house.

All the way to Trinity he went over in his mind what he wanted to say to her, but he knew that nothing he could produce would make any difference. He had no more to offer than before; she would turn him aside with honeyed words and they would be back where they started. The position seemed hopeless: stalemate. Something dramatic would have to happen before anything could change.

It was dark when he turned the corner of her street. Not a soul was abroad but when he looked up its stretch and saw the rose bush hanging over her garden gate, he experienced a strange feeling of disquiet that was impossible to explain. So strong was it, however, that he began to run; filled with fear in case something had happened to the woman he loved. When he was nearly at her front door, he paused and stood stock-still on the pavement. No lights shone in the windows and the place looked deserted. For a second he reflected on how strange it was that you often knew a house was empty before you lifted the knocker. It looked like a body from which the life had fled.

It was no surprise when no one answered his rapping, though he rattled the knocker for a long time. Then he went round to the back, where he knew there was another entrance leading to the basement kitchen. A surly old woman who cleaned and cooked for Daisy – since she'd come up enough in the world to rent her own house – slept in a little room beside the pantry. When he bent down to peer, he could see the flickering flame of a candle burning. Instead of knocking on the door, he rapped hard on the window and soon a face swam into view. He gestured to her to open up and let him in but she shook her head and was about to walk away when he knocked more loudly and shouted at her, 'Open the door. Where's Daisy?'

With a wave of her arm she showed him that he should go back to the front and wait for her there. He stood shaking on the step and listened for her footsteps coming up the hall, and then he bent down to shout through the keyhole, 'Where's Daisy?'

A voice came back, 'She's gone away.'

He was beside himself and started hammering on the door again, 'Gone away where? Did she leave a message for me?' he yelled. The old woman knew him well enough for he'd been there many times.

'She's left you a letter. Wait a minute and I'll push it through the letter box to you.'

He waited on the step for what seemed an eternity. Then he heard footsteps coming back across the hall and the letter box creaked open to show a piece of paper being pushed towards him. He seized it and pulled it clear, saying at the same time, 'Don't go away! I want to talk to you. When's she coming back? She must have told you.'

The woman sounded surly, 'I'm wanting to go to my bed. All I've been told is to clean this place and leave. As far as I know she's gone for good.' Then the letter box clanged shut and Laurence heard the sound of shuffling footsteps disappearing in the direction of the back premises.

To read Daisy's letter he had to stand beneath the street lamp. The note was very short, only three and a half lines written in a childish hand. Many of the words were misspelled . . . 'Dear Larry, Don't be angry. I've gone to Lundun with a man whos going to set me up. I reelly meant what I said to you last night. Love Daisy.'

He read the words over and over again and finally, with a convulsive movement, tore her letter into tiny pieces and scattered it to the wind. Some of the scraps were caught in an upward eddy and went sailing away. In a fury Laurence returned to the back of house and thundered with both fists on the door until the old woman's candle reappeared in the glass panes.

'Stop making that row. You go away and let an old woman sleep in peace,' she shouted angrily at him.

'Open the door,' he yelled, hammering with such frenzy that she was forced to give in because she feared he would break it down. When she opened up a crack, he stepped forward and shoved his shoulder into the gap, 'Who'd she go off with? Was it the old man?' he demanded.

'Of course not. He's as mad about it as you are. He was here tonight as well and got a letter too. It's him that told me to clear out. The little bitch hadn't the decency to pay me even!' The old woman's face was filled with loathing of Daisy.

'If it wasn't him, who'd she go away with?'

'Huh, off she went in a carriage with a real young swell. I heard him say they were catching a train to London – that's the best place for her kind if you ask me. She told me he's a lord or something, but I ken better than believe a thing she says. One thing's certain though, he's got plenty of money or he'd never have taken her away from the old man. That poor old soul's spent money on her like it was water.'

'Did she take anything with her?' Laurence wanted to know if there was any chance of her coming back.

'Every damned thing except the furniture: she's been packing for days.'

He walked home to Leith in a daze, sometimes raging against Daisy or wringing his hands with pain at the knowledge that he'd never see her again. The more he thought about it, the clearer it became that the whole thing had been planned for some time. She'd known about it when they met for the last time. The marvellous love-making had been her way of saying goodbye.

He groaned aloud, startling wandering drunks in the Kirkgate as he walked along reflecting on how happy he'd been only that very morning when he'd held her in his arms. He'd heard her say 'I love you' and he'd been stupid enough to believe her.

213

'Damn you, Daisy. God damn you! You're a bitch and a liar!' he yelled at the silver sickle of the moon.

'I'm worried about Laurence.' Brabazon looked across at Duncan sitting propped up in his bed. 'He's so surly all the time and if anyone speaks to him, he snaps at them. He's drinking too much as well. I've no idea where he goes at night.' Her brow was furrowed and her eyes anxious. For the past few weeks Laurence had been like a brooding storm-cloud inside their home.

Duncan made a sound and she paused to listen to him. She and Mhairi were about the only people who could still easily understand what he was trying to say, although there were days when he was clearer than others. Today he was better and could say in a halting way, 'Something's happened – He's unhappy – Would he tell Henry?'

She shook her head, 'I don't think so. He's worse to Henry than he is to anyone else. I think he's jealous, especially since Henry started paying so much attention to Mhairi.'

The attachment of their oldest son to the girl had not gone unnoticed by his parents. They both liked her and hoped that a match might be made there – she would be perfect for Henry they both agreed.

The objects of the couple's discussion were at breakfast in the room next door. Mhairi was ladling porridge from a big pot. Laurence, who was sitting with a surly look on his face, stared at the steaming pile of oatmeal on his brother's plate and said, 'Don't give me any of that muck.'

Mhairi's hand with the spoon went still and she stared at him without speaking. Henry who was eating, looked up and said, 'That's pretty impolite. It's very good.'

Laurence slammed his teacup into its saucer and said, 'I'm tired of it! I'm not a horse – or a Highland savage. As far as I'm concerned it's muck.'

Mhairi's face was scarlet as she turned to put the pot back on the top of the grate. She was obviously upset though she said nothing and Henry leapt to her defence.

'Don't worry about him. He's a curmudgeon! Give me a second helping. *I* like your porridge.' He held out his plate, but she did not move and stood with her back towards them staring at the fire. Her shoulders were shaking slightly and Henry realised she was weeping. At the sight, his own temper rose and he snapped at his brother, 'Look what you've done. You've hurt Mhairi's feelings.'

Laurence, though he was secretly ashamed of his conduct by this time, was not prepared to admit it. Ever since Daisy had left he'd felt himself driven by some kind of demon that forced him into saying and doing things that he would normally not have considered. He wanted to shout, scream and kick against the world like a spoiled and thwarted child.

'Aach, she's too easily hurt then. Just because I said I don't like porridge – and I don't like the eternal fried herrings she makes either. Herrings and oatmeal. We eat like peasants these days.'

Mhairi had given them fried herrings for their supper the previous evening, though she did not serve them often. However, it was his emphasis on savages and peasants that hurt her more than his criticism of her menu.

'Don't talk like that!' said a furious Henry going round the table and grabbing his brother by the shoulder, 'Say you're sorry. You're just in a bad mood, but it's not fair to take it out on other people who can't fight back.'

Laurence stood up. He was taller and broader in the shoulder than Henry and they stared at each other for a few seconds till Laurence pushed his brother in the chest and said, 'What are you going to do about it then? Going to fight me are you?'

Mhairi, horrified, ran up and tried to step between them saying, 'Sit down, don't be silly. I don't mind if he doesn't want any more porridge, Henry. I'll make something else in the morning.'

'Get out of the way Mhairi!' Henry did not look at her as he spoke. His eyes were fixed on his brother's face. Both were furious by now, and the long years of muffled resentments and jealousies were coming to the surface.

215

'Apologise,' he said to Laurence through gritted teeth. Laurence laughed, 'Look at our knight in shining armour fighting for his lady! I'll knock your head off, brother, if I hit you.'

'Try it.'

'Don't, don't!' cried a frantic Mhairi, trying to save the china which looked in danger of being knocked over. Then, just as Henry took a swing at his brother's chin, she called out in a frantic voice, 'Mrs Nairn, oh, Mrs Nairn!'

When Brabazon came rushing in from next door, her sons were reeling to and fro in the middle of the floor with their arms locked around each other and their heads down. 'What on earth is going on! Stop it this minute! Have you gone mad? And your father's trying to rest next door. What's this about?' she demanded angrily.

'Porridge,' said Laurence as they stood apart, angry but abashed. 'I said I didn't like porridge and he went mad.'

'It wasn't that. He said only Highland savages and peasants ate porridge,' protested Henry.

Brabazon realised immediately why the fight had broken out. She looked at Mhairi who stood at the fireplace with her cheeks scarlet and tears sparkling in her eyes.

'Apologise to Mhairi,' she said shortly to Laurence.

He walked towards the girl with his hands raised and clasped together like a supplicant. His eyes were dancing and it seemed he was enjoying himself.

'I'm sorry for saying porridge is the food of savages – and horses,' he said in a mocking voice.

'Apologise properly,' snapped his mother. She longed to be able to grab his collar and shake some sense into him the way she had done when he was a child.

Laurence gave a grin and sank down to his knees on the floor with an almighty thump. It hurt but he didn't mind. He relished making the girl confused. 'I'm so sorry I've hurt your feelings Miss McKay,' he said bending his head towards her feet, 'Go on kick me, but at least say

216

you accept my apology or my mother's going to take a stick to me.'

Mhairi leant away from him and said solemnly, 'I accept your apology Mr Nairn. I won't give you porridge ever again.'

The gossips of Perseverance Place had their eyes on Mhairi and Henry. They'd noticed that she often went walking with him in the evening and that when he talked to her, he showed an animation that was wakened in him by few other people.

'Henry's aye been that shy with vomen but the vee lassie's bringing him out of his shell,' said Minna Meirstein to her husband.

The old man shook his head, 'He's a feeling laddie. I hope he doesn't get hurt.'

'Vhy should he? He's a good catch for a maid servant. It'd be grand to have a vedding in the Place.'

'I don't think she's looking for anybody yet and it wouldn't matter to her how good a catch he was if she didn't love him,' Abe replied. He was greatly taken with Mhairi and noticed every nuance of the way she behaved. He could tell from the way she talked with Henry Nairn that she was not in love.

His wife however was more practical, 'She's maybe not in love yet, but she's still only a lassie and she's sensible. The time vill come – Henry's a fine laddie.'

In the brewery Brabazon called her eldest son into her office and looked sorrowfully at him. 'What's all this trouble with Laurence? He's your brother Henry. You've got to treat him more tactfully.'

'Tactfully!' exploded Henry, 'You know perfectly well he's been awkward for months, Mother. It's impossible to speak to him and get a reply that's not an insult.'

She nodded, 'I know there's something wrong with him. Do you think you could try to find out what it is, Henry. I'm worried in case he owes money. He wouldn't want me to know.'

That evening Henry waited at the door of the stables but Laurence deliberately took longer than usual in grooming the horses, brushing their silken coats with long, lazy strokes and hissing softly through his teeth as he did so. He knew his brother was hanging about waiting, and he was not prepared to make it easy for Henry. When he did emerge from the stalls, the older Nairn was sitting on a bench reading a newspaper and Laurence said airily, 'Waiting for me, are you?'

'I thought we might go along the Kirkgate for a beer before supper.'

The brothers never went out together and Henry never went into pubs to drink beer. Laurence's face showed his surprise at the invitation. 'Changing your ways brother? All right, wait till I fetch my coat. I could do with a beer.'

They went to The Bells and as soon as Laurence pushed open the door, a group of men at the bar turned their heads and greeted him like a friend, 'Hey, Laurence, what're you having? Sit down at the piano and give us a tune.'

Henry looked surprised. He had no idea that Laurence played the piano any longer. As children they'd played duets together but since the Brewery House instrument had gone to the saleroom, Laurence had never mentioned any interest in music.

'In a little while I might,' called Laurence to his friends. Then turning to Henry he asked, 'What'll it be – Perseverance Special!'

Seated with the glasses at a corner table where they would not be interrupted, they stared awkwardly at each other. 'Get it over Henry,' said Laurence with a laugh, 'You've obviously been told to talk to me.'

Henry shrugged. 'It's Mother. She's worried about you and she has troubles enough as it is. I think you should make things easier for her.'

Laurence's face darkened, 'I've problems too.'

'That's what worries her. She thinks you might owe money or something.'

The answer was a shake of the head, 'Oh, it's nothing

like that. It's nothing she can do anything about. Tell her it's personal and in time I'll probably get over it.'

'You're not ill? You haven't – caught anything?'

'Don't be daft. I don't go with tarts – at least . . . no, I don't go with tarts. I've not got the clap if that's what you think.'

Henry flushed scarlet. He was very shy of sex and could not discuss it with anyone. His own ignorance and innocence worried him and he longed to say to his more experienced brother, 'Tell me what to do. I don't know how to court Mhairi. When I'm with her she treats me as if I were her brother – but I want more than that.'

'Mother's upset. I wish we could reassure her,' was what he said however, staring down into his beer.

'Well, I'm fine. I'm just needing an adventure. When Pat went away I really missed him. I was so jealous of him for being able to go and I haven't got over that really. I want to be free too, free of Leith, free of the brewery, free of my life here!'

The last words were said with vehemence and Henry nodded sympathetically, 'We all knew you missed Pat but neither you nor I can get away, Laurence. You know how Mother needs us now that father's growing worse. They don't talk about it but I can see him fading away. One of these days, very soon, she's going to need us even more.'

His brother shrugged despairingly and his eyes were shadowed, 'I know that. It's all part of my problem. You're a good fellow Henry, but I'm not. I can't help it. Tell Mother I've had an unhappy love affair but I'll get over it. She'll understand that and stop worrying – but don't tell her that every day I dream about getting away from this place, don't tell her that.'

Henry looked at him with dawning sympathy and indisguised admiration, 'A love affair? Who with?'

Laurence stood up and collected the empty glasses so that he could have them refilled, 'You don't know her. Her name's Daisy.' Then as if he regretted revealing even that scrap of information, he turned to his friends at the bar and shouted, 'What would you like me to play?'

The titles of several Music-Hall songs were shouted back and Laurence took off his jacket, rolled up his sleeves and sat down at the piano. He banged out the tunes with such verve and skill, playing from memory and without sheet music, that Henry felt his feet tapping while he finished his beer. When the second glass was empty, he rose to go home for supper. Laurence was still playing with enthusiasm, hair flopping down over his eyes, and he did not look up as his brother left the bar.

Laurence's talk with his brother did little to lift his depression. As autumn advanced his spirits fell even lower and it was galling for him to see how enthralled Henry was with the pretty little Highland piece. He could not do enough for her, deferred to her in every way, followed her with adoring eyes. He was in love for the first time and his enthrallment was painfully obvious.

Laurence regarded the object of his brother's affection coldly as she went about her work in the Nairns' flat. Tiny, slim but big-breasted, she looked as if she'd be comforting and cosy to hold in bed.

But would Henry be any use to her there? wondered his brother.

Her hair was luxuriant and a wonderful colour. Even on the dullest days it seemed to spring and glow with a life of its own like a dancing fire. He wondered what she would look like with it falling around her shoulders and suddenly remembered the legend of Lady Godiva. Mhairi, naked, would look like that he decided; demure and shy beneath a torrent of hair. The vision was interesting and he allowed a knowing little smile to cross his lips as he watched her piling up dirty breakfast dishes in the sink. She saw the way he was looking at her and cringed inwardly, for he made her feel awkward but she did not know why. He rarely spoke to her.

On Sunday afternoons it had become a regular habit for Henry and Mhairi to take a walk on The Links. The approach of winter meant that these walks would have to be curtailed, but every dry or sunny day was seized on with eagerness by Henry – who never failed to issue an invitation on his way out to church in the morning. Knocking on Happy's door, he'd call through the keyhole to Mhairi, 'I'll come for you at half past two. All right?'

She enjoyed their time together for they talked of all sorts of things. He told her stories he'd read in books: she talked to him about Inverlochy. Henry was the only person to whom she revealed her longing for Calum. One afternoon she told him the story of how she'd laid her baby down at the feet of the plough horse.

He was thunderstruck by Stewart's cold indifference to his son. 'He must be a brute,' he said angrily when she'd finished her tale.

She shook her head, 'He was used to having everything he wanted, nobody ever stood up to him. He was like a king on our island.'

'How's your little boy getting on now? Do you ever hear about him?' asked Henry sympathetically.

She smiled and said, 'I've had three letters from my friend Chrissie since I came to Leith. My own folk can't write, you see. Chrissie tells me about them. Calum's the bonniest bairn in the whole island and the cleverest; she says he's a fair wonder.'

'I'm not surprised with a mother like you,' said Henry fervently.

He longed to grasp her in his arms, to tell her how much he felt for her, to ask her to allow him to look after her and shield her from people like Stewart for the rest of their lives, but his shyness made him tongue-tied and awkward. Every time he'd worked out what to say to her, she somehow diverted him from the subject and he could not tell whether she did so deliberately.

In fact Mhairi was aware of Henry's growing feelings for her and dreaded him speaking about it. She liked him very much and would miss their Sunday strolls if they ever stopped, but should he make a lover-like approach to her, she would be forced to examine her feelings too closely. She would have to decide whether there was any chance that she would one day love Henry Nairn. At the moment all she felt for him was a deep and genuine friendship.

The girls in the chocolate factory had always been adamant that there was no such thing as friendship between men and women but her relationship with Henry was, as far as Mhairi was concerned, a perfect example. They could talk to each other without constraint; they were kind and tactful with each other. She thought highly of him in every way, admired his musical talent and his sweet nature – but she did not love him. He did not turn her stomach to water when she caught sight of him unawares, and the thought of going to bed with him was distasteful. That was not any reflection on Henry, however – the thought of going to bed with anyone was horrible. And she decided she'd never experience that sort of love. It must be romantic nonsense that people write about in books, she concluded.

She said as much to Henry one day when they were discussing love in an abstract way. Nellie Warre's son Robert had just that week been married to a girl called Annie from the chocolate factory. Annie, Mhairi had been told, was pregnant and that had precipitated the marriage.

'I don't think there is such a thing as love really. In the end it always comes down to practical things,' she said musingly.

Henry was shocked for he was a romantic. If only I could tell her what I feel! he thought. If only I could say, 'I know what it feels like to dream about someone; to long for the sight of them; to have such a rush of feeling at the way they flash an eye or give a smile in your direction . . . I know all these things because of you Mhairi.' Instead he said with conviction, 'Oh love exists all right.'

'You read too many books Henry,' she told him with a laugh.

He shook his head in protest, 'No, look at my mother and father. They love each other. The feeling they have

222

for each other fills our house and it has always been like that. It's something wonderful really.'

Mhairi was struck into silence by that. Of course he's right, she thought. In spite of illness and frailty, Duncan Nairn was still Brabazon's lover in the most sublime sense of the word. Their affection was a bond that had kept them together through the vicissitudes that could have broken many people. So she nodded, 'That's true. I take back what I said about love. Some people are lucky enough to find it, but they are fortunate and very unusual,' she sighed.

In late autumn, chestnuts from Spain were brought in by the sackful in the holds of ships importing sherry from Cadiz. The sailors sold them to street vendors and as the winter mists swirled into Leith, every corner had a man selling roasted chestnuts from a burning brazier. The smell was mouthwatering as it drifted between the close-packed buildings of the port.

There was a chestnut-seller at a pitch on the edge of the Links as Henry and Mhairi walked along that Sunday afternoon. After they'd paused to listen to a band that was playing away, Henry asked the girl by his side, 'Have you ever tasted hot chestnuts?'

She shook her head, 'No, never. They smell very nice though.'

'I'll buy some. Wait there.'

A line of people stood waiting their turn to be served and as Henry took his place, he felt someone move in beside him. It was Laurence. 'Buying chestnuts for your girlfriend then?' he asked.

Henry nodded. A smell of beer came off his brother. He'd been drinking – and on a Sunday too! Laurence did not bother to lower his voice as he said, 'You're daft about that lassie. Why don't you do something about it? It's obvious from the way you're hanging about her that you haven't – or you *can't*. Can you Henry?' He didn't stop there. 'She's a tasty little piece all right. You'll have to hurry up or someone else'll have her from under your nose. She's no innocent, is she? She'll be fancying a bit by now I guess.'

'She's a very respectable girl,' hissed Henry, angry and scarlet-cheeked.

Laurence laughed, 'They're all respectable girls but they can still like it, you know. She must; she's had a bairn, hasn't she? Remember all that business with the police?'

'Oh God, shut up, someone'll hear you. The baby wasn't her fault.'

'Of course not. She'll have told you all about it.' Laurence bent forward to whisper into his brother's ear, 'I bet she said she was raped. All the tarts on The Shore have a story like that. It makes you weep the first time you hear it – but every time it's the same – innocent girl; wicked man; wham! A baby and then the street.' He pretended to be playing a violin with a doleful look on his face.

Henry angrily pushed him away. 'Leave me alone. I don't know what's wrong with you, but you should think hard about the way you're behaving. Go away!'

When he returned to Mhairi with two packets of hot chestnuts, he saw with a shock that Laurence was standing beside her, hands in his pockets.

In a surly way Henry handed over the chestnuts, ignoring his brother, who said, 'None for me? Maybe Mhairi'll give me one.' He popped his fingers into her packet and took out a big specimen, peeled it quickly and held it to her mouth, 'Taste it, Mhairi. Tell me if it's good.'

She opened her lips and bit into the chestnut. The brothers watched her while she chewed and then she said, 'It's delicious.'

With a smile Laurence put the rest of the half-eaten chestnut into his own mouth. His eyes were fixed on hers all the time he chewed it. She went scarlet with confusion.

While her sons were out Brabazon sat with Duncan, holding his hand and talking to him. For the past few days

224

his speech had been very difficult even for her to understand and the convulsions were more distressing to watch than before. He seemed terribly weary, but it usually soothed him to be alone with her and she was grateful for the emptiness and silence of their flat.

She tried everything to divert him, first reading the newspaper aloud and then, when he still showed signs of restlessness, she started telling him the local gossip. 'Pat Warre's coming home on leave soon. Nellie had a letter yesterday and she's been going round telling everybody her news. She's beside herself with excitement but I suppose it's natural, he's been away a long time. I wonder if he's changed. Everybody in the Place is pleased for Nellie – only Tom Lambert was nasty when she tried to tell him about it.'

Duncan made a sound and she nodded, 'I know, Lambert's nasty about everything. I distrust that man so much. I wish I'd had the nerve to put him out of his flat when he was discharged from the brewery, but it seemed so unfair at the time. He's the only person in this building that I don't like. I think he's evil. It's impossible for me to forget how he attacked Laurence that night on The Shore.'

Duncan's eyes were fixed on her and she knew he was interested, 'I wonder if Pat coming home will make Laurence happier. He's so miserable it's painful to see, and it makes him so sharp-edged. He's always teasing Mhairi, watching her in a funny way all the time. It worries her – and it worries Henry even more. I think that's why Laurence does it.'

Duncan nodded and she patted his hand saying, 'I know you sympathise with him – you always have – but he can be a devil. Poor Laurence, he's too like my father for his own good.'

Duncan's eyes were anxious as he looked at her and his mouth opened to a series of strangled sounds. He was trying to tell her something.

'What is it, my dear? Don't distress yourself. Take your time,' she said softly bending towards him. She grabbed

225

up the book he had been reading before she came in and said, 'Point the words out to me on the page.'

With her guidance, he started to indicate individual words on the open page that lay on the coverlet in front of him. Very slowly his trembling index finger hovered as his eyes searched for what he wanted. Brabazon spoke the message as his finger quivered towards each word – '*Don't . . . let . . . this . . . last . . . too . . . long . . .*'

Their eyes met and she whispered fearfully, 'What should I do?'

He gave a groan and a shudder. Then his eyes went back to the book. He was looking for a specific word, but it was not on the page so he tried to pick out individual letters. After a few false starts she finally made out that he was trying to spell, 'H-E-L-P'.

'Help you?'

He nodded and the finger hovered over the printed page again: 'me – go'. Duncan tried to hold his wife's hand in his. 'P-le-ese,' he stammered.

She knew what was intended and her face was agonised as she gasped, 'Oh, my dearest, how can you ask that, how could I?'

Once again it was letters he looked for. This time they spelt 'P-i-l-l-s'.

Unwillingly, she understood. 'Your pills. It would have to be the veronal, Duncan. But surely you know I couldn't. I love you more than anyone in the world. I'd sooner kill myself.'

Although her dear Duncan was wasting away in front of her, his finger was insistent and his eyes bored into her face as if they had the power to will her to do as he bid. With a gasp and a sob, she yielded, 'All right. I'll save them up. I'll make sure you don't suffer. But you'll have to tell me when – you'll have to be sure. You choose the day. Oh, God, Duncan, why has this happened to us? Why, why, why?'

Brabazon wept until she was exhausted and when Mhairi came in later that evening to find out if there was anything she could do, she found them lying clasped together and asleep. Pity rose in the girl's heart at the sight of Duncan slumped back against his pillows, with his wife curled up at his side – holding his hand in hers.

'So that's what love is like. Henry's right, it does exist,' she thought as she tiptoed towards the door. Very quietly Mhairi let herself out and climbed up the stairs to Happy's flat thinking about her own life. She had not loved Calum's father but she'd been flattered by his attentions, and her innocence had made her the ideal prey for him. The memory of the seduction and her subsequent disillusion still made her flesh crawl. It was obvious Henry was happy in her company and that pleased her because she could tell how lonely he had been before, but she could not encourage him. 'I'll never marry anyone,' she told the lingering shadows of the night.

Though it was growing late, she had no wish to go to bed and settled herself to watch the moon from Happy's window. Around ten o'clock she saw Henry hurrying across the yard from the church and heard his feet running up the first flight of stairs. Later she watched the Cairns coming home, arms round each other's shoulders and singing. Ruthie was resplendent in a bright blue gown that Mhairi correctly guessed had been purchased out of Gideon Warre's winnings. He'd insisted on sharing his purse with Ruthie because she'd been his trainer. The Cairns' boxing gymnasium had been inundated with customers since Gideon's triumph and Ruthie was looking for larger premises.

Much later Mhairi yawned, and was about to go to bed, when she saw Laurence Nairn come into the yard. He was oblivious to prying eyes and lingered beneath the lamp standard that stood in the middle of the cobbles. It seemed to the watching girl that he was talking to himself, for every now and again he threw out an arm in expostulation or beat himself on the breast in anguish. Embarrassed to be spying on him, she drew back into the window embrasure and after a while he pulled himself together before going inside. When Mhairi heard his front door close, she went to bed where she lay awake for a long time

– wondering what was preying on the mind of Henry's annoying brother.

Laurence didn't know why he'd started the game really unless it was to annoy Henry, but teasing Mhairi amused him and went out of his way to think of ways to discomfit her.

It was almost too easy. She blushed readily and he felt he'd scored a victory when he saw the tide of pink flooding up her neck and into her cheeks. By concentrating his mind, he found he could make her so conscious of him that she would suddenly blush without a word being spoken. Sitting at the table in the flat he sometimes lifted his eyes unexpectedly and caught her unawares. Then he would deliberately make his gaze langourous and let it linger over her almost lovingly until he reduced her to such a state of nervousness that she dropped spoons and clattered the china in the sink. The edges of all the Nairns' plates became chipped and Brabazon could not understand why Mhairi had become so careless.

Then, when he had almost brought her to the verge of tears, he would switch off his gaze and ignore her – sometimes keeping up the pretence that she was not there for days at a time. But she could never relax unless Laurence was out of the house, or better still out of the yard and the brewery.

She wanted to tell Henry about the disquieting effect his brother was having on her and when they were out walking one cold Sunday, she broached the subject by saying, 'I don't think your Laurence likes me.'

'Don't worry about him. He had an unhappy love affair with some girl or other and it's made him angry. We'll just have to let him come round on his own. He will – in time. Ignore him. Anyway the rest of us like you very much.'

Being complimented by Henry still made her uncomfortable and Mhairi sounded flustered as she said, 'And I like all of you – very much.'

Henry looked at her with his trusting eyes expressive, 'Do you really?' he asked. It was the opportunity he had been seeking for so long, but she stiffened and he decided against speaking out. Why was she so guarded with him, still, in spite of the weeks they'd been walking out together? He knew he had won her confidence. Why was he not able to tell her of his love for her? What warned him against speaking?

Mhairi looked shyly at him when she began talking again. 'I'm fond of you all – your mother and your poor father, and especially you. The Nairns have been so kind to me. You can't imagine how desperate I was when your mother found me in the brewery that night.'

'It was lucky for us that she did. Nursing Father and running the brewery at the same time was killing her. You've been like a daughter to her.'

Mhairi's eyes were yearning as she looked up at him, 'Really?'

'Yes, really. She thinks a great deal of you – and I can tell Father does too, by the way he looks at you.'

Then she remembered again how Laurence looked at her and a shiver that she could not explain went down her spine. They were almost at the bandstand where a military band from Leith Fort, all dressed in scarlet and gold uniforms, was playing briskly. As they listened to the music, Henry suddenly took Mhairi's hand and she did not freeze against him.

Encouraged by this he started talking urgently in a very solemn voice. 'Mhairi. Perhaps one day we could think about something special between us . . .' He was having trouble saying what he meant.

She let him keep her hand in his and glanced up obliquely. Tendrils of golden hair had escaped from the cheap little bonnet she wore and blew around her cheeks, making her very pretty and childishly appealing. She looked younger than her real age.

'Something special?' she asked. 'But we're such good friends, Henry, why not let's keep it at that.'

He would not be deflected now, 'I mean perhaps we could become – betrothed.'

'I hadn't thought about marrying; I'm not ready for that yet.' She whispered.

He was quick to reassure her, 'That's all right. I won't be able to marry either for a long time but we could be promised to each other. There's no one else in the world I want to marry except you Mhairi.'

The music was still playing but neither of them heard it. Henry was overwhelmed with love, but Mhairi felt an unaccountable panic rise in her. She almost turned on her heel to run away. The only thing that stopped her was that she did not want to hurt his feelings, for he was so good and kind. She respected him and was fond of him, but that was not love. That was not what made people marry each other. She glanced at the other couples near the bandstand and saw them exchanging glances as they swayed to the music. They looked at each other in that strange way as if they were sharing a secret.

'I don't think I'm ready to marry yet,' she repeated firmly.

Henry was anxious to reassure her, 'I understand but when you are, I want you to remember today. I'm not going to rush you. One day you'll be ready and I'll be waiting for you – no matter how long it takes.'

She wanted to weep. He was so kind. 'Oh Henry I'm fond of you, *really* fond of you, but I'm not in love and when I marry I'd really like it to be because I am. Do you understand?'

'You don't love anybody else?' he asked.

'Of course not. I feel that my life's only just starting in a way. You're a wonderful person and I like you very much, but that's not enough,' she said in a gentle voice.

'I'll make you love me,' said Henry with resolution, 'Consider yourself spoken for Miss Mhairi McKay.'

As he took her arm and led her off across the grass, the band was playing 'Drink To Me Only With Thine Eyes'.

1897

Illness, death and childbirth in any home affected all the inhabitants of Perseverance Place. These were events which set up a strange sensitivity within the building, as if a breeze were agitating one branch of a tree and causing every other limb to bend and shiver.

The happenings that affected the women most acutely were pregnancy and childbirth. At first, when a pregnancy was new, a strange euphoria filled them but as the expected day of delivery drew near, a primitive tension gripped old and young in much the same way as a flock of ewes are visibly affected by one of their number going into labour. They would grow febrile and excited in anticipation, as if they were priestesses in some ancient fertility ritual.

It was childless Minna Meirstein who first sensed that Tom Lambert's wife Irene was carrying another baby. In the past Irene had given birth to three children, but all of them had died and her neighbours had thought she was past child-bearing age. Now she looked drawn and careworn as she trudged up and down the stairs.

'She's carrying. I can tell by the look of her. It's in her face, around her eyes,' said Minna one morning to Nellie Warre, gesturing towards Lambert's wife as she carried a basket of dirty clothes across the courtyard on her way to the communal 'steamie', the wash-house two streets away.

Nellie shrugged, 'She may be, but she'd no' tell anybody would she? I don't think I've done more than pass the time of day with her for years.' Irene Lambert kept herself distant from the others, never lingering in the yard on sunny evenings, gossiping and drinking cups of tea; she never helped out when anyone was ill; never opened her door to a caller; never borrowed or lent cups of sugar

231

or other necessities that had been 'forgotten' – another way of saying not bought because of some current shortage of money.

'Poor soul,' said Minna watching the gaunt figure disappearing into the narrow entry to the Kirkgate, 'She has a hard time of it with that brute of a man.'

No one liked Lambert who was now working as a dock labourer and drank his wages every Friday night. It was a mystery why Irene stayed with him or how she managed to run a household with the few coins he threw her way.

'How far gone do you think she is?' Nellie asked, for Minna was often consulted in preference to a doctor because of her unusually acute powers of divination.

'Hmm, I'd say a good five months, but she's tall and she carries it vell. It might be even further on. She's not strong though and she'll not have an easy time. You vait and see.'

'I wish she'd be more friendly. Then we might be able to help her,' sighed Nellie.

Minna shrugged expressively saying, 'There's aye folk that vant to keep their doors closed against their neighbours. They've usually something to hide. Don't vorry about it. She's like that with everybody – not just her neighbours in the Place.'

The word 'neighbours' steered the conversation off in a different direction. Minna was angry about the row that always came up through her floorboards on Saturday nights when the Cairns family returned home after roistering in the pubs.

'Did you hear them last week? Singing and fighting and kicking up such a row that my Abe couldn't say his prayers. They've no idea that Saturday's a holy day for us.'

'They don't think much of Sundays either,' said Nellie. 'They'd a crowd of folk in on Sunday night when you were out. Somebody was trying to play the accordion. It was awful. I worried for poor Mr Nairn – and him so musical!'

They nodded their heads in disapproving unison, looking into each other's eyes until Minna said, 'He's not long to go, poor soul.'

'I know. Mrs Nairn's fair distracted. But that wee lassie's a big help to her. She's an angel of mercy.' Nellie was always in and out of the Nairns' flat and admired the way Mhairi coped with the increased demands of Duncan's incapacity.

Minna pursed her lips, 'I vonder if Henry'll marry that lassie. It vould be the best thing he could do and best for her as vell.'

'Folk don't always want what's best for them,' said Nellie sagely.

What the two old sages didn't know, as they set the world to rights, was that Mhairi was in the Nairns' flat above their heads stirring a pot of custard over the fire and thinking about a letter she'd received that morning. It crackled stiffly in the pocket of her apron and every now and again, she laid down her wooden spoon to re-read it. Each reading only made her more unhappy. The custard took a long time to cook because it must not boil and she wanted it to be creamy. Duncan could no longer swallow anything solid, even the tiniest grain made him choke.

When she judged it done, she spooned some into a china bowl, poured cream around it so that it looked like a floating island and carried the bowl to the next room where the patient lay. His face was ghastly, the closed sunken eyes making it look like a skull. Every time she came upon him asleep, Mhairi's heart missed a beat for she feared that he was dead. Yet common sense told her it would be best if he could only slip away quietly. But though his mind wanted his torment to end, his body was fighting against death.

When she set the steaming bowl down by his bedside he opened his eyes and she saw a thousand questions in them.

'It's a fine day and Mrs Nairn's in the brewery. I saw her out giving orders to the dray men about half an hour ago. Here's your custard. Let me help you up.' Mhairi had grown into the habit of maintaining a running commentary for Duncan and did so whilst propping his emaciated frame against the pillows and tucking a napkin under his chin. She often told him things she talked about with no one else – not even Happy. She'd told him about Calum, describing how his bonny hair clung to his head like a fairy's cap and how he used to grab for her face with his wee hands as if he wanted to pat her cheeks. She knew he listened and understood what she said, though he could make no replies.

'I'd a letter from home this morning. I write every now and again and send a postal order for Calum when I can. This letter's from my friend Chrissie. She's getting married to a laddie up there and they're to have a wee croft like ours. She wrote to tell me my family's gone away. The landlord's taken back the croft. God knows what'll happen to them.'

Tears slipped down her cheeks as she talked and Duncan's eyes searched her face with sympathy. She knew he was longing to offer her comfort and his understanding gave some solace to her pain.

After the sick man was fed, given his pills and settled down to sleep for a few hours, Mhairi had the afternoon to herself. Outside a wintry sun was shining, making her long for the fresh air. Pulling on her shawl, she went out for a stroll in the churchyard. It was close enough for her to be able to get back to Duncan quickly, but it gave an illusion of the country with its spread of grass and clusters of trees. Even better, its atmosphere of gentle melancholy suited her mood.

She sat facing the church on one of the table-top tombstones, and scratched at the velvety moss that spread like a cushion on the surface of the stone. The letter was still in her pocket and after a little while she took it out, though she knew every word by heart . . .

'They were all greeting when they left. Your wee Calum

was brave, like a little soldier. He helped your mother to load the cart. He's a braw bairn, you would be proud of him if you could see him. He's grown quite tall and his hair's a bonny colour, just like yours. His eyes are such a lovely shade of blue. There's nothing of Stewart in his face, but he's the same shape. Folk aye say Stewart's a grand figure of a man so you should be pleased about that too.'

Chrissie also wrote that the evicted McKay family had gone to America. 'They've sailed for New York where your uncle Cathal's working,' said the letter.

New York! thought Mhairi in horror. From her reading of Duncan's newspapers she had a picture of it as a huge and sinful city, even bigger than Edinburgh. She doubted if her parents could cope with it. She folded her hands and sent up a silent prayer for their safety to the God whom she was sure hovered somewhere above the spire of the church.

As her eyes were closed, Mhairi's memories for once flowed unchecked. With an ache she remembered what it felt like to hold Calum in her arms. In her nostrils she could smell again the milky, sweet scent he had after she fed him; most vividly of all, her last sight of him came back. He was held up in her mother's arms with his little baby arm upraised.

The sun warmed her face, but her thoughts chilled her heart. 'Oh God, I wish I could see my bairn. He'll grow up far away across the sea and never know anything about me. What'll happen to him in America?'

She was not angry at her parents for not telling her about their departure in advance. They probably had not been given any notice themselves. The agent would have turned up one morning and announced, 'Get out'. It had happened to other families round about before and Mhairi had witnessed the bewildered way they had to pile up their carts. All because Scotland did not want them.

Chrissie wrote that she knew no address for the McKays yet but if she got one, she would pass it on to

Mhairi. Chrissie's mother and Mhairi's were cousins. There was a good chance that they would keep in touch.

'Dear God, look after them but especially look after my bairn,' prayed Mhairi through her tears. But she was interrupted when footsteps came over the grass towards her. A hand fell on her shoulder and she looked up to see Laurence Nairn beside her.

'What's this? What's up with you?' he asked in a semi-jocular way, but she only gave a sob in reply and so his face sobered. This was serious.

He sat on the tombstone at her side and turned her head towards him by putting one hand on each of her cheeks. She did not fight against him and the tears rolled down unchecked. He wiped them away with gentle fingers saying, 'Come on, don't cry. It can't be that bad. What is it?'

Something stirred inside his heart at the sight of such misery. He'd thought he'd never be able to feel such sympathy for a woman again after Daisy. Without speaking again he leaned towards her and held her close, letting Mhairi rest her head against his shoulder. She lay there sobbing and it was a surprise to both of them that she still did not fight free of his arms.

Laurence began to feel strong and reliable. He liked holding her. After a while when Mhairi's grief began lessening in its intensity, he said softly, 'You poor wee thing. What's the matter?'

At that she seemed to collect herself, realised how much she'd relaxed with him and sat up, pushing back across the stone so that there was a distance between them. 'I've had bad news. I had a letter from home. It's about my family. They've had to go away. They've taken my baby with them.'

'Where have they gone to? You might be able to visit them.'

She looked bleak, 'They've gone to New York. I'll never see them again.'

Any consolation that he had intended to offer, any jollying assurances, were obviously out of place. 'That's

236

very sad,' he said and his tone of voice showed that he meant it.

She drew even further away from him and wiped her eyes. 'I'm sorry for crying like that. I'm just being silly I suppose. The same thing happened to my granny. She sent four sons and three daughters off to America and never saw any of them again. Lots of Highland families can tell the same story.'

'That can't help much,' he said, 'Come on, get up off that stone. It'll soon be dark and there'll be a frost tonight. You'll be frozen if you stay here much longer. I'll walk you back.'

When she stood beside him with her head drooping, Laurence longed to be able to comfort her, to bring back her pert and cheerful look. The desire to tease and upset her was completely gone now and she looked to him like a hurt child in need of protection. He could find no words to make Mhairi's sorrow any less however, and they walked along in silence.

In the Kirkgate, opposite Donaldson's, the butcher's shop, an old woman wearing a long black shawl and a battered bonnet was selling flowers from a big wicker basket. Her name was Ivy and she always smelt strongly of drink – rum was her preference. She saw the couple coming along the pavement towards her and held a bunch of violets towards Laurence. 'Buy some flowers for your pretty lassie,' she wheedled.

He paused and looked at the flowers. They were perfect for Mhairi because they were soft and velvety looking, so he took a bunch and paid Ivy a few coins for them. Then he turned and presented them to the girl at his side.

She stared at them in astonishment and pleasure. 'They're lovely, thank you,' she whispered.

'I'd do anything to stop you weeping,' said Laurence with a smile. When she smiled in return, he thought she looked like the goddess Ceres that was carved on the pediment of a fine building on the crossing facing Constitution Street. 'That's a relief. I wanted to make you happy again,' he said.

It was as if they had both shown weakness that afternoon and later regretted it. Mhairi went about her work as usual the next day, but deliberately avoided looking at Laurence. He ate his breakfast in a hurry and was out of the house before anyone else. During the following days, he tried to be away before she arrived for work in the morning and to stay out till after she'd gone back to Happy's at night. If they did meet by accident, they greeted each other gravely, like strangers. The teasing looks stopped altogether, much to Brabazon's relief for she had wondered what game her son was playing.

Though they tried to avoid each other, however, their paths kept crossing. Mhairi bumped into Laurence when she went out shopping; he saw her climbing the stairs in front of him, or caught sight of her white arms hanging clothes out to dry on the poles sticking from the kitchen window. He felt as if he were looking at something forbidden. Their acute awareness of each other charged the air with a strange, explosive force whenever they met. Minna picked it up and raised her head in surprise one day when she saw them brush past each other in the Kirkgate. For the first time it struck her that they made a fine-looking pair. She hoped that the same idea did not occur to them as well, for she was fond of Henry.

For his part Henry was unaware of the tension in the house whenever Mhairi and Laurence were there at the same time. He continued paying court to her; continued taking her for walks on Sundays; continued dreaming about her at night. He was blissfully in love and confident that she would fall in love with him, too, in time. He assured himself that it had to happen because they were so companionable, liked the same things, and understood each other.

One day he confided in his mother that he wanted to marry Mhairi. Brabazon was not surprised. 'What does she think about it?' she asked.

'She says she's not ready to marry yet – but I'll wait till she is. Besides I couldn't marry now when Father's so ill. Not till . . .' He hurried on. 'I don't mean anything

238

bad by that, Mother – I just mean it won't be possible for me to marry for several years. It's just as well that Mhairi's not ready yet, either.'

'Has she actually agreed to marry you?' Brabazon enquired. The way Mhairi behaved towards Henry was not like a woman in love. It was more the way she herself behaved towards Mark, her brother.

'Not exactly, but she hasn't said she won't. She's said she's fond of me and that's enough for me just now. I really love her, Mother. It's the most wonderful feeling in the world!'

Brabazon's voice was anxious as she tried to calm him down a little. 'You mustn't expect too much, my dear. You can't make people love you just because you love them. Perhaps all you feel is an infatuation. You've not known many girls after all.'

He was genuinely surprised at her reaction, 'But I thought you'd be pleased! I thought you liked Mhairi.'

'I'm very fond of her and so's your father, but I don't want you to be hurt Henry. She could meet someone else and fall in love. She's a young girl.' How could she explain her misgivings to him? She was sure he was reading more into his love affair than was actually there.

Because she, too, was aware of how Henry's love was growing, Mhairi made an effort to find friends outside the Place. She sought out girls of her own age and gathered with them in the evening, window-shopping and chatting, but she was never fully at ease in their company. The walks she'd had with Henry, going around the ancient parts of Leith, were far more to her taste.

Yet she denied herself the pleasure of his company for the sake of keeping him at arm's length while she thought about what to do. She had a major problem and it was his brother. Laurence's dark face; his smouldering brown eyes beneath the finely marked brows; the breadth of his shoulders; the physical emanation that came across from him: all were deeply disturbing to her.

Like someone entranced she found she was noticing how he used his hands; how he gestured with them; when she saw him lay his fingers on a book or a piece of cutlery, she felt her flesh tingle as if he were touching her. She remembered the way he had handed her the bunch of violets as if caressing her; her acute awareness of him made her feel guilty so she acted defensively, bristling if he came too close, turning away when he spoke to her.

Laurence was in as bad a state. The game he'd started with his brother's girl had suddenly become serious and he was ashamed. Now, to his surprise, he wanted to seek her out and hold her in his arms – but she fended him off as if he were dangerous.

She was not like Daisy, not as sensual and languid, and she wakened different feelings in him. Mhairi made him want to protect her, to hold her and soothe away her troubles. He had been deeply moved the afternoon he'd found her weeping over the letter in the churchyard. He'd never felt quite like that before.

Daisy had driven him almost mad with desire, but his passion for her had been a painful thing. He'd never really trusted her and the knowledge that she was fickle and incapable of genuine commitment had only fuelled his infatuation. Mhairi McKay was different.

'Girls like that are not for me!' he told himself angrily and turned away when he saw her coming up the street with a shopping basket on her arm. Why was it that he saw her wherever he went? He could not forget her and took to wandering along the darkened streets late at night. Henry was his brother and Mhairi was the only girl that Henry had ever taken any interest in. How could Laurence be sure that his own muddled feelings did not stem from his rivalry with Henry? Since childhood he had smarted every time his mother had patted his brother's cheek or praised him. 'I'm not jealous of him. It can't be that,' Laurence argued with himself.

Mhairi's late-night musings were also complicated. She did not know if Laurence loved her because she had heard enough rumours about his private life to be suspicious and knew it would be dangerous to fall in love with a man like him. It would be like giving herself up to danger, whereas marrying Henry would be taking refuge against the rigours of the outside world. Henry would never betray anyone he loved.

This burning desire she felt was new and disturbing to her. She dreamed about Laurence when she was asleep and thought about him when she was awake. He so filled her mind that when he did appear, she flew into a panic and ran away from him. She was acutely aware of the fact that they were avoiding each other and part of her hated him for upsetting her life so much. And why did he have to be Henry's brother! If there had to be a choice between hurting herself and hurting Henry, she would prefer to be the one who took the wound. She was genuinely fond of him.

The early part of the year was marked by an unusually bad spell of high winds and driving rain. It depressed Duncan who stared bleakly all day long at the window of his room. Rain ran down the glass as if it were being poured out of a bucket, and there was nothing else to see outside. In an effort to cheer him, Brabazon brought her account books from the brewery and pointed out with delight that the debts were at last all paid off.

'We're clear, my dear, we've done it!' she exalted, hugging his feeble body in her arms.

Then she took some money out of the cash box and ran to the pawn shop to recover his signet ring, and her own jewellery, by repaying the loan she'd had from Abe. But when she held Duncan's finger to replace the ring, she was shocked to find that the flesh had wasted away so much it slipped down over his knuckle and landed on the floor as soon as he moved his hand. She stitched it round with cotton and put it back, squeezing it firmly into place, but she did not say anything cheering like, 'We'll have to fatten you up.'' Both of them knew there was no chance of that now.

On another grey cold morning not long afterwards, Nellie Warre came running into the brewhouse calling out, 'Mrs Nairn, Mrs Nairn, there's a terrible noise coming out of Mrs Lambert's house. The door's locked and I canna get in. One of the laddies'll have to fetch her man or break the door doon.' Since the death of Alex, Nellie had reverted to calling Brabazon by her full title.

Laurence was despatched to the docks to find Tom Lambert while Henry ran back to the flats with his mother and Nellie. By this time the other women of the building were huddled on the landing, their faces white because the sounds that filled the stairway chilled the blood. The horrific moaning interspersed by howls of agony made them stare at each other in horror.

'She's in labour,' said old Happy.

'It's no easy having a bairn, but I've never heard anything as bad as that,' announced Nellie, 'I hope that man of hers hurries up.'

They rattled on the door and called to the woman inside to try and unlock it, but nothing happened except that the yells continued and they all shuddered at each cry. As the minutes ticked away the disquiet of those waiting increased. Mhairi, her nerves stretching to breaking point, put her hands over her ears to shut out the terrible sounds.

At last Laurence came running up the stairs with a key in his hand. He stuck it in the lock and turned it sharply saying over his shoulder, 'He wouldn't come. He's on a crew unloading a tea ship. He said he'd miss a day's wages if he left.''

Nellie snorted, 'He'd no be much help even if he was here anyway.'

In a body the women rushed into the flat, but they faltered in the hallway because of the terrible smell that assailed them. Irene Lambert's body was lying on the linoleum of the kitchen floor in a pool of blood and excrement. She was still alive because every now and again she doubled up in seizures of agony. But she was weakening rapidly for her moans were now more feeble, like the mewings of a sick cat.

Disregarding the filth, Brabazon and Nellie knelt on

each side of the writhing figure and tried to lift her up. Over her shoulder Brabazon called out, 'Go back to work Laurence! Henry fetch a midwife! We'll deal with this. Mhairi boil a big pan of water – and hurry!'

Then she turned back to Irene who was having her face cleaned by Nellie. When the dirt was wiped off, the saw that a livid bruise marked one cheek and there was dried blood caking her hair.

'Oh you poor soul, did you fall down?' asked Nellie.

'He knocked me down,' came a croaking whisper.

The helpers looked meaningfully at each other. Everyone in the building had heard Lambert hitting his wife when he was drunk, but this had been a brutal beating.

'Her baby's coming now,' Nellie told Brabazon, looking up over the slumped body, 'It's no' normal what she's going through. I've seen labour like this before. The bairn must be coming the wrong way up.'

She spoke gently to Irene, 'Was it like this with your other bairns?'

'Yes,' came the groaning reply, 'It's always like this – and they've always died.'

'We'll need a doctor. Tell somebody to fetch one,' whispered Brabazon.

But Irene managed to raise her head, 'No doctors,' she groaned.

Brabazon's face was determined as she told Mhairi, 'Take no heed. We need a doctor. I'll take care of the fee.'

They lifted the labouring woman onto the thin quilt of a rickety bed and Nellie lit a fire in the rusty grate, then looked round the comfortless room in despair. 'There's nothing here for a bairn, no cot, no clothes,' she said to Brabazon who was bending over Irene, trying to soothe her torments.

'She probably thought it would die,' Brabazon replied, anxious because this was no ordinary labour.

'How long has this been going on?' Nellie asked.

'It started last night when he knocked me down. It

wasn't so bad at first but now – oh God, I'm going to die, I'm going to die.'

Her voice rose to a frantic wail that was unbearable for the women at her side. They longed to be able to do something to stop such suffering and felt impotent.

'Help me, help me,' sobbed Irene and Nellie took one of her hands while Brabazon hung on to the other. They were still kneeling by her side when the door swung open and a stout woman bustled in. They knew her by sight and were overcome with relief because this was Mrs Millar, the Leith midwife. For years she had been delivering the town's babies and was talked of like a saint by women she had helped through travail. Because of her the numbers of deaths in childbirth had dropped significantly.

One look was enough for Mrs Millar. She did not waste time introducing herself but took off her coat, rolled up her sleeves and started examining Irene while saying over her shoulder, 'Is the doctor coming? This one's bad. Lie still dear and let me see what's going on here.'

When she was satisfied, she straightened up and told Brabazon, 'It's a breach birth and it's not moving. What happened to her face and head?' She wasn't pleased at the answer.

Three hours later, she'd literally hauled Irene Lambert's daughter into the world.

The doctor who'd arrived in time to help her cradled the baby in his arms. As he looked at it, he shook his head, 'This wee thing's going to have a struggle. It's barely breathing. Poor little scrap.' And he gestured at the cheerless surroundings of the mite's new home.

But the doctor had reckoned without the women of Perseverance Place. By the time he and the midwife had departed – having saved Irene Lambert, staunched her bleeding and eased her pain – Nellie, Brabazon and the others had all moved into the Lamberts' flat. They scrubbed it clean. They lit a fire in the newly shined grate and brought clean sheets for Irene's bed. They cooked soup, made tea for her and when everything was finished, they crowded around the cardboard shoe box on Nellie Warre's knee. Inside lay a miniature baby girl, fists curled under her cheek and eyes closed in peaceful sleep. 'The little thing doesnae look big enough to live, does she?' said Nellie.

Happy Anderson disagreed, 'She'll live. She fought hard for life that one, so she's a battler. She'll no give up easy.'

Nellie tucked cotton wool round the tiny body, dropped warm milk and brandy into the baby's mouth through a glass eye-dropper and laid the box in the warm hearth where the heat of the fire could keep it cosy. When she was finished, she said to Irene Lambert, 'Your bairn's a bonny wee thing. What are you going to call her?'

Everyone looked surprised at the reply. 'After Mrs Millar? What's her first name?' they asked each other but no one knew, and Brabazon sent Henry to find out.

When he came home he announced, 'She says her name's Sophia.'

Nellie laughed, 'Sophia Lambert! That's a grand name for a bairn as wee as this yin. Here's hoping she lives up to it.'

It was nearly midnight when Tom Lambert came lumbering up the stairs. He was drunk and his little pig-eyes glinted when he saw the crowd of people in his house. 'What the Hell's going on here?' he asked.

A babble of voices told him, 'You've got a daughter!' and the gathering parted to show his wife and baby enthroned in the clean bed.

He threw his cap on to a chair and said gruffly, 'You should have left her alone. You're a bunch of meddling bitches. Get out of here before I throw you all out on to the landing. Get out!'

Nellie, furious, put her fists on her hips as she accused him, 'She went into labour because you were knocking her about. We wanted her to tell the police about you, but she wouldn't. If it happens again though, I'll tell them myself. I'll get my son Gideon on to it. It's lucky you didn't kill her and the baby both!'

Lambert loomed over Nellie's tiny frame and seemed

to have to restrain himself from hitting her. In a tone of menace he hissed, 'I know what's lucky and what isn't lucky for me. Get the hell out of here and don't come back.'

When Brabazon woke next morning the mist and rain had disappeared, and there was a coating of silver frost shining like icing sugar on the walls around the courtyard. She smiled and turned towards Duncan saying, 'Thank heavens the skies have cleared at last.'

Then she heard the sounds of Mhairi entering the flat and went into the kitchen where the neatly dressed girl was stoking the fire in the grate while Laurence and Henry sat at the table morosely spooning food into their mouths. 'Wasn't that awful yesterday?' Mhairi asked Brabazon.

'I don't suppose we should have expected anything else from Lambert,' she answered.

'It's really depressed me,' went on Mhairi as she bustled about. 'And it's having a queer effect on Happy. She wouldn't get out of bed this morning although it's so nice and clear. I'm worried about her.'

Brabazon raised her finely arched eyebrows in surprise, 'Worried about Happy? She seemed all right yesterday. What's wrong?'

'She's gone strange. Like I said, the Lambert business shocked her.

'Is she sick?' asked Brabazon.

Mhairi shook her head, 'Not exactly. At least she hasn't complained, but it's awful to hear her talking.'

Brabazon turned away saying, 'My dear girl, she always sounds depressed. You must know that by now. It's just her way of stopping bad things really happening.'

When Mhairi shook her head tendrills of fair hair clustered around her cheeks, 'Oh, I know that. This is different. She's saying such queer things.'

'Maybe she's going senile,' offered Laurence shortly. Brabazon wondered if he was right. Happy must be well over eighty after all, although no one in Perseverance Place had ever been let into the secret of her actual age.

'What sort of things?' she asked.

Mhairi paused in her work and said, 'She keeps on telling me – 'When one comes in, another one goes out!' Then she starts crying and saying, "Oh I hope it's me!" I feel so sorry for the poor old thing.'

Brabazon's blood chilled and the hand holding her cup shook slightly, but she made her voice normal when she replied, 'That's all just talk. She's got hundreds of sayings like that. Haven't you heard "Laugh in the morning, weep before night"? This is only another one! Don't let her worry you.'

In spite of her words, however, she was filled with foreboding as she walked over the yard to her brewery. The morning no longer seemed fresh and crisp but so chilling that the cold permeated the very marrow of her bones.

It was supper time. The stairs of Perseverance Place smelled of the cooking coming from every flat. The lamps were all lit. People were coming home from work and settling down beside their firesides for an evening of peace and relaxation. The old building gave a groan and settled against the bitter cold that held all Leith in thrall.

Out in the Kirkgate the gas jets hissed and shuddered in the insistent wind. The houses looked grey and ghostly as they leaned over the roadway towards each other. Lights in shop windows glimmered weakly, as if disheartened for few people were out buying that evening.

Wrapped up in her long cloak, with its hood over her head, Brabazon Nairn came slipping out of the churchyard gate and ran along the pavement towards the pharmacy. In her hand she clutched a piece of paper bearing Dr Allen's latest prescription for Duncan. Soon she was on her way home carrying a package wrapped in white paper and neatly secured with red sealing wax. As she hurried through the shadows, she counted, 'There's thirty

here in this box and fifteen left. That makes forty-five.'
She always liked to have a fall-back supply for Duncan
was now taking six or more pills a day.

She swept past a drunkard on the street and did not
notice how his eyes popped at the sight of her. The way
she hurried over the burying ground and across the Perseverance Place yard at night in her cloak had started a
rumour that her part of Kirkgate was haunted. Now the
drunk, passed by a dark spectre that was muttering incan-
tations under its breath, crossed himself and swore to
become a teetotaller.

Brabazon did not pause. She was too absorbed in her
own thoughts as she turned into the alley and ran till she
reached the familiar stair leading to the front entrance of
the flats. A glance up at the windows of the tall building
showed her that Nellie's place was brightly lit – each
window blazing like a lighthouse in the dimness. The
Warres liked noise, light and merrymaking – and the
excitement of seeing Pat soon had temporarily swept away
their grief at Alex's death. Every day Nellie's talk was of
Pat and whether he would have changed.

Happy's flat on the floor below was lit as well and
Brabazon watched her shadow shuffling to and fro across
the window. Mhairi would be there too, baking and cleaning, trying to cheer up the old woman who was sinking
deeper and deeper into gloom with every day that passed.
It was as if a cloud hung over her and she looked more
bent, more grey and more mortal than ever before.

Minna's flat next door to Nellie's was in darkness for
she and Abe were still in their musty shop counting up
the day's takings, happily arguing with each other. Brabazon had seen them with their heads together when she
passed and she knew it would be some time before they
locked up and went home.

Ruthie's windows, below Minna's, were blazing even
more brightly than the Warres'. Having the gloomy
Happy living next door had not affected the Cairns, for
they were impervious to her gloom. Depression was a

negative state and none of the Cairns could stay that way for long.

In the Lambert's window on the same floor as Brabazon's a single candle flickered, guttering, as if it were threatened by draughts. Irene had not shown her face since the birth, but the listening neighbours knew the baby was alive because they sometimes heard it crying. It had a surprisingly loud voice for such a tiny scrap. Poor Irene Lambert, thought Brabazon with a shiver as she began to climb the stairs. That brute of a husband must have warned her against becoming friendly with the neighbours and, of course, she would be too terrified to disobey him.

The last window Brabazon looked at was her own, softly glowing, welcoming and safe. Yet the sight of it made her apprehensive. She did not allow herself to recognise why.

Later that night Brabazon paused on the threshold of her bedroom and listened to St Mary's clock striking midnight. The tolling was slow and she held her breath between each strike, willing the silence to go on and on and on, hoping time would stop forever.

When the twelfth peal rang out she shook herself and became brisk again. Duncan was awake and very restless, the trembling and twitching was more terrible than it had ever been. Frantically she tried to soothe him, holding him down in the bed in an effort to bring him some respite from the spasms of cramp.

His face was running with sweat and she wiped it carefully with a towel as she whispered, 'Would you like something to drink, my dear?'

With difficulty he nodded, and she held a cup to his mouth so that he could drink the sweet milky tea that he preferred. She'd poured an eggcup of brandy into it, hoping that the spirit would soothe him into sleep but time passed and there was no lessening of his writhing. Every now and again she rubbed at his emaciated limbs with loving hands, trying to bring elasticity back to the knotted muscles, but there was to be no relief for him.

Brabazon realised she would have to give him more pills.

'You've had so many already, but I'll try another two,' she told him and pretended not to notice the burning look he gave her.

'Bra-ba-zon.' Though the sounds were hardly more than grunts, she knew what he was saying.

'Bra-ba-zon.' It was more distinct this time.

She kept her eyes averted and shook her head. 'No, Duncan, not yet,' she whispered.

'Please' he managed, so clearly that it frightened her. For weeks she had been ignoring the fact that Duncan was in agony, that his illness was growing unbearable, that he wanted to be dead. Tonight however that knowledge could not be avoided.

A sob came from him and she saw that his eyes were as full as hers. With a shaking hand he tried to touch her face and she grasped his fingers, holding them to her mouth and kissing them one by one. 'When you made me promise I didn't think it would ever happen. Life without you will be empty. I've loved you for so long.'

They clung together for a long time and when she drew back she was struck by a new realisation of his daily suffering. It was as if her husband were projecting his experiences into her own mind as they lay side by side in the bed. When the church clock struck one she sighed, 'All right my dear, all right. I'll do it for you.'

Next door her sons were sleeping, Henry behind the curtains of the box bed and Laurence sprawled on the cot in the tiny cupboard as she tiptoed across the kitchen and then returned with a half full bottle of brandy. As silent as a ghost she carried it back to her own bedroom.

Duncan was watching the door for her return and his eyes were sharp as she counted out the pills.

'How many?' she asked him.

Slowly he held up his shaking hands with the fingers spread out. She watched silently as he held them up three times. 'Thirty?' she asked and he nodded, exhausted. To spare him more effort she said hurriedly, 'All right, my

250

dear. Thirty. There will be no mistake.' Her voice was shaking and still she was hoping for a last minute miracle, yet one by one she crunched the white tablets into the glass of brandy. Before she gave it to him, she asked, 'Are you sure?' but the answer was clear in his eyes.

The glass was held out to him like an offering and she said in a firm voice, 'I love you, Duncan.' He was beyond speaking and his hands could not hold the glass. She knew that her last act of love would be to help him drink the potion, and this she did as he took it sip by sip. Then she kissed him on the lips. They tasted sweet because of the brandy. With a sigh, she lay down beside him hugging him close. It was as if they were settling down to sleep as they had done on so many other nights. After she'd extinguished the lamp, darkness folded around them like the wings of an angel.

A man was pushing his way through thickets of bramble and whitethorn, the same bushes that clustered around the little croft house on the island. She could only see his outline and when she called out 'Henry' he came closer. But it was not Henry, it was Laurence and he advanced towards her holding out one hand. 'Wake up,' he said.

Mhairi felt confused and unhappy when she woke from her dream but she did not have long to ponder its meaning because someone was knocking on the door of Happy's flat. She grabbed a blanket as a covering and ran to open it.

Laurence Nairn stood on the threshold. His hair was tousled and he looked as if he had been weeping. He said urgently, 'Please go up to our flat, Mhairi. Mother needs your help. I'm going to fetch the doctor . . .' His face was so grim that she did not need to ask what had happened.

She nodded and told him, 'All right, I'm coming. I'll get my shoes. You go.'

In the Nairns' flat, Henry was kneeling as he raked the fireplace. When Mhairi entered, he looked towards her with eyes that were reddened. He had been crying too.

251

'Oh, Mhairi, Mother's in there,' he said nodding towards the bedroom door.

The girl found Brabazon kneeling by the bed with her head on the falling quilt. A glance was all that was needed to see that Duncan Nairn was dead. She tiptoed up to the kneeling woman and laid a hand on her shoulder, which felt as stiff and rigid, 'I'm so sorry,' she said softly.

'Help me,' came Brabazon's voice.

'Yes. Let me fetch you something to drink. I'll make tea. Will you take some whisky in it?'

'I don't care. Help me look after Duncan.' Brabazon's voice was strange.

'The doctor should see him first,' said Mhairi.

Brabazon's hands were gripping the bedcovers, 'I killed him, Mhairi,' she whispered.

'Oh no, no, don't say that,' the girl spoke soothingly, although she felt shock at the sight of Mrs Nairn on the verge of breaking down.

'I did. I have to tell someone. He pleaded with me. I don't care if they hang me for it. He was so tired of suffering!'

Mhairi knew that she was hearing the truth and wished the revelation had not been made to her. 'Don't talk about it. Don't tell anyone else,' she whispered urgently, kneeling down beside the bed and taking Brabazon's hand.

Brabazon laid her face down on the bedding and sobbed, 'I don't care what happens to me. I did it because I loved him so much.'

Tears were pouring from Mhairi's own eyes, but she was too much in awe of Brabazon to embrace her or try to soothe the agony with kisses and sympathy. She felt her powerlessness painfully. 'Shh, try to be calm. Let me fetch something for you to drink,' she said and ran next door for Henry.

He was standing at the window watching the rising sun streaking the sky with lines of brilliant light and turned towards her to say, 'I know. I know what she's saying.

We've got to stop her. I've made tea. It's on the table and the whisky's in the cupboard.'

Mhairi nodded, 'We mustn't let her tell anyone else,' she said.

'I know. She must be hysterical. Doctor Allen'll calm her. I've just seen him and Laurence coming into the courtyard. They'll be here in a second.'

The doctor's face was grim as he came into the flat. With a nod to the people in the kitchen, he bustled through to the bedroom where Brabazon was still keeping vigil over her husband's body. Laurence stood at the half-open door and listened to what was being said between his mother and Allen.

At the sight of the doctor, Brabazon started to sob, 'I killed him. I gave him thirty veronal tablets.' There was unrestrained hysteria in her voice.

The doctor sounded imperious. 'Be quiet. You did nothing of the sort. He died of pneumonia. It's obvious. I'm going to write the death certificate now.'

When Brabazon's voice rose to a wail, his own became stern. 'Stop this, Brabazon. Stop it at once. Are you trying to make me out to be a criminal? Do you want me to be struck off? I gave you that prescription for thirty pills. I shouldn't have given you so many. Think what you're saying woman. You're putting your sons through hell. If you did help Duncan to die, keep the knowledge to yourself. Let him rest in peace. For God's sake pull yourself together.'

His admonitions worked, for Brabazon became calmer and listened as he went on, 'What I know and what I don't know need go no further than this room. Duncan was my friend and so are you. I've always had the deepest respect for you both. Look, I'm writing the certificate now. As far as I'm concerned, his death was the result of the palsy. If it hadn't happened tonight, it would be tomorrow or the day after.' The doctor's voice was soothing.

Laurence heard the sound of ripping paper and Allen came out of the bedroom with a folded sheet which he

253

handed to Henry with the words, 'That's for the registrar. You take care of it. Keep your mother away from everybody – till she calms down. Watch who she talks to. I've given her a sedative and she should sleep now. She's in a state of collapse.'

He turned to Mhairi who was standing in a corner like a shadow. 'I hope you're hard of hearing and that you've a short memory,' he said sternly. She did not speak, but only nodded. Her heart was full and she wished she were still asleep and dreaming of the island.

Duncan Nairn's death cast a terrible pall over Perseverance Place. The brewery was closed for a week and every flat in the building, even the Lamberts', kept their window blinds pulled down until the funeral. A procession of sad faces filed up and down the stairs to pay their respects to the dead man's family, and so many tributes of white hellebores and evergreens arrived that they had to be piled up in the brewhouse until the day of the funeral. When Brabazon inspected these offerings the smell of them made her stomach heave.

She was calmer and talked no more of having killed her husband, but her sons were afraid that her composure would crack and allowed her to speak to no one alone. They stood one on each side of her during all interviews with friends and sympathisers like grim-faced Praetorian Guards.

On the morning of the funeral she dressed carefully and went early into the kitchen to tell her sons. 'You don't need to worry about me any longer. I won't do or say anything unwise. I'm sorry if I've worried you. But what I did will be on my conscience forever. The only thing I want you to understand is why I did it – it was because I loved him so much.'

Without speaking the boys both held out their arms towards her and she walked into their embrace.

Duncan's funeral was enormous because he was well-known and, in spite of his bankruptcy, well-respected in

Leith. People who had enjoyed his music in church, and savoured his beer in the bars, stood along the pavement to watch his cortege pass by. Men took off their hats and women lowered their heads as the coffin passed in front of them.

In the procession of mourners walked the dead man's brother-in-law Mark Logan with his eldest son, and a crowd of Duncan's ex-business associates, including Willie Ord the lawyer who looked so stricken and wiped his eyes so often that spectators imagined he had lost his closest friend.

Laurence and Henry walked side by side at the head of the procession. They were both concerned about who would take the six cords of the coffin while it was being lowered into the open grave. Henry would have one, of course, and Laurence would take the other. Their Uncle Mark, as a near relation had to be awarded the honour of being a cord-bearer as had his son Roderick, even though this cousin was almost a stranger to the Nairn boys because Mark's snobbish wife had not encouraged great intimacy with the family of a female brewer.

Henry thought, 'That's four cords taken care of but who should have the other two?' He was acutely conscious that his father would not want to be lowered into his grave by Willie Ord or any of the other fair-weather business friends who had abandoned him in his time of trouble. He whispered to Laurence, 'Gideon and Robert Warre should take two cords I think.' Laurence nodded in vigorous agreement. After all the Warres were more closely involved with the Nairns than any other family in Leith.

The cortege made its slow way to the churchyard where the Nairns owned a private family burial plot in a corner near that of the Logans. Duncan was to be interred behind ornate iron railings with his forebears and fellow Leithers all around him.

The weather was bitter. A keen wind carrying ice on its breath blew in from the Arctic and cut through the clothes of the most warmly wrapped up mourners. Mr

255

Templeton, the minister, visibly shivered as he quickly read the burial service. At his signal Laurence and Henry walked together to the lip of the yawning hole while the other cord-bearers stepped up behind them. Roderick Logan was bending down to lift his cord when a man pushed him roughly aside and took it from his hand.

The usurped cord-bearer looked in astonishment and annoyance at the stranger who turned out to be a tall and dashing figure in the scarlet uniform of a soldier. Only when Henry and Laurence straightened up after lowering their father's coffin into the grave did they realise that the sixth cord had not been taken by their cousin. The soldier in his place lifted his head to reveal a tanned face. He gazed solemnly at Laurence for a split second before he dropped his eyelid in a wink. It was Pat Warre, home from India.

The funeral meal was laid out in the brewhouse on scrubbed trestle tables. Mhairi helped Nellie Warre to hand out glasses of Perseverance ale and glasses of rum to the mourners. Brabazon, surrounded by a cluster of women, moved from group to group receiving condolences. Her brother followed on her heels like an anxious dog, saying over and over again, 'You'll have to start thinking what you'll do now, Brabazon. I'll come tomorrow and discuss things with you. Don't forget. Tomorrow.'

She nodded so distractedly that he was unsure she'd heard him so he caught hold of Henry and told him as well and at the same time asked, 'Who was that impudent fellow who took Roderick's cord? What a terrible thing to happen at a funeral!' Henry tried to look sympathetic as he explained although he had been secretly grateful that Pat had prevented young Logan playing an honourable part in Duncan's interment.

As Laurence handed Pat a glass of rum he wanted to laugh, clap his friend on the back, and banish the gloom that had oppressed him for so long. But even though they all knew that death was a release for Duncan, his family could not be seen to show relief at his funeral.

256

'Sorry about making a scene out there but I knew that your father wouldn't want that milksop taking a cord of his coffin,' Pat said.

Laurence's eyes danced, 'You're right. He never even liked Mark much. It's great to see you, Pat. How long are you home for?'

Pat shrugged, 'I haven't made up my mind if I'll sign on again. Let's meet later and talk about it. By the way, who's that yellow-haired lassie helping my mother? She's a bonny little piece.'

Laurence shot him a look and his voice became guarded. 'That's Mhairi. She looked after my father while he was so ill. Henry's keen on her.'

Pat stared knowingly at his friend and his eyes missed nothing, 'And you too? Poor old Henry.'

Happy Anderson was too feeble to attend Duncan's funeral. She'd crept down the stairs to shake Brabazon's hand in silence after the coffin was carried out, and then gone back to bed again. Mhairi was as concerned as ever about her.

'Don't worry, bairn,' Happy had told her. 'I'll just sleep. Oh dear, I didn't think it would be poor Mr Nairn who went before me. Didn't I tell you one goes out when one comes in?'

'You shouldn't talk like that,' protested Mhairi.

Happy shook her head, 'I'm all right. I'm old and ready to go. I'm awful tired. God bless you because you're a good lassie.'

These words were resounding in Mhairi's head as she hurried about making sure everyone had enough to drink. When she proffered her tray of glasses in Henry's direction, she noticed the vulnerable look in his eye as he glanced at her.

Behind him Laurence was talking animatedly to the red-uniformed soldier. They were looking at her too, she realised, and a flush crept up her cheeks. It was something that she was unable to control. Lowering her head, she tried to escape from their line of vision but the soldier's penetrating glance followed her. In a sudden rush of anger

257

and pride she raised her fair head and glared back. As she did so she saw Laurence laugh and she wanted to run across and pummel him with her fists. At that moment she hated him.

When all the mourners had gone home and the brew-house was cleaned up, Mhairi crossed the yard with the other helpers. Nellie and Ruthie who were talking about everything that had gone on and everyone who'd been at the funeral.

'By Jove your Pat's grown into a grand-looking man!' said Ruthie appreciatively. She had an eye for fine young fellows and Nellie showed a touch of alarm as she replied, 'Hasn't he though!' Her pride in Pat was difficult to conceal, however, and she went on, 'I was that pleased when they told me how he'd taken a cord. That fancy Logan laddie was fair put out.'

Ruthie snorted, 'Oh, your Pat'd make ten of him! If he wants to try sparring at the club tell him I'll be pleased to see him.'

'I'll tell him,' lied Nellie, for she had no intention of pushing Pat in Ruthie's direction.

Mhairi was only listening to their exchange with part of her mind. At Happy's door she paused and said, 'I hope she's all right. She was that funny when I left her.'

Ruthie's face became concerned, 'Old Happy? Poor soul, she's that upset about Mr Nairn. She was greeting this morning. I'll come in and have a word with her.'

Silence met them. There was not even a rustle or the sound of a breath in the room.

They looked at each other askance, 'Maybe she's asleep,' whispered Ruthie. But that which they secretly feared had happened. Happy had died in her sleep, curled up in bed like a baby, her hands folded under her withered old cheek.

As soon as Duncan's funeral was over Pat and Laurence slipped away for a drink and so missed the discovery of Happy Anderson's body. They did not leave the Place

together, but met by arrangement in the Kirkgate before
heading off for The Shore. Laurence had changed out of
his funeral suit but was wearing a band of black crepe
around his jacket sleeve as a sign of mourning. Before
they entered the first of the many bars they were to visit
that night, Pat held him back and slipped the band off
his arm. 'Take a little time off, friend. You can go back
to being a good son tomorrow,' he said with a grin.

They were walking from the second to the third hostelry
of the evening when they saw Gideon in his new uniform.
He was patrolling the street in company with another,
older police officer.

'Hey peeler, I'm drunk. Come and arrest me,' yelled
Pat who by this time was well past sobriety.

Gideon pretended not to notice his raucous brother and
fixed his eyes at a point in the sky as he strode past with
a measured gait.

'Look at him. The wee bugger's the champion lifesaver
in Leith,' Pat said nudging Laurence. 'My mother was
telling me that he's aye jumping into the docks to fish out
laddies.' Gideon's face was thunderous by this time and
all the idlers on the waterside watched the scene with
interest.

'How many have you saved?' Pat asked his brother,
running up alongside him.

'Seven,' said Gideon gruffly.

Pat threw himself around in an outburst of hilarity.
'Hear that?' he demanded of the crowd, 'Enough to make
the polis realise that though he's wee he's tough. How
much did you pay them to jump in? Come on, Gid, how
much? If I jump in, what will you give me?'

Gideon's face was scarlet and he snapped, 'If you
jumped in I'd bloody well let you drown.'

Pat and Laurence went on their way with Pat still
laughing. Laurence could see from Gideon's face that
what Pat had said was true, but he felt slightly ashamed
at aiding and abetting in the goading of Pat's good-natured and likeable brother.

As the night wore on they found themselves in the bar

where they'd met Bertha – and Daisy. It hadn't changed at all and as Laurence gazed around, he wished that a blink of the eye would turn back time and bring her to his side again – thin as a willow wand, unreadable . . . Had she ever really loved him or was it just tart's talk? He did not know.

'Do you remember the first night we came here? The night you picked up that big, black-haired woman called Bertha,' he asked a reeling Pat.

His friend clutched his arm and slurred, 'Aw, she was great! There's good tunes played on old fiddles, believe me. I remember that night fine. When I think of it my cock stands up like a flag staff. You went off with the kid, didn't you?'

'Yes, Daisy . . .'

'Daisy. Was that her name?' Pat was laughing and bending over to stare into Laurence's face, 'Hey, what happened with Daisy? You're looking pretty glum.'

Laurence had not talked to anyone about his devastating love affair. Now, with his tongue loosened by drink, he poured it all out to Pat. When he had finished his friend said, 'And she pushed off? You've not heard any more from her?'

'No, nothing.'

'She'll be in some London toff's bed right now. Forget her! She sounds like bad news. You'd be better off with the blonde one in the Place. That's a neat wee armful. Haven't you tried her yet? They're all the same between the sheets you know – even the black ones.'

Laurence shook his head. In a strange way he did not want to discuss Mhairi like that with Pat. 'She's Henry's girl. I don't think she likes me, she's always short enough anyway.'

Pat was slurping his beer and he looked up to ask, 'Do you like her?'

'I suppose I do in a way, she has a funny effect on me. Makes me want to look after her.'

When an expression of horror Pat sat back and banged his glass on the table. 'Watch it! Don't let it happen or

260

you're done for. When they get you like that, you're hooked. Fight it, fight it! Have another drink.'

Laurence did not remember reaching home that night and woke up next morning fully dressed and lying on top of his bed. His clothes smelt of vomit, his tongue felt like sandpaper and his head throbbed. The slightest sound was agony to him but he managed to drag himself over to the stables where he lay down in the hayshed and slept till afternoon. When he woke up and went home for tea, he discovered that Perseverance Place was plunged into double mourning. On the following day there was to be yet another funeral.

'In this part of the world we never do anything by halves,' he groaned.

Happy, it was revealed, had left everything she possessed – about fifty pounds, her clothes and her sticks of furniture – to Mhairi. Her flat reverted to the brewery, but Brabazon told the girl that there was no need to worry about leaving.

'You can stay as long as you like. You can take on Mrs Anderson's tenancy if you want to,' she said, for she was deeply grateful to Mhairi for all her care of Duncan.

'You've a fair dowry now, lass,' said Ruthie when news of the inheritance got out, 'You'll be moving in a husband soon. Make sure you pick one that'll look after you properly.'

Mhairi didn't smile though she knew that Ruthie was joking. Remarks about who she should marry were not something she could find funny at that stage in her life. She was very confused.

Solemnly she replied, 'I don't think I'll be getting married yet. I've had a letter from my family in New York and I was thinking of going there to see them. They say I could get work easily enough.'

It was true. A letter, written in a stranger's hand, had arrived the day after Happy's death. It bore a New York address – a street with a big number – and was short and stilted: 'We are in New York. We are all well but missing home something sore. Try to come over as soon as you

261

can. Calum is growing big and speaks with an American accent.'

Ruthie spread the news of Mhairi's intention to go to America through the flats and in the evening Henry came knocking at her door. 'Can I come in, Mhairi? I'd like to speak to you,' he said politely.

'Please do,' she said.

He looked very solemn as he sat in the chair by the fire. 'I heard about your inheritance. Happy was very fond of you. And Ruthie says you're going to use it for the fare to America.'

'I said I might. I haven't made up my mind. In a way I wish Happy hadn't left me the money. It's all so sudden. I have to think, you see. Your mother's been kind, she says I can stay until I've decided what to do.'

'I know it's not a good time to talk like this but I don't want you to go away.'

Mhairi made a gesture of confusion, a wide spread of both arms and a raising of her shoulders. 'Oh, it's awful having enough money to make the choice. It's such a responsibility.'

He glanced sharply at her, 'Would you prefer to be tied down?'

'I don't know. Sometimes I think I'll sell everything and go off to see my bairn again. Then again, maybe Happy wouldn't like the idea of me selling her things to go to America. I wish I could ask her. I think she left them to me to keep me here really.'

Henry sounded urgent, 'I wouldn't like the idea either. Don't do anything in a hurry Mhairi, that's always a mistake. Wait till the summer. In the meantime, my mother could do with your help. She's going to be in a bad way when the reality of losing Father hits her. She's still stunned at the moment.'

Mhairi nodded. She had not been going regularly to the flat since Duncan died, because she was afraid Brabazon would feel obliged to pay her. But every now and again, she did slip down and tidy up for the Nairns. 'I'm not going to do anything without thinking, Henry,' she said,

'I've been very happy here in the Place. I'm not going to hurry away.'

'I'm glad,' he said, 'I'm not going to bother you but don't forget what I said to you. I really do want to marry you – now more than ever. The brewery's settling down well and it can support a wife for me.'

Mhairi rose in panic and started clattering the dishes on the table, but he stood up and put a hand on hers. 'Please sit down and listen. You don't have to say you'll marry me now. I'll wait for years if necessary, but I want you to know that I love you.'

She looked at him with eyes full of confusion and said, 'I'm very fond of you Henry, I really am but I don't think I'm ready to be married yet. I'm still afraid of men I think.' It was not strictly true but it sounded convincing, and she had no wish to hurt him.

He flushed, 'I wouldn't ever hurt you . . . You're much better than you were. When we first me you wouldn't even hold my arm. If I touched your hand like I'm touching it now, you almost jumped out of your skin.' He was stumbling over his words.

She could only shake her head, 'Don't press me please, Henry, or you'll drive me away to America.'

'In that case, I'll wait till you are ready. I don't care how long it takes.'

The desolation that gripped Brabazon after Duncan's burial frightened her family and friends. She had behaved with great control and dignity during the funeral ceremonies, but after everything was over and life was expected to return to normal, she seemed to collapse. She sat in her darkened bedroom refusing to eat, to go out or receive anyone. When Mark Logan had arrived as promised to discuss Brabazon's plans for the future, he'd got nowhere with his sister.

Her sons knocked on her door and asked questions about the work of the brewery but she barely lifted her tear-stained face from her hands to answer them. United in their concern, they stood together in the kitchen and Henry said, 'What are we going to do?'

Laurence shrugged, 'We'll have to run the place ourselves I expect.'

Dr Allen was called again and he told the brothers to ask the girl who'd looked after their father if she would come back and take care of Brabazon for a little while. 'I don't think your mother's going to be like this for very long but she is on the verge of a collapse at the moment and if she's not helped, I can't answer for the consequences. She mustn't be left alone to brood and she must be fed properly. It's up to you lads to organise that.'

They were genuinely shocked at hearing such things about their mother who had always seemed so strong and invulnerable. She had been the one who carried the responsibility of the brewery and the family, and the suggestion that she was cracking under the strain shook them both.

'Are you going to speak to Mhairi or will I?' Henry asked Laurence when he came back into the flat after showing the doctor downstairs. Laurence was making an attempt to wash dishes and he did not turn his head round but said gruffly, 'Oh, you do it. She's your friend, not mine.'

Henry was pleased at being given this reponsibility. He told Mhairi the story of Brabazon's strange behaviour and the doctor's suggestion.

The invitation was like a new door opening in her life. Mhairi had been genuinely cast down because of her inability to decide what to do and had been waiting for some sign or guidance. On that night it had suddenly come. Brabazon needed her. America would have to wait for a little while longer.

Gentle care and love gradually helped Brabazon Nairn's broken heart to mend. By the time summer came again she was better, though pale and thin. Mhairi looked after the flat and did the cooking, while Nellie and Minna

264

visited Brabazon daily. Their concern showed her that she had really been accepted into the heart of Perseverance Place.

'When I lost my Alex I thought I'd never be able to smile again,' Nellie told her one day, 'but you go on. You never forget but you start living again. And you're still a young woman,' she encouraged, 'with a lot of life to live.'

Four months after Duncan's death Brabazon went back to the brewery for the first time. Her sons showed her around with pride and listened to her astonished congratulations, 'My word, how well you've done! I'm so proud of you . . .' She meant she was proud of them both, but unfortunately she was looking at Henry when she spoke and did not notice how Laurence's face fell.

She examined the account books and noticed that though production and sales had dropped back a little, the position was recoverable. It was time for her to return to work.

Mark Logan and Willie Ord appeared in her office together during her first week back. They wore smiles on their faces, but she could see that her brother was also deeply concerned for her. They had always been fond of each other and though they often did not meet for many months, their affection was unshaken.

Ord made sympathetic noises. 'You're looking tired, Mrs Nairn. You're needing a change. Why not take a trip to the South of France? Menton is the place to go they say.'

She smiled, almost laughing in disbelief at the very idea. 'Not at the moment. Leith will have to do. I've a lot of work to catch up with – though my sons did very well when I was sick,' she added hurriedly because Henry was listening. As she spoke, she eyed Ord speculatively, wondering what he was up to.

It was the same old story of course. He was as tenacious as a bull terrier. 'If you sold Perseverance you'd have more than enough to live comfortably on. You could spend every winter at Menton.'

She put an innocent look on her face. 'Has the price gone up so much?'

'Oh yes, you're a good going concern now – thanks to all your work. It's time you reaped some benefit from it though. I was just saying as much to your brother as we were coming across the yard.'

'And what about my sons? They've been running the brewery recently and they've done very well. They've proved their ability to carry it on.'

'They're young. They'll find other work. I'll speak to my friends. Henry could go into your brother's timber-yard and Calder, the wine importer is looking for a likely fellow. Your other laddie would fit his bill.'

'You've been working on this, haven't you? But I've slaved here for a long time now and I'm not going to throw it all away. My husband's dead and his name is clear. He didn't die in debt, thank God. But this brewery belonged to his family and now it belongs to his sons. It's not up to me to sell it.'

As she spoke she turned and looked at Henry standing silently behind her chair. She could see from his face that he agreed with her. She turned back and said firmly, 'It's not for sale. Not now and not in the future. Please stop bothering me.'

She realised in a sudden flash that if she were to go on living without Duncan, she needed an aim in life. Part of her despair had been that there was no longer a battle to fight. The brewery was thriving and part of her crusade had been won. There was still a remaining goal, however; she had to buy back Brewery House.

When Ord and Mark were leaving she went out into the courtyard with them and gazed around as if seeing her surroundings for the first time. A trickle of smoke rose from the brewhouse chimney and the sun shone on the towering bulk of the flats, as well as on the facade of the elegant house on the other side of the yard. Its windows gleamed, its white paintwork sparkled. Its present owners were looking after it well.

Mark noticed where she was looking. It was as if he

were able to read her mind. Twisting the tip of his walking stick into a gap between the rounded cobbles of the yard he said, 'I could find you a pretty cottage in the country.'

'Oh my dear, I wouldn't like that. I'd miss all my neighbours! This is my place now.'

He ignored that. "Melia and I've a fine garden and there's a view of the Pentland Hills from our drawing-room window. Her health has been so much better since we moved out of Leith.'

Brabazon privately thought that Amelia was a spoilt hypochondriac but she smiled and said, 'I'm glad. You're very kind Mark, but I don't want to leave Leith. Living in the country would make me ill.'

Her brother gave up. He knew he had never had any success when arguing with Brabazon and he was relieved to see her fighting back again, because her collapse after Duncan's death had worried him deeply. If her recovery depended on her hanging on to her brewery, he did not really mind.

A letter from Joshua arrived a short time later. Brabazon guessed that Mark had been writing to their father and opened the envelope with misgivings, not wanting to read more sensible urgings to sell up and retire. She was in for a surprise, however.

'If you want to keep your brewery, you are perfectly right. I have never held with the theory that women should be objects of decoration alone. I've known some formidable ladies in my time and always preferred them to the home-loving invalids who spend their time swooning on sofas. If your mother had shown more grit, I'd probably still be living in Leith.'

It was as if he were speaking to her, and his words gave her both strength and resolution.

Henry continued to take Mhairi out walking on Sunday afternoons and sometimes, to her embarrassment, he tried to peck her cheek in the semi-darkness of the stairway.

'Can't I come in and sit with you for a little while? I promise I'll not upset you,' he asked one evening.

In Mhairi's Highland society, when a young man 'sat in' with a girl at her own home, it was recognised that their intentions were serious. She shook her head, 'I'm sorry. I've things to do. I must do my mending and packing.'

His face was downcast, 'You mean you're really intending to leave? I love you so much, Mhairi. Why won't you stay here and marry me?'

Tears swam in her blue eyes as she looked at him, 'I like you very, very much. You're the only really close friend I've had since I last saw Chrissie. But I've already told you my feelings about marriage at the moment. And now that your mother's so much better it's time for me to move.'

'But why to America? It's so far away. Some man over there will marry you and we'll never see each other again. I'll have lost you.' His voice was anguished. 'You'll never come back.' She took his hand, 'Don't talk like that. It's my family: I want to see them again. I need to see Calum. I'll come back some day.'

She was not telling the truth and she knew it. She was running away from Perseverance Place not because of Calum, but because of the confusion it caused her living there. The dreams of her baby were fading a little and the thought of the voyage to New York made her quake with fear, but she was determined to brave it for she must escape the pain that Laurence Nairn was causing her.

With every day that passed she was more aware of him and more afraid of him. What kind of power did he have over her that he disturbed her mind waking or sleeping? The terrible thing was that he seemed to dislike her now and had not again shown the unexpected gentleness of the day he'd given her flowers.

Henry interrupted her thoughts by extending both hands in a gesture of despair, 'I'm old enough to marry. I'm twenty-two and I want to marry you. You're old enough as well.'

She was eighteen, so what he said was true. Many of the lassies in Leith were mothers by her age. Then, with a shock, she realised, *But I am a mother*, and her face went stiff. 'I'm going to America, Henry,' she said, 'I've bought my steamship ticket. I sail from Liverpool next month.' She had not intended telling him yet. In fact she hoped to slip away without the pain of any farewells.

It hurt her to hear Henry pleading for something she was beginning to realise would never happen.

When he'd left in distress, she started to weep because she was broken-hearted at having to leave the place and the people she loved so much. She walked over to a paper calendar hanging on the wall and began to count the days till sailing date. The realisation of how little time she had left in the Place made her look round at her surroundings with fondness. The furniture Happy had left her was polished and shining; a cushion in the chair showed the mark where she had been sitting before she'd gone out with Henry and a little tin clock ticked the precious time away on the mantleshelf. This was her home, the only place she'd ever felt safe and comfortable since leaving the Highlands. How miserable it made her to think that she was having to go away and leave it.

While Mhairi was musing, Pat Warre came hurtling downstairs from the top floor and rapped on the Nairn's door as he flew past it. Mhairi was startled by the sound of his running footsteps and went over to the window to see what was happening in the yard.

Pat, hands in pockets and cigarette in mouth, was lounging against the wall. He looked arrogant and dissatisfied with life and she realised that she did not like him. He was the only member of the Warre family whom she distrusted.

In a few seconds Laurence Nairn came out to join his friend and took a cigarette from Pat's packet. As he cupped his hands to shield the light of the match that Pat held out to him, an unruly lock of black hair flopped down over one eye and Mhairi's heart lurched. Then he smiled, pushed Pat slightly with one hand and they went off walking briskly towards the alley and the Kirkgate.

'Where are they going? What will they do? Who will they see?' The questions ran unchecked through the watching girl's head and she resented the strength of her own feelings. 'For heaven's sake I don't even like him!' she told herself.

In fact the pair were heading for the pubs and as he walked along Laurence suddenly felt depressed. He was not looking forward to another night's drinking, but Pat was as enthusiastic as ever. 'By God I've a thirst on me. I could do with a *bisti-wallah* following up behind with a skinful of beer,' he said laughing.

After a few months of it, Laurence had had more than enough of Pat's army Hindi, his talk of 'wogs' and 'chi chi bints'. His reminiscences of India were all of barrack-rooms or army beerhouses, whores or sullen servants. The country itself had made little impact on him except that he remembered it as hot. 'You don't think about what a place looks like when it's so stinking hot that your clothes stick to you as if you'd peed yourself,' Pat always said with a laugh when Laurence asked for more interesting descriptions of India's landscape and curiosities.

Laurence felt his greatest surge of annoyance when Pat littered his conversation with Indian words, often saying 'charpoy', 'pani' and 'dhobi' for bed, water and washing. He also talked about old comrades who were only confusing names to Laurence and, when really drunk, always returned to his favourite subject – the brutalities inflicted on prisoners by Afghani warriors.

'They cut off a man's prick and his balls, and stuff them in his mouth. When we caught one of them we did the same thing. You should have seen the blood!

Laurence could tell that Pat enjoyed the cruelty as much as the shock that he caused talking about it. All his old friend had wanted to do since coming home was live a life of riot. He slept most of the day after their nights out, but Laurence had to stagger into work next morning, with head aching and eyes blurred. He was growing weary

270

of dissipation but was determined not to show it, especially when his mother scolded him for the way he was behaving.

'I don't know what's come over you. You could be so different,' she said sadly, not realising that she was driving him on to further excesses.

'If Pat doesn't sign on again and go away soon, I'll kill myself,' he thought when he heard Pat's feet flying downstairs on the evening Mhairi watched from her window. He'd hoped that there'd be no passing knock at his door, but of course there was no chance of that. Not a night had passed without too much to drink; too many women; too many street skirmishes incited by Pat insulting someone in a bar. Pat needed a companion. He needed someone to talk at and show off to.

At first it had been like old times – but only at first, for Pat had changed and perhaps, Laurence thought, I've changed too. Despite all his roistering, deep inside him there was still the little hard kernel of sadness saying 'Daisy'.

His other confusion was more immediate. It was the yellow-haired girl in Happy's flat. He wished he could get Mhairi out of his mind but, like a sea-mist, she kept creeping back in, clouding his thinking.

Pat teased Laurence about Mhairi. 'Coup her one night. That's the way to treat women! They're all the same. They like it rough,' he advised.

'Not her. She's scared stiff of men. She's scared of everybody except Henry.'

Pat was coarser since he'd joined the army. He'd become hardened. Now he grinned into his beer and said, 'Women! That's just her come-on. Grab her one night on the stair and then you'll see. If you don't, your brother's going to get her. Maybe you'll be able to persuade him to share!' He gave a guffaw at the thought.

Something fastidious stirred inside Laurence and he changed the subject, standing up and asking, 'More beer?' He no longer wanted to discuss Mhairi, or any part of his life, with Pat. Their different experiences during their time

271

apart had driven an unbridgeable gap between them. When be brough back two full glasses, he asked, 'What're you going to do now, Pat? You've been at home a long time.'

'Yeah and my money's running out. My mother's getting tired of having me under her feet I think. When I first came back, I was going to look for a place in the docks because I'd thought about home so much when I was away, but now I'm here it seems tame. Leith's not what I thought it was. I'm tired of it already – the same old whores, even old Bertha's still here but she can't give me a stand any more; the same beer; the same faces. I've decided to sign on again. They're looking for men to go to South Africa. I'll go out and see how the Boers fight. It can't be worse than the Frontier. At least I'll keep my cock.'

Pat's departure a week later was a much less emotional affair than his first leaving. Even his mother sighed in relief as he swung off down the stairs. In the yard Laurence shook his friend's hand with a certain sadness, regretting not so much the departure of Pat as he was, but the loss of Pat as he had once been.

The person most relieved to see the back of him, however, was Gideon. All the time Pat had been home, he'd subjected his brother to a barrage of abuse, tried to pick fights with him, and had told everyone who would listen about Gideon paying little boys to jump into the dock and be rescued.

Gideon was patrolling the Kirkgate when his brother strode past with kitbag on his shoulder. Pat grinned, looked sceptically at the police uniform and said, 'Bye Shorty. When I come back maybe you'll be Chief Inspector of Leith Police!' His tone indicated how unlikely that seemed.

When Brabazon noticed how unhappy her eldest son was looking, she asked what was wrong and he told his mother that Mhairi was going away soon. She regarded him with pity. 'She'll maybe come back one day, my dear,' she said gently. He shook his head.

Laurence was standing by the window as they talked and turned quickly round to say 'She won't come back if she's any sense. What's here for her?'

Henry didn't say, 'There's me', but Brabazon could sense him thinking it. The realisation that Mhairi was really going away, made him withdraw into himself again and he spent more time than ever alone at the church organ. His mother's heart ached for him and she wondered if he would ever find happiness. He deserved it so much because he was a gentle, tender-hearted man. She did not blame Mhairi for refusing him, however, because she recognised that the girl was a romantic and she respected Mhairi for her honesty. Her behaviour towards the girl was as cordial and kind as ever.

The news that Mhairi was soon to go to New York went round the building like wildfire. Brabazon told Nellie who told Minna who told the whole of the Kirkgate. The neighbours gossiped about it among themselves and decided that she could not be allowed to sail away without a proper send off. 'Let's give her a party,' said Ruthie Cairns to Minna.

They planned it secretly for it was to be a surprise. A room in the caterer's at the end of Leith Walk was booked for the 5th of November, two nights before Mhairi was due to leave and a little collection was made for a present. It was decided that Henry would be the one to bring the unsuspecting girl to the celebration.

Laurence said nothing but privately decided that he would not go to the party. There was no point because he could tell by the way Mhairi looked at him that she did not like him. He made her feel uncomfortable. Yet he knew that when she left he would miss her. He'd miss the way her yellow head shone like a golden lamp in the dim courtyard on winter evenings; he'd miss the sound of her swift steps coming down the stairs to the Nairn flat in the morning.

He continued making his rounds of the bars; flirting

with the easy girls and going home with one or other of them whenever he chose. Yet there was a part of him always looking out for the Highland girl. His inner self rejoiced when he saw her. He observed her routine, learned her habits, watched her like a spy – although he scoffed at himself for the trouble he was taking. And still there was no real contact between them.

When the time drew near for Mhairi's party, Minna decided that it would be unfair for the guest of honour to turn up at it without a fine dress. Everyone else would be in their best and if she did not know what was happening, Mhairi would probably appear in her old working skirt and black woollen shawl. A hint had to be dropped. She sought the girl out and enquired, 'Have you packed all your boxes, lassie?'

Mhairi nodded. She was looking sad. 'Yes, I haven't much to pack.'

'Have you a bonny dress to vear?'

'I've got that pretty cotton one you gave me when I first came here, don't you remember?'

'I don't mean that kind of dress! Haven't you an evening gown?'

'Goodness I won't need one! I'm travelling steerage, Mrs Meirstein.'

'You never know,' said Minna mysteriously, 'A bonny lassie like you could catch the eye of a millionaire.'

That brought a smile to Mhairi's solemn face, 'Oh, I doubt it. Do you really think I'll need a fancy gown though?'

'I do and I've just the thing in the shop. I've kept the taffeta gown I showed you before. Come in and try it on.'

When Mhairi told Brabazon that Minna wanted her to take an evening gown to New York, Brabazon aided the conspiracy and said, 'I think she's probably right. You should at least look at it. You don't want to hurt her feelings.'

The emerald-green dress had been left in pawn by an actress with a touring company that went broke. Its enormous skirt folded in deep pleats from the tiny waist.

274

It had a low-cut bodice and very full puff sleeves. At the back was a huge bustle in the shape of a bow. Though slightly out of date by the standards of fashionable London, in Leith it looked exotic.

The waist was nipped in by strips of whalebone and closed with tiny hook and eye fasteners that were difficult to operate, but when Mhairi tried it on in front of Minna she found the dress fitted her perfectly. Her breasts were perched up high by the tight-fitting bodice and she gazed down into her own cleavage with apprehension, fearing that modesty would never permit her to appear in public like that.

Minna stood back with her hands up to her mouth and her eyes dancing, 'You're a beauty! I knew I vas right to keep that dress for you?'

'You don't think it's too – bare?' Mhairi asked spreading her hands over her breast.

'That's the best of it. You look like a queen,' protested Minna and turned to Abe who'd just come into the back of the shop. They stood side by side and gazed at Mhairi, so lost in admiration that they did not notice another face staring through the window.

Laurence had been hanging about in front of Donaldson's with his hands in his pockets and had seen Mhairi coming out into the Kirkgate. As she'd greeted acquaintances with her delightful smile, he'd wondered why she never dimpled like that at him. She slipped into the Meirsteins' shop, and curiosity kept him hanging about pretending an interest in their stock. When the vision in green stepped into his line of sight his jaw literally dropped. He blinked and looked harder. 'Unbelievable,' he said aloud.

He waited in the Kirkgate until she left the shop carrying a large parcel which he guessed was the green dress. The dusty window of Abe and Minna's shop was still glowing with gaslight that gilded the array of objects inside with an aura of glamour and romance. Something drew him back to look at the crowded display; his attention had been caught by a mandoline which lay on its side in the front of the window. Multi-coloured flowers were painted on its face and all the strings were intact. He knew he'd easily learn to play it, for making music was no trouble to him.

On impulse he went inside to ask the Meirsteins if it was for sale.

'A sailor pawned it years ago. He's not come back. You can have it for ten shillings,' said Abe.

'Let's try it first,' said Laurence. The instrument was fished out of the jumble in the window and after he'd tightened the strings a bit and given it a tuning, he plucked a cheerful tune out of it.

When he handed over his money, he tried to look casual as he pointed towards the window and said, 'What's that?'

A glitter of what looked like diamonds sparkled into his eyes from two pieces of jewellery lying side by side on a velvet cushion.

'What are they?' he asked again, pointing to them.

'This time it was Minna who bustled forward and looked to see where he was pointing. 'Oh they're lady's shoe buckles. Very dressy, aren't they?' she said.

Laurence nodded. In a sudden vision he saw himself dancing with a girl in an emerald gown who wore those sparklers on her feet.

'How much are they?' he asked in a casual way.

'Oh, only five bob. They're pretty, but not valuable,' Abe told him. The buckles had been in the pawn shop for many months because there wasn't much of a call for such finery in the Kirkgate, except among the whores and the buckles were too old-fashioned for their taste.

Laurence brought them without knowing why and without satisfying Minna's curiosity as to whom they were for. Next morning when he was climbing the stair in the mists of dawn after a long evening spent down at The Shore, he did not stop at his mother's door but went on climbing for another flight till he reached the door of Happy Anderson's old flat. Then he bent down and very quietly slipped the tissue-wrapped buckles through the letter box, holding it up with his thumb so that it did not clatter and waken the sleepers all around.

276

Brabazon dressed for Mhairi's party in her best grey silk gown, and swept into the kitchen to present herself to Laurence, saying, 'I don't want to stay late. You can bring me home before ten o'clock. You said you don't want to stay long yourself, didn't you?'

A queer look came over his face and she thought perhaps he's made other plans for the rest of the evening so she added, 'Just bring me home and go away again if you like.'

'I'll do that,' he said and turned back to the square of mirror above the sink to finish seeing to his tie.

Henry was out with Mhairi. He'd made a pretence of inviting her to a soirée given by the church choir and had prevailed on her to wear the green gown. Laurence had not seen them leave, but Nellie had popped in to tell his mother that everything had gone as planned. She reported that Mhairi was totally unsuspecting and she'd looked very bonny when she'd left with Henry.

Laurence collected his new mandoline before he left the flat with his mother on his arm to walk her the short distance to the party. When they got there they found the rest of Perseverance Place gathered in a state of high excitement waiting for the arrival of Mhairi, whom Henry had taken a roundabout way before heading back towards Leith Walk. They did not have to wait too long. The sound of a door opening downstairs made everyone go silent. Then came the noise of footsteps on the stairs and Henry appeared with the yellow-haired girl. She was resplendant in the green gown and to Laurence's delight she had the glittering diamanté buckles on her shoes.

The couple paused on the threshold while she gazed around before she cried out in surprise, 'Minna, Ruthie, Mrs Nairn, what are you doing here? I thought this was a choir social!' Then she turned to Henry and accused him, 'It's a trick, isn't it?' When he nodded, she burst into tears with her hands up to her eyes. Everybody except Laurence rushed towards her and tried to take her in their arms.

For his part he stood rigid as a statue and then turned

to the band, raising a hand and calling out, 'Start playing.' Two young men were carrying fiddles and a third was seated at the piano. They swung into a tune. It was 'See Me Dance the Polka'. No one could keep crying through that.

The party was off with a swing. The caterer's men carried in a huge cake which Mhairi had to cut. Then toasts to her future happiness were made and when it looked as if she were once more on the verge of tears, the band struck up again. The dancing was led by Ruthie Cairns who swung Gideon into the middle of the floor where they danced with joy and abandon.

Mhairi stared smiling again, her tears forgotten, and Henry held out a hand towards her, asking her to take the floor.

As she watched the general good fellowship of Perseverance Place, Brabazon's heart was gladdened. She looked around and sought out her two handsome sons among the revellers. Henry was still dancing with Mhairi, love apparent on his face. Laurence, with his jacket off and his shirt sleeves rolled up, was on the bandstand playing his mandoline like a man possessed. He looked like his father, but his face had a daredevilish look that Duncan had lacked.

Very soon most of the guests were on the dance floor, hopping or gliding around according to their competence. For the second dance Gideon Warre took up his mother and then, for the third, he swooped down on Mhairi, holding out a hand and crying, 'Come on, take the floor with me. You're not too shy, are you?'

He had gained in confidence, if not in stature, since becoming a junior police constable and today he was putting himself out to make sure that every one at the party had a happy time. Mhairi hopped to her feet quickly, hitched up the corner of her beautiful skirt and took his hand. Her cheeks flushed a deep shade of crimson as she caught Laurence Nairn watching her.

Up on the bandstand Laurence could not take his eyes off the dancing girl. His spirits soared when he watched

278

her flashing feet shod with his buckles. Such pleasure seized him that his playing became infected by his enthusiasm – filling old and young with a desire to dance.

Henry was watching Mhairi too. He thought his heart would break if he lost her. He envied Gideon for having his arm around her tiny waist. Any second she was not dancing with him was a second wasted!

Mhairi was about to dance next with Bobs, Ruthie's enormous brother, when Laurence pushed his way between them. 'Sorry, this one's mine. I'd booked it already,' he apologised and grasped her hand in a masterly way that brooked no refusal. She was drawn on to the floor without protest. His arm tightened around her for the waltz as if he were trying to squeeze the breath out of her body. He started guiding her through the steps and she yielded completely, like a blade of grass bending before the wind. Neither of them spoke for the entire time they danced together but when the last chord was struck, Laurence reluctantly loosed his hold of her and said in a hoarse, fierce voice. 'I've got to talk to you. Wait for me in the hall when the party's finished. I'll walk you home.'

For the rest of the evening she felt fevered, her sight was blurred and her ears filled with a strange humming noise. Surreptitiously she put a hand to her forehead, wondering if she were sickening for some illness. People crowded around, complimenting her on the lovely dress, wishing her well in America. She must have replied because they nodded and seemed satisfied with what she'd said. They smiled at her; she smiled back; they asked her to dance and she accepted. But she was no longer fully aware of her partners or what was happening.

In the middle of the party Abe Meirstein rose to his feet and made an emotional speech about how they would all miss Mhairi. When he'd finished he presented her with a little purse in which lay ten golden sovereigns collected by the people of the Place. She grasped it in her hands and burst out, 'I love you all. I'll miss you. I wish I wasn't going.' The women crowded round, putting their arms about her. Minna, Nellie, Brabazon and even Ruthie were all in tears.

After that Brabazon showed signs of becoming tired so Henry took her home as Laurence was busy leading the band. But he hurried back to the party because he was determined to seek Mhairi out and walk back with her alone.

She tried to lose herself in the crowd because she could guess his intention. She wished that she could suddenly grow wings and soar above the rooftops to fly home on her own, leaving behind her the competition that she had suddenly and unwittingly aroused between the brothers.

When the hands of the clock crept on towards midnight, people began to straggle off home. Only the young ones were left, with Gideon still urging the band on and whirling about the floor with anyone whose feet had not given on up them. Mhairi recognised how thin the gathering had become and slipped off to the cloakroom where she had left her shawl. She pulled it off the hook and ran hurriedly down the stairs. Somehow, she didn't know how, she'd missed Nellie and the others. Alone on the dark pavement, slightly intimidated by the shapes of returning revellers in the shadows, she stood there hesitating.

Ruthie and her brother came down the stairs behind her and exclaimed, 'What're you doing here on your own? Come on, we'll walk you back.'

To her own surprise Mhairi shook her head and heard her voice saying, 'It's all right. Don't worry. I'm not alone. I'm waiting for someone.'

They thought she meant Henry, of course, and went away shouting cheerfully, 'Don't let him keep you out too long then. It's freezing tonight.'

She told herself she had refused because the Cairns were reeling drunk but she'd seen them like that many times before and knew that even in drunkenness, they were cheerful and harmless. She'd have been perfectly safe with them, safer than going home alone anyway.

There was still no sign of anyone else on the stairs and she cuddled her shawl up round her face before she step-

280

ped off into the darkness. She had not gone two steps before a hand touched her arm. 'I've been waiting for you,' said a voice. Mhairi jumped back with a start. He heart was hammering but it sank in disappointment when she recognised the person in the shadows as Henry. 'I'll walk you home. It's late and you shouldn't be out on your own,' he said.

Before she could reply, someone else came down the stairs behind her.

'She's not on her own,' said Laurence.

The brothers stared at each other grim-faced. For the second time since she'd known him, Mhairi recognised real anger in Henry. His jaw was twitching and she could see him clenching and unclenching his fists.

Laurence appeared casual as he took her arm in a confident way. 'She's walking home with me,' he said.

'She's not,' said Henry angrily.

'I've told you she is. We arranged it earlier.' Laurence sounded cool and he smiled as he spoke.

Henry turned towards Mhairi. 'Is this true?'

She nodded. 'He said he'd take me home when we were dancing. I was waiting for him.'

Henry was very agitated. 'But you knew that I'd wait for you. You only had to give me a sign.' His voice was filled with hurt anger making her feel deep pity for him.

She put a hand on his arm and said, 'I'm sorry. I didn't realise. Walk along with us.'

Laurence stepped between them and thrust his shoulders in front of her, separating her from Henry. 'Don't do anything of the kind. I'm taking her home,' he told his brother.

Henry's usually mild face was almost unrecognisable as he swung a punch. Laurence stepped aside and grabbed the upraised arm with restraining hands. 'Steady on, brother. There's no need for that. She'd rather go home with me. Push off. There's a good fellow.'

His calm tone brought Henry back to a realisation of what was happening. With a muffled sound that was

281

almost a sob, he turned on his heel and ran off along the street.

When Laurence turned back to Mhairi, he saw that she looked stricken. 'Oh, how could I hurt him like that? It's your fault! Are you only behaving like this to me to score a point off your brother?'

He became angry now, too. 'Don't be stupid! Can't you see that I'm in love with you? I'm damned sure you're in love with me too. Are we going to deny it because we don't want to hurt Henry?'

She gave a racking rob and gasped, 'You're so conceited. I'm not in love with you.'

'Aren't you? Look at me and say you aren't.' He was bending towards her like an inquisitor. She kept turning her face away so he put a hand on each side of her head and held it steady. Then silence descended on them and they stared at each other in silence for a very long time. Their eyes were fixed on each other in fascination. She saw the anger in his gradually disappear to be replaced by something so tender that it melted her own rage entirely away. After what seemed like an age, he slowly kissed her, bending his face towards her and still holding her head between his hands. His lips were cool and tender and she could feel deep grooves in them as they gently touched her own.

He stood back from her and gazed as if entranced. 'You're the loveliest thing I've ever seen in my life. You've bewitched me,' he said and kissed her again. This time she felt his tongue gently tracing the outline of her mouth and involuntarily her own lips parted. Fiercely, as if she'd given him a sign, he pulled her towards him and began kissing her more passionately, feeling her body go limp in his arms.

They walked the streets till dawn, entranced. Every now and again they would stop to look at each other and he would grasp her hands.

'No America for you,' he said when they reached the docks where the tall ships were berthed.

Her face looked strange. 'I've got my ticket. I have to go.'

He put his arms around her and hugged her close. 'You don't think I'd let you, do you? You're staying here with me.'

'How can I?'

'Easily. We'll get married.' He spoke as if it were something he had all worked out. 'We'll go and see the minister tomorrow – I mean this morning – and we'll get married as soon as possible. Maybe today.'

'But that's impossible. We don't know each other.'

He slid his hands over her shoulders beneath the shawl and whispered in her ear, 'I know I'm going to marry you and nobody's going to stop me. I know you and I are going to bed with each other and it'll be wonderful. Just you wait and see.'

She felt her body clench internally and give a shudder of anticipation. It *would* be wonderful.

'But the steamship ticket. America, Calum . . . everybody thinks I'm going . . . they even gave me a present,' she stammered.

'We'll give it back – or maybe they'll make it a wedding present. Don't make objections, just say *yes*.'

When morning light was flushing the sky, they started to walk back to Perseverance Place. Laurence was still busy making plans. 'We'll tell my mother first. Then you go home and have a sleep. I'll speak to the minister.'

Brabazon was sipping tea at the kitchen-table when they appeared in the doorway. She said nothing, only stared at them wide-eyed.

'Mother, I've asked Mhairi to marry me and she's agreed,' her son told her.

Very slowly she put her cup into the saucer and asked, 'What about Henry?'

Laurence looked at the girl by his side. 'You're not in love with Henry, are you? You're in love with me.'

She gazed at him with bedazzled eyes that were answer enough. 'I'm in love with you,' she said.

283

Brabazon sighed and asked her son, 'It's not rivalry with your brother that caused this is it?'

He put her right. 'No, Mother. I didn't want it to happen; I really didn't. I've been trying to stop it for months and so has Mhairi. That's why she was going to America really, but it's got us now and we can't avoid it. Please be happy for us.'

She rose to her feet, tall and straight but looking sad. 'I'm very happy for you,' she said as she walked round the table to hug them both. 'Anybody who knows real love is blessed. Treasure it. But who's going to tell poor Henry!'

That afternoon when Henry was passing her office, Brabazon dashed out and took him by the arm. She led him inside, sat him down on the chair before her desk and stood with her hand on his shoulder while she broke the news . . . 'Mhairi isn't going to America now.' He looked up with hope on his face but she hurriedly went on. 'She's getting married instead.'

He looked up blankly, his face showing utter surprise. 'Married? Who to?'

She felt deep pity for him as she said gently, 'I'm sorry to have to be the one to tell you but she's marrying your brother.'

Henry jumped up abruptly with his face working. 'Laurence! There must be some mistake. She can't be marrying him.' He turned and strode angrily across the office floor, beside himself with emotion.

Brabazon wished she could hug him to her as she had done when he was small, but she feared he would feel she was condescending to him. 'Oh, Henry,' she said softly, 'you can't make someone love you . . .'

He turned to look furiously at her, 'I thought I could. I thought she'd come to love me in the end. But Laurence hasn't given her the chance. He's stolen her from me, Mother. He's taken her away because he knew how I felt about her. I'll never, never forgive him.'

'Oh, no, I've seen them together. They love each other. They really do, I'm sure of that.'

His mother's defence of her other son did not soften Henry's hurt, however. Angrily he shouted at her, 'She'd be better off with me. She'd be happier with someone who really loves her. I tell you he's stolen her deliberately. It's always been the same with him. He's resented me since we were children. You know that too. I've seen you trying to mollify him. And now he's taken Mhairi!' His voice cracked and he turned away. When he'd recovered a little he managed to ask, 'When's the wedding?'

Brabazon sighed and drew back from him, respecting his need for privacy. 'It's the day after tomorrow. Very sudden. I think he's worried that she'll go to America after all if he gives her time to reconsider.'

Henry shook his head. 'Perhaps she should. He won't appreciate her,' he said sadly.

Brabazon said nothing. It was useless to offer Henry anodyne words of comfort when he had been dealt such a blow and it grieved her to see her tall and manly son so broken. He recognised the concerned look on her face and tried to smile as he told her, 'Don't worry, Mother. I'm not going to make a scene.' Then his face hardened again and he said bitterly, 'But don't expect me to be present at my brother's marriage.'

The swiftness of the wedding meant that by the time the great day dawned, the people of Perseverance Place had not recovered from their surprise that it was happening at all. When Ruthie met a radiant Mhairi tripping down-stairs in her hastily purchased wedding dress to walk to the church, she grinned and said, 'That was a quick trip to America.'

The bride flushed and said, 'Oh Ruthie, it was all so sudden. It took us both by surprise.'

Ruthie laughed and patted the girl's shoulder, 'Don't worry. I was only joking. Everybody likes a whirlwind romance. Good luck to you.'

Mr Templeton looked confused when he started to read the marriage service to the couple. If he had ever contemplated the marriage of a Nairn, it had been Henry marrying Mhairi that he'd seen in his mind's eye – not his organist's younger brother.

Henry was absent. A deputy organist provided the music – rather badly as it soon turned out. The church was not full for Mhairi had no family within reach. Only the neighbours and Brabazon's brother Mark turned out to see them married. The faces of this congregation revealed that they shared the minister's feelings. Not only were they surprised by the turn of events, but many of them also did not approve. Everybody in Perseverance Place was fond of the gentle Henry. They liked Laurence too, but he was generally reckoned to be harder and more able to look after himself. The feeling of the neighbours was that Laurence had stolen his brother's girl from under his nose and that Mhairi had been swept off her feet. It was a sombre crowd who watched the couple taking their vows.

Mhairi listened intently to the words of the marriage service. When she took her vows she meant every single word of them. As Laurence took his, she heard his voice sounding deep and sincere and a wave of emotion swept over her with such strength that she was on the verge of fainting. As she swayed, he reached out and held her hand, making her heart soar with delight – she loved him with a passion that overrode all other feelings, all misgivings and all her guilt about Henry. She loved Laurence and it was a love that could not be denied.

As they left the church to the halting playing of 'The Bridal March', Mhairi remembered with a pang the day she had listened to the magnificent 'Arrival of the Queen of Sheba' played by Henry. 'Oh, the poor dear!' she thought and wondered how she would ever be able to face him again, for Brabazon had told her of the way he received the news of her wedding.

The bridegroom's mother walked out behind her son and his new wife, with Mark Logan at her side. She too was thinking of Henry as she watched how the couple in the church porch stood looking at each other in a dazed way. She saw how Laurence's hand clasped Mhairi's and the way their eyes sought each other's. Oh yes, they were in love all right! She could recognise the feeling and remember how she had stood in the same porch and gazed into Duncan's eyes. A constriction filled her throat and she turned her head away.

A small reception had been organised in the brewhouse, a very muted affair without speeches. The guests took turns in shaking the couple by the hand and wishing them well. When Minna and Abie went up to give their blessing, Mhairi tried to return the going-away purse to Abe but she was told, 'Keep it for a wedding present my dear.'

After what was deemed to be a respectable time, dragged out so as not to show unseemly haste, they walked over the cobbled yard between the lines of people throwing confetti over their heads and climbed the stairs to Happy's old flat. Hurriedly they slipped inside, locking the door behind them. Then they turned to each other and began kissing with frantic and pent-up longing. Their marriage had begun.

1898

The people of Perseverance Place might have been cheated out of a big wedding party, but they were all febrile
with excitement because of the unexpected nature of Laurence and Mhairi's love affair. Highly charged emotions
seemed to run around the building like thermals before
an electric storm and the sight of the locked door of the
lovers' flat reminded them all of secret pleasures, of youth
and lovemaking. It was as if a strongly charged sexuality
were seeping into every house, coiling up the stairs like
Eve's serpent of temptation. Not a person went in or out
without being conscious of it.

Minna and Abe sat before their fireplace and held
hands, remembering the days when their own love was
urgent. As they looked at each other, wrinkled and freckled with age now, he leaned over to kiss her paper thin
cheek. 'You can't blame them really. It's wonderful. I still
love you old lady,' he whispered.

The Cairns' reaction to the charged emotion was totally
predictable. They dressed in their finery and went out to
drink in a noisy gang, hammering on Mhairi's door and
shouting ribald comments through the keyhole as they
passed. Then later, coming home gloriously full of beer,
they shouted even more specific remarks of encouragement. Till early morning they sang and quarrelled happily
before exhaustion claimed them one by one.

In the Warres' flat Nellie brooded more than ever
before on her late husband and avoided going out, because
she was so sensitive to the atmosphere on the silent landing beneath her. When Gideon came to visit her at night,
he often found her sitting sadly by the fireside and she
always wanted to talk about Alex. One evening she told
her son, 'I miss your dad something terrible. I wish you
could do something about how he died now that you're

a bobby. Mrs Nairn's convinced he was pushed down that ladder. She kept on about it at the time but nobody took any notice.'

Gideon felt a painful stab each time his mother brought up this subject, for it was something that was on his own mind as well. Yet he told her gently, 'You shouldn't think about it, Mam, It was long ago. You'll only upset yourself.'

He did not speak of the hours he spent during his night patrols going over and over the circumstances of his father's death. He did not tell her how, in the police station, he'd sought out a copy of the report made at the time. It was written off as an accidental death. There was not even a hint that foul play might have been involved. As he read the matter-of-fact words, Gideon sometimes wondered if he, his family and Brabazon Nairn had dreamed up their conviction that Alex had been murdered – but still the doubt persisted, niggling away all the time at the back of his mind.

One might when Nellie was even more gloomy than usual, he admitted to her, 'I've my doubts about what happened too. I've gone over and over it, but there's nothing specific to go on, just this feeling . . .'

His mother nodded, 'Aye. I know. You hang onto that Giddie. It's up to you to find out what really happened. Someone did it. I'm sure. Who'd know how to get into the brewhouse at night? Who'd want to do your father harm?'

Gideon shrugged, 'Nobody I can think of except Tom Lambert. He was bitter about losing his job, bitter against the Nairns and us. But surely not bitter enough to kill a man?'

Nellie said balefully, 'That one's bad enough for any villainy. Look how he neglects Sophia, his own poor wee daughter. Don't give up, son. Don't forget.'

Gideon echoed her feelings, but he also knew the near impossibility of making mere speculation into something more concrete. 'Don't worry, Mam, I'll not forget,' he told her, 'I think about it every day.'

If Nellie had her troubles, so did Brabazon. She worried about how Henry was going to cope when Laurence and Mhairi emerged from their honeymoon period, and he would be seeing one or other of them every day. While the couple remained hidden away, she sought out her eldest son and said, 'I was thinking you might be able to do me a favour. There's a big exhibition of brewing going on in Burton-on-Trent, and I'd like you to go down and see what new things are on show.'

He was not deceived, 'What sort of new things, Mother? You've not been one for modernisation before.'

She gestured vaguely, 'Oh, utensils, finings . . . they tell me there's modern techniques coming in. I don't want us to be left behind.'

Henry smiled, 'I remember you once saying that sturgeon's bladder finings are the best and that no modern chemical will ever replace them as far as Perseverence Brewery's concerned.'

She bridled, 'We've got to move with the times, Henry. Will you go?'

'I'll go,' he told her quietly, 'But why don't you admit you want me out of the way? It's no use Mother. I'll not change my mind. I'll not get over this in a couple of weeks.'

He was gone when the couple emerged from the flat two days after the wedding. They were so obviously happy that the sight of them crossing the yard hand in hand brought smiles to watching faces at the windows of the building. Mhairi was blushing and shy in front of her neighbours, but they could all see that she was totally entranced by her husband. As she waved him off across the yard to work in the mornings, it was obvious that every moment apart would be spent thinking of his return. For his part, Laurence had lost his challenging air, his tongue was less caustic and he no longer thought about Daisy – this last would have surprised him most of all if he had even realised it.

Marriage made Mhairi bloom. Her eyes sparkled; her skin looked like a peach; her hair glittered with even more than its usual brilliant sheen. Laurence looked at her with delight when they sat facing each other over supper at night. 'I never thought I'd want to be a married man but I love it,' he told her.

'I love it as well – and I love you,' she replied. She could not believe how light-hearted she felt; even her remorse about Henry was rendered less painful when Brabazon told her that he had gone away for a little while. The lovemaking with Laurence was ecstatic and she wondered how it was that she had been frightened of it for so long. It was nothing, absolutely nothing like her experience with Stewart.

Her husband was gentle, considerate and tender as they lay in bed together. He whispered endearments in her ear as he smoothed back her tendrils of hair and caressed her body. At first she followed his lead trustingly, but very soon her hunger for him was as insatiable as his for her. As the days passed she learned to give pleasure, besides accepting it, and each time they went to bed they surprised themselves anew. She revealed herself to him spiritually as well as physically. They made love, then talked till dawn, lying close together under the big quilt. Their delight in each other was unbounded.

They had been married for two weeks when Henry came back. Mhairi met him in the yard on the morning of his return and faltered in her step when she saw him coming over the cobbles towards her. It was impossible for them to avoid each other so she raised her head, smiled at him and paused to say, 'Good morning, Henry.'

For a moment she thought he was going to ignore her but his better nature overcame that first impulse. He stopped and looked longingly at her. She was prettier than ever, and the sight of her made his heart ache. 'Are you happy Mhairi?' he asked.

Her face went solemn and she nodded, 'Yes, Henry I am. I'm sorry about what happened but I couldn't help it.'

'I'm glad you're happy,' he said and went on his way.

He was not so forgiving when he encountered his brother in the brewery. He walked past Laurence as if he were a ghost. The younger brother stopped and stared after him, then shrugged. 'If that's how it's to be, then all right,' he said aloud.

The enmity between the brothers poisoned the atmosphere in the brewery and caused their mother much distress. She knew only too well that the only time her eldest son was happy was when, like his father, he slipped over to the church to play the organ. His old interest and enthusiasm for the business was dwindling away to nothing, but Laurence – inspired by marriage and its responsibilities – was taking over where Henry had left off.

'Would you like to concentrate more on your music?' she asked her bachelor son one day.

'Are you hinting that I'm neglecting the business?' he said.

She shook her head 'No, but I think your father would have been alive today if he'd been able to lead the life he wanted. I don't want you to miss your true vocation. Why don't you go up to Edinburgh for lessons? I know you're a fine musician already but if you want to make a career of it, you'll need to go to someone who knows more than you do. Mr Templeton and I have been talking about it and he has a friend at Edinburgh University with contacts in musical circles. He'd be able to help you, Mr Templeton thinks.'

Henry stared at his mother and then put out his hands to grasp hers, 'Can you manage without me?' he asked.

She nodded, 'We'll manage.'

'You're a magnificent woman,' he told her.

It was an inspired suggestion on Brabazon's part. By the time a few months had passed, Henry was hardly ever at home; for he was continually being invited up to Edinburgh to perform for fashionable congregations. As his fame spread he was much fêted by his admirers, including many young women who flirted outrageously with him. He never pursued these acquaintanceships, however. He had been hurt so badly that he was not prepared to risk his heart again. Nevertheless the stimulus of music, the adrenaline of celebrity had a curative effect and he was able to conceal his jealousy when, barely four months after her marriage, Mhairi knocked at her mother-in-law's door to break her latest news – 'I'm having a baby! Laurence is so pleased. I had to stop him shouting it out of the window last night!'

Brabazon laughed. Laurence as a father was a strange notion, but then another thought came into her mind – soon she would be a grandmother. The shock sobered her, but the idea that another generation of Nairns was about to be born made her glad that she had fought so hard to keep the brewery. Her ambition, dormant during the time of worrying about Henry, flared back into glorious life. She hoped with all her heart that Mhairi would have a son.

The baby was due at the end of the year and Laurence worked himself up to a state of excitement as Mhairi grew rounder and more placid with every week that passed.

He was proving to be a good husband, caring and attentive, and there was nothing he enjoyed more than taking his pretty wife out on a Saturday night to the Music Hall or a concert. From time to time they took the tram up to Edinburgh and attended the theatre. In summer they promenaded like a staid old married couple round the bandstand on the Links. He delighted in buying her presents and they continued to relish each other's company. When Mhairi grew heavy with child, he walked proudly at her side, a hand on her elbow in case she stumbled.

It was a Sunday evening when she went into labour. She had been silent and pensive all day, sitting in the rocking chair with her hands on her belly and after tea she suddenly said, 'I think something's happening. I've been having pains and now they're very close.'

Laurence flew into a panic, 'Why didn't you tell me?'

'Oh, I knew it wasn't the real thing till now.' Mhairi did

not want to remind him that though he was experiencing fatherhood for the first time, she had already been a mother. Laurence did not like her to talk about Calum. It made him frantically jealous although he knew there had been no love between her and Stewart.

'I'll fetch the midwife,' he cried snatching his coat from its hook before she could stop him. She knew there was no hurry and asked him to fetch Brabazon first.

At his mother's flat, Laurence encountered Henry in the kitchen. He looked more polished and cosmopolitan now that he had launched himself on a musical career. He also seemed remote and still acted towards his brother as if he did not exist. Laurence could not stand the strain and blurted out, 'I'm worried about Mhairi. She's in labour.' They were the first words he'd spoken directly to Henry since the wedding.

Henry turned around. His face was expressionless. 'I hope she's all right,' he said.

They stared at each other. Laurence suddenly said, 'I love her you know.'

'I know,' said Henry.

Laurence wished he was able to say 'I'm sorry' but the words would not come. He blamed it on his anxiety about his wife.

Laurence had no grounds for his fears though. Mhairi was young and healthy. Her previous experience of childbirth stood her in good stead: she knew how to conserve her strength for when it was needed and she gave birth to her second son as successfully as she had her first.

Brabazon left Mrs Millar, the midwife, in charge while she ran downstairs to tell the good news to Laurence who'd been told to wait out of the way in her own flat. She found him and his brother both sitting asleep by a dead fire – an empty whisky bottle on the floor beside them. She shook Laurence by the shoulder and whispered, 'You've a son. It's a beautiful little boy – he looks just like my father.'

Her son sat up, grasped her round the waist, sank his face into her lap and burst into tears. He hadn't wept like that since he was a tiny child. When he recovered, he wiped his eyes and told his mother, 'If he looks like Grandfather, we'll call him Joshua.'

The christening of Brabazon Nairn's grandson, Joshua James, provided the opportunity for the celebration that had not taken place when Laurence and Mhairi had married.

The inhabitants of Perseverance Place turned out in style at the church, filling the pews. Mark Logan came, but Amelia did not condescend to grace the proceedings. It was a fine day in late autumn, and food and drink was laid out on trestle-tables in the courtyard. The baby's grandmother provided barrels of beer and his uncle played glorious music in church. Mhairi Nairn sat at the head of the top table with her son, wrapped up in a crocheted white shawl, clutched to her breast. Every now and again, she stared at his sleeping face in delight. How grateful she was that he did not look like Calum! The long suppressed yearning and love for her first baby was now being poured out in adoration of this new child.

At intervals during the party, Laurence came up and stood beside his wife, bending down to gaze at the child in her arms. Their mutual pride was heart-warming and brought tears to many eyes watching them. Even from the Lamberts' window two white faces could be seen behind the dirty glass.

For the first few weeks of her new baby's life Mhairi could not be persuaded to leave him even for a moment. She took him into bed with her at night, she suckled him every time he cried during the day. Laurence would come home at night from work and push open the door of their flat, pausing in wonder at the sight of his wife sitting with her golden hair falling around her shoulders, and the child sucking greedily at her pink-tipped breast.

He knelt by her side and put out a hand to touch her. 'You're like a picture. It's wonderful seeing you like that,' he told her.

After two months, however, they were still divided in their bed at night by a shawl-wrapped bundle. 'Put him on the floor, just for a little while,' pleaded Laurence.

But Mhairi would not hear of it. 'What if he wakes? What if he hears us?'

He was angry. 'My God what if he does! It'll do him good. I hope he learns something. He'll do it himself one day if he's lucky.'

'Hush, don't speak so loudly, you'll wake him. I'll put him in a cradle tomorrow, I promise you.'

When the cradling of young Josh was put off for another week though, Laurence began to show irritation. Mhairi told him she did not want to fall with another baby yet, and he snapped, 'There's no danger of that if you go on like this.' He turned heavily in the bed and sank his face in the pillow. His longing for her was intense. He was even beginning to feel jealous of his own child he realised with a shock.

Eventually they quarrelled. 'My God, is that bairn going to share our bed until he's grown up? Are you going to live like a nun forever?' he shouted.

She stared at him with round, horrified eyes, 'Of course not, it's just . . .'

'It's just that you're going to drive me off to other women if you're not careful. Is that what you want? Is that what you're trying to do?'

The threat brought Mhairi to her senses. She was very aware that she was married to a man with a huge sexual appetite and though she knew nothing about Daisy, she remembered Henry mentioning Laurence's unhappy love affair. She had never asked him about it, however, and he had never volunteered any information. She thought it was best to leave that particular sleeping dog to lie. Now she realised that she had been neglecting him in favour of the baby; rising from bed she lifted her precious bundle out of its cosy nest in the midst of their blankets. Cuddling Josh close, she put him in the cot that had been waiting for him for weeks, then turned back and climbed into bed with Laurence, shrugging her way out of her nightgown as she did so. Their lovemaking was at first very swift, but later that night they achieved a union so loving that they were both moved to tears by the joy it brought them. Two months later Mhairi discovered that she was pregnant again.

The joy she took in baby Josh made her look forward to the next birth, but it also brought back vivid memories of Calum. When she suckled Josh, she remembered her first baby. Her heart was sore at the realisation that he was so far away and they did not know each other. If they were to meet they would be strangers. Sadness shadowed her, she dreamed about Calum at night and at intervals during the day she caught herself thinking about him till one night she tentatively suggested to Laurence that she might soon be able to send for her first son.

'I've an address for my folk. I could send the money for his fare. It'll come from the money Happy left me . . .' she whispered.

To her surprise her husband rose up against his pillows and said accusingly, 'Isn't our bairn enough for you? And there's another one due in a couple of months . . . you couldn't manage all those bairns at once. You've never suggested anything like this before, what's wrong with you?'

'I keep thinking about him. Having a wee baby in my arms brings him back. I'm his mother and I've not seen him since he was three months old,' she explained tearfully.

Laurence grabbed her by the shoulders, 'And do you remember his father? Do you think about him when you're making love to me?'

Mhairi shrank from his rage, 'Of course not. You know I hated it that one time with Stewart.'

'That's what you say now but you let him do it. He got you with child.'

Unwittingly she had wakened his terrible jealousy again and with deep disquiet in her heart she realised that talking about Calum was a great mistake. Her longing for her first son would have to be hidden from Laurence if she wanted her marriage to stay happy.

'It's such a pleasure to me that you're so interested in what's going on here,' Brabazon told Laurence one day as he followed her through the brewhouse watching the various stages of another batch of beer being brewed.

'I've grown up. I'm becoming ambitious, Mother. I want to know as much as I can about this operation. I don't want to be a brewster though. I'll manage the business and leave that to other people. Henry does it well – and Robert Warre does it magnificently.'

She nodded, 'Yes, we're lucky to have him. He's taken up where his father left off. The Warres have a genius for brewing.'

He laughed, 'Well Robert has thank heavens. Pat hasn't and neither has Gideon.'

'Oh, Gideon's doing very well in the police force. I heard that he was promoted the other day. He'll go a long way,' said Brabazon. She did not mention Pat and neither did Laurence.

On her way home that night she met her daughter-in-law struggling up the stairs of the flats. Mhairi was near her time of delivery again and for this pregnancy she had not been well. Her feet and ankles had swelled alarmingly and she found it difficult to carry her sturdy little son up and down the stairs. Brabazon hurried to catch up with the panting girl and grabbed the baby from her. 'You shouldn't be doing this, my dear. Where's Laurence?' she asked.

Mhairi did not meet her eye, 'He's still at work. He said he would be late. There's something he wants to see to.'

Brabazon lifted her eyebrows in surprise, 'Really? I haven't seen him. But your baby's due any minute – he should be here.

'Oh, I'm all right,' said Mhairi and struggled on up the stairs.

Later that night when Laurence arrived in Brabazon's flat, it was obvious he had something important on his mind as he settled down in the chair at her side. 'For the past few weeks I've been doing some talking with Willie Ord,' he began.

She looked up in startled surprise. 'With him? What on earth for? I've never trusted that man.'

'Oh, you're prejudiced because he tried to make you sell out to Gordon's when father first went bankrupt. He was only trying to do a deal. He's a businessman, Mother.'

Her face went stiff, 'I don't like his kind of business.'

Laurence laughed, 'But Ord's done well for himself. He's always ready to weigh in on the winning side.'

'And which side is that?' She was apprehensive in case her son, too, was going to start asking her to sell up.

He's on our side now. He realises you've made a success of the brewery. I've been meeting him because he's offered to help us make a bid for Gordon's.'

She gasped and sat back in her chair with her head swimming, 'For Gordon's? Don't be silly! Where are we going to find that sort of money?'

'Mother, I've been looking at the account books. We have reserves now and we could raise a lot more on our property. We could easily do it. Think of it! We could buy our biggest rival; doesn't the idea appeal to you?'

It appealed to her a great deal but years of caution, years of pinching and saving, were hard to forget. Her habits had become frugal and she was frightened of risk-taking. It was not the same however for her son.

'Let me try mother. Gordon's is having a bad patch. We've beaten them to the best of the market round here. They could be picked up quite cheaply.'

She was not convinced yet, 'But why? Why should we not be satisfied with what we've got? As you said, we're doing well.'

'If we buy them now we remove our biggest competition. Their well is not as good as ours but we could pipe our water along there and double our production. Our well's bottomless, Robert says. It's certainly never run dry in living memory, has it?'

She had to agree. Even in summers of drought the Perseverance well kept on running sweet and pure. Its water seemed to come from the heart of the earth and bubbled to the surface so cold that it was a shock to sip it.

'You really surprise me. I never thought you'd turn out like this,' she said in awe at the change in Laurence. Was this the young man who'd gone out roistering every night with Pat Warre, who could hardly be persuaded to take any interest in his work, who talked with longing about leaving Leith?

He laughed. 'I got married, Mother. I've a family to worry about now,' he said proudly, rising to his feet, 'Can I go ahead then? Can I start the move against Gordon's?'

'As long as it doesn't mean Perseverance is in danger,' said Brabazon. She could see that he needed the challenge: quietly running an unadventurous business would never do for the new Laurence.

And so it was that Laurence was out dining with Willie Ord when Mhairi went into labour with their second child. By the time he returned at midnight, the baby had been born and this time it was a girl. Brabazon presented the little bundle to him and smiled in delight, 'We needed more girls in this family.'

The child in his arms was as serene as a cherub, with pink cheeks and a thatch of blond hair. She was sleeping soundly and her lashes lay on her cheeks like fringes of lace. 'She's beautiful, just beautiful,' he sighed in adoration. Then he went over to the bed and knelt by his wife's side.

She was still weak and put a feeble hand on her husband's hair. 'Do you like your new daughter?' she whispered.

'I'm madly in love with her already. She's a lucky girl, she's going to look like you,' he told Mhairi, holding her hand in both of his.

'What'll we call her?' she asked. Her voice was fading

and she was visibly exhausted: though the labour had not been so long this time, her energy was less and she had endured a worrying pregnancy. As he watched her, Laurence determined that a local girl would be hired to help Mhairi just as she used to help his mother. His mind immediately went to the Warres' teenage daughter, Elsie. She was old enough to go out to work and the money would be useful to her family.

He looked again at the sleeping babe. 'She's so pretty, let's call her after a flower,' he said.

Mhairi smiled, 'That's a nice idea. What do you suggest?'

He nearly said, 'Let's call her Daisy.' The name slipped into his mind unconsciously although he hadn't thought about his former mistress for many months. He bit the name back and thought frantically before he said, 'What about Poppy?'

Mhairi closed her eyes with a happy look on her face. 'That's a lovely name. We'll call her Poppy. Show her to Josh, my dear, we don't want him to feel jealous.'

Laurence cradled his son in one arm as he displayed the baby in the other. He loved being a father – he really did – but sometimes a devil of resentment burned in him when Mhairi made a fuss over their son. He knew it was stupid to be jealous of a child, but the feeling burned there nonetheless. In a way he resented any claims apart from his own upon the girl he had married, the girl he'd won from his brother. If he'd had a choice, he would have kept her to himself forever.

Children were proving to be a responsibility and a tie. They meant that it was not possible to go out walking alone with his wife any longer, to visit concerts or the Music Hall as they had done in their first year of marriage. Nowadays Mhairi could not leave the house without worrying about who was looking after Josh. Even when the boy was left in the care of Brabazon, she would not stay away for more than an hour without fretting continuously.

Laurence put his son back in the cot and went back to

the big bed with the new baby. Then he kissed Mhairi on the cheek and said, 'Go to sleep my dear, I'm going upstairs now to ask Elsie to start coming in to help you . . .'

Not content with that, he decided that the arrival of two children meant that their tiny flat was no longer big enough. Yet the idea of moving away from the Place was unthinkable. He was now as dedicated to the brewery as his mother and could hardly bear to let it out of his sight. Like Brabazon he stared across at the smoking chimney first thing in the morning and last thing at night.

'We need to expand,' he told Mhari when two cots were lined up on the floor beside their bed. His solution was to give Lambert notice to leave. 'We'll take his flat as well and put in a staircase to it. It'll double our space,' he announced to his mother.

Her face showed surprise, followed by fear. 'Are you sure that's a good thing to do? He's a difficult man. He's always hated us ever since I dismissed him from the brewery. Even then I was afraid to put him out of his flat.'

'I won't put him out just like that. I'll find him another place. There's a little flat on the other side of Minna's shop. I'll buy it and rent it to him. Willie Ord'll handle the deal and Lambert needn't know who his landlord is. He'll reckon he's been lucky.'

In fact Lambert took the news badly. He cursed Laurence soundly when notice was handed to him but he moved his wife, his child and his bits of battered furniture to the flat on the other side of the alleyway. He was still part of the Place, however, because he continued to hang around the yard watching everything that went on. No one dared to challenge his right to do so.

Dr Allen told Mhairi that it would be unwise for her to have any more children – at least for a while. Laurence was frightened by this verdict and they started to be very careful in their lovemaking. It put a great constraint on their relationship and their mutual frustration caused them to quarrel.

If Laurence scolded the children, he found his wife usually took the child's part. At this, he would draw his brows together in a dangerous scowl, throw on his coat and leave the house. She rarely asked where he was going.

One evening after a sharp difference of opinion he found himself walking towards The Shore. He did not stop walking till he was outside the bar where he had first met Daisy.

'I shouldn't – I shouldn't . . .' he said to himself but he pushed open the swing door and went inside. It was just the same: noisy, crowded, redolent of bodies and beer. A pianist, not a good one, was playing in the corner and people were singing along as Laurence pushed his way to the bar and laid a shilling on the counter. 'I'll have a pint,' he said defiantly as if he were challenging his wife, his mother and his children all at the same time. He stood out in the crowd of labourers because his suit was smartly cut and he looked like a business gentlemen. He drew curious stares but did not care, turning to glare back defiantly, his elbows on the bar behind him.

A toothless and wizened character sidled up to him and touched his arm. She smelt of cheap perfume.

'Remember me, my handsome lad?' she asked.

He was drinking his beer and his eyes slid sideways to look at her. It was Bertha, her late flowering over now. He had to fight to keep the distaste out of his face. 'I remember you. You went with my friend Pat Warre.'

'And you went with Daisy. You came asking about her afterwards. Did you find her?'

He nodded, 'I found her.'

Bertha laughed, 'It's odd but I was hearing about Daisy the other day. My word, she's some girl. She's living with a toff in Pall Mall now. A lord they say. She's come a long way from a miner's row in Wallyford, hasn't she?'

Laurence signalled to the barman to give Bertha a gin. He pretended to be only mildly interested in her gossip, but secretly he was avid to hear more. Not only was he interested in details of the toff in Pall Mall but also in the revelation about Daisy's background. She'd spun him many different stories about her origins, but growing up in the poverty of a mining village was never one of them.

'Daisy's not from Wallyford,' he essayed.

'Of course she is. It was her ain cousin that told me. Daisy's father was an Irishman that was killed in a pit fall. Her mother went on the drink and Daisy went on the streets.' Bertha gulped down her gin and set the empty glass on the bar with a meaningful look. He nodded for it to be filled again.

'Does she write to her cousin?' he asked.

'Daisy write? Of course not. She's all grand now though. Calls herself a fancy name and everything. I bet she's told her toff some story about being the illegitimate daughter of a duke. That's her style!'

'How do you know that's she's in Pall Mall then?'

'She sends a message to her mother once a year – and money too. All through her cousin. She aye gave her mother money even when she was living with an old fellow up in Trinity.'

Laurence's heart was thudding. He wondered if Daisy's cousin knew about him, but Bertha was still pouring out her story because she knew that as long as she kept his interest he would go on buying her gin. 'My God, the poor old soul in Trinity was fair taken aback when she ran off one night. He never suspected she was playing games behind his back. She could make anybody believe anything could Daisy. Still the same her cousin says.'

It was easy for Laurence to refuse Bertha's offer of a 'good time'. He was anxious, now, to get away from the sordid surroundings that had once had such appeal for him. As he walked home, he found to his disquiet however that his mind was full of Daisy. He remembered her naked and slippery as a seal in the bed beside him; he remembered her pointed breasts and then closed his eyes at the recollection of her deceit. 'Damn you Daisy!' he said to her memory.

1902

It took longer than Laurence had planned to secure Gordon's Brewery but he did it in the end.

On a brilliant spring morning he and his mother stood side by side in the front of the grey stone pile that was Gordon's and stared at it with satisfaction. It was not an attractive old building like Perseverance, nor was it in such a secluded situation because the façade ran along thronged Great Junction Street, but it was bigger and it represented success to them. It represented victory.

Brabazon heaved a grateful sigh as she looked at her son. She was dressed like a queen for this occasion and wore a grey skirt, a grey hat with a plume and a chenille wrapper patterned with mutely coloured roses. As she stood in front of Gordon's, she leaned on a gold-handled umbrella. Mhairi had gone to Edinburgh with her to buy this outfit and they had spent a whole day mulling over possibilities in the exclusive salons of the capital city. Brabazon wanted to look impressive and she had certainly succeeded.

'You've worked wonders,' she told Laurence. He was dressed in a well-cut suit of dark tweed and had grown a curling dark beard that gave him gravity.

'I'm not finished yet,' he said exultantly. 'I'm going to pipe our well water along here and then I'm going to build sheds for the transport. One day I'll have a fleet of lorries. I've been reading about horseless carriages. They make dray horses seem old-fashioned.'

Brabazon looked shocked, 'Oh no my dear, horses look wonderful. I've always loved to see our pairs pulling out of the yard. Motor vans would not be as impressive and anyway, they're always breaking down and making such awful noises.

'You won't have to hear them. As I said, I'll put them in this yard.'

'Oh, goodness me,' sighed his mother, 'You don't seem able to stop. There's only one thing I really want Laurence. I want Brewery House.'

'I know – and you'll get it. The fellow who owns it won't sell yet, but in time I'll wear him down. Ord's working on it.'

She smiled ruefully for she knew the persistence with which Willie Ord worked. He was like water dripping on to stone.

'We must hurry back,' she said turning on her heel, 'It's Henry's big concert in Edinburgh tonight.' She looked questioningly at him, 'I don't suppose you're coming?'

'Mhairi wants to go,' said Laurence slightly shame-faced, because he and his wife had disagreed about whether or not she could attend the concert that very morning.

'She loves music and she knows I'd like her to go with me,' said Brabazon coolly. She and Mhairi had also discussed the concert and their mutual wish to heal the breach between the brothers. To have it dragging on as it was doing year-in, year-out, was hurting them all. Especially Mhairi who was made to feel perpetual remorse about her jilting of Henry; she wished it could all be resolved amicably at last.

'You *should* come with us,' persisted Brabazon, 'It's a great honour for your brother to be asked to perform such an important engagement. The best people in Edinburgh will be there to hear him. I think we should go along and give him our support – *as a family*.'

'We didn't go when we played in the Albert Hall last year,' said Laurence mockingly.

His mother just looked him in the eye and said, 'Perhaps we should have.'

'You want me to go to Edinburgh with you tonight? All right, but I don't expect Henry'll appreciate me being there.'

306

The three of them rode up to Edinburgh in a hansom cab, with Laurence fretting at the slowness. He would have preferred to make the trip by electric tram if not by horseless carriage, but Brabazon still thought of a hansom as being the best way to travel. The church was packed with people dressed in their best clothes and the Nairns filed in self-consciously knowing that all eyes were on them. Henry was famous. There was even talk that he was about to be invited to play in New York soon.

The audience was treated to a night of magic. Henry's playing was truly magnificent and Brabazon felt her throat tighten with emotion as she listened. He had far surpassed his father as a musician now. Laurence sat thunderstruck too. The musician in him could appreciate his brother's artistry.

Mhairi sat beside her husband with her gloved hand in his and tears sparkling in her eyes. Her memory went back to the times she'd listened to Henry playing St Mary's organ – and then, as if he were tuned into her thoughts – he launched into the 'Queen of Sheba' piece. It thundered out, swelling exultantly like a glorious cry and she was swept along with it, remembering the delight with which she'd heard it for the first time. When Laurence looked at her enraptured face he felt a stab of jealousy. She should not be looking like that about anything connected with his brother.

1908

Willie Ord came calling from time to time at Perseverance Brewery and whenever Brabazon saw his carriage bowling into the yard, she steeled herself. She weighed each word he uttered in her presence, for in spite of his association with Laurence, she was still intensely suspicious of him. The habit of distrusting him had gone too deep for her to overcome it now.

He was conscious of her reserve and when he spoke to her was always very careful not to put a word out of place; acting affability itself; enquiring about her health; complimenting her on the reputation of Perseverance Brewery and making appreciative comments on any improvements Laurence introduced. He always spoke of Brabazon's younger son as if he thought she had given birth to a prodigy.

'You must be very proud of your Laurence. He's one of the wonders of Leith, Mrs Nairn!' he said with a puckish grin one day. 'The way he's turned this place into a great success is talked about by all the local traders.'

She stared at him caustically, 'I've two sons Mr Ord and they're both remarkable I'm proud to say.'

'Of course, of course. I hear your Henry has had a huge success in New York. Playing the organ, isn't he? But what's happened to this brewery has been a surprise even to me. Do you remember how I was always at you to sell for your own good?' He twinkled through his round spectacles at her and she realised that though she had always thought of him as being her senior, he was probably not much older than herself. He affected age, that was all.

She nodded with a small smile, 'Yes, I remember only too well. It's a good job I didn't listen to you, isn't it?'

Unabashed, Ord laughed. 'I'd have lost a good client,

that's for sure. But I was only looking out for your good and the good of your children you know. I really was. Now I see I was wrong and I'm man enough to admit it.'

She waited for what she was sure was coming next. It could not be another offer to buy, she knew he'd go to Laurence with that, but her instinct was right for Ord nodded confidentially to her and said, 'Laurence is a family man now, though your Henry's not wed yet, is he? The Nairns shouldn't be living over there.' He made a gesture with his arm towards the Place.

'I like it,' she said defensively. 'It's been good to me and the neighbours are all friends. I'd be miserable anywhere else.'

'There's no need to leave the Place; you'd not be miserable in there would you?' His hand was now indicating Brewery House. Its shutters were closed over the windows and it looked sadly desolate. The new owners, as was their custom, had gone to Portugal for the winter.

'No, I wouldn't,' she admitted. There was no point in trying to lie to him. He guessed the truth anyway. His sharp eyes had discerned her love of the old house long ago, for after all he'd been there the day she left it.

Beaming, he said, 'I've come straight round to tell you that I've just heard the owner's died in Lisbon. His wife and daughters are going to stay there and they want to sell.'

It felt unseemly to rejoice over a death but Brabazon's heart leapt at this news. 'That's interesting, have you any idea how much they'd be wanting for it?' she asked.

'That's not decided yet, but leave it to me. I'll ask around,' said Ord and bustled off on his stubby legs.

Robert Warre came up after he had gone and said with a grin, 'Well, missus, if I ever had any doubts that the brewery's doing well, they'd be gone this morning. I've never seen that auld yin looking so friendly.'

Brabazon did not stand on ceremony with any of the Warres. 'You're right. He's on our side now for some reason.'

Robert laughed, 'I've seen him hanging about. I think he's courting you, mistress Nairn.'

She reeled in shock, 'Courting me? *Him!*'

'Aye. His wife died last year and they say he's looking out for a lady with property.'

She laughed and protested that such an idea was impossible, but inwardly realised there might be a nugget of truth in what Robert said. 'I wouldn't put it past Ord,' she thought and the absurdity of the idea made her laugh. Aloud she said, 'Don't worry, Robert; you're not about to have Willie Ord as a co-owner here.'

During the days that followed, she went through every room of her old home in memory, planning what she would do when she bought it back. On one thing she'd already determined: the house would be turned round. The front door would be put back to its original and rightful position. She knew that a good deal of money would have to be expended so she discussed the project of buying with Laurence. He was agreeable to the expense, although he was not so keen on his mother's plan for turning the house around again. His arguments were financial and he protested, 'The reason they changed it round at all was to cut it off from the brewery yard. They made it a separate property and therefore more saleable. I see the logic of that. If we ever had to raise cash again, as you and Father did eighteen years ago, it would be more difficult to sell if the front door opened into our yard.'

Brabazon was adamant. 'I don't care. I love the Place and I don't want to be cut off from it ever again.'

'All right, all right,' he placated her, 'Do whatever you want. You've waited for it a long time after all.'

The time dragged heavily for her till Willie Ord called again. He was looking conspiratorial for he loved to be involved in a deal. Characteristically he did not come straight to the point though she was burning to ask only one question – how much was being asked for her old home? 'The wine trade must be doing well those days,'

310

he observed as he stared out of her office window at Brewery House.

She played his game, 'Why?'

He shook his head, 'They're asking a lot for your house.'

'How much?' She could not keep the urgent note out of her voice.

'They say it's one of the finest houses in Leith. Folk always say things like that when they're selling. They're also saying they've so many buyers eager to get it that they want it to go to auction.'

'How much do you think it'll make?' she persisted.

'Maybe five thousand if there's enough bidders,' said Ord.

Brabazon's heart sank. She and Duncan had sold the house for a thousand and she'd calculated that at the most it might have trebled in value since then, but five thousand pounds was a lot of money and she said as much to Willie Ord.

'It'll probably not come up for sale again in your lifetime,' he said flatly and she knew he was right. She had to grasp her chance now.

Something told her to hide her feelings however and she shook her head mournfully. 'I don't think it's worth as much as that.'

'Well it's going to auction. We'll have to wait and see,' he told her as he left.

As soon as he was out of the yard she put on her green cloak, which was still doing service in spite of the prosperity of the brewery, and walked over the yard to her old home. As she put her foot on the flight of stone steps leading to the back door, she realised it was the first time she'd stood there since the day she'd walked out of the house with Duncan. She put a hand up to her eyes and stared through the window, but could see little in the darkness inside. So she slipped up the side entry to the garden, where she wandered for a long time among the neatly tended flowerbeds. The soil was still rich because the brewery had gone on sending over loads of spent hops even after Alex Warre had died. 'If it's going to cost five thousand, that's what I'll pay. I must have it,' she promised herself.

Something told her to beware of Willie Ord, however, and when she talked of her suspicions to Laurence, he frowned and said, 'I'll ask around. Willie's all right but he's not above a bit of sharp dealing on a matter like this.'

Next day he was grinning when he stuck his head into his mother's office.'Guess who's acting as lawyer for the widow of the man in Brewery House?'

'Willie Ord,' she said without hesitation.

'Right first time!' said her son.

Brabazon was outraged, 'The rogue! He was only trying to push me into paying a big price because he knew how much I want the house. You go straight round to his office and tackle him about it, Laurence.'

'Don't be so righteous, Mother. That's business. I don't blame Willie. He's sharp, that's why he's valuable to whoever he's dealing for. If we'd paid, we'd have been unbusinesslike.'

Brabazon shook her head, 'There used to be things called *ethics*, Laurence, what's happened to them?'

His face sobered, 'Ethics and being too trusting lead people into trouble. Father had ethics, didn't he? There's not a lot of room for fair play in business, Mother. Now let's work out how we'll buy Brewery House for you without paying Willie's price.'

The next time Ord called to see her, Brabazon greeted him with a solemn face. 'I've been talking to Laurence. He feels there are too many other things we can do with five thousand pounds. For example, he wants to buy motor lorries for the beer deliveries; he says it will be a great advertisement. We'd be the first.'

Ord shook his head, 'What a pity. You're missing a good opportunity. Money spent on property is never wasted.'

She shrugged, 'I can't override Laurence's decision, I'm afraid. He's the boss here now.'

The house was advertised in the property columns of

the *Scotsman*, drawing many viewers to the neighbourhood who sometimes paused to speak to one or other of the residents of Perseverance Place and their questions about the salubriousness of the courtyard were never reassuringly answered. 'It can be a bit noisy and it does smell a bit if they're brewing – but we dinna mind, we're used to it.' said Elsie Warre when she was stopped in the yard by a would-be purchaser.

Laurence joked with Brabazon, 'When buyers come to view, I've told the stable lads to stick a pitchfork through the dung heap. That'll make the yard stink! Why don't you ask Ruthie Cairns to start singing if she sees folk looking around – that's enough to put them off more than a stinking midden.'

'What are we going to do? We can't let the house go without making some attempt to buy it,' she said.

'Don't worry. I've worked out a plan. We'll get someone to act for us at the auction, someone Willie doesn't know. If he thinks we're bidding, I wouldn't put it past him to try to push the price up a bit. I've told him we're not interested – I think he half-believes me.'

The auction was fixed for ten o'clock on a Wednesday morning and was to be held in the front garden of the house. Brabazon felt herself shiver with nerves when she read the sale announcement.

'Don't worry,' Laurence repeated. 'I've everything organised. Just you wait and see . . .'

The day of the sale was fine and people started arriving early. They came marching up the drive from Constitution Street or stood in groups around the courtyard, eyeing each other and growing excited, some of them loudly running down the house in the hope that other potential bidders might be put off.

From her kitchen window Brabazon watched the scene with a sinking heart. Most of the crowd looked so well-dressed and affluent that she was sure five thousand pounds was like tuppence to them.

313

Mhairi had come to wait with her and was well aware of the growing tension. At length she said, 'It would be far better if you and I take the children and go down to be there when the sale's going on. If you're seen to be not bidding, Ord'll be really convinced you're not interested.'

Brabazon agreed but wrung her hands, 'I can't bear the suspense,' she groaned.

Her daughter-in-law laughed, 'Trust Laurence, he'll manage everything.' She had complete faith in her husband's capacities.

When she reached Brewery House garden, Brabazon could see Willie Ord standing in the middle of a group of cronies. Laurence was among them, lounging against a wall and apparently indifferent to the proceedings. From then on, everything was done so swiftly that she hardly noticed what had happened. She thought the auctioneer was rehearsing at first: he waved his gavel in various directions shouting out figures. 'One thousand three hundred, thank you Willie . . . one thousand five hundred, thank you sir . . .' His voice became more animated as the figures rose and while she was still struggling to hear the sum he had reached, he raised the gavel high in the air and shouted, 'Are you all done then gentlemen? Are you all finished?' She leaned forward with one hand cupped over her ear but the wind blew the sound of the final figure away as the auctioneer banged his gavel on the front door of her beloved house. 'Going, going, GONE!' he shrieked and a man standing behind him with a ledger in his arms nodded and scribbled something into it.

As she felt the crowd relax, Brabazon saw the figure of Abe Meirstein, dressed in his habitual black, slip away from the back of the throng and head for the yard. What's Abe doing here? she wondered and began to run after him.

Holding up her skirts she sped like a girl out of the garden and across the yard. When she caught up with him, Abe was toiling up the outer flight of stairs, going very slowly because his rheumatics were bad. Hearing her behind him, he turned. His black eyes were

314

expressionless and they looked at each other without speaking for a few moments. Putting one hand to the neck of her dress as if to prevent herself from fainting, Brabazon asked, 'Who bought it Abe?'

'I did.'

She drew in her breath with a deep gasp, 'How much did you pay?'

'I paid two thousand seven hundred and eighty-five. Not bad, eh?'

The tears filled her eyes. 'Very good. I'll give you three for it.'

Then he nodded, just once, and said with a sudden smile, 'There's no need for that. I was bidding for you. You've just bought yourself a fine house, Mrs Nairn.'

She ran up the steps and threw her arms around him, breathing in his scent of snuff and mothballs. 'I love you Abe! I really love you,' she sobbed.

Suddenly the doorway was full of people. It seemed that everyone except Brabazon knew that Abe had been deputed to do the bidding for Laurence. A jubilant Minna came down to hold her husband's hand; Nellie and Elsie were jumping about in glee calling out, 'You did it!'

Mhairi and the bairns were standing smiling in the yard and Laurence came running across to join in the celebrations. From her position on the steps. Brabazon turned to them all with her arms spread out, crying in delight, 'Oh Laurence, you're a clever boy! Thank you so much. We'll have a party to celebrate this, my darlings. And we'll hold it in Brewery House.'

At that moment it seemed that all her years of hard work, and the troubles she'd endured since Duncan's bankruptcy, had been swept away. She felt young again, her life was full of promise for Brewery House was hers once more. 'I've done it, Duncan, I've done it!' sang her heart.

Brabazon went round to Willie Ord's office to fetch the key of Brewery House personally and was rewarded for her pains by seeing the look of utter astonishment on his face when she explained her presence.

He looked her up and down and, after a moment, grinned, 'Well, you can't blame me for trying, can you? Well done Mrs Nairn! You've got a bargain,' he told her.

The house was cold, empty and echoing but to Brabazon it was a place of magic. She wanted no one with her as she walked from room to room saying hello again. Finally she climbed to the top floor attic where she'd stood so sadly long ago. Her eyes gazed over the trees on the Links to her parents' house – sold now and lived in by someone else. She could find it in her heart to feel deep pity for her mother and was able to recognise how she'd suffered from frustrated love for a man that didn't love her back, and how that love had finally turned to implacable hatred. Brabazon's father still wrote regularly from St Petersburg but his last letter said that he'd recently been ill and now she wished that he could come back to his native Leith and be entertained in her fine home.

'What a lot of trouble love causes us,' she mused. She thought about her own sons and the breach between them which had never been properly healed. Henry spent most of his time now out of Leith, travelling and giving recitals all over the world. Success had assuaged some of his suffering but on the rare occasions when he did come home and was forced to meet Mhairi, his mother could see the pain in his face.

Returning to the Place, after the revisited grandeur of the other side of the yard, Brabazon found her flat suddenly seemed very small, but it was cosy, comfortable and very welcoming. She took her cherub candlestick from the mantelpiece and turned it slowly in her hands. 'I'll put it back where it used to stand tomorrow,' she promised herself.

The Brewery House party was planned to take place three weeks later, as soon as all the legal formalities were completed. She wanted to hold it before the builders moved in, for she was sticking to her determination to re-open the old front door. On the day of the celebration, sounds of preparation filled the yard. She'd ordered trestle-tables and quantities of food from a local baker; the beer was to be provided by the brewery. Laurence was again in charge of the music and though the famous musician, Henry, had come home from London, where he was giving lessons to aristocratic pupils, he had nothing to do with the programme. His taste was too highbrow for the sort of party that was planned.

Brabazon spent the day fussing that all was ready. She looked so radiant that even Laurence blinked at the sight of her. He'd found her in the drawing-room admiring the surroundings she'd regained. 'It's lovely,' she sighed.

'When are you going to move in yourself, Mother?' asked her son.

'Oh, not yet. The builders have to do their work first and then the painters will come. Anyway I've no furniture. Perhaps by next summer everything'll be ready. You and Mhairi and the children will be living in the house with me by then, too, I hope.'

He laughed, 'You're amazing. You work yourself to death to buy this place back and then you don't rush to live in it.'

She smiled, 'I suppose it does seem strange but just knowing it's mine again is enough. I'm savouring it like a child eating a piece of cake bit by bit. I want to take my time. When I move in, the house has to be perfect. Meanwhile I'll go on staying in my flat as I've always done, and look out at my house every day. But I'll know it's mine. I'll know that it's waiting for me to move in.'

When it became dark, music began pouring out of the open doors of Brewery House, its strains filling the courtyard of Perseverance Place. In groups of twos and threes people began arriving for the party, straggling down from the flats or climbing out of carriages and walking into the imposing building. Many of the guests had never been in it before but others, like Dr Allen and Mr Templeton had known it well in the old days.

Even for them stepping into the hall was like going into

fairyland because of the crystal chandelier which hung blazing from the ceiling, its crystals tinkling and glittering in the draught from the front door. Enormous garlands of flowers and ivy were looped in swathes down the banisters and on the white-painted walls. It was impossible for anyone to step into Brewery House that night without leaving all their worries with their coat in a heap at the foot of the staircase.

It was a very mixed party. Sergeant Gideon Warre of the Leith Police came with a flirtatious girl who waved an ostrich-feather fan; Sergeant Roddy and his wife were there too. Of course all the neighbours from the Place came – with the exception of the Lamberts but they did not have to be asked because they had moved away, only a short distance it was true but at least out of the building. When Willie Ord arrived, his white hair sticking up on end, he sought out Brabazon's brother Mark to whisper, 'A damned fine-looking woman, your sister! Do you think she might be open to an offer?'

Mark smiled, gratified for Brabazon's sake but shook his head, 'I don't think she'll ever marry again. She was devoted to her husband.' He had come to the party alone, because Amelia's health would not permit her to contemplate such an occasion. Mark had not coaxed her to change her mind because he now had a cosy arrangement with a lady living at the foot of Leith Walk in a neat little flat which he'd purchased for her some time ago. His plan was to spend the rest of the night there after Brabazon's party, and he wished that he'd been daring enough to bring his lady friend to the festivities with him.

The guests all stood in line to shake hands with Brabazon and her sons in the hall and everyone who saw her was pleased by how fine she looked in a dark purple velvet gown. It was plainly cut and unadorned with ribbons or loops, but that set off her magnificent head and erect carriage very well.

Afterwards, Henry Nairn moved urbanely from group to group being a good host. Fame and travel had not changed his kind heart and he hurried about finding chairs for some and drinks for others. To the chagrin of the giggling girls from the church choir however, he treated them all the same. He was impervious to attempts at flirtation.

The Perseverance Place neighbours at first tended to cluster together until Henry broke into their clique and dispersed them through the crowd. Soon Ruthie was slapping backs and telling risqué stories with business friends of Mark's. Nellie quickly found a soul mate in Dr Allen's sweet-faced wife and Elsie took to the floor with Mark's second son Peregrine – whose arrival at the party disconcerted his father somewhat until he realised that the boy was as anxious to keep out of his way as his father was to be avoided.

Abe and Minna were treated like royalty, given the best chairs and introduced to each guest. Brabazon would never forget Abe's role in winning back her house. Soon the old couple lost their reserve and were gossiping as easily as they did in their dusty shop. Sitting beside them was Donaldson the butcher with Lil who was squeezed into a low-cut, figured satin gown that glittered and shimmered whenever she moved her massive body. Around her neck sparkled a necklet of paste diamonds that would have rivalled anything in a theatrical outfitter's stock.

Mhairi missed the family reception line and was the last guest to arrive at the party because it had taken so long to settle the excited Josh and Poppy. The dancing was well under way when she stepped into the drawing-room and the first sight that met her eyes was her husband in his shirt sleeves, hair hanging down as it had always done when he was younger, playing the piano with such total concentration that he did not notice her arrival. Oblivious to other admiring eyes, she hurried over to where Brabazon stood surrounded by a crowd of people that parted like the Red Sea to allow Mhairi through.

'You look lovely, my dear!' said Brabazon kissing her on the cheek. Mhairi was dressed in a kingfisher blue silk gown with roses tucked into her bodice. The minute waist of the dress gave her a fashionable hourglass figure and swept back into a long train that swept the floor. She'd made it herself with the assistance of Nellie, and an admiring Elsie, and it set off most magnificently the crown of golden hair that was piled high on her head, showing her creamy neck and shoulders. On her feet she wore blue shoes adorned with diamanté buckles. She hoped Laurence would see them and hitched up the front of her dress a little so that they would show.

At that moment he struck a last chord on the piano and swivelled around on the stool to gaze at the gathering. His eye went first to Mhairi and her beauty pierced his heart. It was as if he were seeing her for the first time. She was transformed from a resident of Perseverance Place into a dazzling figure of romance. He walked proudly over to her, slipping an arm around her waist and nuzzling his face into her hair. She bent towards his touch and glowed with delight. It was plain to see that they were still in love.

As he played for the next few dances, he kept seeing her sweep past his line of vision in the arms of some man or other and started to feel the pangs of jealousy, but it was not until she took the floor for the fifth time that his passion burst into full fire. Henry was her partner and Laurence saw only too clearly the bedazzlement on his brother's face, and knew that he still loved Mhairi.

He clashed both hands together on the keys in a thunderous discord and stood up saying, 'I'm tired. I'm taking a break.' Then he stepped down from the dais and went to claim his wife.

He called to the band; 'Play something we can dance to.'

They struck up a mazurka and ignoring Henry he swung Mhairi off, making her feet leave the floor by the fury of his dancing. She clung to him with a frightened expression and whispered urgently, 'Not so fast, please, Laurence. I'll fall.'

'You'll not. I'm holding you. Don't you trust me?'

'What's wrong with you?'

'What should be wrong?' he asked through gritted

teeth, 'Don't you know I saw the way you were looking at my brother. What's going on with him? What're you trying to do?'

She was amazed, 'Nothing's going on. He asked me to dance and I did, that's all. He's an old friend, I would not refuse him.'

'I don't suppose you would. There's more to it than that. I can tell by the way he was looking at you . . . come on, dance faster Mhairi, dance faster.'

By the time the music ended, her hair was flying loose and tears filled her eyes, 'You're being very stupid,' she whispered to her husband when they stopped at last.

'Stupid, you think I'm stupid! I'll show you who's stupid' he spat back and left her standing in the middle of the floor while he descended on the girl that Gideon Warre had brought to the party. For the rest of the night he danced and flirted with her, pretending to be unaware of the hurt so obvious on his wife's face. She was rescued by Henry who saw her distress and engaged her in earnest conversation about his travels.

Otherwise it was a very good party for all. At about two o'clock in the morning people started straggling home until finally there was no one left except the Nairns – and the Cairns who would have gone on all night with a little encouragement.

'I'm going straight to bed,' announced Brabazon yawning widely and unconscious of the tension between Mhairi and Laurence.

Back in their own flat, the couple became engaged in the most vicious and violent quarrel they'd ever had. For the first time Laurence saw the hidden side of his wife – the deep streak of stubborn determination that had made her lay her beloved baby down at the feet of a plodding carthorse.

He started the argument by going straight into the attack, 'I was watching you. I saw him talking to you all night.'

She turned on him and said with steely coldness, 'He only did that because he knew I was hurt. He saw that

321

you'd been cruel to me and that I minded you flirting with that silly girl of Gideon's.'

He snorted 'Gideon's girl! She was just a little tart. He shouldn't have brought a girl like that to Mother's party.'

'You disgust me! You slobber all over the girl and then call her a tart. I suppose you know all about tarts.'

'I never pretended I didn't,' he was glaring at her as if he wanted to wound her.

She shrivelled inside and turned away from him, erecting a barrier between them. 'I don't want to hear about it. I might never forgive you, I might never forget.'

Something hard in her face made Laurence wish he had never started the fight. He put out a hand and tried to take hers, but she deliberately avoided him. They undressed in silence and climbed into bed, taking care to keep well apart though he longed to touch her. For her part she longed to be touched, but was not going to be the one to make the first move. He'd done wrong; it was Laurence who should apologise. She was lying fuming at his failure to realise this when, in the middle of the night, he rolled towards her with a groan and said, 'You're being silly. Let's make up.'

If only he had phrased it another way she was to think later. If only he'd said '*We're* being silly,' the fight would have been over and they would have slept in each other's arms. It was unjust and instead of softening to him she deliberately turned away, hunching up one shoulder and pulling the blanket off him. A breach was made in the fabric of their marriage.

The next day they were perfunctory with each other, but had no time to argue because the pace was hectic. Everything had to be taken out of the big house and the rooms swept clean. Brabazon, who was supervising the operation was radiant, talking incessantly about her party, who was there and what was said. She still did not notice the coldness between her son and his wife.

When all was out, Laurence drove the cart loaded with chairs and tables back to the premises of the baker who'd rented them out. He did not return for hours and Mhairi was in bed with her eyes tight closed by the time he let himself into the flat. He climbed in beside her and the beer he had drunk made him fall asleep instantly.

It was almost three o'clock in the morning when Mhairi was wakened by a terrible rushing sound and the smell of burning. In the square window opposite the bed, the sky outside was bright red and coloured sparks were flying across it like a series of shooting stars. With a scream she shook her husband awake and ran to grab her children. Laurence raced from door to door in the building, hammering on the panels and yelling, 'Fire, fire!'

Out in the yard with her children, both wrapped in blankets, Mhairi saw that it was not the brewery that was ablaze as she had first thought but Brabazon's beautiful house. Flames were shooting up to the sky and every window was a square of red, orange, purple and yellow. The interior was already gutted and fire leapt from a hole in the roof like an inferno.

Others were gathering in the yard, frightened and staring. Brabazon stood with the old green cape over her nightgown, transfixed by the scene. Henry had gone for the fire engine and came running back up the alley shouting, 'They're on their way. Let's start filling buckets.'

Brabazon turned towards him and said bleakly, 'There's no point. We can't save it. It's gone now; it's gutted.'

'Maybe not, but we've got to stop it spreading,' he shouted back at her.

The scene in the courtyard was like a vision of Hell as man and women formed a line and passed buckets of water from the brewery to the burning building. In spite of their tremendous efforts, however, the inferno refused to be quelled and eventually the blaze could be seen from as far away as Edinburgh. Brabazon led the children out of the Place and along to Mr Templeton's manse where he took them in with expressions of sympathy and comfort. Abe and Minna, who were too old to fight the fire, were also sent to the manse.

Leith Fire Brigade came running up the alley from the

Kirkgate to take over the fire-fighting and Gideon, at the head of a posse of policeman, also arrived. When he saw what had happened, he paused in horror. Already he could tell that the position was hopeless and when dawn came the terrible extent of the damage was revealed. Only the outer walls of the lovely old house still stood, blackened and stark. The heart of the house was only a pile of rubble from which smoke rose like a funeral pyre.

Brabazon stood beside her sons with their arms around her. She needed their support for she felt old and very tired.

'I'm sorry Mother. By the time we saw the fire it had taken too strong a hold,' said Laurence. His face and forearms were cruelly blistered but he did not yet feel any pain. That was to come later.

'At least we saved the brewery and the building,' whispered Brabazon. She was too exhausted and depressed to think of anything else.

The fire went on burning for three days before it was doused completely and it was not until then that the investigating team could move in.

Brabazon and Gideon watched them at work. 'You hadn't left a fire still burning or a candle not snuffed, had you?' he asked her.

She shook her head with conviction. 'No. I was very, very careful Gideon. The fire was not lit again after the party and when we tidied up there were no rugs on the floors to catch alight. I can't understand what's happened.'

'Neither can I.' said Gideon bitterly, poking with his boot toe at a pile of ash, 'It looks as if someone set fire to your house. There are some crazy people around who enjoy doing a thing like that.'

'Someone who doesn't like me perhaps?'

'Maybe not even that. It could be someone who likes watching fires burn. Was there any stranger around when you were all trying to save the house?'

She shook her head. 'No, I don't think so. There was

just the neighbours and my sons – and Tom Lambert came to watch but he didn't help.'

'Lambert?' Gideon's voice was sharp.

'Yes. I saw him standing in the alleyway with his hands in his pockets. He didn't lift a bucket but he stood there for a long time till the Fire Brigade arrived. Then he went away.'

'And by that time the house was doomed, wasn't it?'

She shook her head sadly, 'Yes, I'm afraid it was.'

When he left Brabazon, Gideon walked to the block where the Lamberts now lived and climbed the stairs to their flat. When he rapped on the door it was opened only a chink and he said in his most official voice, 'I'm here on police business Mrs Lambert. Where's your man?'

She whispered, 'He's in the docks working.'

'Where was he the night Mrs Nairn's house burned down?'

'He was out drinking. It was pay-night.' From her tone it was obvious that was a sufficiently good reason for a husband to be absent from home.

'All night?' questioned Gideon.

'Aye, sometimes he doesn't mak' it hame'

'How did you know about the fire?'

The woman opened the door a few inches more and he could see her white, frightened face staring at him.

'Somebody knocked on my door and told me to get out. I took my bairn and went into the Kirkgate. Then someone took us to the manse. We were there till morning.'

'And you didn't see your man?'

She shook her head. 'No.'

When Gideon thanked her and turned to descend the stairs again, she opened the door fully and called after him, 'Oh, dinna tell him I spoke to you about this, will you?' She sounded really afraid.

Lambert was in the middle of a gang of men unloading a timber ship and when Gideon spoke to the ganger he called the sullen man out of the line.

'Leave me alone you little bastard!' hissed Lambert,

'You'e aye persecuting me and I'm losing money standing here gassing with you.'

Gideon was calm, 'This won't take long. Where were you on Friday night?'

Lambert pretended to be puzzled by the question, 'Friday? Which Friday?'

'You ken fine which Friday. The night of the fire.'

'Oh when Mrs Nairn's grand hoose burned doon. I was in The Anchor howff. You can ask there if you don't believe me. Some of the lads in the gang here were there too.'

'All night?'

Lambert shot a glance at Gideon's innocent face, 'No. I went off with a woman after, didn't I? My wife's a dead loss these days. You ken what it's like – or maybe you don't!' He laughed at his own sally and turned to see if his mates had heard him.

'Which whore were you with? Will she vouch for you?' Gideon asked calmly.

'Oh she'll vouch for me all right. It was a wee blonde one called Alice. She's on the corner by the swing bridge most nights. Go and ask her – but watch out, she'll have you by the balls before you know what's happened – if you have any balls that is.' He was jeering loudly for the benefit of his friends, but Gideon remained impassive.

'Mrs Nairn says she saw you in the Place watching the fire,' he told Lambert.

A look of evil flashed through the pig-like eyes, 'She's a liar!'

'Oh, I doubt that,; said Gideon.

'Then she was imagining things,' conceded Lambert.

Of course the whore called Alice backed up Lambert's story. He had been with her all night, she told Gideon. He could not make her change her mind.

Mr Templeton, the minister, went to seek out the Nairn brothers and found them together in the brewhouse. Henry had cancelled his appointments in London to stay in Leith for the moment. Their mother was causing them considerable concern and that brought them together.

'I hope you don't think I'm interfering,' said kind Templeton, 'But I've just been speaking to your mother. She's in the church praying again.'

The brothers stared back at the minister with their expressions showing how worried they were. 'She's not well. The doctor says she's exhausted,' said Laurence.

'She's had a very great shock,' said Mr Templeton, 'She's suffering from some sort of sense of guilt. She seems to think that the burning down of the house was a punishment from God for something she's done. I've been trying to persuade her that God isn't like that, but all she can say is that she's brought it on herself. It has something to do with your father, I understand.'

The brothers looked at each other askance. They were terrified in case she went around Leith talking to people who would not be as discreet as Mr Templeton.

'We've been discussing her. We think she ought to take a holiday. Always walking around the yard and seeing the ruins of the old house is preying on her mind. She'll not be better till she gets away,' said Henry with conviction.

'I agree. That's a very good idea. Will someone go with her?' asked the minister.

'I'll go,' said Henry. 'Our Uncle Mark's been here and we're trying to make arrangements now. We think she should go to Russia. Her father's still there and it would be a good thing if she could see him. He's not been well and she's very fond of him.'

'Has she agreed to go?' asked the minister, remembering the distracted woman in the pew of his church.

'She doesn't know anything about it yet,' said Laurence. 'We're going to arrange her passage and then present her with the news. My Mhairi's going to pack her cases. All she'll have to do is board the ship.'

When the preparations were completed, Brabazon shrank in horror as her sons told her that she was sailing to Russia, 'but I can't leave Leith,' she whispered.

'Mother, that's what you need. You need to get away. We want you to go to Russia and see your father.'

She shook her head, 'I can't. It's too far.' The idea of even stepping out of the Kirkgate terrified her now.

Laurence bent down and took her hands in his, 'You're going even if we've to carry you to the ship. Henry's sailing with you because he's got a series of concerts in Germany and he'll travel on there after he leaves you in St Petersburg. Think about it Mother, think about seeing your father again. He's not well Uncle Mark says, and he's been asking for you.'

She lifted her head, eyes wide, 'Asking for me? Has he really?'

Both of her sons nodded, 'Yes, he has. He wants to see you. You'd be letting him down if you don't go.'

She remembered the dashing father she'd worshipped when she was a child. She remembered the way he laughed when he threw her up in his arms, how he enchanted her by his joking. He had been the only gleam of light and gaiety in their gloomy, manner-conscious home. 'I'd like to see him once more.' she said.

Even then they had not won. She was still protesting when they ushered her up the gangplank of the ship bound for Russia. Before the family left her on board with Henry, she bent down to her grandchildren and hugged them close. To a solemn-faced Poppy and Josh she said, 'I'll tell your Great-grandpapa about you both and what a fine young fellow his namesake is.'

Tom Lambert had always taken great pleasure in beating his wife, but after Gideon's visit to the dock and the questions about where Lambert had been on the night of the fire, the beatings became more vicious and frequent. Instead of staying out most nights as he had done for years, he began coming home early, only half-drunk, and goading the terrified woman. No matter how she tried to placate him, she could do nothing that did not give him reason to hit her. His was a rule of terror over both Irene and the growing Sophia.

One night Irene reached the end of her tether and did not run to answer the door when he came knocking at it. He was forced to use his key and came staggering in. He was more drunk than usual and asked her in a slurred voice, 'Why didn't you open the door, you bitch?'

'I'm feeding the bairn.'

'Where's my supper?'

'There isn't any. I've no money. You didn't give me any this week.'

Grinning as if she'd made a joke, he walked up to his wife and grabbed a handful of hair, pulling her head back fiercely. She grimaced, but did not cry out because she knew that excited him to even more extreme violence.

'Get my supper and stop your cheek,' he hissed, tugging at her hair. He then deliberately turned over Sophia's plate and allowed the milk to run down on to the floor, rubbing it into the bare boards with his foot.

Irene shook herself free, calling out to her crouching daughter, 'Run away, run away and hide, bairn!' The girl fled towards the bedroom where she huddled down with her arms around her head trying to shut out the terrible noises which she knew were about to follow as Lambert advanced remorselessly on her mother, driving her into a corner. There Irene huddled from him, shielding her head with raised forearms. Her passivity excited him and he bunched his fists so that he could hit her harder.

He also kicked at her body with his heavy working boots and did not stop until he felt one of her ribs crack beneath his onslaught. Behind him the child screamed, 'Stop it, stop it!'

He turned on her then, fists raised, 'Get back in there or I'll hit you too,' he told her and slammed the bedroom door so that he could attack his wife uninterrupted. When his rage was spent, he opened his front door and slung her body on to the stair well. 'Get out and don't come back,' he shouted as he locked the door against her semi-conscious figure.

Gideon Warre was walking the beat along the Kirkgate to Tolbooth Wynd.

'There must be some way to prove it, there must. I'm sure Lambert's involved . . . I can't let the bugger put it over on me,' he fumed inwardly. His failure to explain the mysterious fire at Brewery House was a frustration to him and his persistent pleading at the police station for a renewed investigation into what was considered the open-and-shut case of his father's death, was beginning to cause irritation with his superiors. Yet the same persistence that had made Gideon stand up to the Champion, now made him go on ferreting away, asking questions and never allowing the cases to be finally shelved.

That night he had planned to take a short cut through the maze of little wynds to the police station at the corner of Queen Charlotte Street, but an impulse made him retrace his footsteps towards Perseverance Place. He was going to take another look at the burned-out ruins of Brabazon's house . . .

He approached through the churchyard, walking around the perimeter of the wall till he came to the clump of ivy which concealed the secret door to the brewery. He stooped down and tried the handle. As usual it was unlocked. When he opened it, he heard the sound of someone moving about in the brewhouse and called out, 'Anyone there?'

His brother Robert's voice came back and Gideon smiled. Robert was a dedicated worker like his father had been. He could barely bring himself to go home at night.

Gideon breathed in the familiar smell of brewing hops with pleasure as he crossed the floor to where a light glimmered. Robert was perched on top of a stepladder watching the creamy suds of yeast slowly heaving up and down inside the brewing vat. They still fascinated him in spite of the many times he had seen them and his gaze followed their hypnotising undulations for a long time before he turned to call down to his brother.

'This brew's going well but I just wanted to check.

Now that Mrs Nairn's away, I don't want anything to go wrong.'

'You're as bad as Father,' said Gideon.

'I hope I don't end up the same way though!' replied Robert coming carefully down the ladder.

Gideon's face went heavy and stern. 'That was a funny business. I've never been happy about it.'

'I know,' replied his brother, 'But there's nothing you can do. Don't brood lad. Come on through and I'll give you a pundy to help you on your way.'

With the beer comforting his stomach and his mind full of childhood memories, Gideon let himself out of the monks' doorway fifteen minutes later. He enjoyed a leisurely stroll through the moonlit churchyard but when he was almost upon the Kirkgate, his euphoric mood changed. He heard the sound of someone gasping in agony and saw a dark shape huddled at the foot of one of the graves. Running across, he found a woman crouched on the ground. He put a hand on her shoulder and bent down to look into her face. It was Irene Lambert. She was fighting for breath, her face so badly bruised and caked with dried blood that she was hardly recognisable. When Gideon tried to lift her, she cried out in such pain that he hurriedly loosed his grip. 'What's happened to you?' he asked.

'Oh, Gideon, get me a doctor, and go back for my bairn . . . he's got her in there' Her words were gasped as if she were only able to breathe from the top part of her lungs and he could see that her injuries were serious. And now he knew who had inflicted them . . .

He had to leave poor Irene while he ran to the police station but when he returned it was with two constables and a canvas stretcher. 'Take her up to the hospital,' said Gideon, 'I'll go to the flat and fetch her bairn.'

It took a lot of banging on the door before Tom Lambert was roused from his drunken sleep. When he did open up he glared angrily at the cause of the row and demanded, 'What the hell do you think you're doing?'

Gideon could see the frightened face of Sophia behind

her father. He shoved a foot into the doorjamb and said, 'Your wife's in the hospital. She's badly injured and she wants to see her bairn.'

Lambert did not bat an eye, 'She was drunk, she fell doon the stairs,' he said.

'Why didn't you go to help her then?'

'Why should I? I've just told you she was drunk.'

Gideon's voice was steely. 'Listen Lambert, you can't pull that one again. That woman's been beaten up and we both know who did it. Come with me now or by God, I'll beat the hell out of you the same way as you beat her.'

Lambert was a coward and young Warre's reputation as a fierce fighter was well-known. Without further protest he fetched his coat and walked beside Gideon to the hospital, with a sobbing but speechless Sophia trailing beside them. Once there, Gideon was stern and said, 'Stay here in the corridor till I ask the doctor how she is. Don't go away.'

Lambert's wife lay stretched on a high metal bed with nurses fussing around her. A white-coated doctor was wiping his hands as Gideon came in and he shook his head saying, 'This one's bad. She's got internal injuries. I don't think I can save her.'

Gideon leaned over the body on the bed and saw that her eyelids were fluttering, 'Can you hear me Mrs Lambert?' he whispered. The fluttering increased and he said urgently, 'I fetched Sophia. She's here now. What happened? Did he beat you up?' He knew the answer but needed her testimony.

Just then there was a noise behind him and Gideon turned to see that one of the nurses had brought in Lambert and Sophia. The girl ran towards her mother and took her dangling hand. Lambert stood in the doorway.

'Get him out of here,' snapped Gideon in rage and when Lambert was told to go, he leaned over Irene again whispering the same questions.

Irene's eyes slowly opened and she looked into her

daughter's face and then over at Gideon. 'I fell,' she groaned.

He groaned too, 'Don't be daft, woman. Tell me the truth and I'll charge him.'

'I fell. He'll kill my bairn . . . like he killed your dad.' The words were barely even whispered and Gideon had to bend his head to hear them.

He turned towards Sophia and then to the doctor saying urgently, 'Did you hear what she said? Did you hear it?'

Sophia laid her head on the side of the bed and wept but the doctor who was in the far corner of the white-tiled room, turned and said angrily to Gideon, 'I don't know what you're playing at. That woman's dying. Let her do so in peace for God's sake.'

Gideon was desperate. He put a hand on Sophia's heaving shoulder and said, 'You heard her. She said he killed my father, didn't she?'

Sophia looked towards the door through which Lambert had been taken and sobbed, 'No, no, go away . . .'

Irene's eyes were closed now and her breath so rasping that she could no longer speak.

The doctor pulled at Gideon's sleeve. 'If you don't stop this, I'll have to make an official complaint. She *won't* say he did it. Don't waste your time and don't upset her any more. They never tell. They're always too scared.'

'Christ, I can't believe this,' groaned Gideon sinking his head into his hands. He felt so near to unearthing the truth for which he'd spent years searching, but still it was to be denied him.

Irene Lambert died without speaking again. When it was over Gideon rose to his feet and strode into the corridor where Lambert sat slumped on a bench.

'Your wife's dead,' said Gideon.

Lambert nodded. The doctor had told him.

'You killed her. You're a murderer.'

'Did she say that?'

'No, she didn't but I know what happened.'

'I'm telling you she fell down the stairs when she was drunk. The bairn saw it. She'll back me up.'

333

Gideon's heart sank. Sophia still remained at her mother's bedside, but he let her be. It was very plain to see that she was as terrified of her father as her mother had been. There was no chance of getting the truth from her.

Face tense and drawn, Gideon leaned over the seated man and said very slowly and quietly, 'If anything happens to the girl. If I hear you're ill-treating her like you ill-treated her mother, I'm telling you Lambert that I'll get you one night in a dark alley and you'll not live to tell anybody about it.'

Lambert glared back, his eyes red like a maddened animal's. 'That'll be some fight,' he whispered.

The ship carrying Henry and Brabazon Nairn was the last to sail up the Neva and into St Petersburg before ice closed the river for the winter.

It was early November and the cold had come early that year, but it arrived together with a flinty sun that glanced off the thin golden spires and pinnacles that rose from the heart of the beautiful city.

The voyage over the Baltic Sea had been stormy and Brabazon had spent most of her time in her cabin. She was glad to step ashore and into her father's arms.

He held her tight and said with a sob in his voice, 'I've been longing to see you, my dear.' He was still tall and straight, but painfully thin and haggard. It was obvious that he was ill yet he still looked exotic and dashing in his floor-length sable coat and enormous fur hat. Greeting Henry too, he led them over to where a small fur wrapped figure stood surrounded by young women.

If Brabazon had ever consciously wondered what her father's lover looked like, she knew as she met Olga that her imagination would never have come up with anything near the truth. She would almost certainly have conjured up a woman of exquisite beauty – tall, dark-haired, a match for Joshua in every way. But Olga, his second wife and the woman for whom he'd broken up his first marriage and left his home, was small and dumpy with a heart-shaped face and twinkling brown eyes. If she had any claim to beauty it was her lips, which curved in exquisite sweetness. Now they were smiling at Brabazon and it was impossible not to smile back. As she did so, Brabazon remembered the discontented downward curve of her mother's mouth. No wonder Joshua preferred Olga.

The women all clustered round her, exclaiming and laughing, and Olga said something in French, too rapid for Brabazon's schoolroom understanding to follow. Joshua laughed. 'She says you're both like me – too tall to kiss easily!' But nevertheless Olga stood on tiptoe and managed to hug the newcomers to her.

The young women in the welcoming party were Joshua and Olga's daughters, three pretty girls who were highly excited by meeting their half-sister from beyond the sea, and one of her sons. When they realised that Brabazon could speak French, though haltingly, they talked to her very slowly, repeating words so that she could more easily understand, 'Father has been so eager to see you. He's talked of nothing else for days. We think you're his favourite child!' They said this gaily and it was obvious there was no jealousy in their hearts.

A fleet of carriages was lined up on the dockside and the party streamed towards them, carrying Henry and Brabazon along in their midst. Almost before the two visiting Nairns knew it, they were transported to an imposing front door which was opened by a footman in satin and a curled white wig. Even Henry was fazed and Brabazon stared. She knew her father was prosperous but this was beyond her imaginings!

Joshua, on the steps beside them recognised their amazement and turned to say, 'This is Olga's house. She's a Grand Duchess and has always lived in great style but you mustn't let that upset you. She's the dearest and kindest woman in the world.'

Olga was very rich. The only daughter of a man who owned huge estates in the Ukraine, she had spent her early life travelling from one enormous house to another until she'd met Joshua Logan at a winter reception in St Petersburg. Although each was married already it was what she was fond of describing as a *coup de foudre*. They fell in love instantly; became lovers that night and eventually defied convention by living openly together. In spite of her rather staid appearance, Olga was as much of a rebel as Brabazon's father. She had four children by him before they married – as well as one by her first marriage – but she was related to the Romanovs and no one dared criticise anything she did. Her husband, a feeble man, but more amenable than the intransigent Maria Logan who would never agree to a divorce, was pensioned off to a place in the Crimea where he was still living happily with a series of French mistresses. The liaison and later marriage between Olga and Joshua was delightfully happy.

Olga saw the signs of sorrow and pain on Brabazon's face and set about soothing them away. She was a past mistress at giving pleasure. Every day she planned a treat for her visitors and they soon found that everything that was elegant, everything that was fashionable in St Petersburg, was French. The language of the court was French; the manners were French; the best carriages were French; the clothes of both men and women had to be from Paris to be considered smart at all.

A dazzled Brabazon was led from shop to shop by her father's wife, and presents were piled into her arms. She was robed in gowns of such magnificence that she was astonished when she saw the reflection staring back from the mirror at her. 'Is that me?' she wondered stepping forward for a closer look.

Olga was delighted at the transformation she was bringing about and could not stop. Like a fairy godmother, she wanted to change Brabazon's life. Holding out a gown of garnet velvet, she cried 'You're so elegant. You must make the best of yourself. Look, try this dress, it's a wonderful colour – and then I'll take you to my jeweller for a necklace of stones to match. Your father says I'm to spare no expense . . . he was always so upset that you wouldn't accept help from him when you needed it, you know.'

Brabazon shook her head, 'I couldn't when Duncan was alive; his pride would have been hurt.'

Olga nodded, 'Your father understood my dear, but indulge him now by letting him spoil you a little.'

The weeks passed full of pleasure both for Brabazon and Henry. He was taken to the St Petersburg Conservatoire of Music where the teachers and students listened enraptured to his playing and fêted him. Then he was whisked from the house of one admirer to another, taken to concerts and ballets, dined and wined, always surrounded by enthusiasts. To him and to his mother, the brewery and Perseverance Place gradually receded and the smell of burning left Brabazon's nostrils. As her new family claimed her, she stopped waking every morning with her mind full of worries about what was happening at home and accepted at last that Laurence would be able to cope very well in sole charge. She hoped he did not overreach himself for he'd taken over Gordon's completely and was running the two establishments as one. Not content with that, he'd written to say that he was considering expanding even more, and was investigating the purchase of a small brewery in Musselburgh. 'By the time you come back, we'll be a huge concern, Mother,' said his letter, and she quailed as she read it. She was not sure that she wanted her little Perseverance Brewery to be transformed.

Henry had grown even more in assurance since his arrival in St Petersburg and though he had originally said that he would stay for a few weeks, and then return to his concert schedule, his date of departure had been put off several times. He was flourishing in Russia and it even seemed as if his broken heart might heal at last, because his mother noticed with pleasure how he danced and flirted with the charming young women of Olga's circle. At one recital they'd attended, Henry had also been invited to play. Pride had overwhelmed Brabazon when he'd chosen a Schubert piece that had left everyone spellbound.

337

After it was over, a tall man with a neatly clipped white beard had come over to Brabazon and bent over her hand.

'I understand that you are the mother of that young man. You must be very proud of him,' he said smiling gravely.

'I am,' she said simply.

The stranger sighed, 'I have a daughter of whom I too am very proud. She is an artist. It is wonderful when one's children do things that one cannot do oneself, is it not? But perhaps you can play music like your son?' He was speaking English in a slow, halting way.

She smiled and shook her head, 'No, not at all.'

'And I cannot paint!'

He introduced himself as Count Alexei Orlov and led Brabazon across the room to meet a girl among the crowd around Henry. 'This is my daughter Antonia, the painter,' he said with pride.

The petite person in a cream silk gown and wearing roses in her dark hair, patted him on the arm, 'Don't Father, you'll make me embarrassed,' she said.

The evident fondness between father and daughter warmed Brabazon's heart and she smiled at them.

The count particularly wanted his daughter to travel, 'She has been to France, and to Germany. Next I would like her to go to London, because she tells me there are many wonderful galleries there that she wishes to see. One day I will send her if I can find some suitable person to act as her chaperon. She is very young, not yet twenty,' he told Brabazon.

Next day he and Antonia had come to call. To Brabazon's surprise Henry had offered to join their sightseeing party and sat beside Antonia in the carriage, taking obvious pleasure in her company. Though she was not as beautiful as many of the other girls who crowded around him, Antonia was full of personality and had been well educated in music as well as art.

As Brabazon had watched Henry unbending, laughing at Antonia's sallies, she knew he'd not seemed so carefree for years. Not since, and Brabazon hardly dared think of it, not since he had first taken young Mhairi McKay out walking on the Links.

1911

During Brabazon's absence in Russia, Laurence brought in a contractor who cleared away the debris of Brewery House and razed the site. What was left when the last of the heaped carts rumbled away was only a broken wall – staring across at Perseverance Place like an unpeopled stage set. Then Laurence called in an architect and gave orders that another house should be built on the site.

The architect was delighted with such a commission. 'I can see a really elegant villa here, Mr Nairn,' he enthused, 'In red sandstone perhaps with a Gothic façade and a stylish mansard roof.'

Laurence shook his head, 'I've an old print that'll show you exactly the sort of house that I want,' he said and led him into the brewery office where a picture of the house hung in a dusty corner. He pointed to it. 'I want that.'

'But it's Georgian.' protested the architect.

'Old-fashioned or not, that's what I want. And it must be exactly the same. If you can't do it I'll find someone else who can.' Laurence did not have time to waste arguing about mansard roofs and the architect took the commission, though he grumbled a lot about the restrictions put on him. What was worse was that Laurence Nairn was in a hurry, 'I don't suppose she'll stay away for long. It must be finished, or as near finished as possible by summer,' he said.

Protests that this was impossible were swept away by the laying out of more money. 'I hope the profits will stand this. It's goodbye to motor lorries this year again,' thought Laurence as he signed the contract for the rebuilding of his mother's house.

He was feeling strangely disgruntled with life. The delights of success, now that he had them in his grasp, were beginning to taste stale. When he was at home, Mhairi and the children found him short-tempered and demanding. He was especially hard on his son, young Josh.

Mhairi decided to talk to him about his ill-temper. One Sunday evening when the children had gone out, she laid a hand on his shoulder as he sat in the fireside chair. 'What's wrong?' she asked.

He shrugged, 'Nothing's wrong. I'm tired, that's all.'

'But you're so irritable with the children. They're good bairns, they don't deserve it. You're always snapping at Josh especially.'

He flashed his dark eyes at her, 'There you go again! The children! Josh! Do you ever think of anything else? You're too wrapped up in them. It's not like it used to be when there was only us.'

'Things change,' she said patiently, 'We've responsibilities.'

He rose and pulled on his jacket, 'Responsibilities! I'm tired of them.'

'Where are you going?' she asked.

'Off to hear the speakers on the Links. I want to have an argument with somebody. I can't get a decent one here.'

She stared uncomprehendingly at his back and he turned to look at her, 'Come with me. We'll go and listen to them talking about religion and politics – all sorts of things but not about children or about beer. The band might be playing.'

'I can't,' she shook her head, 'Josh and Poppy will be back in a few minutes and they'll need their tea.'

He was striding fast across the Links, walking off his anger, when he heard a sharp whistle and turned to see a figure in a scarlet uniform waving an arm in his direction. His heart lifted. It was Pat.

'I didn't know you were back,' he said with a broad smile when they were standing looking at each other.

'I came back today. I'm bored already!' Pat laughed, white teeth flashing in his tanned face. He was the very model of the perfect soldier and as usual he had a strangely unsettling effect on Laurence. Looking at Pat he felt he had missed out on the opportunities of life, because he'd stayed in Leith and done nothing. The achievements he could have been proud of a few hours before shrank to nothing now in his estimation. Pat's very presence – his swaggering walk, his immaculate appearance, the caustic comments he made in a loud voice – had the same effect on the Place as a stone thrown into the middle of a peaceful pond. And it grew worse over the days that followed.

As usual he assumed that Laurence would be ready to go out drinking with him every night, and looked genuinely astonished if his invitation was refused.

'I'm busy. I've work to do,' Laurence said the first time he wanted to avoid going out with Pat. Nights spent in the bars of The Shore were no longer the sort of thing he enjoyed.

'Work? You'll be a long time dead, laddie,' said Pat brooking no refusal.

The next night Laurence sought for an excuse, he said, 'My wife doesn't like me going out every night.'

Pat rocked back on his heels. 'I never thought I'd hear you saying you were under some woman's thumb!' he scoffed. So Laurence joined him, though grudgingly and feeling out of place. He was secretly anxious to avoid his old friend but Pat was unconscious of this.

'Why don't you say "No"? Why don't you stand up to him?' Mhairi asked her husband after he rose next morning complaining of an aching head.

Laurence, however, would not admit that he had been dragged out against his will, though he knew that to be the case. 'He's my friend and anyway it's good to get out of the house. There's nothing here but you scolding and bairns chattering and yelling from morning till night.'

Mhairi felt her skin shrink at his words. She protested, 'But they're your bairns too, and they love you.' He did not reply.

For the two weeks of Pat's leave, the atmosphere in the

342

Nairn home was poisoned by his presence. Laurence was unsettled and angry; torn between taunts about how domesticity could spoil a man, and his own enjoyment of life with Mhairi – which he felt he must deny, even to himself. Pat tried to urge him to flirt with the whores as they'd used to do but he refused and his friend said scornfully, 'I don't know how you can stand getting into bed with the same woman every night for a lifetime!'

Laurence replied lamely, 'but we're comfortable together. I don't want to let her down. She trusts me.' He was reluctant to talk to Pat about his real feelings for his wife. They were private; almost sacred. Talking about them to Pat would sully them.

The soldier scoffed into his beer, '*Comfortable!* What a word. You're not meant to be comfortable with women. You should screw 'em and leave 'em. That's the best way.'

It struck Laurence that there was something wrong with Pat. Although he professed an urgent need for women as sexual outlets, he did not actually like them and it was obvious that he had never felt the delight that Laurence had experienced, and still enjoyed, with Mhairi or the agonised rapture he had gone through with Daisy.

It was a relief when the day came that Pat had to return to his regiment in the South. Before he went away, he regaled Laurence with his reflections on the possibility of another war. 'There's been nothing to do since we beat the Boers, but we'll be fighting the Germans soon, you mark my words. By God, I'm looking forward to it! There's no pleasure in peace for a fighting man. We'll show the world how to fight!'

When Pat marched off across the courtyard, Laurence was at the mouth of the alley talking to the builder in charge of the reconstruction of Brewery House. The two friends shook hands in farewell and he was surprised at the mixture of feelings he had about Pat – regret for the past, for their lost friendship and relief that Pat was leaving. Relief predominated.

'Don't get yourself shot!' he said jocularly.

343

'And don't you let yourself be mollycoddled by women. You're under the thumb of your wife and your mother. You should break out before it's too late,' was Pat's advice to his boyhood friend. Then he strode away in the direction of the station while Laurence gazed after his ramrod back. 'Break out before it's too late . . .' the words echoed in his mind. Too late for what? he wondered.

The porters at the Caledonian railway station in Leith were used to coping with rich and fashionable travellers. Every day they pushed huge cabin trunks along on their trolleys for affluent people travelling to and from the boats that docked in the harbour. Yet the woman who hailed a grey moustached porter one April evening was an unusually impressive sight even for the cosmopolitan port. She had the air of a duchess and behind her in the carriage could be seen a mound of crocodile suitcases with sparkling golden clasps.

As if she was used to being the centre of attention, she paused dramatically on the platform when she alighted from her first class seat. With great composure, she adjusted the amethyst-coloured velvet coat that was wrapped tightly around her in such a way that it made her look like an exotic lily. An enormous collar of silky dark brown fur framed her face and pinned into the fur was a bunch of Parma violets that exactly matched the colour of the coat. She wore a toque hat decorated with a cluster of more violets and tiny striped ribbons of French silk. The haughty face that looked out beneath it was skilfully made up and enigmatic.

As the porter hauled suitcase after suitcase from her compartment, he noticed their opulence. Each bore a crest topped by a tiny crown and the initials DDC. When all the cases were piled on to his trolley, he turned to her and asked, 'Where to, madam? Do you need a cab?'

'Where's my handbag? Where have you put it?' she asked in a very high-class accent.

344

His eye searched among the cases. There was a jewel case, but no handbag.

'Perhaps you left it in the carriage,' he suggested and climbed back into the train to search but there was nothing to be seen except a crumpled copy of *The Times* lying on one of the seats.

The woman began to lose her composure. Her voice rose in panic. 'But everything of value is in it! *Everything*!' her sang-froid had deserted her and she looked on the verge of panic.

The porter was a kind man who hated to see ladies upset. He tried to soothe her, 'Keep calm, madam. It must be here somewhere. When did you last see it?'

'In London I think. I didn't need money after that because I was travelling with a gentleman who paid for everything. I had no need to go into my bag. Oh, heavens, what has happened to it?'

'Did you have to change trains anywhere?' asked the porter.

She shook her head. To his concern he saw that tears were beginning to fill her beautiful eyes.

'Was there anyone else in the compartment with you?'

'Only my friend, my husband's brother, but he left me at Newcastle.'

'He wouldn't take the bag with him by mistake?'

She dismissed the idea and the concerned porter searched round for inspiration. What he found was the station master, resplendent in his frock coat, top hat and striped trousers, surveying his domain from the open door of his office.

'Just a minute madam,' said the porter soothingly and ran over to ask his superior for help.

Mr Thomson was an admirer of pretty women and something of a snob. The sight of a beautiful lady in distress, surrounded by crocodile suitcases bearing crests acted on him like adrenaline. He offered to telegraph every station down the line between Leith and London, enquiring about a missing handbag.

Wiping her eyes with a lace-edged handkerchief, the

lady shook her head at his offer. 'That's most thoughtful of you but, no, there's no need. I've just this minute realised what's happened. I'm so silly. My husband always tells me that I'm not capable of walking out of the house on my own. I've been too sheltered . . . too spoiled, but I remember now. I must have left it on my dressing-table at home. My maid will be frantic!'

'Can I telegraph your maid?' asked Mr Thomson.

'What a splendid idea! But, oh how silly of me, she's gone to her aunt while I'm out of town and the Cadogan Square house is closed up. I've the aunt's address in my jewel case though. You could perhaps cable her there and put my mind at rest. I'm sure she'll have my handbag with her. She's absolutely reliable, a perfect treasure!'

The men escorted her to the station master's office and watched entranced while she took a golden key from a chatelaine at her slim waist and unlocked the jewel box. They caught a tantalising glimpse of sparkling treasures nestling among pads of green velvet as she slipped her fingers under a flap inside the lid and triumphantly brought forth a slip of paper.

'Thank goodness I have this at least. If you would be so kind . . .'

She handed the paper over to Mr Thompson who read, 'Miss Charity Wilkie, care of Mrs Adamson, 33 Laburnum Gardens, Lewisham . . . I'll do it straightaway, madam.'

The lovely lady gleamed at him, 'You are so kind. But I can't pay for the telegraph. I haven't a penny piece.' She spread out her hands as if this unthinkable position was something to be laughed about.

Mr Thomson obliged her by doing just that. 'Don't give it a thought, madam. I'll see to it. It'll be a pleasure to put your mind at rest.'

Her confidence was obviously returning and she prattled gaily to the entranced men. 'You must think me such a silly! And my husband the General will be furious when he comes off the steamer *Peregrine* in three days' time.'

'You're waiting for your husband then, madam?' The

station master knew that the *Peregrine* was expected from London on the date she said.

She nodded brightly, 'Yes, he's coming up from London. I hate sailing – it makes me so sick – so I came by train. It's much nicer on the railway. You meet such delightful people.' Her glance embraced Mr Thomson meaningfully. He visibly melted.

'Have you somewhere to stay?' he asked.

'My husband said I was to book a suite in your best hotel. It's The Adelphi, isn't it? I sent them a message reserving the rooms – but what can I do now? I can't pay. Do you think they'll allow me to stay there until General de Craigny arrives?'

She had a bedazzled Thomson eating out of her hand by now. He assured her, 'You mustn't worry about a thing. I'll have a word with the manager – but a lady like you oughtn't to be alone without money. Let me lend you some . . .' He rushed over to his desk and pulled open a drawer.

She made deprecating gestures, 'Oh, no. I wouldn't dream of it. I can stay in my room for three days. It'll teach me a lesson. I can just hear the General saying so. He's always scolding me.'

The two men looked sympathetically at her. Poor woman, she was obviously bullied – probably married to an older man. They formed an unflattering picture of him in their minds.

'I insist!' said Mr Thomson gallantly handing her twenty-five pounds. You couldn't offer such a grand lady any less, he reckoned.

She smiled so delightfully at him that he felt his head swim. 'You're too kind. My husband will be so grateful – or perhaps he'll be a little jealous! He's so protective of me.' Her eyes flirted with them both and they felt light-headed.

Very cordially they loaded her and all her baggage into a cab and Mr Thomson handed the cabby a florin with instructions to take the lady to The Adelphi Hotel and be quick about it. As she was driven away, from the cab window she waved a gloved hand. 'Now that's what I call a real lady,' sighed Mr Thomson to the porter who nodded in vigorous agreement. They both waved back.

Laurence Nairn was working in the brewery when a small boy came running into the yard and asked one of the labourers, 'Which yin's Mr Nairn?'

The labourer was a cautious man and said, 'There's two Mr Nairns. Which yin do ye want?'

'Mr Laurence Nairn. The lady said he'd black hair.'

'He's in the office over there . . .'

Laurence was absorbed in his papers, 'What is it, lad?' he asked when approached by the youngster.

'There's a lady in The Adelphi Hotel wants to see you. She sent me to tell you.'

'Och away you go! This isn't April the first. You're a week late.'

The small boy was persistent. 'There is! She gave me a shilling to come and tell you. She's in suite sixty-three.' He had obviously been well coached and repeated the number in case Laurence did not get it the first time.

'You tell your lady that if I'm passing The Adelphi Hotel I might look in,' said Laurence with a laugh, and went back to working. Little boys in Leith were notorious for playing japes. He'd done that sort of thing himself when young and Pat had been particularly good at it. 'Off you go now,' he said again in a not unkindly way to the urchin.

When he went home that night Mhairi was looking distracted and seemed not to hear him when he spoke to her. 'All right, ignore me! What's wrong now?' he snapped angrily and sat down to his supper.

'I didn't want to tell you, but it's Josh,' she said.

He groaned, 'What's he done?'

'Gideon sent a policeman round to tell me Josh kicked a football into the conservatory of that big house opposite the Links. He's smashed a pane of glass and the woman's hopping mad.'

Laurence laid down his fork and knife with a thump, 'My God, he'll be in prison next. Where is he?'

Her blue eyes were round and she was obviously anxious to protect her son from his wrath, 'He's gone to bed. He's awful upset. He didn't mean to do it. He said he'll pay for the glass and apologise.'

'He damned well better! He's out of hand that boy. It's all your fault. You spoil him,' raged his father, forgetting his own tempestuous youth.

As they stared at each other over the supper table, Mhairi's eyes were full of entreaty. She wanted him to treat his son with understanding and she pleaded, 'But he's a lovely kind laddie, Laurence. You don't value him enough. If you were to lose him..'

He glared at her. 'Oh that's it, is it? You spoil him because of your first bairn, the one who went to America. That's what's wrong with you.' He was furiously angry because any reference to Calum enraged him. His jealousy had grown over the years; he often accused Mhairi of dreaming of Calum and her first lover.

'You're brooding about that man who had you first!' he shouted. The fact that she was weeping, the fact that she tried to persuade him that he was wrong, did nothing to soothe his fury.

Next morning the same small boy came back looking for Laurence again. 'The lady says you've to come at once. It's very urgent,' he recited.

Laurence was in the yard with the builder who was trying to justify his claim for another advance of money. The job of rebuilding the house was running late and Laurence was anxious in case it would still be only half-finished when Brabazon came home. He was very irritated and glared at the scruffy child saying, 'Get out of here? Go back and tell your lady that I don't know anybody who's like to put up in The Adelphi. She's got the wrong man.'

'She hasn't, mister. She said I was to find Laurence Nairn of Perseverance Brewery. She said to tell you she's somebody from the past that you've forgotten about.'

'Piss off,' said Laurence. But the boy's words interested him. If it wasn't a joke, who could it be? Was it his mother playing some sort of prank? Unlikely.

That night, because there was still a coolness between him and Mhairi, he went off alone for a walk after supper without mentioning the mystery message to his wife. Somehow, he did not know quite how, he found himself going in the opposite direction to the Links. Soon he was outside The Adelphi. The uniformed doorman standing in front of the gleaming brass and glass front door bowed slightly haughtily to him, for Laurence was still wearing his office clothes. The feeling that he was being disdained as a customer spurred him on. With his most lordly air, he pushed open the door and felt his boots sink into the deep pile of a scarlet carpet that ran along the hall to a desk where a uniformed clerk sat like Cerberus at the gate of the Underworld.

'I'd like to send a message to the lady in suite sixty-three,' Laurence announced.

The clerk lifted an eyebrow, 'Lady de Craigny you mean?'

Laurence was staggered but hid his amazement. This must be some eccentric aristocrat in search of a large quantity of beer, he decided and said, 'That's right. Send up and tell her I'm here. The name's Nairn.'

The clerk snapped an imperious finger at a pageboy in a round cap and brass-buttoned jacket. When the boy came back he was jiggling a shilling in his fingers. 'Lady says he's to go up,' he told the clerk, who looked annoyed. It was not hotel policy to allow men and women who were not married to each other to spend time together in the bedrooms, but a Lady's word was law and Laurence was guided up to the door of suite sixty-three.

When the sound of a voice came from within in answer to his knock he entered to find an empty sitting-room. Long windows with lace curtains fluttering in a faint breeze looked out over the busy street below. A lady's magazine lay open on one of the chairs. Laurence stood in the middle of yet another ankle-brushing carpet and coughed. Nothing happened. Then, after what seemed an eternity, he heard a sound from the next room of the suite, and the intervening door opened slowly. A beautiful woman in a white lace negligee stood framed with a hand on each doorjamb, so that she looked as if she were posing. Her figure, visible through the lace, was arrow-slim but shapely.

She smiled at him and said in a strong Wallyford accent that sounded incongruous, 'D'ye still love me, Larry?'

His heart was booming. He blinked in disbelief and then he gulped. 'Daisy! It's not you?' He could not move towards her for he was unsure that she was there in life, that she was not a vision.

Her accent, now, was well-bred English. 'In the flesh,' she drawled, and with a gurgling laugh ran towards him, arms extended. He felt the bones of her pelvis pressing into his crotch, her fingers twining themselves into his hair and her mouth pressing on his. Daisy always knew how to make a man's passion rise by the way she kissed. He forgot his wife and his family, he forgot everything but Daisy and his desperate need for her.

'Don't talk, don't talk,' she kept saying as they struggled out of their clothes. They were so eager to make love that they did not even reach the bed in the next room, but fell where they stood on the floor of the sitting-room.

Daisy gave a muffled scream when he came in her and he remembered that she had always done that. It made him feel like a conqueror, the most powerful man in the world. They clung together, panting, for a long time, until she leaned back on an elbow and brushed his hair away from his eyes with a tender hand. 'You're still the best fuck I ever had,' she told him.

'I'm the one who's meant to say things like that, not you!'

'Darling, don't be bourgeois. Women can use the same words as men for the things they like, you know.' She used the highfaluting voice that she could turn on at will.

'Oh Daisy,' he groaned burying his face into her breast,

'Why did you go away and what's more to the point, why have you come back?'

She stroked his head and asked, 'Aren't you pleased to see me?'

His voice was anguished, 'I'm married, Daisy. I've a wife and two children.'

'That's no surprise. Someone as beautiful as you would have to be married and a father long ago.'

'Why have you come back?' he asked again, sitting up to look at her as she lay spreadeagled.

'What would you say if I told you it's because I've always remembered you – because I've always loved you best.'

'If you said that and it was true, I'd want to kill myself right now because we've wasted all those years.'

She jumped to her feet and strolled, absolutely and unashamedly naked, over to a table on which there was a cigarette box. 'Don't be silly, darling. Don't be so dramatic. I've no use for you as a corpse.'

'Come back and lie beside me. I want to hold you,' he told her and she lay down in his arms, puffing cigarette smoke over his head towards the ceiling. He felt thrilled by her daring and abandon. 'What are you doing here?' he asked her again.

She laughed, 'The hotel thinks I'm waiting for my husband, the General off the steamer *Peregrine*.'

'Are you?' Jealousy stabbed him at the thought.

'Of course not! From what I've told people about the General, he sounds terrible. An old bully with a red face and probably impotent as well.'

'So, what's really going on?'

She sat up with her arms around her knees and teased him, 'I've come back to fetch you. I'm tired of being an old man's darling – any old man's darling.' Then, more seriously, she went on, 'I thought we could go into business together you and I. I've collected a bit of money together.'

'What sort of business?'

'I don't know really, but we'd find something. I've been

352

thinking about you so much recently, dreaming about you. I've always loved you, you know. I've bought a house in Lewisham. There's ten girls in it and they bring me in a good bit. It's a busy area, lots of lonely men looking for women. But I want to travel. I like Monte Carlo and you'd like it too. Come with me Laurence, you're the one I want.'

'You mean you want me to pimp?'

'Don't be silly. Of course not. No, I want *you*. I want us to be together. I'm tired of working and now I'm ready to enjoy myself.'

He looked at her in disbelief, 'Why did you take so long? Daisy, get this into your head. I'm *married*, I've responsibilities and a family. I can't just grab a bag and go to Monte Carlo with you.'

'Why not? You love me don't you? You make love as if you do anyway.' She bent to kiss him on the lips and stroke his face as if he were a baby, 'And I love you. It's true. I've never forgotten you. Come with me darling.'

At two o'clock in the morning, he got up from Daisy's luxurious bed and dressed himself. She watched, dark eyes unblinking, and when he was lacing his boots, asked in an unusually serious voice, 'Are you not staying with me?'

He bent his head, 'I've got a wife, Daisy. And responsibilities.'

She sat up and grasped his arm, 'I love you. You love me. I came back for you and I won't come back again. Remember that.'

He groaned and shook his head, 'I can't just leave them – Mhairi and the bairns, my mother . . . I need to think about it. I have to go away and think,' he told her.

'You've only got one day, that's all. When the *Peregrine* gets in and there's no General de Craigny aboard, I'll have to be well away from here. If you decide it's me you want, come back tomorrow evening. I'll wait till then.'

The town was silent as he walked the familiar streets.

Only the odd cat hunting in the shadows flitted in front of him as he crossed the Kirkgate. He entered by the alley and stood in the courtyard staring up at the windows of the Place. There was a light in his own window, glittering out like a beacon telling him that his wife was worried about him. The resentments that had built up so gradually because of his own jealousy seeped away as he climbed the stairs. He loved her – but he loved Daisy too. In his tired mind he battled with himself, trying to work out the true state of his emotions.

He thought with pleasure about going to bed with Mhairi, how comforting it was to cuddle her warm body and feel her arms around him. The sweetness of their relationship could still catch him by the throat, but then he remembered the transports of his night with Daisy and experienced an entirely different feeling. She made him rampant even in memory. His longing for her was like a fever in his blood.

He was white-faced when he pushed open their bedroom door and found Mhairi lying awake and he pulled off his clothes without speaking. He slid in beside her and she moved away. He rolled towards her, wanting to take her in his arms, to plead with her for forgiveness, for he was suddenly overcome with remorse. But Mhairi had a sharp nose and she smelt perfume on his skin. Her heart chilled. She put out a hand and deliberately pushed him away from her. 'You've been with a prostitute,' she said accusingly.

Next morning she did not waken him at the usual time, and the flat was silent when he opened his eyes and realised he'd overslept by at least an hour.

'It's gone seven-thirty. Why didn't you wake me?' he stormed when he went through the kitchen and found her there.

She shrugged, 'Why should I? You were out half the night.'

Neither of them were prepared to talk about what she'd said in bed. 'Damnit, I'll be late for work!' he shouted again.

354

She said nothing but turned her back and clattered some dishes in the sink so loudly that he wanted to shake her and cry out, 'Make me want to stay with you, Mhairi. Don't you realise that you're driving me away?'

But her face was cold when she turned to look at him, 'You should be ashamed of yourself,' was all she said.

He did not want to ask what she meant. Hurriedly he rose from the table, took his cap off the back of the door and ran to the brewery.

The day passed like a nightmare – sometimes he knew he had to stay in Leith but then a memory of Daisy would cross his consciousness and he knew it was impossible to allow her to go away for a second time. He remembered his grandfather Joshua and the story he'd told in the Edinburgh restaurant. Joshua had given up everything for love – he'd left his wife and children, his home and his business. All for love. Now Daisy had come back for *him*! She was giving him an opportunity that could not be denied.

In the late afternoon, he was still undecided what to do. From the brewery window he watched his son and daughter go into the Place on their way home from school at Leith Academy. Poppy was so pretty, soon she'd be a replica of Mhairi the first time he'd laid eyes on her. Josh, too, was a goodlooking boy, tall and becoming manly. He resembled Laurence's grandfather strongly. Josh would take care of his mother and sister and would probably prefer it if Laurence went away, for he'd be old enough to go to work soon and they'd been scrapping with each other for a long time.

Laurence's heart was beating fast when he finally made his decision. He sat down at his desk and began to write . . . 'Forgive me, Mhairi. Things are not working out between us and you'll be better off without me. I still love you and the children, but something's happened that has taken me by surprise. I had a mistress once called Daisy. That was before we married, but she went away and I thought I'd never see her again. Now she's come back and she wants me to go away with her. You must have all my share of the brewery. I don't want anything. Please don't think any more ill of me than you can help. Your loving husband, Laurence.'

When he read what he'd written it struck him that to sign himself 'your loving husband' was an unfortunate choice of words but he did not want to strike out the 'loving' in case he hurt Mhairi's feelings even more, and there was not time to write another note. He folded it up and wrote her name on the outside. Then he walked off across the yard and simply disappeared.

Mhairi spent a second miserable night, sleeping only fitfully, waking at every creak or groan of the old building, and lying back deeply disappointed when Laurence did not come through the door. By midnight she was weeping; by dawn she was furiously angry; by six o'clock she was quaking with fear convinced that something terrible had befallen him, that he was dead. At half past six she woke Josh and told him, 'Your father's been out all night. I'm afraid he's had an accident.'

The boy dressed hurriedly. Before he left the building he went up and rapped at the Warre's door to rouse his closest friend, Robert's son Sandy. They had grown up together and were as close as Pat and Laurence had been when they were boys. 'My father's not come home and my mother's worried. Help me find him,' Josh whispered when Sandy's sleepy face came to the door.

First of all they went to the police station where Gideon was the sergeant on duty. 'That's not like your dad,' he said with a frown, 'I'll put a man on to it.'

Then the boys searched the neighbourhood streets, went hunting among the gravestones of the churchyard and questioned people on the dockside.

It was an old tramp who gave them their first clue. 'I saw a man like that driving off up Leith Walk in a hansom about four this morning. With a woman. They came from The Adelphi.'

When this was reported to Gideon, he sent a constable along to the hotel. The desk clerk nodded when given Laurence's description. 'He was here the day before yes-

356

terday to see Lady de Craigny. *If* that's her name, which I'm beginning to doubt because she's done a bunk and left us without paying her bill. She had expensive tastes too – champagne and all meals in her room. It comes to sixty-four pounds, including what she borrowed from the manager, and there's nothing left behind to show for it except a lot of empty suitcases.'

When Gideon went to Perseverance Place with this terrible news, he found the reason for Laurence's disappearance was already known. At breakfast-time, the brewery clerk had come running over the yard with a letter in his hand. Mhairi slumped in shock when the meaning of the written words struck home. 'He's left me. He's run away with somebody called Daisy. He's gone to London,' she sobbed to Poppy who put out her arms to embrace her stricken mother.

'He must have gone mad, Mother; but don't worry, Josh'll fetch him back.'

Mhairi drew away, her face white and set, 'No, I don't want him back. If he prefers someone else to me, he'd better stay with her.'

By mid-afternoon the whole town was talking about Laurence Nairn's disappearance with the glamourous stranger. Mr Thomson at the station was thunderstruck. 'But she was a perfect lady! When I telegraphed her maid, I received an immediate reply saying she'd left her handbag on the table in Cadogan Square.'

'Anybody can send a telegram,' said Gideon Warre, who was making enquiries about the mysterious woman. 'How much did you give her?'

Bit by bit he worked out the extent of Daisy's depredations. Twenty-five pounds from the station master; another thirty-five from the bewitched hotel manager; her hotel bill; a bracelet worth seventy pounds bought on approval (payment awaiting the arrival of her mythical General); a man's leather travelling bag with a set of silver-backed hairbrushes, said to be for the General and also to be paid for when he sailed into Leith.

Of course, when the *Peregrine* did berth that afternoon, there was no General of any kind on board.

'Judging by the tales she's spun and the number of folk she's deceived, that Daisy would've made a fortune on the stage,' said Gideon grudgingly to his astonished mother. Nellie could not hear enough details of the scandal.

'Oh poor Mhairi! Poor Brabazon!' she wailed, 'I'd never have believed it of Laurence. He was such a fine laddie.'

'Even fine laddies have their breaking point,' Gideon told her.

His next task was to find out who Daisy really was and his memories of Pat's youthful escapades led him to make enquiries among the whores of The Shore. It was not long before he was directed to Bertha, who was full of gossip. 'My word, Daisy Donovan's a fine one! She'll stick at nothing that lassie. Her cousin's not heard anything of her for years, and she never came near the Kirkgate if it was her in The Adelphi. But it sounds like her style. She'd some nerve had Daisy, but she must've run out of capons to pluck if she's come back for Laurence Nairn. Mind, she was aye soft about him. Never charged him a penny! He must be the only man who ever got her for free.'

Mhairi's neighbours were kind. They did not talk to her about Laurence but gathered around like a phalanx of protectors, warding off gossip and curious eyes. She listened with a rigid expression to all the information Gideon gleaned. In her heart she was suffering agony however, and at night she lay in bed going over everything that had been said between her and Laurence for the past six months. If I'd been different would he have stayed? she wondered. Then a feeling of pure anger would engulf her and she longed to see him again so she could scratch at his face, pull his hair, beat him with her fists.

Strangely none of her rage was directed against the unknown Daisy – she did not imagine what she looked like and did not allow herself to think of her rival at all. As far as she was concerned, this was a matter between herself and her absent husband. What he had done was a betrayal of trust, a casting away of their marriage vows and her heart felt as if it had been broken in two. She stayed hidden in her flat, away from the world. After three days of mourning, she wrote a letter to Brabazon.

Almost a year had passed since Brabazon and Henry had arrived in Russia. In mid-summer, Henry had reluctantly left to fulfil his series of concerts in Germany but promised to return in the autumn and persuaded his mother to stay on in St Petersburg until then.

'I can't stay away from Leith for so long,' she protested.

But these protests were swept aside by Olga who told her privately, 'You can't leave yet, my dear, your father's very ill – though he himself doesn't know how gravely. His doctors say he cannot last out another winter. Please stay with us a little longer.'

It was true that Joshua was failing visibly, but his old fascination was undiminished for his daughter. Every day they spent together she felt was a gift to her, she was so enjoying the company of the father she had dreamed about when she was a lonely child.

Brabazon was playing cards with Joshua when a servant came in with a letter for her. She lifted the envelope and said, 'It's from Mhairi. That's good! I love her letters. They sound as if she's speaking to me when I read them.'

'Do you want to read it now? We'll stop playing,' said Joshua. His face was grey and lined but he smiled.

'No, let's go on. Even though I'm losing!' Brabazon knew the card playing distracted him from his suffering for a little while. Like everyone in the family, she was acting a part, hiding the imminence of his death from him, doing everything possible to amuse him and assuage the attacks of pain that gripped him. Though she was often homesick now, Brabazon was determined not to leave St Petersburg until her father's suffering was over. When Olga had told her the doctors' verdict, she had written home telling her family not to expect her until next spring – it was unlikely she would be able to get away before ice closed the Neva. That letter, she reflected as she dealt the cards, must have crossed with Mhairi's.

They finished the game and Joshua won. Exhausted, he was wheeled off to bed by his manservant and then, leaning back in her chair, Brabazon opened her letter. Her heart sank in disappointment at seeing a single sheet, she enjoyed the screeds of news that Mhairi usually sent.

This time the words she read were anguished. Mhairi gave a short account of Laurence's disappearance than wrote: 'He's gone. He'll never come back. I'm broken-hearted and I don't know what to do.'

Without further ado, Brabazon found Olga and told her, 'Something terrible has happened. My son Laurence has disappeared.'

'Disappeared! What's happened to him?'

'He's run away from home with some woman called Daisy. I must go home at once. There's no time to be lost.'

Henry, in Hamburg giving a concert, was telegraphed, and though he sent back an immediate reply telling his mother to wait until he came to fetch her, she was too agitated to brook a day's delay.

'I must go now on the first ship. I *must*. They need me.'

Olga knew that one of Joshua's timber ships was bound for Leith on the following day and sent orders that a cabin be reserved for Brabazon. After that the house was plunged into confusion as maids rushed here and there packing up, while Brabazon sat with her newly discovered family, hugging each other and weeping.

'It will be so sad to leave you all – and at such a time,' she told them. 'But you must understand my dilemma. Mhairi and her children are distracted. I have to go home.'

On the morning of her departure, Alexei Orlov came to see her and said sadly, 'I hear you're going away. I'll miss you. So will my daughter. We were becoming very close, Brabazon. I'm sure you've realised that.'

Her heart was sore as she held his hand. She had come to respect this man more than anyone she had met since

Duncan's death. Now that they were parting, she knew how much she had flourished in his company: how his attentions had made her feel like a woman again. Both of them had been trembling on the brink of an autumnal love which could have as been glorious as the brilliance of dying summer. That must be put behind her now, however. Sadly she nodded, 'I did realise it Alexei, and I won't forget you. But perhaps we're too old for romance.'

He shook his head, 'Oh no, one can never be too old for that. I've been a widower for many years, but I have never found anyone with whom I wanted to share the rest of my life until I met you.'

'If things had been different . . .' she sighed.

'Don't talk about it as if it is over. When you have settled your family and your son returns home, you must return to Russia.'

She shook her head, 'I don't know what's waiting for me in Leith. And I doubt if Laurence will come home soon. He's not the sort who comes back with his tail between his legs,' she said sadly.

Alexei's eyes were concerned as he told her, 'I wish I could travel with you myself but I cannot leave my post with the Tsar. There is a great deal of intrigue at court at the moment and he needs protection. There's been an assassination plot that we foiled at the last moment, and he needs friends. If I leave now, it could be dangerous for him.'

Brabazon reassured him, 'I'm quite capable of travelling alone, and when things are calmer at court you must come to Scotland and see my home town. But it'll be a great deal less spectacular than what you're used to,' she told him. It had taken her a while to accustom herself to the Russian love of brilliance and display.

'I know I'll see you again, Brabazon. Things are not finished between us. One day we'll meet and perhaps be able to spend what's left of our lives together,' he said solemnly.

She looked at him with clear eyes and nodded, 'I hope so, I really hope so Alexei.'

That was all he required from her. Seizing her other hand, he told her, 'Before you go away, I want to take you out for a short trip, my dear. Please don't refuse.'

She mounted a little gig beside him and they drove off at a fast clip to an imposing building in the middle of Morskaya Street, the most fashionable shopping area of the city.

He handed her down from the gig and proffered his arm for her to take as he led her into the shop. It was a jeweller's and filled with the most beautiful things that she had ever seen. All around her were glass cases with contents that sparkled and shone.

Alexei told her, 'This is Fabergé's. This is where the jewelled Easter eggs that the Tsar gives to the Tsarina every year are made. I want to give you a present that will always remind you of your time in St Petersburg. I've picked it out. I hope you like it.'

A man in a frock coat came over smiling, for he recognised Alexei. 'Is this the lady who is to have the pendant?' he asked, 'Come this way, madam, and try it on.'

In a cubicle closed off from the shop by a velvet curtain, Brabazon had a beautiful pendant hung round her neck. It was shaped like a heart and made of a crystal encased in veins of finely wrought white gold. 'It's a Russian snowflake,' said Alexei, 'and it will never melt.'

The timber ship made heavy weather in the early autumnal gales and it was ten days before the mist-wreathed coast of Scotland hove into view. Brabazon, wearing Alexei's gift around her neck, suffered the long voyage with impatience, pacing the deck anxiously whenever the wind made it safe to do so. The captain and the crew looked after her attentively for they knew she was the daughter of their employer, Joshua Logan, but no amount of cosseting could allay her apprehension.

When she saw the outline of Leith appearing as they steamed up the shores of the Forth, a feeling of dread so strong that it almost overwhelmed her and made her wonder 'What am I going to find?'

Laurence's family had been escorted to the docks by his Uncle Mark to meet Brabazon's ship. Although Mhairi was trying very hard to put on an impassive face, and had succeeded in doing so through the past days, she broke down in anguished weeping as soon as she saw the familiar figure of her mother-in-law. As the two women embraced Mhairi sobbed her grief, 'Oh, why did he do it, why has he gone away?' Dry-eyed, Brabazon held her daughter-in-law tightly, trying to give her comfort. But there was nothing she could say.

1912

The sun came gleaming in through slatted window shutters and made a pattern of light and shade on the marble floor. Outside there was the sound of the sea washing against a shingle beach. It was going to be a warm day.

Laurence Nairn stood by the window buttoning his shirt and although it was morning and he should have felt full of energy, he sighed as if exhausted.

'How long are you planning to stay in this place?' he asked.

Daisy's voice came from the bed, 'No idea. I like Monte. There's such a smart set here at the moment.'

He sighed again, 'They're all mountebanks, Daisy. The really smart people don't go where you and I go.'

'You're a wet blanket,' said Daisy angrily, sitting up against the pillows, 'All you ever do is complain. Look! The sun's shining. We won a thousand francs at chemmy last night: all we've got to do is go out and spend it.'

'I don't like Monte Carlo,' said Laurence sullenly.

'Prefer Leith do you?' she asked in her real Wallyford voice that only came out when she was trying to taunt him.

He walked over the floor towards the cupboard and pulled out his jacket. It was beautifully made of cream tussore silk and had been bought by Daisy. She liked him to look smart, to dazzle every female eye. 'At least Leith's honest. This place is full of tricksters trying to impress each other.'

'Honest! How dull. Honest people are poor and boring, and they die young. If I wanted to be honest I'd have stayed in Wallyford.'

He left the room without speaking, but she glared angrily after him, shouting, 'Who pays for all this? Who keeps you Mr Honesty?'

The promenade was empty except for a few men in faded blue jackets who were brushing the paving stones. It was still early and most of the people Laurence knew did not rise till noon. He sat at a café table beneath a palm tree and ordered coffee. While he drank it his mind went back over the past year. When was it that he had begun to see Daisy in her true light? Could it really have started the very day they'd left The Adelphi – when he realised that she was running off without paying her bill? I must have been mad! he said to himself for the thousandth time.

The knowledge that he'd made a terrible mistake had begun to hit him even during their first train trip from Leith to London. Lovely as she was to look at, Daisy had a cruel philosophy of life. When she talked of other people, it was with utter cynicism.

'People are such fools. They believe anything you tell them if you have the right sort of appearance to back it up. I must buy some more good luggage. It really makes eyes open in hotels! What a pity we couldn't bring all my crocodile cases away with us,' she'd said settling back and spreading out her beautifully tailored skirt.

At first he'd found her sexuality impossible to resist, even when disillusion was dawning. She knew the power she had over him in bed and used it to the full. Bit by bit he realised that she was working him in the same way as she worked her other victims. She did not believe that sex would ever pall for him.

Now Laurence was beginning to hate her; sipping his coffee, he sat bleak-faced and considered his situation. He'd burned his boats. There was no way he could go back to Leith. He had heard nothing of his family since he'd left, but his mind often went back to them, wondering how they were. He read the newspapers avidly in search of notices of Henry's concerts but found none. Had his brother given up his career? Perhaps he'd gone back to help with the brewery? How was it surviving? There was Josh to inherit it, of course. Josh, his son, would be fourteen. Poppy, pretty little Poppy, was a year younger. And

Mhairi, what about Mhairi? Had she found another man to keep her warm at night? Then again, what had become of his project to reconstruct Brewery House? Had anyone carried on funding the work?

He ordered another coffee and told the waiter to bring him a cognac as well. The pain of thinking about home was too much to bear. 'You've been a fool, an absolute fool,' he said to himself, and let the cognac slip down his throat like a warm stream. It did not cheer him, but it stiffened his resolution. This, he told himself, was the day that he was going to leave Daisy Donovan – but he had told himself that before.

He was still sitting in the sunshine with his leghorn straw hat tipped over his eyes when one of the men they often met gambling in the casino came strolling past. He paused at Laurence's table, pulled out a chair and asked, 'Mind if I sit down?'

Even if I did I wouldn't be able to stop you, thought Laurence but he nodded in sullen assent. He did not like this character, who had a vicious tongue.

'Where's your lovely sister this morning?' asked the intruder with a smile.

'She's not my sister.'

'Isn't she? I heard her saying she was to that English m'lord at the tables last night.'

Laurence stood up and said, 'She's my mistress.'

'Didn't say she wasn't that as well, did I?' was the sneering reply.

Daisy was still in bed, entwined in a snarl of silken sheets, when he slammed back into the room.

'Don't make such a noise!' she groaned. He strode over to shake her, demanding, 'Why do you tell people I'm your brother?'

'Who said I did?'

'That snake, that gambler who's always hanging around. The one who says he's a Polish count.'

'Oh, don't worry about him.'

'I don't! I want to know why you say it: is it because you don't want me to scare off possible customers?'

'They like the idea. It gives them a thrill. They like a bit of smut,' she said brutally.

He groaned and put his hands to his head in despair, 'That's it Daisy. That's the end! I'm getting out.'

She did not seem either surprised or distressed. Instead she rolled over on her shoulder and said, 'You're growing into quite a bolter, aren't you?'

'It's getting harder and harder to persevere,' Brabazon said to herself with a wry laugh in her brewery office a few months after her return from Russia. She looked bleakly out of the window, reflecting that there had been nothing but bad news since her return.

First of all a letter had come from Olga with the news of Joshua's death. It was not unexpected, but Brabazon grieved nonetheless. In her father's will he had instructed that she should receive an income of one thousand pounds a year for life from his estate, but she had hardly given a thought to her new riches. Money was no longer of pressing importance to her. There were so many other things on her mind.

Alexei wrote frequently and his letters were full of forebodings about the political situation. 'I'm worried about Antonia. I don't want her to be in Russia if there's going to be an insurrection. I'd like her to go where she could perfect her painting – she's outgrown all the teachers in St Petersburg. They say her talent is remarkable and that it should not be wasted.' Brabazon leaned her head in her hands and thought about where Antonia could go – to Paris, or Florence perhaps?

She was wearing mourning again because although the Place had still been reeling from the shock of Laurence's disappearance, tragedy had struck again when Minna Meirstein dropped dead in her pawnshop. She was leaning happily over the counter gossiping with a customer when she'd suddenly slumped forward, life extinguished like a light.

Abe was inconsolable, sitting alone in his darkened flat

day after day. Mhairi took over the care of him. It diverted her mind from her own problems and she was one of the few people with whom the old man could talk easily. He had always liked the girl with the yellow hair.

Brabazon's greatest feeling of disquiet, however, was on account of Henry. Her eldest son had cancelled all his playing engagements and returned to Leith to help her run the business. He did not try to justify his decision. He refused to discuss it at all.

'I don't want you to give up your career. You're famous! It's terrible that you should stop in the middle of such international success.'

'I've chosen to come back, Mother,' was all he ever said.

Perseverance Brewery was thriving under the competent care of Robert Warre. The Gordon's operation was profitable as well but the smaller Musselburgh brewery, which Laurence had bought shortly before he'd ran away, was faltering and had to be sold.

As she looked out of her window, Brabazon could see the half-built skeleton of Brewery House. At first it had touched her but now it haunted her like a memento mori, yet she had no heart at the moment to complete its reconstruction. That would have to wait for calmer times – if they ever came.

Her office door opened and Poppy pushed her head around to say, 'Are you all right, Grandmama? I was passing and thought you looked lonely.'

Brabazon held out her hand to the girl and smiled in genuine pleasure at the interruption, 'Sit down my sweet and tell me what you're doing. How's school?'

Poppy shrugged, 'I'm not a great scholar, but I'm very good at painting. I want to be an artist. I'd like to study Art but people say there aren't any really top class woman artists.'

'That's not true. I know a very good one in Russia. I wish you could meet her too.'

Poppy was interested, 'There's some good women painters in Edinburgh as well. But Mother doesn't want me to do that. She thinks I'd be better doing something like teaching.'

'Are there any good schools of Art in Edinburgh?'

Poppy nodded, 'Oh yes! They're famous.'

'We'll have to see what we can do then,' said Brabazon. Poppy had given her an idea.

Mhairi was in her flat, shifting ornaments from one shelf to another. They did not need moving, but she could not sit still and fretted if her hands were idle. It was when she was on her own that she thought about Laurence most. It seemed to Mhairi that their entire married life had been a pretence on his part. She convinced herself he had not loved her. He'd only married her to spite Henry.

Yet there was no getting away from the main point. She had loved him, and still did. Her pain and love mixed together and made her lot almost insupportable. Only helping Abe provided her with any real distraction. She sometimes sat with him in the pawnshop in the evenings as Minna used to do, and listened to his stories of life in Lvov. He told her how he'd first seen Minna, a lovely young thing with chestnut hair, walking along the dirt road of their village. He described their flight from persecution, the hunger they'd endured, the hopes they had shared. Yet Abe, too, was failing in his health. The cough which had always racked him in Leith's damp winters was particularly bad that year.

Dr Allen shook his head when he looked into the shop to check up on him. 'Keep taking the linctus Abe,' he counselled.

It was a great grief to Minna, Abe told Mhairi, that they'd never had any children. When he died his money was to go to a Jewish charity which looked after orphans, and he took great joy in observing the children of the Place and the Kirkgate. He knew them all. Poppy was a favourite with him and he spent a lot of time talking to her about pictures, showing her illustrations in the old books that were piled up on the floor of the shop. If a picture came in for pawn, he and Poppy would discuss it and she learned a great deal from him. One evening he told her mother, 'You should send that child to a proper Art school. She has a wonderful eye.'

Mhairi shook her head, 'She'd never make any money if she went to Art college. I want her to become a teacher. It's safe and secure.'

Abe, surprisingly, dissented from this view. 'Security isn't everything. There are some people who are stifled by it,' he said.

There were plenty of poor, thinly clad urchins in the Kirkgate but the child who brought the most profound look of pity to Abe Meirstein's eyes was Sophia Lambert. She still lived with her father in the flat they'd moved into from the Place.

'That lassie's no friends. She's living a life of terror. I can tell by her eyes,' Abe said to Mhairi.

'Her father's a brute! Gideon says he killed her mother but the police couldn't prove it – and I know Gideon thinks he's done other terrible things as well. Living with him would make anybody afraid.'

'I wish I could do something to help her; I've tried to speak to her and she runs away from me,' the old man sighed.

'I know. Josh was saying the other day that he's tried to talk to her too, on the way back from school, but she never answers him. He thinks she's terrified in case someone tells her father she's been talking to a Nairn. You know what he's like about us.'

'She's a bonny lassie too,' said Abe, 'If she could learn to laugh, and stop trying to hide herself from the world she'd be a beauty one day.'

Mhairi smiled, 'That's what interests Josh I think. He's intrigued.'

She was right. Her son was very intrigued by Sophia, who was a tall girl with long waving hair of an unusual reddish-brown colour and a very pale skin that seemed luminous. She rarely looked directly at anyone but when she did, her eyes were very pale blue, fringed by dark lashes. These eyes were always troubled, the eyes of a girl with awful secrets.

Her teachers had no success in winning her confidence. If she went to school with bruises on her thin arms and legs, she would only say that she'd fallen and bumped herself. If she was found weeping in a corner, they could never elicit any reason for her grief. She was as secretive as the Sphinx. Her troubles were not for sharing, and the teachers soon lost interest because Sophia had learned how to make herself as unobtrusive as possible.

Josh and his friend Sandy speculated about her, because they were coming to the age when girls were of overwhelming interest and Sophia was growing more eye-catching every day.

They started waiting for her in the Kirkgate and offering to carry her shopping basket up the steep, twisting stair of her building. At first she recoiled from them as if they were trying to rob her, but the weeks passed and she seemed to grow used to them till eventually they were able to make her murmur a reply to their greetings.

Finally, one evening Josh succeeded in wresting the basket from her grasp. 'Let me carry that. It's heavy. What have you got in there – a stone of potatoes?'

She flushed and he realised that he'd made an error. She probably lived on potatoes because they were cheap. She gave the basket up to him, however, and even smiled as the boys walked beside her to the entry to her building. Once there though, she grabbed her burden back and said hurriedly, 'Don't come any further. Someone will see you, and they might tell.'

'Tell who?' Josh asked, but got no reply.

He and Sandy talked about her all the way home. When she'd smiled, her face had lit up and she'd looked quite different. They were divided between pity and admiration for her and she became a damsel in distress to them. Whenever they met her in the street after that, they hurried over to talk, to engage her interest and win that smile again. She rarely obliged.

On Christmas Eve, Josh lingered in the alleyway hoping to see her. It was dark when she finally slipped

371

down to the shops with the basket on her arm. He ran after her and caught her up outside Donaldson's.

'I've a present for you,' he said and slipped a little bag of tangerine oranges wrapped in silver paper into the basket. He was sure she would not have the money to buy any for herself. She stopped and asked, 'Why should you give me a present?'

'Because I like you and because no one else'll probably give you one. It's Christmas tomorrow.'

Her face crumpled and she looked as if she were about to weep.

'Don't cry,' he said hastily. He hated to see women's tears and his mother's long weeping over his father's disappearance had harrowed him.

She wiped one hand over her eyes and smiled instead, 'Thank you, you're kind. But please, don't stay here with me. My father's out and I don't know when he'll be back.'

'But why? What would he do? I'm not doing any harm and neither are you. We're only talking.'

'He doesn't like me to talk – not to anyone . . . please go away, *please*!' Her voice was genuinely panic-stricken. Josh placated her by saying, 'All right, don't worry, I'm going. But you shouldn't let him bully you. You'll have to break away one day.'

1913

Abe died in the bitter January weather and once again the Place was in mourning.

'It seems we've no' been out of the black for years. We no sooner get over one death than there's another,' said Nellie to Ruthie.

'You get times like that but thing's will be better again soon,' was Ruthie's optimistic reply. She did not believe in taking a gloomy attitude for too long. Nellie was more deeply downcast, however, because she missed Minna sorely and was lonely without her. Brabazon spent most of her time in the brewery and Mhairi was too sunk in misery to be able to bring much lightness into their society. She'd just been perking up a little when she was cast down again by the death of Abe, for she'd grown very fond of the old man.

Yet Ruthie was right, things do change. The agent of change at Perseverance Place was Antonia.

Brabazon broke the news of her imminent arrival to Henry one morning after the post was delivered to the flats.

'We're going to have a guest from St Petersburg soon. Antonia's father has accepted my offer that she stay with us for a few months while she looks into the possibility of having painting tuition in Edinburgh,' she told him when she looked up from Alexei's letter.

Henry's face expressed his pleasure and surprise. 'I like Antonia. She'll be a great asset to the Place. They'll never have seen anyone like her.'

Brabazon looked a little apprehensive. 'I was worried about how she'd like living here. It's not the Hermitage is it? But she and her father have both assured me that she's delighted to come. In fact I know that Alexei's anxious to send her out of Russia at the moment. He's convinced something violent is about to happen soon and fears for the Tsar.'

'Where is she going to live when she's studying?' Henry asked.

Brabazon wrinkled her brow. 'Mark offered to have her out at his estate – Amelia would love that because Antonia's an aristocrat, and she's such a snob. But it's too far. She really needs a sort of studio so I thought about Abe and Minna's old flat. It has four big windows looking north – north light's what painters want, isn't it? And it's fairly big. She'll be comfortable there. Nellie'll love to have a Russian as a neighbour.'

Henry laughed, 'The Place won't know what's happened to it. That's a wonderful idea Mother.'

Abe had left a letter to be read on his death saying, as he'd told Mhairi, that the Jewish orphanage was to have any money he possessed. The pawnshop was rented and so was his flat, but his furniture was to go to Mhairi and two pictures hanging in his bedroom were for Poppy because of her eye for art.

When Brabazon and Mhairi went to clean out the rooms in preparation for Antonia's arrival, they found that the furniture, once polished up, was of good quality; the cutlery was solid silver and the pieces of china turned out to be Dresden or Meissen. Abe and Minna had kept the best things from the shop for themselves. But the pictures were dirty, in chipped gilded frames. Both women frowned as they looked at them. Holding up the smaller of the two, Brabazon wrinkled her brow and said, 'I don't think Poppy'll like this one. It's very gloomy, a lot of dragons and tortured souls struggling about in a pit. It looks as if they're in Hell.'

'This one's a bit better, but it's very dark,' said Mhairi holding up the other, 'It's a Virgin and Child. The child looks rather odd, as if it's a miniature adult, but the Virgin's pretty.'

They put the pictures down in a corner facing the wall and Brabazon said, 'We'll take them away later. Let's start cleaning now. Antonia arrives the day after tomorrow and I'd like everything to be perfect for her.'

Antonia came dashing down the gangway of the Russian timber freighter with her arms out and her face aglow. She looked lovely. She grabbed Brabazon first and cried out, 'My dear Bra-bay-zon how I wish you'd go back to Russia and marry my poor father. He's so lonely without you!'

Then she turned and embraced Henry saying, 'I've been longing to hear your music again. You're a genius Henree.'

After that she hugged every member of the family as if she had known them all their lives saying, 'Mhairi, I've heard all about you and your beautiful hair. Let me see it, yes, it is lovely.'

The children were enthused over until Josh's cheeks grew scarlet with embarrassment but it was impossible not to like Antonia; she was so ebullient, so genuine in her praise, so lavish with her emotion. She was a fresh breeze blowing into their lives, sweeping away the staleness and depression that had hung around them all for too long. Poppy fell in love with the stranger the first moment she set eyes on her and thought that Antonia was elegant in her little forward-tilting hat with a veil and her duster coat of pale grey – worn over a Parisian gown that looked like a long narrow tube.

The Nairns swept their guest along the quay with Antonia talking twenty to the dozen all the time. Her English was good, but her accent was strange and sometimes she was quite difficult to understand. Whenever she saw a look of incomprehension, she laughed, tried in French and then in Russian, before going back to English again. She was like quicksilver, enchanting and dazzling at the same time.

When they were all seated in a large hansom cab, she began fishing in her handbag saying, 'Bra-bay-zon I have

375

brought you a present from my father. I'm sure you will like it.'

She started to scuffle unceremoniously through the contents of her reticule till Brabazon put a restraining hand on her arm, 'Not here, my dear. We'll do all that at home. Now we're going to Perseverance Place.'

'Per-sev-eer-ance Place? Such a name! What does it mean?'

Josh leaned over and said proudly, 'It means sticking power, resolution, determination to see things through.' He'd always loved the name of the place where he was born.

Antonia fluttered her eyelashes at him, 'That I like. I'll enjoy Perseverance Place I think.'

When they drove into the Place, she gave a cry of surprise and pointed to the half-repaired Brewery House, 'And what is that? It's very fine, like some of our Russian houses almost, except for its dull colour.'

'That's my old home. It burned down, but it's being rebuilt.' Brabazon told her.

'I hope you finish while I'm here. I'll help you furnish such a fine house. It will be a project – is that the word? – for us,' was Antonia's reply.

In Brabazon's flat she began searching through her purse again and finally, with a cry of triumph, fished out a handful of sparkling jewellery.

'Here it is! Father sent it to you, Brabazon. It's a parure of diamonds and it once belonged to one of our Tsarinas.'

'A parure?' asked Brabazon receiving the glittering waterfall into her hands. The girl nodded, 'A necklace and earrings – they match, see.' She held one earring up to the lobe of her ear, and with the other hand displayed the necklace which was made of rosettes of diamonds ending in a large stone shaped like a pear.

Brabazon gasped, 'It must be worth a fortune.'

Antonia laughed, 'Not a fortune, but it would pay for the repair of your house and for its furniture as well if you decided to sell it. He's sent me off with several pieces like this. He says it's my dowry. He's so gloomy, Bra-bay-zon. He keeps on saying that revolution is on its way.'

Brabazon held the beautiful pieces of jewellery cupped in her hands and smiled at dear Alexei's daughter. It was like having a part of him with her.

With her foreign clothes and continual chatter, Antonia added a spice of glamour and excitement to the courtyard. Her gaiety, her kindness, and her ability to look like a fashion plate in all weathers, endeared her to everyone. They vied for her attention – even the normally unimpressed Ruthie and Rosie, whose brothers were bowled over too. Nellie liked her because she made a special friend of Elsie who was about the same age as Antonia, but the person who could not bear to leave her side was Poppy.

Because of the rivalry for Antonia's attention everyone envied Henry on whom fell the task of squiring her. She was forever wanting to set out on expeditions and coaxing him to go as well. He obliged with a will, as carefree as when he'd been in Russia. He even started going over to the church and playing the organ again, something he had not done since his return home to take over the business side of the brewery. Antonia went with him and sat listening enraptured. When he finished she clung to his arm and told him how clever he was, how he moved her with his music.

A few weeks after her arrival, Antonia walked across to the brewery to seek out Brabazon. She had been into its cavernous interior several times before, but still found it as confusing as a maze and wandered around for a little while before she located her quarry helping to add sizing to the barrels in the cellar.

'When you're finished, I want you to come and see something with me,' said Antonia sitting down on an upturned box in the corner.

Brabazon raised an eyebrow, 'See what? Is it far away? I'm rather busy.' When told it was a surprise, she laughed. 'Your surprises are always good.' She thought of the carelessly carried diamond parure which had been valued at one thousand pounds, and was currently lying in an Edinburgh jewellery shop awaiting a buyer. When it was sold, Antonia insisted that the money be used for the new Brewery House.

When the sizing operation was finished, the two of them walked across the courtyard arm in arm. 'Where are we going?' asked Brabazon.

'Only to my studio. I've something to show you,' said Antonia.

On the top floor she opened the door with a flourish. Since moving in, she had coloured the smoke-stained walls with soft pastel washes and had painted stencils in a freize along the top of them. With the window frames and floorboards now varnished pale-blue, the Meirstein's gloomy old home looked like the interior of a doll's house.

'I love what you've done here. It's become so light and happy,' said Brabazon stepping inside. Antonia was beaming. 'No, I haven't brought you here to admire the decoration. Look what I found in a cupboard!'

Propped up on a chair were the two canvases that Brabazon and Mhairi had laid aside when they'd cleaned the flat. Mhairi had stuck them away and forgotten about them in the excitement of Antonia's arrival.

'I've been cleaning them. I couldn't believe what came up when I rubbed off the dirt. I'm sure this one's a Bosch – and this, this might be a Botticelli!'

Brabazon gasped, 'But those are Poppy's pictures. Abe left them to her. We forgot them . . . what did you say they were?'

'My painting master at home has a passion for Botticelli, and I'm sure this is genuine but I'm going to take it up to Edinburgh and ask someone else's opinion. It needs cleaning by an expert too. I'll take Poppy with me if the pictures are hers. I'm so pleased for her. She's going to be a rich young lady.'

They went the same afternoon and when they returned, they rushed into Brabazon's flat with their faces aglow. 'Guess how much the pictures are worth, Grandmama?' gasped Poppy.

'Five hundred pounds?' essayed Brabazon.

'Five thousand each at least!' was the exultant reply, 'The man asked me if I wanted to sell. I said I'd think about it, but I am going to sell the one with all those horrible devils in it. The other one's lovely though, and Antonia says it'll never lose its value. If I need the money I can sell it some time in the future. In the meantime I can love it.'

As well as having a discriminating eye for paintings, Antonia was an excellent artist herself. Her father had not exaggerated when he'd praised her. When summer came she was often to be found sitting in the courtyard making sketches of Perseverance Place and its people. Poppy watched every thing she did and soon was sufficiently encouraged to set an easel up beside her.

Antonia told Mhairi, 'Your daughter has a great talent. Already her sketches are better than mine. You should foster her ability and find her a good teacher. She must have proper tuition.'

Mhairi held one of her daughter's studies of flowers in her hand and said in amazement, 'Isn't it lovely! I'd no idea she could do as well as this. Can't *you* teach her, Antonia?'

The answer was a shake of the head, 'She's past me now. She's too good. She needs a proper art master.'

After a few days she was back with a suggestion, 'Poppy can come with me to Edinburgh for tuition. My tutor in Castle Street will take her even though she's so young. I showed him some of her work and he was most impressed. He's quite expensive, but Poppy's talent must not be wasted. The money she gets from the Bosch will pay for it and there will still be plenty left.'

When Henry announced to his mother three months later that he wanted to marry the Russian girl who was revolutionising all their lives, Brabazon grasped her son's hands in delight. Then she paused and said, 'Have you asked her?' for she remembered the unhappy time when he pursued Mhairi and refused to accept that she did not love him.

379

'Of course,' he laughed, 'and she says she'll have me. I'm a good bit older than she is, but it doesn't matter to her. All this is her idea really. I was far too shy to ask her myself, so she asked me!'

When Mhairi heard the news, she embraced Antonia with delight for she felt no jealousy, only pleasure that her one-time suitor had found love in the end. 'I'm so pleased for you both, so pleased,' she told the smiling couple.

St Mary's Church was decorated with white lilies and tumbling pyramids of ferns and ivy for the ceremony. The bride wore cream satin with lace flounces and an enormous picture hat. When she stepped out of the church on Henry's arm, she was radiant, beaming up at him like a brilliant sun. Standing side by side at the church door they glowed like blessed people. Henry, who had waited so long for happiness, could hardly believe that he had found it at last and kept smiling on his new wife as if she were something from a fairy-world that might be snatched away at any moment.

Mark's wife Amelia made an exception to her rule about boycotting Nairn family celebrations and turned up for this wedding dressed in the height of fashion, and gushingly eager to make the acquaintance of the bride.

'What a pity your father could not come over for the ceremony,' she told Antonia who smiled sadly and said, 'He could not leave the Tsar, but he knows Henry and is delighted at my good fortune in marrying him.'

That delighted Amelia who went around all her fashionable friends for weeks afterwards repeating that the bride's father was indispensable to the Tsar of Russia. Normally she tried to forget her Leith connections but such was Antonia's cachet and the pull of her Romanov connections, that the Nairns became a positive advantage.

When the bridal pair came back from their honeymoon in the Highlands, Antonia plunged with enthusiasm into helping Brabazon with plans for the redecorating of Brewery House which was almost rebuilt at last. Mother and daughter-in-law almost had their first disagreement over

380

this because Antonia insisted on modern ideas that Brabazon consistently turned down saying, 'No, my dear. I
want everything to be old, Georgian if possible, just like
it was when I came here as a bride. The only thing I still
possess from the original house is a candlestick from my
mother's house. I'm going to put it back on the drawing-
room mantelpiece and rebuild my home around it.'

Antonia was disappointed, but she good-naturedly
accompanied Brabazon to Dowell's saleroom in Edinburgh's George Street where she enthusiastically bid for
gleaming pieces of mahogany furniture, winged arm-
chairs, breakfront cupboards and an enormous sideboard
with lion's feet. Like the pieces she bought with such
discrimination, she was both beautiful and rare. Henry
was lucky at last thought Brabazon as she watched him
walking home across the Place with his lovely young wife.
Then an unbidden thought came into her mind – where
was Laurence? Was he happy tonight?

'I'm not tempting fate again. We won't have any big
parties this time,' said Brabazon as she gradually transferred her possessions from the flat to Brewery House.
She also felt that it was no time to be light-hearted when
there was talk of war in the air. Over a period of weeks
she drifted to and from one place to the other until the
night came when she settled down to sleep, not in the
building but in the magnificent bedroom of her new home.
The Nairns' old flat was given to Robert Warre and his
growing family, but Antonia kept her studio although she
and Henry moved their living quarters to Brewery House.
Mhairi however refused to go.

'We'll just stay where we are,' she told Brabazon. She
privately thought that going up in the world from a turf-
roofed bothy to a mansion was too much for her to contemplate. The flat in Perseverance Place was all that she
wanted.

The other neighbours understood Brabazon's wish for
an unpublicised departure and Gideon talked about it

with his family in Nellie's flat. 'No wonder she's scared after what happened the last time. I'm going to have a word with Lambert,' he said. Sandy. who was listening to the talk, reported to Josh that his Uncle Gideon, the bobby, was going to put the fear of God into Tom Lambert and warn him against doing anything to upset the Nairns.

That evening the boys saw Gideon, resplendent in his uniform with gleaming buttons, stride purposefully up the Kirkgate and into Lambert's flat.

'What do you want?' snapped Lambert, looking up from his supper.

'I've come to give you a warning.'

'What kind of warning?'

'A general warning. If anything happens to any property or any person in Perseverance Place, I'll come looking for you and even if you've an alibi as watertight as a diving bell, I'll get you. I promise you that.'

Lambert's eyes were bloodshot and mean, 'You'll fix me up. Is that what you're telling me?'

'I'm glad we understand each other,' said Gideon and walked away.

Every day the newspapers were full of the forebodings of war and Antonia's normally happy face became clouded when she read the news from the Balkans. One day it announced that the German army was re-arming and growing in numbers. She shivered and told Henry, 'I'm so worried. Something terrible is about to happen. I hope my father will be safe through all this.'

Henry reassured her. 'He's with the Tsar, my dear. I should think that's the safest place to be in times of trouble.'

'I wish he could come over here – if only for a visit,' she said but she knew that Alexei would not leave Russia at such a time of upheaval.

The months of tension crept on and the news never became any more reassuring. It was a depressing winter and the wet spring did little to lift the feeling of depression. Especially affected was Mhairi, whose spirits sank to a very low ebb. She rose early every morning and stared out of her window in the mistiness of dawn. Sometimes she imagined Laurence was standing in a corner of the yard. Then her heart would leap, she would give a gasp and prepare to run down to meet him. But when she looked more closely, it was always an illusion.

Her children despaired about their mother. 'It looks as if she's never going to get over it,' said Josh to Poppy.

'Grandmama says she will in time. We've to be kind to her and she'll cheer up,' said his sister.

'I wish I could tell Father what I think about him. I'd let him have it!' said the angry boy. He was almost sixteen now and tall for his age. When the women of the family saw him crossing the courtyard, they were so proud of him for he made them feel safe. Soon, thought Brabazon, he'll be old enough to share the running of the brewery with Henry, and Robert Warre. Then I'll be able to retire. She did not think about what she'd do when that day arrived.

Perseverance beer was a firmly established favourite now, not only in Leith and Edinburgh but also in other regions of the country. They had built up a market and kept it because of the unfailing quality of their product. The brewery's money troubles were finally at an end and Brabazon could contemplate expenditure without worrying about whether she was being rash.

The dullness of the spring did not depress the spirits of the young people. Poppy was absorbed in her painting lessons, while Josh and Sandy recreated the joyous youth of Laurence and Pat, running around the narrow streets of Leith together like young conquerors. Josh's interest in the Lambert girl had not diminished. She was growing into a woman and the beauty of her eyes still fascinated him.

'It's a pity she's scared of everybody,' he told Sandy.

'I think you're smitten with her. You should choose somebody a bit easier to know,' said his friend jokingly.

'She's a mystery, that's why I'm interested,' said Josh and continued his campaign of trying to win Sophia's confidence.

One Saturday night he met her in the Kirkgate standing in front of a fruit stall and contemplating its colourful display. When she saw him coming, she hurriedly picked one orange off the top of a pile and asked the vendor, 'How much for this?'

'A farthing.'

She fished a coin out of her pocket and paid for it, but Josh was at her elbow asking, 'Wouldn't you like more than one?' He reached over her shoulder and grabbed another two in his outspread hand. 'I'll have those as well,' he said and gave the stall owner a halfpenny after he slipped the oranges into the girl's basket.

'You shouldn't do that,' she said.

'Why not? I hope they're sweet.'

She looked around and said, 'Leave me now. I don't want to be seen . . .'

'What's the matter? I won't hurt you.'

The pale eyes searched his face and she whispered, 'It's my father. He hates me talking to anybody. He thinks everybody's watching out for him. If he knows I've been talking to people, he hits me.'

'Christ, he's a bastard!' said Josh.

She did not deny it but repeated, 'Please go away. Thank you for the oranges, but please leave me alone.'

Mhairi was walking home from the bioscope at the same time as her son was talking to Sophia Lambert, and she stood in the alley watching them. When Josh came running towards her, she put out a hand and grabbed his arm, saying urgently, 'Don't go near that girl, Josh. Her father's evil. He hates the Nairns. Really hates us. I'm terrified of him – I'm sure that he'll bring us even more misfortune if he's given the chance.'

Josh put an arm round her and hugged her to him, 'Oh Mother, you go to too many moving pictures. Gideon's watching out forLambert. He can't do anything to us.'

384

Mhairi was not soothed however, 'Just stay away from the girl,' she said again.

Josh deliberately changed the subject, 'What was showing tonight?' he asked her. Mhairi had become a regular patron at the bioscope at the end of Leith Walk where she sat entranced by the stiffly moving images on the screen. Her interest had begun when a letter came from one of her sisters in America telling her that Calum had started working as an extra with a movie company.

'He rides horses and falls off them, that sort of thing,' wrote Annie, the youngest sister who now corresponded with Mhairi about once a year.

It was unlikely she would even recognise her son if he did appear before her on the silver screen, but its magic quickly seized her and the dramatic stories helped her to forget her own misery. For a few hours she was transported into another world.

The misgivings of Alexei Orlov were proved correct. In the middle of July, 1914, the Tsar mobilised over a million troops and in the first week of August, the world was plunged into full-scale war.

Over the following weeks the newspapers carried pictures of cheering young men queuing up outside recruiting offices to join the army. But Antonia, who was a great newspaper reader, reacted with dramatic Russian vigour: 'Look at that! Poor things, they have no idea what war will mean. They are doomed!'

Henry looked at his wife seriously, 'I hope it's over before any of the boys we know have to go,' he said, thinking about Josh.

She gazed at him with her eyes swimming and reached out a hand to grasp his over the breakfast table.

On the other side of the yard Josh and his friend Sandy Warre talked continually about the war. They were frantic to go. 'My Uncle Pat's in France. I heard my grandmother saying so this morning. He's been longing for a fight and now he's got one,' said Sandy. Both boys had

seen the gloriously uniformed Pat, the very picture of a
hero, on his visits to the Place and he stayed in their
memories as a figure of glamour and derring-do. To be
fighting in France alongside Pat seemed the acme of male
adventure to the boys.

'We'll be old enough to join up soon,' said Josh, 'Then
we'll show the Germans!'

On a chilly autumn night they were wandering along
the Kirkgate and found themselves in Tolbooth Wynd,
going in the direction of The Shore. Like the other boys
of the Place before them, they felt its magnetic appeal.
They loved to observe it – but from a safe distance. Darkness was falling when they turned into its tawdry length
and as they reached the first bar, a knot of fighting men
came bursting out of the door. They staggered around
locked together with arms around each other, sweating
and swearing. One of them was Tom Lambert, skirmish-
ing around on the edge of the mêlée. When he saw the
watching boys, he stepped back from the other fighters
and ran up to Josh. His face was scarlet and filled with
venom. It was obvious that he was wild with drink and
uncontrollable.

He grabbed Josh by the front of his jacket and hissed,
'You're the one that's been after my lassie? Want to fuck
her do you? I can tell you one thing, no Nairn's going to
lay a hand on her. The Nairns think they can have everything, but they're not going to have Sophia. I'll see to
that.'

He pushed Josh roughly in the chest with an open
hand. Sandy stepped behind him and tried to grapple
with him from the back but, like his Uncle Gideon, Sandy
was small in stature and Lambert brushed him away like
a fly. Josh put up his hands to defend himself but then
he saw that Lambert had a short-bladed knife glittering
in his hand. The boy looked around for a way of escape,
but he was pinned against the wall by the charging man.
Desperately he punched out to fend off this attacker and
the blow caught Lambert in the stomach. He reeled and
gasped, putting one hand over the place where the blow

had struck him. 'You little bastard! I'll get you for that,' he said and came on again, the knife glittering in his fist. Josh managed to push himself off the wall and charged forward with his head down. He knew his only chance was to run Lambert down and he'd have to risk being stabbed. As he came near to the weaving man, his arms were swinging wildly and Sandy was beside him, punching too. Between them they drove Lambert towards the edge of the dock. 'Shove him over, shove him over,' panted Sandy and went in with his head down like a charging bullock. Josh stood square on his feet and swung a punch at Lambert's face. Miraculously it connected with the jaw and, looking totally surprised, Lambert staggered back – throwing his arms up into the air. He gave a groan and fell on to his back on the stone pavement. The knife flew out of his grip and spun down into the greasy water behind him. As he went down, Lambert's head crashed against a bollard in the roadway with a terrible crunch. The boys watched him roll over and very slowly topple over the dockside. When they rushed to the edge, he had disappeared below the surface but a fountain of spray was rising to show where his body had hit the water.

An uncanny quietness hung over them. The other fighters had fought their way on up the street and could be heard yelling and shouting in the distance. No one except Josh and Sandy had seen what had happened with Lambert. They leaned over the edge and stared at the water, now still. Then they looked at each other and Sandy said, 'Serves him right. I hope the bugger can swim.'

'He had a knife,' said Josh with his voice faltering.

'I know. I saw it. But we'll have to haul him out,' said Sandy, staring into the filthy water. Josh began stripping off his coat, but he was stopped by Sandy's hand on his arm. 'Look!' he whispered in a scared voice. They peered down and saw Lambert's body floating just below the surface of the water. He was face-down. On the back of his head was a gaping wound.

The boys hauled him out and carried his body along to the life-saving station where the attendants worked on him for a long time, but nothing could be done. A doctor called to the bath-house pronounced that Lambert was dead and that death had been caused, not by drowning, but by an injury to the head.

When Tom Lambert's body was taken to the mortuary, Police Inspector Gideon Warre had taken over the investigation into the death.

Apart from the boys there were no witnesses. As usual, when violence took place at The Shore, people disappeared, became tactfully blind and deaf. There was little chance of finding anything out from local residents.

Gideon questioned Josh and Sandy closely about the retrieval of the body. Sandy resolutely denied that there had been anything suspicious about Lambert's death. 'He was drunk. He fell into the water. He must have struck his head on something down there,' he said staring his uncle in the eye. Josh Nairn said nothing, only shook his head when asked if he had seen the man fall.

'I've no doubt he was drunk,' said Gideon heavily. As far as he was concerned, Lambert's death meant the removal of a nuisance. It was retribution for the trouble the man had caused the people of Perseverance Place, the Nairns in particular. Yet, if he *had* been killed – even accidentally – as Gideon suspected, the police could not look away. He was duty bound to continue his enquiries and, little by little, over the following weeks whispers began coming to his ears.

A prostitute offered to buy immunity from a charge of loitering by telling what she knew about Lambert's death. Gideon interviewed her and she told how she'd watched a young lad drive the drunken man back to the water's edge with punches, and stand doing nothing while he'd disappeared under the water.

'Were you sober at the time? Can you swear to what you saw?' asked Gideon.

'Who's sober in The Shore after dark?' she asked.

'Could you identify the young man who did the punching?'

'No. It was dark and I was quite a bit away.'

'Off you go,' he said closing his notebook. She was on her feet in a trice, 'Does that mean I'm getting off?'

'Push off before I change my mind,' was the brusque reply.

A month later another woman came into the station with the same sort of story and Gideon knew he had to act. Lambert had been pushed, he had been fighting with a laddie, she said. Then she described the boy: 'Tall, fine-looking with black curly hair. It was Laurence Nairn's boy I think. He looks a lot like his father did when he used to hang around the bars on The Shore.' She was prepared to swear it was Josh who threw the blow that put Lambert in the water.

When the subdued police inspector climbed the stairs to Mhairi's flat, he was in mufti. The familiarity of the stairway carried him back to his childhood. Nothing had changed, he thought, as the silence was broken by Ruthie Cairns' voice raised in some sort of raucous song. She'd never been able to sing and age had not improved her.

Wishing that he did not have to undertake this terrible job, Gideon knocked on Mhairi's door. She smiled at him when she answered it. Wiping her hands on her pristine white apron, she invited him in. He did not accept. Instead he asked her, 'Is your laddie at home Mhairi?'

She nodded, 'Aye. What do you want him for Gideon?'

'Nothing for you to worry about. Just ask him to come out and meet me at the bottom of the stair. We'll go for a wee walk.'

Josh was a braw laddie, a good type, thought Gideon as he watched the boy come swinging down from the upper flat. It would be a terrible pity if this one unfortunate accident should spoil his entire life. Nothing would be achieved by punishing Josh for the death of a villain like Lambert.

They fell into step together without speaking and

headed for the churchyard where Gideon knew they would be unlikely to be overheard.

'What was your quarrel with Tom Lambert about?' he asked when they were safely away from other ears.

To his relief the boy did not lie. 'It was over his daughter really. He was drunk and started taunting me about her. He hit me and then I saw he was going to stab me. He had a knife. I'd no alternative but to hit him as hard as I could. He cracked his head on the bollard before he fell in the water.'

'He was a wicked bastard. He'd stop at nothing. He killed my father but I could never prove it. He killed his wife and I'm sure he set fire to your grandmother's house, but there was no way we could get him for that either. He was cunning. Leith's well rid of him.'

Josh stood staring down at his feet. Then he said, 'He was beating his daughter. She told me.' Gideon was not surprised, 'Aw, poor lassie! What a life some folk have.'

Josh nodded, 'But it's no comfort to me that he deserved to die,' he said.

'The doctor's report said the damage to his head was what killed him,' Gideon said.

'I know. What are you going to do?' asked Josh. Gideon replied in a quick and hurried way, 'I'm a policeman, Josh. It's my duty to apprehend wrongdoers. It's my duty to find out the truth.'

'I'll admit it. I'll not deny it. I'm tired of knowing that I killed him. I'll stand trial, go to prison or whatever I have to, but I didn't mean to kill him.'

He didn't mention hanging, but they were both grimly aware that was the punishment for murder.

'They'll not hang you for manslaughter,' said Gideon quietly.

'But it'll be prison, won't it?'

'Aye, for a long time I'm afraid.'

The boy squared his shoulders. 'I'll still admit it. There's nothing else for it.'

Gideon shook his head. 'Listen laddie. Get out of Leith before somebody other than me cottons on. Join the army,

390

they're desperate for men. I'll forget our conversation. Think of your mother and your sister. Think of your grandmother. Haven't they suffered enough in the last few years without any more? I shouldn't be doing this but I'm giving you a chance, for God's sake take it.'

1915

The recruiting sergeant accepted Josh Nairn's word that he was eighteen years old and before he had time for regret he was swept into the 7th Royal Scots – Leith's local regiment.

He went back to Perseverance Place and told his mother that he had joined the army. He did not tell her why but she knew from the strained look on his face that she should not argue, should not make a scene, should not threaten to go to the authorities and tell them his true age. Instead she gathered him in her arms and wept over him, her head on his chest and her tears wetting his shirt.

Training was stringent and he looked older, harder and far more formidable when he returned to the Place in early May to take his farewells before setting off with his regiment for France. The neighbours were made solemn by the sight of him – the first boy among them to go to the war. The Warre women felt a clutch of fear at their hearts as they realised Sandy would be the next to leave in a khaki uniform. They gathered around, patting Josh on the back and consoling his mother who could not help but show her fear. Already the papers were filling up with news of casualties in the trenches and she dreaded that he would become one of the terrible toll whose photographs, looking young and optimistic, appeared in every edition of their local newspaper, the *Leith Burghs Pilot*.

Before he left, proud and straight in his suit of rough khaki, his tightly wound puttees and jaunty forage cap, Josh distributed presents bought from his army wages. Nosegays of flowers for Brabazon and Antonia, a little sketch pad for Poppy and a copy of the *Movie Fans' Journal* for his mother.

At eleven o'clock on the night of the 21st of May 1915, he boarded a troop train and left Leith for Flanders. His family waved him off, trying to look brave and fluttering their handkerchiefs as the train pulled out of the station. When they walked home through the darkened streets, Antonia broke the news that she and Henry had been keeping to themselves for several weeks – she was going to have a baby. It was due in November she said, and Brabazon burst into noisy tears. The emotion she had been holding back during Josh's departure broke forth in a torrent.

On the train, Josh was sharing a compartment with another seven men, some of whom he'd known all his life. They had equipped themselves with a case of beer – Perseverance Special, Josh was pleased to see.

'Drink up. We'll make a night of it. It's a long way to London,' they told him.

In spite of the noise of their singing, he fell asleep quite quickly as the train rushed southward. The driver was a man of fifty-three who'd once driven Queen Victoria and later King Edward VII. He was highly reliable and careful, but even his skill could not help him as he drove on towards the other train on the line in front of him. Two negligent signalmen had neglected to clear the way for the speeding troop train. The fatal minutes ticked away as the engine raced down towards Gretna Green, the English border and disaster.

The tremendous crash of a collision with a stationary train at sixty-five miles an hour threw carriages into the air like children's discarded toys. Many of the men slumped asleep in their seats were never to waken. Perhaps they were the lucky ones because before the others could scramble from the wreckage, the night express from Euston ploughed into the wreckage. Its enormous engine mounted the pile of already broken carriages.

With blood streaming from shattered limbs, or screaming in agony, the survivors fought to escape. That was when, in the carriages nearest the engine, a fire broke out and was soon raging through the wooden debris, greedily engulfing the struggling men.

A farmer living at Quintin's Hill, beside the line, was

wakened by the noise of the collision. When he ran to his window, he saw a column of smoke and flames rising into the black night sky. Fragments of carriages, upturned engines and scattered bodies lay all over his pasture. It looked more like a battlefield.

Rescuers came from far and near and worked till noon next day, dragging bloodstained and mangled bodies out of the collapsed carriages. They were laid in pathetic lines along the grass of the railway embankment until coffins could be found for them. As the women of the farmhouse made tea and provided food for the rescuers and survivors, tears ran down their cheeks constantly. When a roll call of men from the train was taken at midday, only fifty-five answered. There had been more than five hundred aboard. The others were either dead or injured.

Doctors laboured endlessly, comforting the dying, amputating limbs without anaesthetic; nurses ran to and fro; local people came out with bundles of torn-up sheets to be used as bandages and went up and down the rows of injured men handing out cigarettes. Everyone was struck by the stoical way the soldiers accepted their injuries. They lay smoking, eyes towards the sky, uncomplainingly waiting for their turn to be taken to hospital where many of them were later to die of their injuries.

By afternoon the corpses had been transferred to a large hayshed and when the first count was made there were over a hundred corpses lying beneath its raftered ceiling. The farmer and his wife were in tears as they looked down the pathetic huddled rows. 'Some of them were only laddies,' sobbed the shocked woman.

Josh Nairn was killed outright. He lay in the barn beside his friends from Leith, far from Perseverance Place and his family – who were as yet unaware of the tragedy. He was identified by personal items in his pocket, because his body was one of the few that had not been burned or scorched by the flames. His name was therefore high on the list of casualties that was telegraphed to Leith police station.

The port was going about its normal business that Saturday morning. Though it was still early, Brabazon was dressing to go over to the brewery; Henry was already in the cellar checking on his barrels; Mhairi was making tea for herself and Poppy. At Brewery House Antonia was still in bed for she was feeling unwell and terrified of doing anything that might endanger the child she was carrying.

Nellie Warre was yawning and thinking about the day ahead; the Warre men were hurrying to and fro in the brewery, sniffing the air and telling each other it was going to be a grand day for brewing.

Leith docks were full of ships unloading for the war effort. In the police station, Inspector Gideon Warre was listening to his Chief briefing him about official suspicions that a German spy was operating in the port. Then a boy from the telegraph office came running in with a terrible look on his face . . . Gideon read the message with horror and disbelief. Inside his head he voiced his fear in misery, 'I hope I've not sent the Nairn's laddie to his death.'

He alerted his men to the tragedy and told them to be ready to break the news to the bereaved families, but he kept the task of telling the Nairns for himself. Grimly he hurried to Perseverance Place and sought out Henry. 'There's been an awful train crash. That troop train young Josh was on has smashed into another one near Gretna Green. They say there's hundreds of lads dead, but we've no casualty list yet. I hope your Josh isn't one of them. I'm sorry Henry. Do you want me to help you tell the women?'

Henry's kind, reliable face went ashen. 'Antonia,' he thought in a panic and rushed over to Brewery House, but fortunately his wife was still in bed and her newspaper lay unread on the table. As he lifted it he saw that the terrible news was printed in the Stop Press column at the side. Quickly he threw the sheets into the fire burning in the drawing-room grate and watched as the flames consumed the terrible news they contained. A forlorn hope that it might all be some terrible mistake stopped him from breaking the news to his mother and Mhairi. He went back to work and waited, for he knew Gideon would tell him as soon as any more specific news was received. At twelve-thirty his fears were realised because Gideon came back. He was in full uniform and he looked terrible.

Silently he stood in the dim, cool cellar and stared at the man looking back at him. No words were exchanged but they understood each other. Then he passed Henry a slip of paper. 'What's this?' Henry asked.

'It's a train pass to take you to Carlisle. His name's one of the first on the list of dead. Someone has to go and identify him. I'll come with you.'

Henry put both hands over his face and sobbed in anguish. He had loved Laurence's boy as if he'd been his own son. 'My God, my God, how'll I tell them?' he gasped.

'I'll do it for you,' offered Gideon, but Henry shook his head. 'No, it's my place to do it. I'll find the words. Leave me now, Gideon. I'll meet you at the station later.'

He told his mother first. It was a miracle she had not heard the news already, but she'd been busy all morning in the grain loft, tasting malted barley and crunching the seeds between her teeth. It was a job she always enjoyed.

'It's not as good as it used to be. This war's making a difference to lots of things and now we've got this brewing quota to worry us. It's cutting down our production something terrible,' she said to her son when she saw his head popping up above the trap door in the floor.

'Mother, I want you to be very strong. I know you can do it. There's bad news,' she said.

'Is it Laurence?' she whispered.

'No, it's Josh. There was an awful train crash last night and he was in it.'

'Is he badly hurt?' her voice was stunned and disbelieving. He knew he must not tell her lies.

'He's dead, Mother.'

'Josh? Dead? It's not possible. He's only sixteen years old. He can't be dead.'

Her eldest son took her hand in his and said, 'I can

396

hardly believe it myself, but it's true Mother. There's nothing we can do. Now we've got to tell Mhairi.'

Brabazon moaned like a hurt child. 'I can't stand it, I can't stand it. Not Josh, not the bairn! Oh God will you never stop hurting us?'

'Don't say that Mother. We've got to tell Mhairi. Do you want to come with me?'

She suddenly looked very old and frail but she nodded bravely, 'I'll come,' she said.

Mhairi had not left the flat all morning, and was sitting in her chair in the kitchen window watching the comings and goings of the yard while she ate her lunch of bread and cheese. To her surprise she saw Ruthie Cairns coming in looking distraught and wondered what had happened. She was on the point of going downstairs to enquire and offer comfort if necessary, when Henry and Brabazon arrived.

Her mother-in-law put both arms around her and said, 'My dear, I love you. You're as precious to me as my own child. I want you to be brave now. Henry's just heard there's been a train accident. Josh was in it.'

Mhairi's eyes were enormous and terrified as she stared from one to the other. She read what she most feared in Brabazon's stricken face.

'Is he dead?'

'Yes, he is. I can't believe it but he is. Gideon got his name from the list of casualties.'

'Oh God, I hope he didn't suffer,' said his mother and fainted clean away.

An electric tramcar was trundling along Lewisham High Street with a goodlooking, dark-haired man at the controls. It lurched to a halt beside a stop where a woman with blonde hair piled high beneath a smart hat stood waiting. The driver looked at her and felt his heart contract with longing. 'She's got hair like Mhairi,' he thought.

It was a fine sunny day and he could imagine what was going on in Perseverance Place. His mother would be bustling about in the brewery; the air would be heavy with the smell of hops; the women of the building would be sitting at the stair foot gossiping and laughing. Was his wife among them? Had she found some other man to take care of her? It had been about three years since he'd left but he had not written home or heard any news of Leith. 'I made my bed and I've got to lie in it,' he told himself many times when feelings of depression claimed him.

He swung the brass handle of the tram controls and started it up again. A shower of sparks flew up into the air from the long metal arm connecting with the overhead wires and he rattled on to the next halt. It was strange, thought Laurence Nairn, in spite of how long he'd spent trying to persuade his mother to invest in modern methods of transport that he was now in charge of an electric tram, but longing to be back behind a pair of hefty carthorses. His tram passed the house owned by Daisy de Craigny and he gazed without emotion at the lace-curtained windows and the neatly planted front garden. Daisy, if she was not in Monte Carlo, would still be in bed although it was eleven o'clock in the morning. She did not rise till noon.

As ever, the knowledge that he'd made a terrible mistake was eating inside him like a wound that would never heal. He was lonely and he was bitter but he could not go home.

At the end of the run, he guided the tram into the terminus building and switched it off before jumping down and joining a crowd of other drivers who were standing in the big doorway enjoying the sunshine.

They were talking about the war and one man held a newspaper that carried enormous black headlines on its front page.

'Bad news again is it?' asked Laurence.

'Terrible. A tragedy. You're from Scotland aren't you? All these poor bastards were from up there,' was the reply. The man held the sheet towards Laurence, his stubby finger indicating the lead story. 'Train Crash at Gretna

Green' screamed the black headline. 'Hundreds Dead' said the sub-headline.

Down at the bottom of the page was a list of casualties. Laurence folded the paper in half and held it up to his face to hide his expression from the other men. His stomach was churning with a terrible premonition. His eyes were misted and his mouth dry as his shaking finger traced down the closely printed list. The name Nairn was there. His finger stopped at it.

On Monday the news of the Gretna Green disaster reached the troops fighting on the Western Front near Artois. In a trench lined with wooden planks Sergeant Major Pat Warre read the list of casualties and started to shiver uncontrollably. With sudden terror he realised that he wanted to weep, and that a lump seemed to be stuck in the middle of his throat. Outside the rain beat down and around him men were sitting hunched over their rifles, heads bent and shoulders up. Soon he would have to drive them over the edge of the trench and into the teeth of the enemy fire.

'*I can't go*,' he said to himself, 'I can't go out there again.'

As he stood up one of the men raised his head. There was hatred in the soldier's eyes and Pat knew why. Yesterday he had shot the man's friend, a young lad who'd broken down and refused to go into the attack.

Pat had cursed him soundly, called him yellow and, in order to frighten him, he'd raised his revolver to the boy's head with his finger on the trigger. The boy refused to do as ordered; he'd kept on shivering – just as Pat himself was doing now – and weeping like a child. Pat shot him.

The soldier in the floor of the trench still glowered at his sergeant and a light of realisation came to his eyes when he saw how scared Pat was. Pat turned quickly around, pulled out his revolver, stuck it in his own mouth and blew his brains out.

The victims of the train crash were to be buried on the 24th of May and it seemed a cruel irony that a day of such devastating tragedy could be so bright and beautiful. It should have been a day to rejoice the heart, to make men glad to be alive, for Leith basked in the rays of a kindly sun and the blue waters of the Forth estuary glittered and sparkled like a sheet of opal. The port was putting on its best face to bid farewell to its sons. The people, however, were unconsoled. They were all in mourning. Flags flew at half mast, shops kept their shutters up, the streets were deserted and homes had their blinds pulled down to shut out the glorious light. There was hardly a household unaffected by the disaster, because those who had not lost a relative themselves all knew someone who had. The death toll of men from Leith itself had risen to one hundred and fifty and there were some critically ill survivors still fighting for their life in hospitals near the site of the crash. The men who had died had all been young, with their lives in front of them. The community, always close-knit, was stunned with shared grief.

The worst affected among those who mourned were the people whose men were officially listed as missing. They knew only too well that this was no grounds for hope: it meant that the bodies had been completely consumed by the fire that raged through the wrecked trains. There was no hope, there was only despair and terrible horror at the idea of the deaths their loved ones had endured.

There was desolation in Perseverance Place. Every window was blank, every blind and shutter closed. The building looked as if each living soul had deserted it. A silence as sinister as a funeral pall hung over the brewery and all the surrounding buildings. The world was in suspension. Not a blade of grass or a leaf on a tree seemed to quiver in the still morning.

Mhairi Nairn had spent a sleepless night, lying with her daughter for company in the bed she had once shared with Laurence. The pain in her heart was so terrible that she hardly dared to breathe deeply in case the agony

400

stabbed her to the vitals. She could think of nothing except her dead son. When Poppy woke in the light of early morning, she saw her mother, already dressed in her mourning clothes, sitting like a waxen figure in the chair by the bedside. She sat without moving or speaking and in her gloved hand she clutched the pass which would allow her to go into the hall where the coffins lay, and afterwards to the graveside at Rosebank Cemetery where the interments would take place.

Brabazon had wanted Josh to be buried in the family plot but the army authorities persuaded her that it was best if he shared the military funeral of the other soldiers. He would be the first Nairn for centuries not to lie in St Mary's churchyard.

From the bedroom Mhairi could see Josh's old coat and cap still hanging on the back of the front door, and a drawing he had done for her, when he was younger, pinned on the wooden panelling at the side of the kitchen window. It was yellowed and curling at the edges now, but she loved it because he'd said it was her – a matchstick figure with a mop of bright yellow hair. He had written 'Mother' on it in a childish hand.

In her bedroom, on the dresser, was the photograph he had taken only a few days before he went away. In it he stood smiling, like a young gladiator in his khaki, and now he was dead. The dam of pain inside his mother burst out in a groan of agony. She bent her head and the tears that ran down her cheeks were scalding hot. Poppy, hearing the noise, came running in from the kitchen. She too was swollen-faced but knelt beside her mother and said in a brave voice, 'Don't cry Mother, don't cry. I love you.'

Mhairi gulped convulsively and reached for her daughter's hand. Poppy felt impotent as she sat on the floor with her mother clinging to her and sobbing as if her heart would break. Eventually the girl asked, 'Can I get you something to eat? You'll need food. It's going to be a long day.'

Mhairi shook her head. 'No, no, I can't swallow . . . oh

my dear Josh, oh my bairn!' she keened in a voice of such agony that Poppy's strength left her and she wept too.

The mourners had been told to assemble in Dalmeny Street Drill Hall at one o'clock so at a quarter to, Henry's footsteps were heard on the stairs going up to Mhairi's flat. As if this were a signal, the other flat doors opened and the neighbours stood framed inside, all in black as well, their faces expressing sympathy and grief. Poppy opened the door to her uncle who walked into the bedroom and, without speaking, held out a hand to Mhairi. She rose, took his arm and they walked out together with Poppy following behind.

In the courtyard Brabazon was waiting alone, a gaunt black figure of tragedy, but with her head held high and her face impassive. She took Henry's other arm. Antonia was unwell. She had fainted at the breakfast table and was put to bed, with a maid detailed to make sure she made no effort to rise and follow the mourning party.

The Nairns, with Mark Logan escorting Poppy, walked slowly to the mouth of the alley and one by one the neighbours came out of their houses and filed in behind. The Warres, wiping their eyes as they walked, came first; followed by the rumbustious Cairns whose faces were heavy, all laughter forgotten. At the entry into the Kirkgate, the Donaldsons stood and Lil gave a terrible sob when the dead boy's family passed her. They all filed out of the Place and no one looked back to see if the windows behind them contained the faces of those who'd once lived there: Abe and Minna; Happy Anderson; Alex Warre and Duncan, the dead boy's grandfather who used to sit and stare down into the open space for hours at a time.

It did not take long to walk to Dalmeny Street and on the way they followed other families who were making the same terrible journey. The Drill Hall doors stood open with uniformed soldiers standing at each side to inspect the passes of those seeking entry. When the Nairns filed into the dimness, each of them quailed for they found themselves in an enormous space with one hundred and seven coffins lined up in the middle of the floor. The train crash had claimed over forty more dead than these coffins, but the fire that raged through the crashed train had swallowed up many bodies without trace – some men had simply disappeared in the inferno but they, too, were in the minds of the mourners crammed inside the hall. Josh's was one of only fifty-eight coffins that bore flowers, because the rest contained remains it had not been possible to identify positively. As a result many of the people in the hall had no focus for their grief. They did not know on which coffin to concentrate their thoughts and prayers. The sound of their weeping soared to the ceiling like a terrible anthem.

Around the coffins were placed potted palms and from the rafters overhead, military flags hung down in mournful folds. It looked as if an army had lain down in strict parade order. Each coffin was draped with a Union Jack and when she entered the hall, Mhairi's eyes sought for the circlet of roses that the family had sent for Josh.

Eventually she found it and wished that she had not, because the sight of it made her realise again, with fresh horror, that her child lay beneath the flowers.

The families had to wait huddled together, listening to the weeping and not knowing if it was their own voices they heard or those of other people, until a quarter to two when the service began. Two ministers, both of them chaplains to the 7th Royal Scots, officiated and because one of the dead was a Roman Catholic boy whose body had been identified only by a shamrock charm attached to a chain around his neck, the Service for the Dead was also read by his local priest. Then the stricken relatives stood and watched for almost two hours as parties of soldiers carried each coffin from its place on the hall floor to waiting military ambulances which would take them to the burying ground. All the while a military band played laments which barely muffled the sounds of grief from the press of mourners. Some people fainted – men as well as women – and both Brabazon and Mhairi felt their heads become light as if they were floating in another dimension. Their grief made them weightless, took them

403

out of their actual bodies, but they managed not to faint and stared ahead with set faces knowing that was the only way to survive the terrible experience. Henry, watching them, realised what they were going through and was glad that he had insisted on Antonia staying at home.

It was half past three when the throng of mourners and notables emerged on to the street. They stood blinking a little as their eyes became accustomed to the blaze of the sun after the gloom of the necropolis behind them. More throngs lined the pavements, for thousands had come from near and far to show their sympathy. When the procession formed and began to move off, a deep sigh swept these watchers; they swayed together like a forest of trees in the wind. All the ships in the harbour, at the same moment, sounded their steam hooters in a long, low note of lament and the mournful note drowned out the music of the slow pacing bands.

Led by ambulances bearing the coffins, the procession of grief walked along Dalmeny Street, across Leith Walk and up Pilrig Street – which was lined with trim villas and pretty gardens. Each bow window contained a horrified group. Many were openly weeping; even the policemen who lined the route had tears trickling down their cheeks as the pipe bands marched slowly past playing Scotland's heartfelt lament for other young men lost in the fifteenth-century battle of Flodden . . . 'The Floors o' the Forest are A' Wee'd Awa'.'

The people behind the dead walked in time with the music, without registering the pity that was being poured out towards them by the thousands of spectators. Anxious to mourn with dignity in so far as they were able, they supported each other. Henry Nairn had his mother on one arm and his sister-in-law on the other, both women walking with raised heads and fixed expressions, willing themselves onwards. Poppy walked behind them on the arm of her Great-Uncle Mark.

When they reached the broad gates of the cemetery they saw Sophia Llambert and their friends from the Place standing beside a uniformed Gideon and watching for

404

them. The knowledge that there were others grieving with them, gave Josh's family strength. They needed it because when the procession turned into the broad walk down the middle of the burying ground, they found they were walking directly towards a huge bank of russet earth – the communal grave.

A feeling of panic rose in Mhairi. Her strength of will ebbed away. She wanted to tear herself from Henry's arm and run, run, run. To reach the sea and fling herself into it! For a few seconds she knew it was impossible to sustain any more agony and leaned forward as if to ask her mother-in-law what to do. Aware of Mhairi's increased anguish, Brabazon whispered, 'Be brave a little longer – for his sake.'

It took so long for each coffin to be laid to rest that the strain began to tell on many of the mourners. Some of them collapsed on to the short cropped grass and lay defenceless while their relatives fussed around trying to revive them. Others broke down in frenzied weeping that could not be stilled.

Finally, a line of soldiers stepped forward, raised their rifles towards the sky and fired off three volleys of shots that reverberated over the cemetery, bouncing off the gravestones and memorials, echoing around the tall buildings in the streets. When the shock waves finally subsided, the band began playing again and this time the music was 'Lochaber No More' followed by the awesome solemnity of 'The Dead March from Saul'. Then a lone trumpeter sounded the Last Post. The most terrible funeral that Leith had ever seen in all its long history was over.

People let their muscles relax and their shoulders slumped as they looked at each other for a lead. The officers and dignitaries shuffled their feet awkwardly and started to straggle away in groups, not talking, not looking directly at anyone. The bandsmen and the bearer parties, turned smartly at a command and marched off. Only the mourners were left standing staring aimlessly, wiping their eyes and wondering what to do. Until they went the grave diggers could not begin the mammoth task of filling in the huge hole.

Slowly people began to talk to each other, to grasp hands and weep. Complete strangers embraced and shared their grief. The catharis of the funeral had removed barriers and broken down reserve.

Henry wiped his eyes and turned first to his mother and then to Mhairi, with an arm extended to each. Brabazon grasped his right arm gratefully. She had not shed a tear since the procession began and now felt as dry as tinder, like a dead woman. Gathering her strength for the effort of leaving, she raised her eyes to stare out in the direction of the sea. Over there, she thought, was Alexei. She put a hand on the crystal snowflake around her neck and sent her thoughts winging out to him. Somehow that gave her comfort.

When she turned to Henry she saw there was a strange expression on his face. He was looking down the path towards the gate, but he only said, 'Come, Mother. We'll leave Mhairi a moment.' He led Brabazon forward while Mhairi, unheeding, stood alone on a slight rise of ground. She was like a graven figure, her head turned to the place where her son had been laid.

Poppy was frightened and ran back to pull at her mother's sleeve and urge her, 'Come away Mother, come away now.'

Henry stepped forward to restrain the girl and told her, 'Leave your mother, my dear. Come and wait with us.'

Mhairi continued to stand alone while the crowd drained away around her. Henry watched first her, then looked back up the path towards the gate. A man was running along it, hair flying and face contorted. Henry pulled his mother and Poppy aside so that he could pass. He did so, looking neither right nor left. Nothing would deflect him. He was intent on reaching the solitary woman.

She heard him coming but did not turn her head. When he reached her he stopped and spoke in an urgent voice,

'Mhairi, my Mhairi, It's over, my dearest. Let me take you home. I've come to take you home.'

Then she fixed her blazing eyes on his. Her face was expressionless and she stared as if she did not know him, could not understand the words he was speaking. He gazed back at her, pleading again and willing her to react. 'Mhairi, my dearest, speak to me. This is the most terrible day of our lives. I need you.'

Slowly her eyes lost their fury and filled with tears; slowly her muscles relaxed as if she were letting out a long pent-up breath. Her body seemed to soften; she reached a hand towards him. He extended his and their fingers touched, then entwined again. Both of them were weeping now, but not just tears of mourning.

She spoke at last. 'Oh Laurence, I prayed that you would come.'